Cold Air Return is a coming-of-age story that rings true from its first words. It is the summer of 1960 in north central Pennsylvania and twelve-year-old Eugene and his friends are on the cusp of adolescence. Cigarettes are smoked. Innocence collides with responsibility. The bonds of boyhood are tested by the dimly understood forces of race and class and religion. The first twinges of love are shadowed by an adult world where evil is real. O'Keeffe builds his story deftly, each character drawn with knowledge and care. The climax is at once foreshadowed and unexpected, leaving our humanity exposed. I could not put this book down.

—Kurt Landefeld, author of *Jack's Memoirs: Off the Road*

OTHER BOOKS BY PATRICK LAWRENCE O'KEEFFE

*History of Ottawa County: The First 175 Years* (2016)

BOTTOM DOG PRESS

# COLD AIR RETURN
## A NOVEL

## PATRICK LAWRENCE O'KEEFFE

**HARMONY SERIES**
**BOTTOM DOG PRESS**
**HURON, OHIO**

**CREDITS:**
General Editor: Larry Smith
Cover and Layout Design: Susanna Sharp-Schwacke
Cover Image: *Geraniums On A Country Porch*,
painting by Doug Strickland
Title Page Illustration: Karen O'Keeffe.

**ACKNOWLEDGEMENTS:**
I am most grateful for all the help I received in the writing and publication of this novel:

My wife, Karen, who read the first drafts as I wrote them, and told me when they were good reading, and also when they weren't; my children, Bridget, Katie, Sarah, Patrick, and Tim, whose responses to my first manuscript were so valuable and encouraging.

Fellow writers, who offered crucial insights: Nancy Dunham, Rich Norgard, and Kurt Landefeld as well as other friends and fellow writers at the Firelands Writing Center, who carefully read and listened to my submissions, gave me such good advice, and exhorted me to keep going.

Bill Wright, the late Sandusky poet, labor activist, and peace activist, from whose war experiences the character of Owen Ahern was partially developed.

The folks who so enriched my childhood that I just had to pick up the pen: my parents, Eleanor and Jack; siblings, Peggy, Jimmy, Mary Ellen, Kay, George, Betsy, Mike, and Eileen, and our live-in cousins, Charlie, Susie and Ellen; friends, neighbors and the many fascinating characters who made up the local culture of Ulster, Towanda, and Bradford County, Pennsylvania in 1960.

All the teachers throughout my life, especially those in English and foreign languages at Holy Cross Seminary: John Corcoran, Bill Simmons, Dave Verhalen, and Tom Waldron.

Larry Smith, publisher, fellow writer and friend, who also leads the group at the Firelands Writing Center, and Susanna Sharp-Schwacke, fellow writer, friend and editor.

The University of Notre Dame Archives, source for the details of the 1960 Notre Dame—Pitt football game, which briefly appears in the novel.

## 2016–Melody Falls, Pennsylvania

"Somebody wants to know about Uncle Dan," my daughter Emily called to me from the top of the cellar stairs.

Why would anybody be asking about Dan? And, what could I tell them, anyway? I decided to take the call, but asked her to explain that I would be a few minutes.

A push on the Gojo pump, a thorough hand cleaning of stubborn grime from an ancient Briggs & Stratton 5-horse that lay in pieces on the work bench, and I went upstairs. Emily had gone to the kitchen to get a coffee. Entering the home office — it was her office, now — I reached for the desk phone.

"Eugene Ahern speaking."

"Mister Ahern, thank you for taking my call. Let me introduce myself—"

I cleared my throat. "Your call concerns my uncle?"

"I apologize for any inconvenience. I'm Timothy Turley, with the Holy Cross Fathers, from our Provincial House in Indiana. I was hoping to talk with Daniel Ahern. Would he be available?"

"No, I'm sorry, Dan doesn't live here."

"So, he lives nearby, perhaps?"

"Dan's been out in Oregon for years, Portland mostly. Retired now, down near Coos Bay. He's...you might say, a bit infirm these days."

"Sorry to hear he's doing poorly."

"What can I do for you, Father...Turley, is it?"

"Timothy Turley. Call me Tim."

Moving around the desk, I sat down in the well-worn leather executive chair. An Emily-rescue from the attic, the chair was my father's favorite when this had been his office. I leaned back to a sigh of old upholstery.

"So, tell me, Father Tim. Uncle Dan left the priesthood many years ago. May I ask why you're looking for him after all this time?"

"It concerns something that belongs to him. But before I go any further, I should ask: did your uncle ever marry? Any children? You see, I need to speak with his closest relative."

I reached back for the double cord from the window blinds, twisted it around my fingers. "Something that belongs to him, you say?"

"Let me explain. Father Robert Walters, one of our missionaries, passed away quite a while ago. Perhaps you knew Walt, or knew of him?"

"Sorry, no, I never knew a Father Walters, or anybody named Walt." Why would he think I might have known the man?

"It happened back in 1982. Very tragic. Well, a few days ago, our archivist came across an item that Walt had designated be given to Father Dan, your uncle."

A tinge of acid came to my throat. "An item belonging to my uncle has been sitting in your archives for—what would it be?—over three decades?"

"Please let me explain, Eugene."

"Father Tim, suppose you just say what it is."

"A manila envelope. You need to understand that Father Walt was in Guatemala when he died. Santa Maria Nebaj."

"Sorry, never heard of it."

"He had sent home the envelope and asked that it be put among his stored items, designated it be given, in the event of his death, to Father Dan. He was apparently unaware that your uncle had left the priesthood just a few weeks prior."

"In the event of his death...he was in some kind of danger?"

"You could say that. It was 1982. Guatemala was in the midst of terrible strife, with government forces in control of roaming death squads. Walt suddenly disappeared, vanished into thin air."

I swallowed. My voice dropped down a little. "So, this Father Walters, the man you call Walt: they killed him?"

"We—when I say we, I mean our religious community's administrators at the time—suspected so, but didn't know for sure. Last month we found out." Father Turley paused. I heard a dry cough beyond the mouth piece, and then his voice returned: "The incident had been well concealed, until recently. Walt was caught up in a genocidal sweep, and interrogated. He was eventually...executed, you could call it."

"Jesus," I whispered.

The phone line remained quiet.

"Please excuse my language, Father."

"Your language is quite appropriate, Eugene."

"Tim, I'm sorry for what happened."

"Walt was a revered man. He had gone to Guatemala specifically to take over an abandoned orphanage. We—the Holy Cross Fathers—lacked a presence in Guatemala, but Walt was determined to serve the needs of children he'd heard about being so misplaced by the chaos. He talked his superiors into giving him the go-ahead. A temporary assignment."

"Again, I'm sorry. Must have been quite a guy, this Father Walters."

"Yes, he was. An orphan himself, you know. Two years at Saint Joseph's in Scranton, not far from you. That institution serves a different need now, though still run by the Immaculate Heart Sisters. Very stingy with their records, but they finally did tell me that Robert Walters originated from your hometown. I have the letter right here: placed from Melody Falls, Pennsylvania, November, 1960."

Releasing my grip on the window cord, I sat forward. Memory started percolating through the kids I'd known back then. "Robert Walters, same age as me, you say."

"They could have changed his name. That would have happened if, say, something from his circumstances put him in danger, or for any number of reasons. If so, Walt's original name was never forwarded to us." Another shuffle of paper. "He entered our high school preparatory program here at Notre Dame as Robert Joachim Walters, fourteen years of age, let's see, September, 1962. Highly recommended by Father Daniel Ahern."

"High school preparatory. That would be the little sem?"

"Oh, so your uncle told you about Holy Cross Seminary."

"He tried to recruit me. A brief visit there when I was a kid."

"Holy Cross closed in the late 60s, shortly after Walt had gone on to the next level. Nothing's left of the little sem now but a stone marker, and the backstop where they used to play ball."

We were both quiet for a moment.

"Father Tim, just what can I do for you?"

."What should I do with the envelope, Eugene? Walt's unmistakable cursive on the front, 'Give this to Daniel Ahern, if I don't make it back.'"

"Sounds like he wanted my uncle to have it, all right. Do you suppose it's something — you know — private, or personal?"

"I could open it," he said, "but won't do so without authorization."

"In answer to your earlier question, no, Uncle Dan never married. So, I am Dan's closest blood-relative," I said, mulling it over, "along with my sister. She's thirteen years younger than me. Lives out in San Francisco, a graphic artist..."

He remained patient, waiting for me to decide what to tell him, responding to my small talk with some of his own: "I'm very familiar with the Bay Area. In the 90s, I did some graduate work at Berkeley."

Making up my mind, I felt my shoulders relax. I gave him the phone number of Uncle Dan's residence in Coos Bay, Oregon. "You have to understand, my uncle has good days and bad days. Maybe you can catch him on a good day. If not, his live-in friend, his caregiver, would know best what's to be done with the envelope."

He thanked me, and then said, "Eugene, since your uncle was so well acquainted with him, I was somehow hoping to hear that you and Walt had been friends. A shame you never knew him."

The receiver back in its cradle, daughter Emily appeared in the doorway, sipping coffee just as her mother used to do: cradling the mug sideways, she savored its warmth in her hand, fingers wrapped around and poking through the loop, leaving the handle to stick out.

Memories arose, burst into the clear, feeding on Father Tim's telephone voice: "A shame you didn't know him." Within that moment, the past unfolded itself, the way daylight blooms through a morning window, displacing a long night of dreaming.

"Everything okay, Dad?" At the hazy edge of my vision, I was aware of Emily, over the mug's brim, trying to catch my eye through curling vapors.

Wait a minute. The missionary who was killed in Guatemala: Walt, they called him, short for Robert Joachim Walters. Could that have been *his* name? The sisters at the orphanage… they had Anglicized it, merely converting it from Spanish into English!

"But, Father Tim, I *did* know him."

# PART ONE:

## ENCLOSED IN RED GLASS

## Chapter 1, Hasty Recovery
### 1960–Melody Falls, Pennsylvania

On a hot, muggy afternoon, Grandma Marja was seen working in her garden with no clothes.

Doctor Willingham had advised, "When it gets too hot for you, go in and take a nap, Missus Ahern."

Sometimes she would do as he had said. More often, she would remove her clothes, put them aside and keep on hoeing. For a while my parents were the only people in the whole of Wilmot County who didn't know that everybody else knew about it. And everybody did, thanks to Missus Tull.

Missus Tull's husband Oswald farmed the steep, rolling quarter section just north of us on the wrinkled eastern slope of Belknap Ridge. Since her somewhat early retirement as the fifth grade teacher from the Melody Falls Unified School District, Missus Tull had developed the practice of roaring over the township roads at a high speed with no apparent destination in mind.

Passing our house, she suddenly slammed on the brakes and halted her blue '57 Rambler in a cloud of dust and flying gravel. Grandma peered at her a while through the split-rail fence, then waved, to which our neighbor responded with a scarlet-faced shriek, "Hey! This is America! Get some clothes on!"

Grandma did not care to be reminded that this was America. She'd been here all of her adult life, and took Missus Tull's shriek to be a rude attempt to make her feel unwelcome. But she'd learned long ago that the best defense in the face of such behavior was to pretend not to understand. So she smiled, shrugged her bare shoulders, and continued to nibble the edge of her hoe around the Swiss chard, ever so proud of her touch at raising greens.

"But you can't do that!" I later heard my father exclaim through the house's duct-work, his tone inflamed by our neighbor's incessant reports to the community about Grandma's full appreciation of fresh air. Missus Tull, after screaming at Grandma from the rolled down window of her Rambler, at last had found purpose for her formerly aimless forays behind the wheel: tell everyone who would listen – and even some who wouldn't, or would rather not have – that Marja Ahern did her gardening in the nude. This tale for a time inspired a dusty increase in traffic to our otherwise out-of-the-way dirt road.

"It's my garden, isn't it? Don't I always fold my clothes and place them in the tool shed? It's not like I leave them scattered around. And besides, Benjamin Franklin frequently took air baths too."

From my bedroom, I could listen to conversations below through a register in the wall. Sheet-metal chasms converged at a Kalamazoo wood-burning furnace in the cellar, which Grandpa Carroll had installed when he had built the house for himself and Marja back in 1913. My father had recently replaced it with a propane-fired hot-water heating system that promised "dust-free, even heat, and elimination of drafts," so said the man from Williamsport who had installed it. He had left in my bedroom wall a cold air duct that was also attached to an abandoned register in my father's office

My father said, "Benjamin Franklin? Air baths?"

"Well, you'd know that if you'd paid attention to your lessons, if you hadn't spent so much time when you were a youngster running around with that Baxter Hoy, and had applied yourself to your lessons."

"I got 99s in History, remember? And I'm positive that no such thing was ever mentioned in any of my lessons."

Full quiet took over the home office below me. I could hear them shuffle in their chairs and sigh to each other, the sounds of human anger slowly cooling down.

Then, he spoke more softly. "Something else, *Kulta*." A Finnish pet name for her. "Please don't call Eugene beautiful lad anymore. This is America."

"But, I'm an American," she complained.

"Beautiful lad is not an acceptable term here for a twelve-year-old boy."

"I always called you that, Owen," she said. "Why can't I call Eugene my beautiful lad, too? I always called you my beautiful lad."

"That's why I'm telling you this," he said, leather executive chair creaking to a forward lean. "By the time I was old enough to argue my case with you, I had already been in for a great deal of suffering at the hands of other boys my age. I would like to spare Eugene the same fate. He's no longer two, you know."

"Boys your age—bah! That friend of yours, again, Baxter Hoy...he's turned into a no-good nobody."

Things went quiet, and in my mind's eye I could see Grandma pouting, lower lip sticking out, pink and glistening.

Grandma's hair was white. As a kid, I assumed this was because she was seventy-six. A life that long would make it turn white, you would think. Not in her case.

A few days after the scolding incident was a bright Saturday morning. We sat on the outer corner of the screened-in wrap-around porch, Grandma in her wicker rocker, I in a wood-slat Adirondack chair. She had just finished the front pages of the *Clarion*. I had finished with the comics and sports page. She looked at me the way she did whenever quiet crept in where you'd expect conversation. When talk just doesn't happen, you're supposed to look away, or start up around some new topic.

But the secret rule did not apply to us. Grandma could look at me all she wanted. She was not like anybody else. I don't know how or when it had started. I had probably been too young at the time to know it was even a rule, and so Grandma had just allowed me to not follow that rule, the way she did many secret rules. She even allowed me to call her Marja if I felt like it.

So here we were on the porch in late morning light, talk about what was in the newspaper having petered out between us. We looked at each other. The pale blue in her eyes suddenly deepened. She reached back, snared her white braid and brought it across her front. It started out thick by her wrinkled neck and tapered down to where a piece of heavy purple yarn held it fast, leaving a wispy tail. She examined the texture of the braid, twisting and feeling it with crooked fingers.

"My hair has always been white," she informed me.

"Not when you were a little girl?" I asked.

"Even when I was a little girl, although it had a hint of the winter sun in it then, but otherwise like pure snow."

Her blue eyes held onto mine as her ancient face softened to mild amusement. "I'll bet you thought I was white-haired only because I'm an old lady." Eyes flashed, savored the satisfaction derived of telling me things she knew would make me rearrange my understanding of her. Her face melted all its crevices and crags into a trickle of laughter that momentarily spilled between us.

"But you have been an old lady ever since I can remember."

Laughter. "Yes. I often forget your life is so short compared to mine, my beautiful lad."

Her eyes suddenly deepened again, and then cheeks flushed and she said, more quietly, "I forgot, I'm not allowed to say that anymore. Beautiful lad, I mean. It's against the rules, don't you see."

The secret rules, she meant. She was as good at all the conventional rules as anyone born here, maybe even better than most, just as she spoke better English than most Americans.

That was from having read the newspaper aloud every day and listening to the radio since it had been invented, in recent years favoring Arthur Godfrey, who spoke so distinctly. But it was those secret rules—the hidden ones—that she still had a tough time with. Grandma arrived here from Finland when she was twelve.

I looked into her blue eyes looking at me. What would it be like for me to suddenly go to Finland? And then, by the time I was seventy-six, to have spent a lifetime uncovering and understanding the secret rules they had there, and maybe still find some of them confusing.

For as long as I could remember, she would tell me I was her beautiful lad, and I never told her not to. When I was alone with my Grandma, we were on vacation from everybody else. What they considered proper might as well have been a piece of luggage abandoned at the seldom used Lehigh Valley depot down in Melody Falls.

I said, "Did people think you were old even when you were young, because you had white hair?"

Grandma laughed and put down the folded paper. "I was once young, and even pretty."

"Yes, in that photo on your dresser you are a pretty girl. When I was a little kid, I didn't know that was you."

Laughter tumbled from her. "Oh, that picture of me and your grandfather: we'd gone straight from the courthouse in Wyotanda to a photography shop on Pine Street. I was so young." She lowered her voice to a whisper, "That was right after we lied about my age at the license window."

"You lied, Marja?"

"Well, yes...but promise you won't tell anybody, Eugene." Her eyebrows lowered. "If the authorities ever found out, they could come and confiscate it."

"Confiscate it?"

She looked at me as if I hadn't been paying attention. "Why...our marriage license, of course!"

I nodded.

"Did I ever tell you?" she said, recovering a normal tone. "One day, I was on a train."

Yes, she had told me. I'd heard it many times already, but each new telling would have more details attached to it, allowing me a clearer picture of her in those olden days when my grandma was young.

"In the lavatory," she said, "I looked into the mirror and saw a girl swaying with the movements of the train, a girl who had suddenly become oh so radiant. I saw a girl who had been talking with a rough Irishman—rougher than a cob, I tell you—Carroll Ahern, coal miner from Hazleton, who had taken a seat across the aisle. We had talked, oh, it must have been for hours, through all the little stops the train used to make in those days. And then in the lavatory, I put water on my face, and in the mirror I saw a swaying girl who suddenly had decided she was no girl at all. She was a woman, a woman who had suddenly splashed herself with water!"

"My grandfather...he was rough?"

"Oh, he was terrible, entirely unrefined. And an Irish coal miner, about as rough and crude as a person could be, don't you see. He was funny to look at, all those lumpy muscles stuffed into his father's suit that was too small for him, on his way to enroll at the Sheshequin Institute. He was supposed to study bookkeeping there. But he would end up spending the tuition money on something else entirely."

She stopped and let her gaze go past me, the look she got whenever she suspected that she may have said too much.

But then she laughed. "He smelled like coal and sweat and drink, and when he spoke he mixed cuss words right in, and then he would suddenly turn red with embarrassment and say, 'Oh, please excuse me, Sister,' in a hasty recovery of good manners."

I laughed. I never knew my grandfather, Carroll Ahern, who had died before I was born. Something in her face, whenever she spoke about him, drew laughter out of me, and Grandma loved to make me laugh with her stories.

"He called you Sister? Grandma, did he mistake you for a nun?"

Marja suddenly let go of her white braid. She looked past me, and was quiet.

A week after my talk with Grandma on the porch, Uncle Dan came home from Indiana for a visit.

My father gave me a warning: "Your uncle lives life on a superior level, Eugene. Let's take care, this time, not to disturb him with a lot of childish concerns."

He said it as if it was something we would be doing together, but he actually meant it for just me.

My father moved a meeting with other lawyers into late afternoon so he could be home at the farm for an extended lunch to welcome his brother home. Grandma Marja presided in the center position at the dining room table, where she beamed over her family. My mother served tuna sandwiches — she made a point of reminding us it was Friday — and bottles of Schlitz beer for the four adults, a glass of lemonade for me.

At first my father and his brother were silent, attentive to their sandwiches, gnawing at the corners of the bread with an occasional "umph" or "huh," while delicately tipping beer bottles to their lips. We were all like strangers at a lunch counter, a bubble of quiet broken by occasional comments from one or the other, words that further discussion might hitch itself to.

Uncle Dan winked at me. My father didn't see, because it happened in such a brief instant, one that reestablished the club whose two members shared a secret, long-unspoken understanding: I was his favorite, and he that special relative who, for as long I could remember, would come home from Indiana as if for the sole purpose of seeing my face light up when we saw each other.

Real talk finally burst through an opening pierced by Uncle Dan. "Casey Stengel has all of baseball laughing at him."

My father raised one eyebrow at him.

Dan and my father both used to be Yankee fans, but living in the Midwest had eroded that away for my uncle in favor of the White Sox, the team in the '59 season that finally broke Stengel's string of pennants.

"Ole Case has gone daffy," Uncle Dan said, "using that platoon system. What happened to putting your best talent on the field, regardless of who you're facing on the mound?"

"You mean, the way Al Lopez does with Chicago," my father jeered. "Strictly a one-dimensional team, those White Sox. No surprise when the Dodgers clobbered them last October."

Their faces flushed, voices grew loud and lilting and spackled with jibes and laughs. Tuna fish suddenly disappeared in full bites now. Bottles of Schlitz suddenly bottomed up toward the chandelier and through amber glass displayed a gurgling displacement of liquid.

Uncle Dan winked at me again. This time my father saw it, and his eyes found mine, settled on me just enough to remind me of his previous admonition.

The Ahern women relaxed against the backs of their chairs, sighed, nibbled sandwiches and sipped their Schlitz from glasses as they watched and listened to sibling banter. Before long, female attention wandered away from the two brothers' baseball talk to their own discussion of how the Swiss chard, early peas, melons and beets were doing this year. I washed down my tuna fish with lemonade, on the lookout for another wink.

When lunch was over, my father hugged his brother — he very seldom hugged anybody — and drove off in his light-green-over-dark-green '56 Buick Special to that rescheduled appointment with important people at his law office in Wyotanda.

I followed Uncle Dan out to the barn, where I sat on a cushion of empty feed bags. He didn't mind at all, because he knew I knew well enough to be quiet as he read from his breviary. A black book with page edges tinted red, he would read sections prescribed for each day. Much of the red was worn away at the corners.

"Even though we each act separately, all of us read it together," he explained to me before he started. "We all recite the exact same thing."

"A secret club," I said.

He laughed. "Throughout the world, except Red China, where books have been confiscated and the practice banned."

Once he got started reading, he paced to and fro on the open floor between the hay mows, in the area where we had a make-up court for basketball. He was in dungarees and a blue work shirt, items he had purchased at JJ Newberry in Wyotanda on an earlier visit home. The fabric never seemed to show much wear. Maybe there was not much call for farm boy clothes back at the university, where he taught biology.

Book open to the day's assignment, he dutifully recited the words, carefully pronouncing Latin phrases in a whisper. Sometimes, he abruptly stopped and stared into the book, and recited a phrase all over again, pronouncing each syllable and consonant distinctly.

"Why do you repeat some of it?" I asked him after he'd finished that day's recitation.

"To get it right."

"What will happen if you get it wrong? How would the rest of the club even know? Especially the ones in Red China."

"They wouldn't know. But I would."

I figured Dan's nature was, in this respect, like that of my grandfather, Carroll Ahern, who Grandma Marja had told me was acutely stubborn and particular.

She had described how, when he built their permanent house in 1913, he couldn't lay the field-stone foundation without stopping many times to redo things. She had tried to help him, but it was too frustrating. Something about practicing the craft that had belonged to his family in the old country made him impossible, she'd said to me, and he would yell at her. "So, one day, I yelled right back. I told him, 'I quit!' and went off to enlarge my garden. He would only have himself to huff and puff at."

And my father had once told me about him and Dan, when they were kids, helping their father with the foundation to the new barn. His job had been to help set the stones while Dan mixed mortar, both of them working long hours every day for an entire summer. Sometimes Grandpa would suddenly knock some of it down and start over. "When it came to setting stone, your grandfather was hard put to be satisfied."

I was sure it was one of those stories designed to impress me with how hard he and Dan had had it under Grandpa Carroll, the point of which was to have me appreciate just how easy I had it.

"To any of us, the foundation would look perfect, a work of art," my father had said. "It was like his own father was looking over his shoulder, telling him it was flawed."

So, the same way Grandpa Carroll set foundation stones, Uncle Dan performed his recitation from the black book: stop, go back, and redo sections. He was never quite satisfied, as if someone was watching over his shoulder.

In most other ways, it seemed to me Uncle Dan took after his mother, Grandma Marja. Both had white-blonde hair, smooth, proportionate faces and pale blue eyes that suddenly seemed to brighten through the simple act of looking at you. I thought of them whenever I revisited that art book that nobody knew I had hidden in the engineering section up in the stacks at the Wyotanda Public Library. Opposite a photo of naked women without arms, made of marble, was one of an ancient urn, a tall vessel, perfectly symmetrical with graceful, flowing lines that attracted your eye to it at once. That was Marja and Uncle Dan: they looked like they had been fashioned by an artisan.

But my father looked more like my Grandpa Carroll's photos, wide and lumpy, eyes hiding serious thoughts. Both my father and his father appeared to have been shaped more by the elements, the way potatoes look a lot like the ground you dig them out of.

Dan closed his black book and carefully placed it in a wye of rough-hewn beams. Eyes shiny, he looked around at the inside of the barn that he, as a boy, had helped construct.

"Now that school's out, what are you doing with your free time?" he said.

You have to be careful when a grownup asks you a question like that. Answer too quickly and you could let them barge into your privacy to take you over with whatever they have in mind, maybe a planned program of improvement—yours.

But I was his special nephew, after all, a favored person, the other member of our two-man secret club. When Dan asked me that question, I figured he actually wanted to know.

"Sometimes I play basketball," was the first thing to come to mind under a horizontal beam where the basket was fastened to a wooden backboard. He and my father had mounted it there when the new barn was completed twenty five years ago in anticipation of Melody Falls High School's plan to start a team.

"By yourself?"

"Sometimes, by myself. Other times with Quin, or Hangy, or Adam, and a few other guys."

"Not with your father?"

"Not...usually."

He looked at me thoughtfully, and said, "Your father was quite a basketball player in his day. Hangy? Who's that?"

"Hangy Hobbes. Well, his real name is Harold."

"Old Man Hobbes' kid? He doesn't like his name Harold, I take it," Dan said.

"No. It's not that." I started to grin. I forced myself not to. Uncle Dan lived life on a superior level, my father had said.

But I was too late. He'd already caught me at it, and he grinned too. "I don't want to know how Harold acquired the name Hangy," he suggested.

I couldn't control my face any longer. "Yes. You would be right in saying that."

He muttered to himself, "Some things never change."

He looked around, eyes shiny again, then at me. "I used to play basketball here too. Often by myself, just like you, trying to up my skills."

"It must have paid off. Dad told me you were good."

He smiled, eyes glowed like embers.

"Your father was in France," he said thoughtfully. "It was wartime. He never saw any of my games. Could be distance and his imagination embellished my actual play. Marja sent him clippings from the *Clarion*. Besides, I'm talking about much earlier, when I was a kid. I used to practice hard by myself, or sometimes with Sheffield Hoy, to be ready for when your father and his friends would allow me into their game."

"But you're much taller than Dad. He couldn't have been much competition."

Dan laughed. "You forget. Your father is five years older. I was just a runty little kid trying to keep up with my big brother."

I couldn't imagine my father playing basketball. He'd been athletic, all right, from what I'd picked out of conversation about his youth. But, basketball? A game where you don't just have to run, but be quick, make changes of direction, fake, jump and shoot? Maybe I couldn't picture it because he was over forty now, an old man, no longer the muscled farm-boy of old photos, more the stuff of pillows on the couch in his law office. Uncle Dan was still young, tall, athletic, smooth and symmetrical…like that urn.

"Still keep it in the same old wooden box, I see," Dan said as he raised the lid and retrieved the basketball.

He turned the ball in his hands, eyed the trademark. He bounced it to me. "Show me your best shot."

A support beam—the one with a wye that held his black book—marked the in-bounds for half-court. From there, I let fly an arcing ball that boinged off the rim, bounced high and came back down to Dan.

"From way back there?" he said. "That's your best shot?"

"I make it most of the time."

"That's a good place to be good from, but only if they don't know it's coming. If that's all you've got, it's easy for anyone to anticipate, which makes it easy to block."

He bounced me the ball. "What else?"

"I'm a guard," I said, complaint restricting my voice. "It's pretty much that or, if they go for a block, I pass it off. I'm too short for anything else."

His eyes lost their blue. He motioned for me to give up the ball. I bounced it to him.

"You have to have an inside game. Without it, you're just a one-trick pony, and everybody knows the trick, Eugene. Don't you ever drive on the basket?"

"I'm too short. All those arms and legs over me."

"Stop saying that. Do you think Bob Cousy says that? Besides, you won't always be short. You will be taller someday, and by then it may be too late to learn the inside game. Learn it now, while it's difficult, and then when you grow, it'll be second nature."

He spoke in a voice I was unfamiliar with, insistent and demanding, his face flushed with disapproval. I felt my own face flush too, from loss of position. I was supposed to be his favorite nephew.

He changed to a softer tone. "What's the place on the floor where you feel most intimidated by all the arms and legs?"

"Under the basket," I said.

He motioned me to join him under the basket. I felt like a calf being herded into a pen.

"It's the hardest place to shoot from," he said, "especially for a short guy like you are, and like I used to be. Not just arms and legs. All those faces and eyeballs above you."

He handed me the ball, and stood a few inches from me, long arms spread out in the air.

"What are you going to do?" he demanded.

I quickly dribbled and turned to shoot. He blocked my shot.

"I figured you'd do that," he said.

"I figured you'd do that, too."

"Then why'd you go through with it?" His face red.

He had me stand under the basket again and handed me the ball.

"What are you going to do?" he demanded, more insistent this time.

I thought a moment. I faked one way, then to the opposite, and dribbled back to the first way, turned and shot. The ball didn't go in, but it was close after bouncing off the backboard.

Dan retrieved the rebound, and said, "Good. I wasn't expecting that."

Then he chided me for not going after the rebound myself, "Once you get your shot off, do you just become a fan? Go after the son of a bitch!"

His teeth and lips hissed the words. I'd never heard him, or any other priest, say son of a bitch before.

He repeatedly put me in situations under the basket He scolded me for not hustling, corrected me for moves that were too obvious, or just plain stupid, instructed me how to fake, how to put the ball up onto the backboard while facing away from it, how to put a twist in the ball so it skimmed off the backboard toward the basket, and how to imagine where I was in relation to the basket at all times.

We worked on it through the afternoon. We took off our shirts. Dan's male torso, his fuzzy, hard slabs of muscle, made me conscious of my awkward, lesser-defined flesh. Sweating, breathing hard against each other, we drilled until my father came home from work in his Buick and, thinking the barn door had been left open, came to close it.

"Teacher and pupil," my father's voice, a dark figure in the doorway light.

We stopped. My father looked back and forth between us, first a glance at me, then a look at his brother. He peered at me again for a long moment.

"Quick learner," Dan finally said. "A little more practice, and he'll have that Hangy kid crying in his Knickerbocker."

My father allowed a measured laugh from the front of his mouth.

"And keep on practicing," Dan said firmly to me. "Keep learning new things. Invent new moves, and try them out. Improve the ones that work and save the ones that don't for another day."

He bounced the ball to his older brother. "Take your best shot, Owen."

My father held the ball, eyed the basket, a glint in his eye. The glint flickered out, and he bounced the ball to me, and told me to put it away.

When I came back from the wooden box, Uncle Dan had buttoned up his blue shirt. The two of them were quiet, glancing at each other.

Uncle Dan didn't know my father had never played basketball with me.

# Chapter 3, Lumumba

Uncle Dan, after a few days' rest on the farm—my father had assigned him to cutting brush, forking manure, chopping wood and repairing a shed roof—seemed ready to return to his teaching duties. He left for the summer semester at Notre Dame out of the Lehigh Valley station in Wyotanda, my parents and I waving to him from the platform. The line of green and black passenger cars gave off a sequence of clanks as it was stretched out by the start-up pull of the engine, and crept forward. At the last moment, through the window, he gave me a wink.

Of almost-equal importance to the two-man secret club that Dan and I belonged to was a four-kid, close-knit group of guys from school. Hangy Hobbes, Adam Stippil and Quin Gutierrez all lived within walking distance.

The Hobbes Dairy Farm was the neighboring quarter-section to the south of ours, along the eastern slope of Belknap Ridge. The township dirt road that ran past our house hugged the mountain's contour, a dusty track curving westward up one side of a ravine to where it crossed over a corrugated culvert pipe that allowed Hobbes Creek to run under it. From there, it did a switchback downhill again before resuming its southerly meander through the woods and past the Hobbes place.

But that loop and the switchback stretched it out to almost a half-mile. I always trekked a straighter route, more aligned with the flight of the pigeons between our barn and Hobbes'. The downhill part of the journey lent itself to quick, long strides pulled along by gravity. You had to be careful to not be tripped by weeds and grass wrapping about your ankles, and not let yourself be snagged by the bottom strand of barbed wire fencing at the lower edge of the hay field.

The woods down there had a way of slowing me down. I stood still in sudden cool, green shadows. Except for the lapping of water over stone at the bottom of the ravine, all was silent. Everything that lived in here knew I had just come in, and waited to see what I would do.

The forest could not hold its breath for long. It either soon forgot about me or, more likely, grew impatient. It was its own world, just like the sunlit, cultivated and fenced world I came from, and the forest accepted that it had to keep going with its life whether I was there or not. Insects found their voice in whispers and hums, along with sounds of chipmunks, mice, and squirrels, all mincing the air with busy doings. A blackbird sang out a question. Further on, a woodpecker rapped for morsels hidden under old bark. Above, sunlight speckled the leafy weave of maple, oak, ash, alder and butternut, and from the steepest sides of the ravine, the bushy long needles of white pine. They say that, before the loggers came in the 1860s, this mountain had been covered in ancient pine.

I picked my way down into the ravine. Sunlight, mostly screened out by the canopy, sneaked through in small, winking patterns onto stone moss and purple lichen. The forest floor, layered in leftovers from seasons past, made the ground slippery as I climbed down. I gripped pine roots exposed by the wash of roaring current during spring runoffs. At the bottom, rocks turned into stepping stones over the rushing water, and once across, pine roots provided handholds for pulling myself up the other side. Emerging from the forest, I entered into the bright day again, slithered under barbed wire, and climbed Hobbes's pasture up to their house.

"Harold has a job to do," Hangy's stepmother, Crystal, said as soon as she opened the back door. She had me sit at the kitchen table. "Mr. H. has him cleaning stable today."

Harold was Hangy's real name. He was Harold, Junior. He became Hangy to kid-friends some while back when we were all pissing together into an empty peanut butter jar that we poured down one of the many rat holes behind Old Man Hobbes' corn crib. It suddenly occurred to us—to Quin and Adam and me—that Harold did it differently than we did, that his stream was out of control, impossible to aim, until he pulled back a mysterious scallop of skin hanging off the end.

Crystal Hobbes moved swiftly about her kitchen. She had been helping out with farm work today, as she often did during the busy summer months. Instead of a house dress, she wore a blue denim work shirt and dungarees, which belonged to her husband, Old Man Hobbes. The work clothes were faded and far too big for her. The shirt hung well off her shoulders in loose billows of material, sleeves rolled up past her elbows. The dungarees started out bunched at the waist under a worn leather belt, then rounded out in favor of her hips, back pockets stretched tight over rear slope, and pant legs falling loosely to rolled cuffs. Her blonde hair—if not dressed for farm labor, it would have fallen in curls around her neck—was tightly pulled back into a lush nest of ringlets held in place by a green band. From her side pocket, the corner of a folded-up red bandana peeked out, easily retrievable for tying around her neck to hold her shirt collar closed against hayseeds and dust.

In the summer, particularly during haying season, I often saw her afield, where she worked as hard as any man. She never seemed to allow farm work to excuse her from housework, either, or gardening and canning, or mothering her two young ones, four-year-olds Elsie and Elise. Hangy, who was her stepson, was old enough that he didn't need much mothering anymore, nor did he want any. And Lucinda, her sixteen-year-old stepdaughter, had never allowed Crystal to mother her at all, not since the day Crystal married the old man and moved into the house six years ago.

Crystal placed two fig bars on a plate and a glass of lemonade in front of me. "You'll have to down this in a hurry. Mr. H. has me raking the north hayfield, trying to get it all baled and into the barn tomorrow ahead of the rain. So, I'll have to go right back at it as soon as the twins are cooled off. They got so hot on the tractor, I just had to bring them in and let them play in the tub."

"The twins go along with you raking hay?"

I hoped she would ask me to stay in the cool house with them. Around me they were never brats, the way they were for their older brother, and their older sister would have nothing to do with them. For me, they would sit quietly, one on each leg, and I would have them help read the newspaper. One arm around each of them would leave me just enough room to hold onto the *Clarion* and read aloud.

Often, when I'd finish an article, one or the other would ask a question, almost in a whisper. The last time we had read together, a report from Associated Press about the Belgian Congo had them bending their necks back to look up at me with huge blue eyes, and when I was finished, they had asked me to read it again. They loved it when I read aloud the name Lumumba, and after the second reading, made me repeat it over and over until they said it along with me.

"Lumumba," their blue eyes looking at me.

"Oh, they're old enough now. They can ride with me." When she spoke of her twin girls her eyes lit up. "They stand on the M's axle housing, one on each side. I make sure I feel two sets of hands grasping both shirt sleeves at all times. Makes it tough to turn the wheel fast at the corners of the field, but I keep her down in low gear."

Like her husband, she referred to the tractor as either "her" or "the M." To Old Man Hobbes and Crystal, the Farmall Super M held the importance of a living creature, maybe even a person. Their secondary tractor was an orange Allis-Chalmers WC, which Old Man Hobbes had purchased for his father—who had always farmed with horses before that—just before enlisting in the War. For years, the WC had enjoyed the premier position among the equipment on the Hobbes Farm. So, the purchase of the new M shoved "Old Allis" down in rank, like a milk cow whose production was on the decline. Crystal and the old man had an agreement that whenever she did field work, she got the M because it had a starter, leaving Old Allis, with its stubborn manual crank-starter, to her husband.

I finished the fig bars and lemonade. Crystal quickly took away the plate and glass. When you went to the Hobbes's house, you got lemonade or tea. Water from their well had a bit of iron in it, so you wouldn't want to drink it by itself. Turning it into tea or lemon water would help cover up the taste. No Hobbes would offer you milk, or drink it themselves. Like most dairy farmers, to think of it as a beverage disgusted them.

"They're starting to fuss," she said as she quickly washed the plate and glass, dried them and put them away.

She was quick in everything she did. When someone hurries, their motions are jerky, but Crystal's quickness was smooth. She moved through chores as if things just happened around her the way they were supposed to, the way water in the ravine swiftly moved among the rocks. I was careful to not be caught gazing at her, at that look on her face, a look of readiness for the next moment. Under light cast from the kitchen window, a wisp of hair on her cheek appeared and disappeared with her movements.

Into the heart of that sudden vision of her, when motion and readiness and the look on her face were all joined in the way light from the window wanted to favor her, memory dropped a cold iron weight. In a cloud from a shared Pall Mall under the Third Street Bridge one afternoon after an altar boy meeting, Quin Gutierrez and I had talked about Crystal.

"Do you suppose she makes her old man take that dirty cap off when they do it?" Quin sneered.

And I sneered back, "Maybe the old man doesn't have to take his hat off at all, because he does it—you know—the other way around, like we saw in Al Cousineau's magazine."

From there, it had been all lip curls and laughs. Through cigarette puffs we tried to outdo each other with even uglier things to say. Now, in Crystal's kitchen, memory of that talk was like finding barn-floor filth floating in a pail of milk, bits of manure floating on top of the cream.

Here in the daylight, in her house, Crystal's movements and female roundness in those oversize man's clothes that smelled like fresh-cut hay pulled my eye to her. Having finished her work at the sink, she turned to look at me, making my ears flush.

Her eyes brightened. "Tell you what, Eugene. The old man must be totally parched by now. I hate to ask, but will you watch the twins for a few minutes, just until I can switch out jugs of iced tea for Mr. H.? He's down at the drainage ditch, cleaning out the sluice pipe. I'll be right back."

"I can watch them."

One moment, she was Hangy's stepmother, and in the next, a woman. I'd not seen her like this before, soft and curvy, a vision pulling at me. Not Crystal Hobbes.

Miss Hendershott, yes. My sixth grade teacher had been bursting into my day dreams, and night-dreams too, and would have me squirming, as much from the surprise of her suddenly wanting to be with me as from trying to imagine what we would do together.

Pulling the jug of iced tea from the Kelvinator, Crystal called up to her girls to get out and get dried off and dressed so they could come down and "help Eugene read the *Clarion*."

Chirping of the twins from the tub upstairs stopped, replaced by the scamper of bare feet on the floor.

With a jug of new iced tea for Old Man Hobbes, Crystal went out the back, screen door whapping the stop. I heard the whine of the starter, followed by the rumble of the M as she headed down the lane that led to where he was working on the sluice at the drainage ditch.

Upstairs, the twins were very quiet. I went into the parlor and sat on the sofa, and looked out to the hallway. Two pairs of bare feet appeared up high on either side of the stairs, followed by two sets of legs, cautiously descending.

"You going to help me with this paper?"

Feet and legs abruptly stopped, froze in position. Whispers came from the staircase, then the feet and legs scurried back upstairs.

When I turned to the Sports, to yesterday's box scores, peripheral vision over the top edge of the paper had Elsie and Elise back down the staircase again, closer this time, moving carefully down, exposing their puffy little bodies like cherubs on the ceiling mural of Saint Agatha's Church.

I rattled the paper. They froze, looked at each other and whispered, then ever-so-slowly continued coming down.

On Saint Agatha's ceiling, two doughy cherubs, one on each side, sneaked forward from behind God, who stood atop the clouds. No doubt, they had been told by some grownup angel to stay far behind the Almighty and out of the way of all His busy doings. But, unable to contain themselves, they floated out from the edges of the scene into glorified air, faces forever locked by the splendor of it all in a state of angelic wonder. Fluffy wings sprouted from their backs, wings that didn't look anywhere near strong enough to support them in flight. But the miraculous nature of their home in Heaven obviously had persuaded reality to adjust itself for the occasion. A large banner swept across the bottom of the picture proclaiming "*Gloria in Excelsis Deo,*" at the feet of God, its tasseled ends swirling up to hide the sex of each cherub from the curious gaze of naughty minds like mine among worshipers below.

Elsie and Elise came down the stairs in complete silence, except for tiny whispers I couldn't decipher. Careful to not spook them, I kept watch over the edge of the paper without looking directly at them.

"Those two girls are going to miss this story," I said to myself aloud. "Too bad. It's another one about the Belgian Congo."

When they reached the floor, they suddenly ran, each to one side, and hid behind the edges of the wide doorway that separated the parlor from the hall. Possessed by giggles, they each sneaked out, naked, a look of awe similar to that of the ceiling cherubs, but with a primitive gleam in their eyes.

The instant I looked up from the *Clarion* and acknowledged them, they both retreated in a duet of louder giggles back into hiding on either side of the doorway. Blushing faces came out again, large blue eyes shiny for my reaction. I focused on today's episode of *Curly Kayo* in the comics, and held the *Clarion* up so I could just see them over the top of the paper. After a wait, unsure of my response to their antics, they retreated again to their hiding places, from where they whispered to each other across the wide doorway.

Curly Kayo, waving to a fan in the crowd, lost his concentration just long enough to be jolted by a sudden left jab from Slacky Binder. It dulled his reaction, left him open to a split-second right cross that rocked the Champ off his feet. In the second of two frames, Curly was down, his normally chiseled look fallen limp against the mat. Solid block lettering arose from the crowd: GET UP, CURLY....GET UP!

Having agreed on their next move through whispers, and other mysterious forms of communication known only to them, they each protruded a butt. I gave them a low growl, having learned to mimic our old hound, Lowdown. The butts disappeared into dollops of laughter, which drew from my throat a sudden explosion of Lowdown's bark, whose ferocity any stranger approaching our property would be familiar with. The twins appeared together in the middle of the doorway, shiny blue eyes wide. I pretended to still be looking at the paper, which I slowly lowered. As I raised my eyes, I let them have a more menacing growl, the one Lowdown would hold in reserve for expectation of real danger.

The Hobbes twins stared at me, two cherubs missing their wings. Pink mouths opened for screams that came out separately, but reached my ears with exactness that made it a single, piercing note. They turned around and ran up the stairs. As they clamored higher, their courage grew. Near the top, they screeched that I would not be able to catch them: a dare for me to chase after.

In the *Clarion*, Beetle Bailey drove a Jeep, Sarge in the passenger seat. Once it was my turn to join the army, would they let me drive one? My father had already taught me how to drive the old rusty Jeep we kept below the barn for field chores, so they wouldn't have to train me on the clutch or gear pattern, or how and when to engage the transfer case and low range. With all my experience on the farm, I'd be perfect for driving a sergeant around. It would sure beat all the walking and tired feet my father and other veterans talked about.

The rumble of the Farmall M outside grew louder as it arrived back in the yard. Upstairs, the twins, who were supposed to be dressed by now, supposed to be helping me read the *Clarion*, scurried to get ready. Crystal came through the back door from the yard, empty jug in her hand. She quickly washed it out, then looked into the parlor at me.

"You didn't allow them back in the tub, did you?"

"No. They're just taking their time getting ready. I warned them they were missing the Belgian Congo story."

She yelled up the stairs. "What are you two doing? Eugene looks awfully lonely reading the paper by himself."

She looked at me again and laughed. "I should have known they wouldn't be ready. They haven't pestered you, have they?"

"Not much," I said.

"Oh, you wouldn't tell me anyway."

She went back to the kitchen, and I moved on to *Steve Canyon*. The twins, now dressed, came down, looked at me with round eyes. I winked one eye, then the other, so they would know I hadn't ratted on them. When Crystal came to the hallway, she wagged her head and herded them back upstairs.

"A shirt on backwards, and one missing sock," she laughed over her shoulder.

"They'd better hurry it up," I said. "Running out of time for the Belgian Congo story."

I heard the three of them rustling around upstairs, and then their mother said "Well, you'll have to ask him." The rustling moved to the stairs, grew quieter, and then came down to the hallway, quieter still, and then into the parlor. "Ask him," Crystal said from the doorway. "Ask him nicely."

"Eugene," came a whisper.

I put down the paper. They stood before me, side by side, tiny breaths lightly puffing. Elsie, wide-eyed, looked at me, while Elise looked at her sister.

"Can we help read about that Belgian Congo?" Elsie said.

"Say please," Elise reminded Elsie.

"Please," Elsie added.

"But, I thought it was time for you girls to help your mom rake hay again."

They both looked back at Crystal standing in the doorway.

"You have a few minutes to help Eugene first. So, you'd better get going."

In an instant they were past the paper and each on one side of my lap, bunching material from the knees of my pant legs in their hands as a way to hold on in case I started bouncing them. My arms out around them to hold the *Clarion*, I folded it back up and took it to the front page, where an AP Wire photo in the center of the page's upper half presented an image of Prime Minister Lumumba.

"That's him," I said. "He's the one we've been reading about. Lumumba."

"Lumumba," they both said distinctly and at the same time.

I gave them one bronco bounce. They giggled and grabbed on tighter, and scissored their legs more tightly around my thighs.

"Now why won't their brother play with them like that?" Crystal complained from the doorway.

I looked up at her briefly without answering. No way would I rat out Hangy. He didn't see the twins as his sisters. They were just extra people who got in the way, like their mother, who was not Hangy's real mother, and so her two girls were not really his sisters, except that they all shared Old Man Hobbes as a father. Not that I would tell her. She already felt bad enough that Hangy's sister, Lucinda, hated her, and had said so.

I got away from Crystal's question and started in on the newspaper story, reading it aloud. She soon gave up on me answering and went back to the kitchen, where she cleaned and straightened and ran water and banged utensils toward supper, all with swift motions that held onto one edge of my attention, the rest of it occupied by the Belgian Congo. I left out bloody parts. I changed a short paragraph about mutilation into a story of a man who was tickled by his captors until he couldn't stand it any longer, and told where the gold was hidden.

The Hobbes twins turned around and looked at me with eyes full of wonder. I gave them another bronco bounce, which had them laughing as they tightly clawed dungaree denim again. Crystal came back into the parlor and stood, listening to me read to them.

"Ready to go, girls?" she finally said.

They gripped me tighter.

"Time to help your mom rake hay," I said, and put the paper down.

"No," they both whisper-whined.

"But if you don't rake the hay, the hay baler will go hungry."

They turned and each gave me a serious eye.

"The baler will go hungry?" Elise asked.

"And then the cows."

They quietly dismounted.

Crystal stooped on one knee to tie Elsie's shoe. "No loose laces allowed aboard the M."

The way she knelt and leaned, which rounded her shoulders inside Old Man Hobbes's oversize shirt; the way she tied the miniature shoe; the way her mouth formed words, and her eyes looked so satisfied with a simple task as fingers moved swiftly, the wisp of hair on her cheek wicking light from the window—it all had me looking at Crystal, had me, from across the room, feeling the squeeze as if we were putting arms around each other.

She looked up. Her eyes pierced me in the instant before I could look away. She stood and put her hands on her hips. "Quin and Adam were here earlier. I told them the same thing I'm telling you. Harold has to clean stable today. That bedding and manure's been packed in there since winter, and Mr. H. wants it spread onto the lower fields where we have already finished haying." Her face drawn into seriousness, she said, "I mean it, I don't want you holding up Harold from filling up that manure spreader. I don't need a furious old man on my hands."

"I'll help him. That way, Hang—I mean, Harold—will get done even faster."

Her face melted back into that look of calm readiness. "As long as your mother doesn't call me up to complain that your clothes smell like cow shit."

Her girls put their hands over their mouths and looked up at her.

"My mother won't call you." I had no way of keeping such a promise.

"Well, if you're going to help Harold, just remember, you're here to work." And then Crystal smiled at me. "Eugene, you can always come back any other day to play."

My face burned. Play? It was not like we would be moving toy trucks around a dirt pile, or setting up Hangy's Lionel train assembly, or scaling hay bale cliffs in the barn to rout dug-in Germans from the mow, the way we used to when we were little.

Play? These days, I smoked Pall Malls. I cursed, "Jesus Christ," and knew the batting average of everyone on the Yankees. I did not play. I was twelve.

## CHAPTER 5, HOUR OF NEED

Through the wide gated doorway, Hangy's face was red, but whether from anger or hard work I couldn't tell. My earlier eagerness to help him quickly wilted when I saw how ugly of a job it was.

"You're up to your knees in it this time," Quin Gutierrez said, black eyes gleaming through his glasses.

"Yeh, funny. Real funny." Hangy oofed as he banged the manure fork against the steel lip of the spreader.

Quin sat on the top rail of the gate, Adam Stippil beside him, from where they'd probably been at it a long time, making manure jokes as a commentary to Hangy's chore.

"Goddamn farming. I hate it," Hangy muttered.

"Shouldn't say His name like that," Adam said, no doubt adopting a serious tone from his father, the Reverend.

Again, Hangy clanged the fork against the top of the spreader to loosen stubborn manure clumps.

When Quin saw me coming up to the gate, he winked and said, "Hey, Genie. How 'bout you running up to grab us a cig from the milk house."

"Should we be smoking in here?" I wouldn't have asked, but was hoping to get out of having to walk back up around the barn to where we kept our stash of Pall Malls up in the milk house cupola.

Hangy answered for him. "No, you are not! My old man would kill us all for smoking in here, especially me. He'd grab the nearest handy tool for whipping my ass to hamburger."

One of those rare occasions when a grownup's rule was on my side.

"Aw, what's it going to hurt?" Adam squealed.

Hangy's face reddened a little more. "My old man sees you smoking near the barn, and you'll never be allowed in here again."

Quin laughed, and Adam's laughter was like a puppy right on the heel of Quin's. Quin said, "Guess what, Adam: Old Man Hobbes catches us puffing a fag, and never can we come back in here."

"Not ever again?" Adam said.

"Not ever. Banned forever from...what is this place? Cow-shit Empire."

Quin laughed hard at his own remark, and slid along the rail a little, which made Adam move too, which made a space for me alongside Quin, who always liked to be in the middle.

"Goddamn farming," Hangy said again, and dug the fork into the manure, inter-layered and packed hard with a year's layers of straw bedding.

"Shouldn't say that," Adam said seriously. "The Lord's name."

Hangy ignored him.

As I took my place on top of the gate, Quin nudged me with his elbow and turned to Adam, "Look around, only be-gotten son of the Reverend. Does this place look anything like the inside of your old man's church?"

"Doesn't matter," Adam said. "Our Savior sees and hears everything."

"And as he looks down on us," Quin said, "you know what he says right about now? Holy shit! As far as the eye can see."

"Shouldn't mock like that."

Hangy stopped forking manure for a moment and wiped his blue work-shirt sleeve across his forehead.

Adam changed the subject. "Everything is so damp in here, I don't see how we'd be likely to set the barn on fire from one smoke."

"No smoking anywhere in or near the barn." Hangy glared at him. "Besides, isn't smoking against the rules of your church? Wonder what your Savior thinks of that. Wonder what your old man would think."

"Not my Savior, but our Savior," Adam said. "And my father, he's called the Reverend, not my old man."

Hangy looked sharply at the three of us sitting on the rail watching him work, lines of sweat flowing out of his blonde hair and down his face. "Well, my old man does not allow smoking in here, and if you guys burn down his barn, it's hello Barry Town for you."

None of us laughed. Eli Zorn, a kid three years ahead of us, had done eight months downriver at Barry Town for gashing his mother's shoulder with a sod spade. She had nagged him for the last time about changing his socks.

One day, under the Third Street Bridge, Eli had told us, "You learn the rules real quick down there. The first rule is: none of the other rules matter. It's whatever they feel like do-ing to you. And, believe me, at Barry Town, they do feel like doing it to you."

Then, he had clammed up, would not tell us what things they had felt like doing to him. He would only drag on his cigarette, then study the lazy column of smoke blown out through a small, round opening formed with tight lips.

"You want to stay clear of that place," was the most we'd been able to get out of him, until we'd finally given up and climbed the dirt bank from under the bridge, leaving him alone with his thoughts.

Hangy was not happy forking manure. The sadness coming off him spread over to us. Adam and Quin and I sat on the rail in quiet.

Finally, Quin said, "You have another manure fork?"

Hangy's eyes lit up at the prospect of help. "You guys aren't going down to the pond?"

"We were planning to, but that was before your old man decided to make you move Mount Manure out of this stable and into the spreader."

Quin shifted into the voice he used when he pretended to give a speech. "Gentlemen, the situation before us calls for an alternate plan of action. I propose, in fact, that the situation is a perfect fit for fulfilling the promise that is at the heart of our august organization, the Dumble-Doers of Greater Melody Falls Township, whose motto, to which each of us has sworn and remains forever loyal, doing dumb things with purpose."

The speech had Hangy stopping to lean on the fork handle. Adam and I were already laughing. Quin loved to give pretend speeches, play to us with gestures and expressions full of importance, a recipe of combined mannerisms he'd gathered from grownups, teachers, politicians interviewed on Sunday news television, and especially the way Father Kearns talked, who, according to what grownups said, had been trained by Jesuits.

Hangy, not in the mood to laugh, at least grinned, his almost-invisible blonde mustache gleaming with sweat.

"Wait a minute," I said. "I propose that helping Hangy move his manure pile was not what anybody had in mind who swore the oath."

Quin messed up my hair. "Spoken like the true son of a lawyer."

"It's not my manure pile," Hangy said. "It's my old man's manure pile. I'm just the kid who has to move it."

Adam spoke up. "Well, it does fit the idea of doing dumb things."

"And with purpose." Quin raised his hand toward the joists that held the upper barn's plank flooring above us, "although, what precise purpose is being served by it remains a matter known only to your father, Old Master Hobbes himself."

"I move we go to the pond," I said.

Quin said, "And leave our sorry fellow Dumble-Doer here on Poop Hill all by himself?"

"I'm all for helping Hangy as much as the next man," I lied, "but we'll all have the stink of it on us, and wear it home on our clothes."

Hangy looked at me sharply. I looked away. Hangy went on forking manure without saying anything.

Quin decided, "This calls for a parley at the milk house."

Hangy stopped and spat. "Can't have a parley at the milk house. What if my old man comes along and finds me not here?"

"You don't even get a break? What if you have to take a leak?" Adam said. "Even my old—the Reverend—isn't that mean."

Hangy, one hand resting on the fork handle, turned and swept his arm in a half-circle. "What do you see? A year's worth of cow shit and piss two feet deep. Does it make sense, if I need to take a leak, that I'd be going off somewhere else to do it?"

"How about getting a drink? He can't keep you from doing that."

"This here is Hobbes Farm. Not Hobbes Hotel." He pointed at the galvanized water tub along the wall.

I said, "But what do you use for a dipper?"

Hangy laughed at that, planted the fork deeper in the manure so it would stand on its own, went over to the tub, knelt down on one knee, removed his hat and put his face to the water. He sucked up a mouthful and swallowed.

"Christ Almighty," Quin said.

"Shouldn't say that," Adam said.

"Will I be struck by lightning?"

"You could," Adam said quietly.

"Well, Cripe'n-itey, then. Okay with your reverence if I say that?"

"Wait a minute," I said. "Your old man won't be walking all the way back up here, not just to check on you. He'd only come up if he thought it was about time to pull the spreader out to the field. That manure spreader isn't even half-full."

Quin messed up my hair. "That's you, Genie, always figuring things."

Hangy thought a minute. He looked at the less-than-half-full spreader. He looked at me. "He wouldn't be walking anyway. He drove Old Allis down to the ditch."

"That's even better!" Quin said. "We'd hear it start up, if and when his majesty decides to pay us a royal visit."

Hangy's eyes widened. He gave the manure fork handle a kick. "That means there *is* time for a parley at the milk house."

A ten-foot square structure with a cupola at the center of its roof peak, the milk house was a separate building from the barn, out beside the driveway, a location that made it accessible to the Melody Falls Creamery milk truck. A stainless-steel tank, recently installed to accommodate new state health department rules, took up half the floor space, its refrigeration compressor huffing against June swelter. The milk house was a perfect place for Dumble-Doers' parleys. It was cozy. We had privacy for planning our dumb doings. Cigarette smoke easily found its way out by way of natural draft from the cupola that drew fresh air in through vents at the base of the walls.

So here it was, a regular meeting of the Melody Falls Township Dumble-Doers. Regular, in the sense that it had not been scheduled and involved taking a break from what grownups — in this case, Hangy's old man — expected. Regular, in the sense that it involved passing around a Pall Mall.

We sat around the milk cooler on three-legged stools, which were left over from when milking used to be done by hand. Hangy, removing his boots so he wouldn't scratch up the stainless steel cover, climbed onto the cooler and reached into the milk house cupola to retrieve a Pall Mall. He handed it to Quin, who dug out his Ronson, lit up, dragged on the cigarette, and passed it around.

On the first pass, it was our ritual for each person to inhale deeply, and then intone the words, *"In hoc signo vinces."* When we had first started this ritual, Adam had been reluctant to join in because it sounded like something Catholic to him. But once we showed him that the words actually came from the back of the cigarette pack, and that it meant "In this sign shall you conquer," he was all right with it.

After the secret words were spoken, as exhaled smoke broke into puffy syllables and rose up over our heads in a blue cloud, regular parley conversation started.

Quin, holding the cigarette, stood and launched another speech.

"Gentlemen, this here is the problem. On the one hand, we are eager to assist a fellow Dumble-Doer in his hour of need. On the other, none of us wants to go home smelling like the south end of a north-bound herd of cattle."

Our laughter fired up the speech-giver's eyes through his glasses.

"Now, gentlemen, no doubt you are all anxious to offer many alternative solutions to this problem. What say ye?" He passed the cigarette to Adam.

"Burn the barn down," Adam said. He passed the cigarette to me.

"Let our friend Hangy hang," I said. I passed it to Hangy.

"I'd better get back," he muttered shakily through exhaled smoke.

We were quiet for a moment, serious need for a real solution having overwhelmed the comedy. The compressor continued to huff.

Quin, the cigarette back in his possession, said, "Let's focus on our goal: the pond."

The pond. Pall Mall went around again as we all thought about the pond, our mixed plumes of exhale climbing in a gentle swirl to the cupola.

"Yes, the pond. Our goal is the pond. Once Hangy completes his dance with a shit pile, we're all headed for the pond. But, gentlemen, I put it to you here and now that a pond is not for recreation only."

"It's actually there for the cows," Hangy said.

"So noted," Quin said. "A matter of small relevance, however. As we frolic—"

"As we what?" Adam said.

"As we Dumble-Doers savor the pursuit of doing dumb things in the luxurious confines of the cow pond, our garments may be judged as being of no use to us at all. Lest we otherwise suffer their stable stench all the way home, we will have ample opportunity to wash them in the same pure waters in which we find ourselves bathing."

"We can leave the clothes on the bank to dry as we swim!" Hangy said.

I knew by now there would be no way out. We would be helping our fellow Dumble-Doer in his hour of need move manure. "You have any other forks, Hangy?"

"Manure forks is one thing we've got plenty of around here."

The compressor, having fully charged the coils on the milk tank, shut off. All was suddenly quiet. Puttering came to us from the distance, an echo off the woods. Old Man Hobbes had cranked up Old Allis's noisy engine and was on his way.

## CHAPTER 6, RICH LADIES IN NEW YORK AND PARIS

We'd washed our clothes, wrung them with our hands and laid them out on the pond bank.

We looked at each other, Quin and Hangy and I. Adam kept his underpants on. He didn't know that a ribbon of purple on his flesh peeped out of the waistband of his underwear onto his lower back, or that two smaller ones snaked out a leg hole onto the back of his thigh. The three of us could only look at each other. Nothing to be said.

We stepped into the water from the bank, all four of us a little teetery, arms windmilling the air for balance at the sensation of mud underfoot, of being sucked into it, of knowing it hid sharp stones. Quin, as always, soon gained his pond feet, sloshed ahead, bent at the waist and slid headfirst under the surface without a splash. Long, sinewy arms in slow, even strokes parted the water as it slid over him, and he crossed the pond.

Hangy went out to the middle, dunked himself, then came up again, blond hair plastered to his head. He looked around, got his bearings and went in the direction of Quin in splashes and kicks, round farm-boy muscles rolling along the surface. They soon conjured up a race against each other, which had no definite start or finish. At the end of the pond, Quin declared himself the dubious winner. Hangy just laughed at him and at the fun of it, their asses white in the sun.

Adam, still with his shorts on near the bank, dunked himself a few times, then sat in the shallows, forearms resting on his knees, face drawn into seriousness.

I was the slow one, a cautious intruder into territory foreign to me, unable to overcome the strangeness, gooseflesh, and uncertainty of breath that I'd always experienced upon first entering water, even warm like this, which the sun had been slowly heating ever since the March thaw. Finally dunking myself, I tried out long strokes and kicks Uncle Dan had shown me after supper one summer evening, when he and my parents and Marja had gone down for a swim over at our place. It came easier to me this time. After just a few tries, I shook off a year's rust from the moves he'd taught me. It was so much easier without my father watching. I swam laps out of the way of the other two swimmers. Muscles in my back and arms warmed to the effort of pulling myself through the water, legs learned to refine the kicks, to convert what started as jerky motions into rhythmic pulsations in tune with arm strokes. The surface gave up its resistance, embracing me as I moved through it.

Once I tired, I joined Adam in the shallows, and sat in the water. Mud crept up between my ass cheeks.

"That's why they call it bottom mud," Marja had told me when I was a little kid.

Memory from those days pictured Marja and me playing in the water on hot days. The mud in our pond was slimier than here at the Hobbes farm. Over many decades since Grandpa Carroll had first dug it out, our pond had slowly filled in with fine silt. According to my father, it was now only about half the area and depth it had once been when he and Dan had learned to swim. But over here, every two years Old Man Hobbes scoured his pond out with a drag-line bucket, which he pulled by a steel cable attached to the draw bar of his Farmall. That left the mud here grittier.

Quin and Hangy, out in the middle, splashed and jawed at each other, dove for stones, competed with how far they could throw them without the benefit of being able to plant their feet.

I looked at Adam. "How come you have those bruises?"

He looked away from me, ears reddening. "Bruises?"

"I thought I should tell you. They're obvious, that's all."

Adam looked toward the noise coming from the others. "Slipped on the stairs."

He stayed watching Quin and Hangy, ears flushed, thinking up more things to tell me. "Skidded on my ass, all the way down the stairs, the cellar stairs, you know, under the church. Those stone steps. You know, taking a load of wood down to the furnace."

A load of wood down to the furnace...in the summer? I was careful not to look at him directly. Just nodded.

"What time do you suppose it is?" he said.

"Maybe two, there-about."

"You figure two? When it gets anywhere near three, I've gotta go."

His chin dropped a little, and he looked at me under his eyebrows. "I'm not supposed to be over here."

"Why not?"

"I'm supposed to be working on something."

"Oh, the Reverend—he always has you working on something."

He nodded, then looked away thoughtfully.

"What happens at three?"

"Nothing at three. The Reverend comes home by four, and I want to play it safe and be sure I'm home when he gets there."

Adam didn't know I knew that his father, the Reverend Stippil, Melody Falls Township's one and only full-time employee, was way behind on the grading project. I'd overheard one end of a phone conversation between my father and one of the other township supervisors. From what I'd heard, they were discussing overtime for the Reverend.

But I didn't tell that to Adam. To tell anybody would just let it out that I could overhear what went on in my father's home office down below my bedroom. Father Kearns had advised me in Confession that eavesdropping, if you did it on purpose, was just like lying. It was lying in reverse.

"Technically, you're not telling a lie," he had said. "But you're still engaging in falsehood, still deceiving others, allowing them to think you don't know something about them that you actually do."

Everybody said the Jesuits had trained Father Kearns to always know what he was talking about. But I hadn't yet decided if I was engaging in falsehood or not, because I wasn't ready to say I eavesdropped on purpose. What I did know for sure, though, was that lying was my biggest flaw, especially since I'd moved on up from being just a kid, and was on my way toward being a grownup.

"...through my fault, through my fault, through my most grievous fault..."

That was my most grievous fault, all right. Lying. I was so damned good at it. I knew how to think out what was going on around me, and then place a juicy one right into the mix. But, as I grew older, the things going on around me were getting more complicated. I'd been lucky more than once that I hadn't been caught and exposed for the liar I was. It was something I'd have to work on for sure.

Quin and Hangy, breathing hard, came over and sat in the shallows with us.

I said, "You guys know about Adam falling down the stairs?"

Adam looked at me sharply at first, then relaxed. Now that he knew the bruises were visible, he also realized he would need to explain the same story to them that he'd told me. They were quiet, glanced at me now and then, as Adam described falling down the stairs in his father's church cellar. With a new telling, he added that he'd been stocking the cellar ahead of time for next winter, which made it more plausible.

"I'd seen that on you," Quin said, helping the tale settle in. "Like some kind of bruises."

"Me too," Hangy said. "Didn't say anything, because I figured you didn't want to talk about it."

Adam shrugged. He stood up and took off his shorts. No need to hide the bruises any more. He was more hairy than us, his privates lush with wiry curls. He'd started to get hair way back when he was eight, when the rest of us were still completely bare, and in awe of him.

"I'd better get all this out," he said. He squatted down and washed caked mud out of the seat of his shorts. When he finished, he went to the bank and laid the garment out with his other clothes in the sun. His bare ass was a field of purple splotches and swirls.

"Christ Almighty, Adam," Quin said. "Be careful next time on those church steps."

"Shouldn't say that, Quin."

"Cripe'n-itey, I mean."

"Cripe'n-itey," Hangy echoed. "Is getting wood the job the Reverend picked out for you for the summer?"

"Job?"

"You know, he's always picking out a job for you to do whenever school's out."

"Not really a job," Adam said. "It's one of my chores. In the winter I have to keep a fire in the furnace of the church on Wednesday and Sunday, and the furnace in the house all the time I'm not at school—that's when my mother takes care of it. But I have to make sure there's always wood at the ready. My sister and me both have to do it."

Quin suddenly laughed. "Agnes May, too? She has to get firewood with you?"

Adam described to us how he and the Reverend felled trees in the woods behind the church; just the crooked ones, leaving straight ones to grow for timber. They trimmed the felled trees, cut small branches into lengths ready for burning, and cut up the heavier logs with a two-man cross-cut.

"After we haul sawed logs up to the yard, it's my chore to split them, and mine and Agnes May's to carry the pieces in."

"She's strong enough to carry wood?" Quin said with big eyes. "That skinny brat sister of yours?"

"Maybe skinny, but she's got long arms and legs, and she's strong." He took on a disgusted look. "A lot stronger than she pretends. She doesn't do her share, that's for sure. She only has to stock the kitchen stove, that's all, and gather kindling, if you can call that work."

Quin looked around at us. "Agnes May carrying firewood."

"I thought she was supposed to help your mother with housework," I said.

Adam shrugged. "Dishes. Clothes. Weeds the garden. Mops the floors. Cleans the Church. Helps with canning. Not much at all. Not compared to me."

"Adam." Quin leaned forward. "Does she have her girly ass all marked up too, from tripping down the stairs?"

The three of us laughed. Adam wagged his head.

"Maybe she's more sure-footed," Hangy said.

Laughter.

Adam spat into the water.

We sat in the pond and talked the afternoon sun across the sky. Turtle heads bobbed to the pond surface. We threw stones, which had them dunk momentarily, but they soon came back up, and kept their distance, looking at us. Swishing sounds came from over the bank. Lady Bella, the Hobbes's lead Holstein, came up onto the bank, eyes large as she looked us over. More heads, more cows, all looking, all ears forward, as if some explanation should be forthcoming about us sitting in their drinking water. They lined the bank, while behind them, throaty noises from those of lesser rank, who hadn't been able to see the spectacle, asked what the hold-up was.

"They'll walk all over our clothes once they decide to move in on us," Hangy said.

Quin jumped up. "They'll bust up my glasses."

We stood and yelled and flailed arms and hands and threw stones, chasing them off the bank. They soon regrouped further down and, once their leader decided it was time to enter the pond, they followed her in. The center of the pond was too deep, so they avoided it, formed a semi-circle by keeping to the shallows. Once settled, up to their bellies in water muddied up by all the movement, they ignored us. With heads lowered, they took on water, sucking and slurping. When they had their fill, they rose up again, snaked long tongues into nostrils, swung glassy eyes toward us for occasional curious looks, and swatted tails at clouds of flies ever buzzing their hind quarters.

We sat back down in the water.

Except Quin. "Gentlemen. What we are witness to here today is a breakdown of the natural order of things. As our founding fathers so rightly and most astutely observed, all men are created equal. As a matter of fact, so convinced were they of this basic truth that they committed it to paper, to which they affixed their John Hancocks."

"Excuse me, "I said. "May I have the floor to make a single point?"

"To the Honorable Eugene Ahern, esquire, one of our own esteemed Dumble-Doers, I hereby yield the floor—I mean the pond—for one of his, no-doubt, well-researched, perfectly formulated, and loaded-with-bullshit observations."

Quin sat down in the water as I stood. "In the interest of accuracy, only one of our founding fathers affixed his John Hancock to said document. He was a man truly of utmost honor, courage, fortitude, and good looks, never to be forgotten, his name was...now I just had it on the tip of my tongue...oh, yeah, John. Well, you know, John something. The rest of them all used other names, like Ben Somebody, and, well, you know."

Quin and Adam laughed. Hangy threw mud at me, and I sat down.

Quin's eyes lit up as he retook the floor—the pond.

"Be that as it may, what the founding fathers also said, by specifically leaving it out of said document, was that the creation of all men as equals did not include, and in fact excluded, any critter of lower ilk, by which I refer to Holsteins. They are forbidden to be considered equal to us, nor any of their kind, be they Jersey, Angus, Guernsey or Texas Longhorn, or any of a half-dozen other breeds who represent lower forms of life. I put it to you, my fellow Dumble-Doers, these stinking critters have no rights in this here pond. We had first dibs."

He sat back down.

"Lowly critters or not, they do bring in the milk check," Hangy said and threw mud at Quin.

In a matter of seconds, we were all up, and mud flew in all directions, some of it bearing tiny pieces of grit that stung on impact.

"Agnes May!" Hangy whined.

We whirled to face away from the bank and plopped down into the water, all in one motion.

She stood on the bank in the spot where Lady Bella had been earlier, her long cotton dress printed with tiny flowers, braid coming out from under the gray bonnet that the Reverend required her and her mother to always wear, which fell over one shoulder. She looked at us with big eyes.

The four of us crab-crawled, dragged our asses in the gritty mud, out to deeper water.

Adam said over his shoulder, "You're not supposed to be here, little sister."

"Are you boys taking a mud bath?"

"You're not supposed to be here!"

"I read how rich ladies in New York and Paris are fond of mud baths. It was in a magazine on the Bookmobile. They put cucumber slices over their eyes."

"What is it you want, little sister?"

"I'm not your little sister. Only a year younger. Mom sent me to find you. I figured you'd be here, because you're not supposed to be, and sure enough, what do I find?"

"Well, what is it, then?" Adam whined.

"On account of Mrs. Hough being sick, the Reverend is coming home early from the grading project on Stonefall Road, because he has to go and see her, on account of her daughter called up and said she can't wake her up. Mom told me to hurry and fetch you before he gets home so he'll be none the wiser that you haven't even started cleaning the church windows."

"I gotta go," Adam said.

He stood, scooped handfuls of water to wash away the mud. When he'd gotten a respectable amount of it off, he went to the bank for his clothes.

She rasped to her brother, "Goodness. None of them have anything on either?"

"Well, you aren't supposed to be here, sister," Adam rasped back at her.

## CHAPTER 7, RED HORN CLIPPINGS

"Why do you have so much, Grandma? Who's ever going to eat all of these?"

"It's a bin buster for sure." Her blue eyes relished applying a successful-farm-crop saying to her vegetable garden.

You'd think snapping pods to empty peas onto a pan would be easy work. And it was, for a few minutes, maybe even a half-hour. Then, the kitchen stool grew hard, the muscles in my neck and back ached, the heat more oppressive.

Her face dripping with sweat, she instructed, "Get down and move around every so often."

I'd done as she said, walked about the summer kitchen, rolled my shoulders, and rolled my neck...more often as the morning ever-so-slowly dragged on and wrapped us in the swelter.

"This is the last batch," I said aloud to myself, but more to remind her that she'd promised earlier it would be the last.

"You used to enjoy helping me," she said, voice fuzzed a little with hurt.

"That was before I knew better."

She laughed at that. It bubbled past the hurt, and her eyes lit.

"You're at that age," she said. "Your father and your uncle were like you. It starts out with a boy's eyes filled with eagerness, his body almost running out of itself to help out. At a certain stage in his life, he loses that enjoyment. He loses it to other things."

"My father and Uncle Dan helped you can peas when they were little?"

"Just like you," she said, "they were eager to help. As they grew, they helped your grandfather with the farm more and more. And, like any boy, they grew to where their eagerness was directed at other things. Away from what I was doing, or their father, off to what their friends were doing, and then beyond, to a much larger world, you see. Just like you, lad."

"Did Dad smoke when he was twelve?"

Marja laughed, covered her missing bottom tooth with the back of her hand. "I found the pipe he'd made for himself, a small, round piece of maple bored out for a bowl and drilled for the stem, which he'd carefully fashioned from a dried-out reed."

"You found his pipe? Where did he hide it?"

"The porch rail, tucked behind the corner post. When I showed it to your grandfather, he told me to leave it be, that I was his mother, not his jailer."

"You ever find cigarettes?"

"Oh, heavens, no. Back then, cigarettes were not something a boy could afford on whatever money might come his way. No, he was barely able to scare up the pennies for a bag of tobacco clippings."

"Clippings."

"You could buy clippings in a brown paper bag at Snead's Mercantile. The bag I found said Red Horn Clippings on it. They were odd pieces and stems left over after the leaves had been cut up for various products. People weren't so wasteful in those days, don't you see."

"Where did he hide the Red Horn Clippings?"

She put her finger to her chin and tried to remember.

"Did he listen to the Yankees on the radio, like I do?"

She laughed and put her hands on either side of my face. "We didn't have a radio when Owen was a boy. Your Uncle Dan, now, he was the one who listened to ball games, on that wooden Philco, the one that's up in the attic now. We had Mister Roosevelt to thank for electrification, which came through in 1937. Dan was still a boy, but your father was almost done with high school."

"Don't know if this is enough for the last batch," I said.

Maybe I would be able to include the batch I was working on in the first batch for tomorrow, and get out of making up the last batch for today. I was sure, by now, Quin and Hangy and Adam were already at the ball field, wondering where I was.

She didn't answer. She stood still at the table, where one empty jar had yet to be filled. I wished I could hurry her along without being too obvious about it. An image continued to play from the back of my mind that had me arrive at the ball field to three sets of eyes asking why I was late. Because I'd been helping my grandma can peas?

Her face was blank. Blank and white.

"Marja?"

She whispered, "Put the stool behind me."

"The stool?"

She held onto the edge of the table, hands like bird claws on a top fence rail. She bent at the waist, quivering, and moved onto the edge of the stool.

"Are you sick again? Should I tell Mom?"

She didn't answer. Sweat, which all along had been running down her face, now beaded on her skin and pooled in the crags of her neck.

"I'll tell Mom to call Doctor Willingham."

"No, no." Pushing against the table, she slid herself further onto the stool.

"We'll finish this canning tomorrow," I decided, borrowing my father's tone for when he made up his mind about something important.

"Tomorrow, we'll only have more to do." Her voice was tired.

"You've been sick, Marja. You should be resting, not canning in this heat. You're not all over your dizzy spells, are you."

At my scolding in a voice that neither of us was used to, she blinked at me.

"Besides," in a gentler manner, "all the peas you've already canned, we'll never eat in a whole year."

"Mustn't waste." Her voice more firm.

"But, we still have three-quarters of a shelf from last year. And beans, and tomato sauce, and green tomato relish, and corn, and even beets."

She stood again, handed me the last canning jar and a scoop. "Spare two thumbs at the top, a space for the steam."

She got down off the stool and walked in slow sliding steps to the stove, where she checked the pressure gauge on the cooker that had been cooling, then to the rack to where jars from the previous batch rested. She pushed on their caps with her thumb to make sure none of them binked, which would have indicated a no-seal. Grandma moved more slowly now than she used to, an old lady, but was still pulled along by what had to be done.

I finished filling the last jar of the last batch. A handful of peas left over in the bottom of the pan I emptied into tomorrow's picking bowl. Once again, she'd had the quantity figured pretty close, just by eyeballing it.

Marja talked as she worked, a lilt of enjoyment regaining her voice. "Rougher than a cob, your grandfather. Supposed to use that money he'd saved up, along with what his family had given him, to enroll at the Institute. His family wanted him out of the anthracite mines, especially after the recent troubles. The owners had been hiring Slavs, first as scabs, then as regular workers, and the Irish and the Slavs didn't get along at all. His family wanted something better for him, better than all that brawling between the Irish and the Slavs over crumbs fallen from the tables of the rich."

"Baxter Hoy said the Irish were nothing but a bunch of drunks and brawlers."

She turned to me with a worried look. "Don't repeat that, Eugene. It's taken all this time for your grandfather to earn respectability. Promise you won't tell anyone of his early circumstances."

"I promise, Marja." Grandpa had been dead a long time already, so I figured it didn't matter anyway. But I was in the habit of making promises to her, even if I didn't always know exactly what she was talking about.

"He was supposed to become a bookkeeper. That's where he was headed the day I met him on the Lehigh Valley." Her eyes lit up. "He was bound for the Sheshequin Institute. Oh, his family was so upset when they found out later."

"What did they find out?"

She looked at me with surprise, as if I hadn't been following her story.

"What he'd done with the money. The money for his schooling, Eugene. That he'd placed a down payment on this farm, of course, instead of enrolling at the Institute. Especially his mother, your great-grandmother Bridget Ahern. She never forgave me."

I had heard bits and pieces of this before, from conversations at the dinner table, discussions between my parents, or between my father and Uncle Dan, or from Marja's own comments. Grandma had the habit of placing snippets of information into the middle of other subjects when she spoke about her past, like someone reading from a history book who skipped about among the chapters.

She said through tight lips, "I think she hated me, that Bridget."

"She hated you, Marja?"

"Or, just couldn't see her way to forgive me. Oh, her son, she forgave, but me, never, not after I had ruined him."

I laughed. "So, it was you who bought this farm."

She looked at me sternly. "Aren't you listening? No, it was Carroll who bought the farm, with the money he and his family had saved up for bookkeeping school."

"But, you had ruined him," I laughed. "How did you go about ruining him?"

Marja said, "My female ways, you know. As far as she was concerned, I'd given up my virtue to trick him out of his farm. When she found out I'd grown up on a farm myself, in Finland, that made her suspicious. And I wasn't Irish, which was the clincher. It made me the villain in any cause that didn't go her way, and no cause on earth was more important than her son Carroll's future as a bookkeeper."

She went back to her jars, quiet again, as if she'd said too much.

Quin, Hangy, and Adam were at the ball field by now, scratching their heads, looking down at the edge of the woods, expecting me to appear any minute, to see me slide under the lower barbed wire strand.

"Now, just on account of what I say, don't you go thinking poorly of your great-grandmother Bridget Ahern. She did bring into this world and raise a wonderful man. She didn't like me because she just couldn't bring herself to be angry with her own son. Her anger went toward me in place of him."

She arranged the cooled batch of jars in a basket, and headed for the cellar door. I took the basket away from her, which drew a pinched-face look from her.

"What did she look like?" The question interrupted her irritation at me for taking away the basket.

"Mother Bridget? Tall and round and big-boned, red patches for cheeks, and blue eyes, and hair that was losing its red color to gray. But I only saw her once. They came here to Cloven Hill Farm to seek out what had happened to all the bookkeeping plans, and to the money they'd seen him off with a few years earlier at the Hazleton train station."

"You never went to their place, to Hazleton, for a visit?"

"Well, no. Now, make sure you write the year on the lids— what year is this?—1960. Your grandfather did go to see them now and again, but I stayed here. Carroll was very supportive of his mother, especially after her husband Sean had died, and soon-after lost her youngest, Eugene—same name as you—who was mustard-gassed in the Great War. We had a farm to run, animals to feed and cows to milk. Without that milk money, a farm goes under in no time. So I never went with him on his visits home."

Down in the cellar, I moved the oldest jars of peas up to the top shelf, out front. After I'd written 1960 on the lids, I placed today's first batch with those she had placed yesterday, on a lower shelf at the back. Coolness down there raised goose flesh under my sweat, so I hurried along.

When I brought the empty basket back up to the summer kitchen, she had undone the screws to the pressure cooker lid. I mimicked what I'd often witnessed from Uncle Dan on his visits home. "How can I let a beautiful lass do all the work, when there's a handsome lad right here to help?"

"Handsome lad, indeed." She covered her mouth and laughed hard, and sat on the stool, face pink and eyes shiny, as I removed the lid for her and used tongs to remove the hot jars.

She took up with what she'd been saying earlier. "Your Grandfather's folks only visited here once, back in 1913. We'd been here a few years by then, and proudly showed them the farm, some of it still in old stumps from the loggers who had stripped this land decades earlier. We told of our future plans with it, but they remained quiet and wagged their heads. Did you move the oldest out front? I neglected to do that yesterday."

"Yes. And dated the lids on the new ones, and put them in the back. So, you never visited Grandpa's childhood home, not even for a wedding, or when somebody died?"

"Never."

"They never came back here to visit the farm, after that one time?"

"Never."

"Not even when your children were born?"

"No. They thought—more Bridget than Sean—that our children would be tainted. Through the bedroom wall, I'd heard her tell Sean, just loud enough so I would hear it, that Finnish people have mostly Lutheran blood flowing in their veins, and any offspring from such a marriage would likely grow up to be lukewarm Catholics at best."

"So, she didn't like you because you were Finnish. I didn't know you were a Lutheran, too, Marja."

"I wasn't. I'd been raised a Catholic in Finland; we were few and far between among all those Lutherans. But that didn't matter to her. She didn't know what she liked or disliked. As I said earlier, Bridget was angry over her own son spending his tuition money on this piece of stump-ridden, rocky land. A bookkeeper would have meant so much more respectability than a farmer, at least in her eyes. But she couldn't bring herself to be angry at him, so that left me."

Marja suddenly laughed. "Through our front window, she remarked to Sean that she could see right through that cleft in Belknap Ridge into the next valley." Laughter had her bending at the waist, covering her missing tooth with her hand. "Then, Carroll told her that I had insisted we name our place Cloven Hill Farm. Mother Bridget's eyes seemed to go from blue to black except for the fire coming out of them. She said the name was surely appropriate, because it sounded like a place where Satan himself would choose to vacation."

"What would great-grandmother Bridget think now, do you suppose?"

"Now? She's been dead for thirty years, lad."

"Yes, but what would she think? I mean, your first born not a farmer, not a bookkeeper, but a lawyer. Your second born, Uncle Dan, a priest! Wouldn't she be surprised?"

Marja laughed. "Now, that would surely frost her buttons, wouldn't it!"

Her face drew into seriousness. "You're mistaken, Eugene. Your father was not my first-born. Nor was Daniel my second."

I looked at her, quiet.

"They were the ones who survived. I'm sure you didn't know. I bore others. Before, between, and after your father and Daniel."

"Others. How many?"

Her eyes sharpened at me. "Why would it matter how many? Any time I've told someone about it, they always ask how many. It is not like a business, or a sport. Each birth is a child, a renewal of its mother and of her mother and her mother...and its father too, of course."

"Did my question make you mad, Grandma?"

She smiled through tears. "Oh, no, lad." She came and placed her hands on either side of my face. "I'm remembering, that's all."

"Marja. I didn't know you'd lost babies."

"You could not have known. It has been kept from you. I don't know why we hide such sorrow. I was so lonely, you see, every time I lost a baby. I cried so hard for each one, but nobody else did. Old Doctor McNally explained to me that something must have been wrong: those babies were not intended to live. I was just supposed to accept that. But I cried. I cried so long and hard for each one, and then would be told not to, as if I had no right to feel such a vast loss."

"Doctor McNally, the veterinarian?"

"Old Doctor McNally, yes. He was the veterinarian, but not the veterinarian that you know. That's his son, the new Doctor McNally."

"But, Grandma, why a veterinarian?"

"Tending to our dairy herd's needs, of course. And the draft horses as well."

I laughed. "I thought you meant they had a veterinarian at the hospital where you had your babies."

Her eyes deepened. "No hospital, Eugene. We couldn't afford it. And no kindly old doctor like a TV's *Gunsmoke*, where he rides a carriage out to the farms and delivers babies and gets paid in chickens, or does it just out of pure kindness."

"But, you could afford a doctor for the cows and horses." My voice rose to a complaint.

"All my babies were born here, right here in our house, in what is now your father's office. We had a midwife, Mrs. Hough, from down in Quarrel Creek, for most of them."

"Mrs. Hough...that old lady with a '49 Ford?"

"I don't know what kind of a car she drives, Eugene. She's the only Mrs. Hough I know. I did see her, in later years, pass by in a station wagon, the old kind, with wood sides. But I hear she's suddenly bedridden, never goes anywhere anymore."

"That's her. An old Ford station wagon. It just sits in her garage these days."

"Old Doctor McNally, the veterinarian, he meant well by me. He was right about the babies not being meant to live. It's nature's way of breeding out weakness. He was actually a very kind man. He'd forget to charge for his services. And on our wedding day, the first time I met him, he saved our gelding, you know. Your grandfather was so worked up about Eyepatch, worried he'd lose that horse, because it wasn't eating. There'd been a dry spell, and Eyepatch had a habit of rolling about on his back. He'd twisted one of his intestines around a lump from all the dust he'd eaten."

"Are we finished, Grandma?"

"Just about."

"Must've been one stupid horse, if he'd been eating dust."

"Well, not on purpose. The grass was covered with dust. You know how it does when you have a dry spell. Dirt had collected in a lump, and his intestine twisted around the lump from his rolling on the ground."

I placed the last seven jars into the cooker for her. She checked them to make sure I'd tightened the lids just so.

"Can I go, then?"

"Yes, I think you're finished for today. So, here I was, a girl in her white dress. We'd just come up the hill from Melody Falls in your grandfather's wagon. The pastor from Saint Agatha in Wyotanda — Father Francis Xavier Newton, he was — had come up the river to meet with us in the little Melody Falls mission church. He'd agreed to pronounce the words of the Church's official blessing, but not the full Mass. You see, I'd not been able to produce a baptismal certificate all the way from Finland. Imagine, a girl he didn't know, not even an Irish girl, wanting to marry an Irishman he'd never seen before, and a rough coal miner to boot. The Father took one look and figured, and rightly so, it was better to marry us than not. He claimed he could read the intention in my eyes, that it was going to happen with his blessing or without, you see. He was a jovial man who smelled like brandy before ten o'clock in the morning."

"I gotta go, Marja. They're waiting for me at the ball field."

"So, here is Old Doctor McNally. On the very day of our wedding, he had finally responded to Carroll's request to stop by and tend to Eyepatch. We came home from our wedding, and here he is in the pasture with a funnel and hose. He gave that poor critter the enema of his life, Eyepatch screaming and kicking against the harness used for such special occasions."

She peered through the window, drawn to Oswald Tull's green tractor off in the distance. He was pulling a mower through his hay field behind a John Deere Model A, engine popping along.

"First cutting a week late, as usual," she muttered. Grandma hated the Tulls.

The sound of the tractor echoed off the far woods and re-echoed through the gulley between our farms.

"Up to then," she said, as she kept her eye on Oswald and his mower, "between your grandfather and me, we held onto enough ridiculous notions to thoroughly confuse a whole crowd, let alone just the two of us."

She turned away from the window and spoke in a Confessional rasp, like you'd use so the priest could hear but hopefully nobody else, as if Oswald Tull, a quarter-mile away, might have been listening. "That's why I told you all about it, when you were still little and I saw you starting up your curiosity in the bathtub. I did the same for my Owen and Daniel, don't you see. It's wrong for grownups to let silly ideas go to seed in young minds from all that secrecy. They only flourish into fantastic impressions later on."

By now, they would have given up on me, would be deciding whether to start a game of scrub with only three players. I retrieved my baseball glove from the corner.

"Oh, I'm sure we'd have bumbled our way into it somehow, just because nature would have pushed us the way she always does with youth, confused or not. But I'm so thankful Doctor McNally stopped by on that special day to undo the horse's intestinal blockage. When we arrived home from our wedding, he saw us, and right after he pulled out the hose so Eyepatch could blow out what ailed him, the doctor looked us up and down, at our wedding clothes and, without our even asking, told us the details of how to go about it."

"You had to give the horse another enema later?"

She put up her hand up to shush me, then cupped the side of her mouth to better give direction to a whisper. "He came right out and told us how to go about it…how to act as bride and groom on our wedding night."

She looked through the window and, satisfied that Oswald Tull hadn't overheard, resumed a conversational tone. "A scientific point of view, I suppose. He figured he'd erase any silly notions we may have accumulated." She breathed a deep sigh. "Well, you go on, my lad. I'll finish up for today."

I headed for the door. By now they'd started a game with only three, and here I was coming along late. Whoever was in the lead would be pissed about starting all over. No way would I tell them about canning peas. It would have to be some other story. I was pretty confident I would come up with a good one.

"In the woodpile," she said suddenly.

I stopped in the doorway and looked back at her.

"In the woodpile, in a tin. That's where my naughty son hid the bag of Red Horn Clippings. But, don't you let on that I found it. Your father still doesn't know that I know. Promise me you won't tell."

"Oh, I promise, Marja."

"Scrub!"

No response from Quin or Hangy.

"Scrub," I offered again.

This time they looked at me, then at each other, then back to me.

Hangy, facing the sun, which made the ends of blonde hair under his hat appear white, curled his lip into a grin, and emitted a breathy laugh. Quin's half-Mexican face was in shadow, black eyes cast toward me through his glasses.

Neither spoke. My declaration to be first batter died and quickly decomposed. We sat in the spotty shade of a chokecherry tree growing out of a pile of rocks that helped hold up the Melody Falls Watchful Christian Fellowship backstop.

"Not enough people," Quin decided. "Looks like you'll be playing with yourself."

Laughter from Quin and Hangy.

My ears turned hot. "And I hurried over here thinking you guys might have already started without me. Well, now we've got three men, so let's go. Lots of times we've played scrub with only three."

"Trouble is, it takes forever to get anybody out with just two men on defense," Quin decided.

Hangy laughed and nodded toward me. "Except when Eugene's the one who's up to bat." Blonde fuzz above the grimace caught a glint of sun.

"And let's tell it like it is." Quin's black eyes glared. "Not really three men here. More like two men and a boy."

They hit each other's arms, fell back and rolled side to side.

I looked away. I could have been at home on the porch, *Tips for Transfer Case Repair and Maintenance* in my lap, borrowed yesterday afternoon from the Bookmobile. It was a book I'd asked for some weeks ago after watching Quin's old man Roberto, or Bert, as everybody called him, rebuild the transmission out of my father's Jeep.

"Musta done some four-wheeling on the highway," Bert had said, and showed my father the end of a shaft that had been tortured to the breaking point, the gear that had been mounted on it already tossed into a pan of bad parts, it teeth permanently blued from too much heat.

"I only use this Jeep on the farm," my father had protested. "It's not like it's road-worthy. It's not even licensed."

Bert lifted his filthy hat off his head and held it aloft with thumb and forefinger, just long enough to give himself a three-finger scratch above the ear. "Well, whoever had it before you got it musta left it engaged on a hard-surface road. That's all I'm saying, Owen. Got the tranny so hot, the steel in that shaft turned to butter, then twisted itself in half. So, where'd you get this heap?"

"Rooney's Junk Yard. A flip-over, scrapped out by the insurance company. Ole Rooney patched the structure back together for me."

Bert looked the Jeep over and shrugged. "That explains the catawampus look to it, all right."

The book, smelling of grease and hand-cleaner, would have offered exploded views of gear boxes, with pinions, shafts and bearings that trailed off to their own side-canyons of illustrated logic. Grandma Marja in her wicker rocking chair, at rest from canning, reading glasses on her nose, would have rattled the *Clarion* front to back, worried the pages as she softly pronounced every word.

Instead, I'd hurried over here to sit in the long grass behind the backstop where Quin and Hangy made fun of me. In the distance, under the eaves of the church, Adam unfolded a twelve-foot splintery ladder with jerky motions. Reverend Stippil, as he had left for work this morning, had ruined the day, if not for us, certainly for Adam, with an assignment for his son to start scraping and painting the clapboard siding.

Quin, at the side of my vision, looked toward me. The humor was gone from his eyes, replaced with sadness. The expression on his face often mirrored my own feelings, as if sometimes he needed to check with me to decide how he really felt. I looked at him. He smiled crookedly, tried to hang onto my eye, but I wouldn't let him. Not after the way he'd been making fun.

"Scrub!" he suddenly called.

"Scrub two!" Hangy responded automatically.

"Scrub three." I resigned myself to the simple reality. Enough time had elapsed since my own earlier call for scrub that, by now, my claim to be first batter up had expired.

Quin gave me that grin that was supposed to get me to go along with his enjoyment. I looked away.

Over by the church, Adam glanced at us as he climbed the ladder. We left the long grass and headed for the shed behind third base. Three of us in a line, Quin and Hangy and I, moved like a six-legged caterpillar along the edge of the dirt field. Up on the ladder, Adam scraped old paint in pitifully slow motion.

I stopped. Quin and Hangy, sensing my drag on the progress of our migration, turned, questioned me with their eyes.

"You guys are right," I announced. "It's too much work to get anybody out with only two defenders. We need at least four men."

Quin twirled his wrist like it was a mechanical tool. When it stopped, his finger pointed in the direction of the Adam on the ladder. "Well, I'd say that poor chicken's neck was already wrung this morning. It seems the Reverend damned his only begotten son to an eternity of painting his church. So much for our fourth man."

From the ladder Adam looked over at us. Slow scraping slowed even more, almost to a stall.

Hangy took an irritated half-step and jerked his head toward the shed to get our six-legged migration going again. Quin peered at me through his glasses. He reached and fluffed my hair.

"What's going on up there, Genie? Up in that head of yours."

"I heard my old man making township-supervisor talk on the phone last night to Adam's old man—I mean, the Reverend. He said he'd let himself get too far behind grading Stonefall Road. You know, he's working that section down between the covered bridge and Route 6."

Hangy, hands on hips, glared at us. "Come on, let's go!"

I ignored Hangy and talked to Quin. "That covered bridge is too far away for the Reverend to have time to come home for lunch. No way he'll be back here before supper, not if he wants to get himself back on schedule, especially with the voice my old man was using on him...you know, like he was pissing right into the phone."

Hangy did not want to hear it. Sidling in the direction of the shed, pink-faced, he tried to jerk our attention that way. "So what?"

But Quin's black eyes flashed at what I'd been saying. "We have all day!" My idea had just converted itself into his. "All we gotta do is get hold of more scrapers and brushes."

Hangy stared at us. Then he caught onto what we were saying. "My old man's got plenty of that stuff. In his workroom in the barn."

Down came Adam Stippil, his rapid, jerky descent teetering the ladder in place under the eaves. He threw down the scraper, and ran to us. "Scrub four!"

We'd have been better off to paint now, play ball later...you'd think. No way did we want the Reverend to find out the three of us were helping Adam, which would only inspire him to ratchet up his only begotten son's work schedule.

Suppose we played ball and one or more of us got called home, or it started to rain, or the Reverend came back early for some kind of congregational emergency...maybe a problem with Old Lady Hough again, who was still in a deep sleep at her house down by Quarrel Creek. Suppose she finally woke up. Suppose she died. Meanwhile, we wouldn't have done enough painting to make it look like Adam had been slaving away all day long as the Reverend had intended.

In front of the shed, I appointed myself the Man of Reason. "A couple of hours, that's all. Adam and I stay here to get started. We scrape and paint, while you two go get whatever else we need from Old Man Hobbes' work room, then all of us together. We can make it look like a whole day's work in just two, three hours tops."

The worst thing about being the Man of Reason is the awful silence that follows one of your pronouncements. All three looked at me with one face.

Hangy said, "Let's go," and Adam, eyes lit by the flame of freedom, said, "Yeh," and shoved past, opened the shed and started going through the baseball equipment.

Quin held back. He stood in front of me, squared himself, and placed both hands on my shoulders. "What you've done, young man, is lost focus," he explained. The yellow sun reflected off his glasses. His breath feathered my face. Reason had no chance. In the face of Quin's mockery, it soon broke apart, and had us both laughing.

The words and tone of voice, came straight from Father Kearns, from Saturday morning catechism class. No such mirth—not even a hint of it—would have found its way into the real thing. When Father Kearns singled you out, when those beefy hands clamped down on your shoulders, it fired up that initial sense of awe we had all felt—we Catholic males, anyway—the day of his arrival in Wyotanda five years ago, a week after Father Moreno had been found in the confessional slumped over, drooling into the pages of his breviary.

Back then, excitement had made the rounds among the grownup males of the Saint Agatha parish. "Is our new Pastor that same Kearns boy? Could it be the same Billy Kearns? You know, the kid from Pittston, All-State. Then, All-America at Fordham from the Rams' glory days under Sleepy Jim Crowley. The kid we used to read about in the *Clarion*. The same Billy

Kearns from the '37 undefeated team, the one who destroyed those Purdue boys with his tackling at the Polo Grounds? Could it be?"

It was.

Beefy hands would descend from above and clamp onto your shoulders. A round, spectacled red face — the Boilermaker Buster himself — would breathe on you in a calm, instructional tone, a recitation of how you had lost focus, which he would complement with a litany of particulars.

I was lucky enough to know just how to say, "Yes, Father," in a whispery voice, and to plead with my blue eyes into his lens-enlarged gray ones, and so escaped ever being knuckle-rapped for what he called "emphasis." It was a fate that others not so lucky had later said made them see a flash of light.

And now, Quin's guidance there behind third base, which was offered in that same instructional tone, loosened up my practical concern for favoring work before play. He was right. I had been in error, had lost focus, forgotten what was impor-tant, after all. Our presence here was clearly meant for...well, some higher calling. God Himself must have chosen us to play a game of scrub, not paint one of His churches. Certainly not one of His Protestant churches.

"Yes, Father." I blurted into Quin's face. Letting go of my shoulders, Quin transformed himself from pretend-priest into pretend-umpire, cupped his hand beside his mouth and yelled out, "Play ball!" Then, he rapped me on the head. It was no-where near as hard as the Fordham Rams Boilermaker Buster would have done, but I saw the light.

People told me secrets. Grandma Marja said it was my honest face. Honest face? Not from being honest. Just the same, people told me secrets, and I'd learned to keep them, though sometimes it got a little sticky to do so.

When Hangy turned his back on the batter to check our positions in the field, Quin caught my eye from the batter's box and elongated his face. I nodded. What Hangy didn't know, as he got ready to pitch, was Quin's secret. I was the only other person who knew: Quin had recently learned a new hitting technique, had practiced it to perfection.

The art of hitting began not with just batting the ball, but hitting the pitch, Ted Williams claimed to a reporter in a recent issue of *Sports Illustrated*. When I had read the article, that should have been the end of it, except I made the mistake of telling Quin. He had me pitch to him last Friday through an endless afternoon in which he could never quite be satisfied with his own success. "I don't want Hangy or Adam—especially Adam—to know about it."

And so we did it in secret. We lugged a bag of balls from the Fellowship shed all the way over to my place. In the upper story of my father's horse barn, one-hoppers off the wood floor whizzed past my ears, foul-tips ricocheted off the beams and rafters, line drives walloped the back wall.

When my father came home toward evening and heard the noise as he was getting out of the Buick, he came into the barn and made us quit. As we rebagged the balls, he said, "Before you come in for supper, go around back and hammer in all the nails you loosened." After supper, he took another look for himself, and had us go back over most of the nails heads a second time.

And what Quin didn't know, as he got ready to hit, was Hangy's secret: he had recently learned a new pitching technique. Quin had elongated his face from the batter's box while Hangy's back was to him. Quin couldn't see how Hangy looked at me and raised his eyebrows. I nodded.

I only had to nod once, and each of them thought it was for him.

Hangy had come over to my place on Sunday to show me a rising fastball.

"Against a good hitter, well, you know he's gonna get some kinda wood on the ball. You just gotta make sure it ain't good wood," Alton Gibbs, Hangy's cousin's fiancé's best friend, had told him between swigs of Pabst Blue Ribbon at the Hobbes family picnic. Gibbs, while never having made it to the majors, had pitched a season and a half for the Binghamton Triplets, where he claimed he had faced many a minor-league hitter who later had moved up to the bigs, although he failed to mention who any of them might have been.

Hangy placed his first two fingers across the stitches on top and made sure to keep the grip symmetrical. He brought his arm over as he strode forward. The target was a wood-block handhold on the sliding door of my father's horse barn. Thanks to your eye's expectation of a downward arc, the pitch fooled you into thinking it rose as it smacked into the wood.

He fell into a trance. Over and over he strode with his tree-trunk legs toward the handhold and released the ball into a vicious backwards spin that scorched a straight line, whizzed and smacked against the wood, like a firecracker going off. As I retrieved errant bounce-backs, I watched him work up a sweat. Such punishment soon dismantled half the wood-block handhold, forced it to cough an array of splinters onto the ground, and left a carcass of yellow fibers and bent nails. Pitches that missed made dents in the door's veneer.

Breathing heavily, he stopped and stared at the ball, turned it over in his fingers. He looked at the vestiges of the handhold still clinging to the door, then at the ball again, its nicked and scuffed hide developing scuffs of red barn paint.

"Watch this."

The ball whizzed in a straight line, but broke to the left just short of target, making another dent in my father's door.

"Are you making it do that?"

When he got the ball back, his mouth curled into a grin as he turned it over in his fingers and eyed it with love. "Maybe I am and maybe I'm not. That's for me to know, and for whatever sorry son of a bitch holds the bat to find out. It depends on if I put exactly the same pressure on top with both fingers."

My father came out of the house, lines in his face from a Sunday nap. He looked at the barn door. Hands on hips, he stared at us.

Hangy turned. "Almost milking time. Don't tell Quin or Adam about this—especially Quin."

My father watched him leave the yard, and head down through the field toward home at that slow, deliberate pace of his. "That Hobbes kid is built like a dump truck, isn't he. Look at the way he walks, all that power in his legs: like a gravel truck grinding along in low gear."

Unsure if he was talking to me, or maybe to himself, I nodded my agreement as I stood still atop my skinny legs, eager to not discuss what I had allowed Hangy to do to the barn door.

When Hangy was gone, my father peered at the shambled handhold. He brushed his fingertips over the dents in the wood around it. Tomorrow, after court, he would be stopping by the lumberyard with a couple of months' worth of my allowance. I would have some repairs to do. "Maybe you and your friends could think about damaging their parents' property next time. You know, find a way to spread the destruction around a little."

At deep outfield Adam stood in position, hands on hips, and waited for things to get started. I looked out at him, and he looked back at me with that hard face and round eyes that held the secret he'd shared the last day of school, when he'd said, "I have to tell you something, Eugene."

After hand-out of report cards, Melody Falls School let out all the grades a little early into one last explosion of playground noise, excited voices, screech of rusty swings, sway of the go-round and see-saw, before the last bell announced everybody could finally leave for home.

Bus Number 2 for rural kids, Sheffield Hoy behind the wheel, had not arrived yet. The thought of liberation from school for the whole summer suddenly nudged Adam and me to wrestle each other. But it was against the rules on school property, so we went down the bank in front, out of sight, where we rolled and pushed and gripped and tripped and tried to hold each other down. We both collapsed against the bank before long, our backs soaking up coolness from the grass.

"There is something special about me," he said, eyes in a stare at the sky.

"I figure everybody feels that way, don't they."

"No, I mean for real. This is different. Something most people don't know about."

I complained, "How can you say what most people do or don't know?"

"I'm just telling you, that's all. The Savior has special plans for me."

He turned his head and put his eyes on me. I turned away, couldn't look back at him. Catholics just don't do this.

"Do you believe me?"

"I guess so, Adam."

"No guessing. Do you or don't you?"

I shrugged.

"Bet it's kinda hard for you to believe," he said, and finally looked away.

Was there something from sixth grade catechism to cover the situation? I should have paid closer attention. Father Kearns had warned us about the Protestants, how they would lure us into heresy, but I couldn't remember the particulars. I would have expected it from one of those wandering, self-appointed preachers who sometimes banged on our door, or Adam's old man, the Reverend Stippil. Not Adam. Not a kid like me, not somebody I wrestled and smoked cigarettes and talked about the Yankees with. Maybe he really did believe it.

Finally, I turned to him. "What kind of a special plan?"

He looked at me again, eyes intent. "I'm to be an instrument of salvation. It came to me one night in the dark, after the Reverend had prayed over Agnes May and me before he took away the lantern."

"The lantern...don't you guys even have electricity?"

"Not upstairs."

His face was hard, eyes round, rounder than I'd ever seen them. Finally, he put his arm over his eyes and sighed. "But I'm such a sinner," he said. "Just when I'm about to go to sleep."

We were quiet, breaths coming back to normal after a rest. Why me? Catholics didn't talk about these things, even if you thought it in your own head, even if it was true. You only discussed it with God alone, not with other people, certainly not the kid you started out with in first grade, who you wrestled with on the last day of school. You never admitted to being a sinner. Only in the Confessional, where you told as little as possible while staying within the rules. Your job as a penitent was to make the priest drag it out of you, make him do *his* job.

Adam looked at me, looked hard again. "It's not as easy as it sounds to accept forgiveness fully, Eugene. For our sins, I mean. We are all such sinners. We are powerless, which is why we must accept what He has chosen for us, salvation in the Lord."

He stared, like he was trying to look right into my soul. I turned away and looked up at the sky, unable to stand any longer those eyes rounded like I'd never seen before.

So, here he was, standing in the outfield, that hard face and round eyes silently reminding me we were all sinners. It passed again between us in an instant. Instead of thinking about the best way to field a grounder and where to throw it, he was being special again.

I turned away, looked in at the batter, and spat into the dirt.

Quin, as he took warm-up swings near home plate, looked over at the Stippil house. "Adam, what's she talking about?"

Agnes May, on the porch, was too far away for us to hear what she was saying as she snapped beans from the pile her mother had made for her on a table there.

"Nothing," Adam said from the outfield. He crouched over, rested forearms on his knees, and stared into the weeds. "Little sister talks to herself sometimes, that's all."

I kept quiet. Agnes May had also unloaded a secret on me. A few months back, she had told me about Philip.

It happened one afternoon down in the basement at Melody Falls Elementary, during the school year, way back in March.

The side hall, which led off the main lower corridor, belonged to the janitor during regular school hours. But if you were one of the bad kids who had to help clean the classroom, it was not unusual for Miss Hendershott, our sixth grade teacher, to send you downstairs after school on a mission to retrieve a broom, mop, or handful of rags. It meant passing down through a shadowy hall to the even more shadowy steel door with a dingy yellow sign that said in black letters, BOILER ROOM.

Pushing open the warm steel door placed you in the presence of the iron behemoth itself. Above its dirt-laden top was affixed a bulging apparatus wrapped in dirt-gray material, from which rose up multiple arms of pipe with flaking white scabs of insulation. From the face of the boiler, a large, weepy eye peered out through grime and cobwebs, in which a swing-needle pointed to steam pressure from an array of black numbers situated over a rainbow arc—blue for low pressure values, yellow for intermediate, and red for high. A mismatched pair of lesser gages displayed, through smeared circular lenses, water level and temperature. And yet another circle of light, the size of a dime, seemed to always be looking at you as it glowed red.

Its name was LANDIS, according to a raised-letter metal mustache directly above its grimacing mouth, through which it demanded from the janitor frequent feedings of anthracite, and whose tooth-gaps offered you grooved glimpses into a smoldering hell. Positioned squarely in the middle of the floor, LANDIS proclaimed exclusive mastery of its domain as it belched, hissed and farted into the swelter.

The boiler conceded one dark, dusty corner of its realm to the cowering presence of mops, buckets, brooms and dustpans that were jammed beneath shelves loaded with jugs of floor stripper, waxes and soaps, and other articles of housekeeping. They all huddled around a filthy concrete sink. From that corner, you grabbed whatever Miss Hendershott had sent you down there for, and then you left the room—quickly. The hot steel door was spring loaded to slam itself shut with a bang.

I was a bad kid that day in March in Miss Hendershott's sixth grade classroom. The Universe, having locked itself in gray shards of ice and snow and frozen mud for a winter of eternity, had suddenly offered, through slightly open windows, a whiff of new, earthy smells. I couldn't define what it awakened in me, but no doubt it goaded me toward misbehavior.

Miss Hendershott's blue eyes had tiny specs of brown in them, which you would normally not notice unless she was close to you — and who would ever want any teacher to be that close? But this afternoon, as she moved about the classroom, in and out of rectangles of sunlight falling through the windows, her blue eyes looked green, and then, if she turned a certain way, almost golden. And, oh, Miss Hendershott's cheeks: a rose blossomed in them.

Two seats over and one up from me, Agnes May Stippil shot up her hand, a move she had practiced throughout her academic career with such frequency and with such force that both her skinny long arms were now slightly bent backwards at the elbow. Although the same age as me, she was Adam's "little" sister. Adam, a year older than the rest of us, had been held back to repeat a year in first grade.

"The sun is making me hot," she complained to Miss Hendershott. One of the rectangles of sunlight shining through the windows had found Agnes May, illuminating streaks of almost-red in the long, brown, braid that fell from under her gray bonnet.

Our teacher, without dropping a syllable from her talk on the Amazon Basin — Adam always mispronounced it "Amazin' Basin" — moved slowly to the outside aisle and pulled all the window shades. It filtered the sun's brightness into a strange yellow hue that threatened to envelop the classroom in stifling closeness. So Miss Hendershott opened the lower sashes just a bit more, letting in all that much more of the promise of spring.

From one of a collection of mountings above the blackboard, a map of South America was unrolled. The Great Basin came under the scrutiny of a wooden pointer whose stiff rubber tip slid over the tributaries leading to the river. As she spoke of dense tropical forest and steaming jungle, Miss Hendershott's free hand toyed with a tiny button at the top of her white sweater.

"The daytime temperature is typically near 100 degrees," she informed us, "with humidity at 100 percent, worse than even the hottest August day here in Pennsylvania."

The button slipped free from its button hole. Then a second button. Slowly but surely, as the Amazon flowed through sodden, steamy jungle, Miss Hendershott's deft fingers made their way down the row of tiny buttons until the last of them was undone. The white sweater opened to her soft, round shapes in a yellow dress just as the stiff rubber tip showed us where the great river emptied into the sea.

"Pay attention, Hobbes."

The rest of the class, each of us relieved that lightning had chosen for the present to strike only Hangy Hobbes, pretended to muster a common focus on the green, veined blob that was Brazil and covered most of the fat part of South America. A gentle, sweet-smelling breeze pushed one of the window shades away from the sill, and allowed it to settle back again. Then it softly reversed itself, and sucked the bottom of the shade into the window's opening, making little puffing sounds. The sweater lost its place on her shoulders and came down off the mid-sleeves of her dress. She placed the white-knit garment on the back of her chair.

"Stippil! Gutierrez!" Lightning struck again—a double strike—getting closer to me. "How many square miles did I just inform you the Amazon is estimated to drain?"

"Umm..."

She answered for them, "Two and one-half million." When she finished gnarling at Adam and Quin, she faced away from us toward the map for a moment to regain her thoughts, which gave me the opportunity to turn to the others—Hangy and Adam and Quin—and sign a double thumbs-up, a celebratory gesture fired by the sudden unveiling of Miss Hendershott's wonderfully female arms with tiny sprinkles of hair. It was the first time we'd seen them since before Thanksgiving.

She turned to face us and resume her subject. But the kid-brat, Agnes May, had other ideas. Her hand was up again, on the end of one of those skinny little slightly bent-backwards arms.

"Miss Hendershott, they were signaling. Harold Hobbes and Eugene Ahern and Quin Gutierrez and Adam Stippil."

Agnes May had no problem fingering Adam, as if he were just some nobody in a lineup of miscreants instead of her own brother. The rest of us innocent—or somewhat innocent—miscreants were caught in sibling crossfire.

Miss Hendershott looked us over one by one, and then spoke to Agnes May. "Did I call on you?"

"No, I'm sorry Miss Hendershott. But Eugene did something with his thumbs."

My thumb now found itself busy removing a loose lash from the corner of my eye.

"Well, Miss Stippil, at least they aren't tattle-tales, now, are they." She turned to me. "Don't rub your eye, Mister Ahern!"

Our teacher sighed. She took up her pointer and, happy to be back in the Amazon, placed her free hand on her hip. In the way she stood, and in her relative position at the front of the room, and in my relative position among the rows of her pupils…well, it all added up to an alignment of chance rarely granted a young boy's existence, and never for more than a glimmer. The placing of her hand on her hip bent her arm just so, and made her mid-sleeve sag. I had all to myself soft, female, inner-arm flesh, all the way to her armpit, a mysterious dark interior that didn't quite hide a frilly edge of white material. The moment rapidly filled with intensity. But then Miss Hendershott turned…and the moment vanished!

The intention was not to disrupt the class. But I had an obligation. My duty was to the others—to Hangy and Adam and Quin—to not let pass the heralding of a magnificent near-sighting of the place where Miss Hendershott's actual round breast hid from us in the steamy jungle. All I did was issue the horse cough. Twice. But it was enough to bring the pointer down on the teacher's oak desk top with a sharp crack. Agnes May jerked in her seat.

This time it was me whom lightning struck. Miss Hendershott came down the aisle and stood over me and my Geography book with her pointer. "You have been chosen, Eugene Ahern," as if I was being knighted, the stiff rubber tip threatening to burn a cross into the top of my head. "Whatever you and your friends thought you were getting away with has just ended. You are hereby appointed today's classroom cleaning official!"

So, there I was after school, a man alone, trying to do his duty. I came out of the Boiler Room, a special brush for sweeping under the desks in hand, when Agnes May, the tattle-tale, materialized in the hallway shadows. She knelt and peered into the tines of a massive radiator that occupied a dusty recess for heating the downstairs hallway. When the hot steel door banged itself shut behind me, she suddenly turned to look at me with one eye, the other hidden in shadow cast because of a lone fixture on the ceiling.

Back in the Boiler Room, LANDIS gurgled. The radiator in the recess answered with a clank. Agnes May turned her face back to the tines and whispered something into their dusty spaces.

"What did you say?" I thought she had meant it for me.

She gave me a furtive one-eye look again. "I was talking to Philip." She turned toward the radiator after speaking the name. "Nobody knows about him. Well, now you do, but nobody else."

Her lower legs, hidden in that full-length dress of hers, stuck out into the hallway, hem having pulled up far enough to reveal socks a dingy yellow from too many washings in poor well water. I quickly stepped over her legs, intent on getting away.

"Eugene."

From the hall intersection, I looked back at her. Her face, now under the full glow from the light, had a thousand tiny freckles. I'd never noticed before.

"You won't tell anyone, will you?"

"Umm..." She had always been such a brat. I thought about all those times she had put a bent-backwards arm up to tattle.

"About Philip." She turned her face toward the radiator again and then back to me, lips pouting. "You won't tell anyone about Philip, will you?"

"I guess not." What would I tell, anyway...that some imaginary person lived in a radiator?

"Please? Please promise you won't tell."

"No, Agnes May, I won't tell anyone. I promise."

In the play of light and shadow in the school basement, her eyes shone like the brown pebbles, shiny and wet, down in Hobbes Creek.

"It can be our secret, Eugene. For so long, I haven't shared a secret with anyone. Not with anyone real."

"I won't tell. I promise."

Agnes May smiled at me for the first time.

## Chapter 11, Cup Adjustment

That afternoon, Quin extended the bat over his head, behind his back, twisted it, turned it, set it against his shoulder blades as he flexed muscles, motions he copied from major leaguers on the *Game of the Week*. From the bunched sleeves of his tee shirt globes of un-tanned shoulders showed white under the sun. Down his arms were shades of increasingly dark brown all the way to his hands. The white shirt, which bore SAINT AGATHA in crimson block letters across the front—as if the fabric had been emblazoned in the virgin blood of the martyr herself—tapered down from his chest, cotton forming itself to torso, like a men's undershirt ad in the Sears Catalogue, until it disappeared into a green army surplus belt that held up his dungarees.

My shirt, identical to his, billowed like a rich lady's drapes. I was jealous. It was not a suffering kind of jealousy, not like the hot feeling in my throat when Agnes May somehow got a 99 in Geography to my 94 on Miss Hendershott's year-end report card.

With Quin, it was more like yearning. A kind of jealousy that had a sweet taste to it, that almost felt good. Yes, a yearning. All that talent and skill and cleverness and those flexing muscles teased me into wanting to be like him. I wanted to share in it. I wished it was alright for us to be close the way girls were close. Girls seemed not afraid to touch in the middle of conversation, or even hold each other for a moment. Of course, I would never even think of doing that. Boys who are friends are nothing like girls who are friends. Maybe it's the outer softness that girls have: when they grow close, it allows them to feel and share an inner firmness. The stronger the bond between boys, the more fragile it is, their hard outer shells so easily broken.

No, it was not what I felt toward Agnes May whenever she outdid me in school. She was just a girl. The feeling about her was envy, pure and simple, which was one of the seven deadly sins, according to Father Kearns. With Quin, it was nothing sinful, no feeling inspired by some fiendish devil thumping along underground. No. With Quin it was very much spawned in the daylight. When we were apart, I wanted us to be together. When we were together, I wanted us to be close, to laugh in each other's faces, share the same activity, or just do foolish things. I wanted to reserve a pocket of the world for just us.

Hangy's first pitch whizzed over the plate. Quin followed the flight and arc of the ball all the way in, educated his own timing "to his adversary's motion and delivery," just the way Ted Williams had instructed. The ball plunked hard against the bottom of a wheelbarrow, which did double duty as our catcher and strike zone. It was propped up on its nose, back legs at rest on two folding chairs called to duty from the church basement.

"Strike," Hangy called from the mound.

"You got away with one," Quin said. "Lucky for you. Lucky it didn't land somewhere in the woods just about..." He pretended to consult a wrist watch "...now!"

Hangy laughed, "We wouldn't want to scare the squirrels and chipmunks, would we," and, with a grunt, let go another fastball.

Quin followed Ted Williams' advice to the letter: he held the bat back until he was ready to commit, head down as the motion of the swing began in his long legs, opened his hips only as the bat started to come around. Long arms, gristle and sinew, bone and tissue like they were held together by rubber bands, extended into a snap of the bat. A sudden "crack!" of good wood on the ball converted whiz to hum. It passed over my head to the outfield where Adam took one step before he resigned himself, hands on hips, to watch it clear the privet hedge.

As Quin trotted to third and then back to home — the equivalent of rounding the bases if this had been a fully manned game — he cupped a hand to his ear. "You boys hear that...just below the roar of the crowd?. Silence! You can almost hear squirrels and chipmunks scatter, looking for the nearest hole to hide in."

Our outfielder squeezed through the hedge. When the ball came back over, I caught it on a bounce and took it back to Hangy. We held a conference at the pitcher's mound, waiting for Adam to find his way back through the hedge.

Hangy turned to me, away from the hitter, and fingered the ball. He showed me his grip, thumb underneath, first two fingers on top. He curled his lip into a grin and spoke low. "Watch this." Against the red stitches, a slight crook in his index finger, while his middle finger stayed straight.

Quin stepped back up to the plate. "One for me," he reminded us. "*Nothing* for everybody else."

I went back to my position. Launched out of motion that started in Hangy's legs, it looked just like the previous pitch.

Quin's eyes lit behind his glasses as he followed it in. As before, he timed it perfectly, started a long stride, and snapped his wrists.

The bat clunked. The ball plopped off the end of it, and fell into a series of tired hops to the right side of the field. It continued out over the dirt of the designated wasteland, that sudden-death area past the infield to the right of second base, where we did not have enough players to position a defender. It rolled to a stop in the weeds, like a sulky, disobedient dog who didn't know where to run away to.

Before the hitter could even throw the bat down, Hangy stepped off the mound toward home to claim his turn. Quin, without a word, and according to a rule he was always sure to impose on the rest of us, trekked out to the wasteland to retrieve his own errant hit. He threw it back over his shoulder without looking, and moved over to left, to his new position, last man in the field. Adam moved up to play a short field. I moved up to pitch.

This was scrub. No such thing as a warm-up on the mound. When it was your turn to pitch, you pitched. On four tosses, I missed the wheelbarrow and walked Hangy, putting an imaginary runner for his team on third. When he stood at the plate for the next at-bat, he laughed as he watched me struggle. He rested the bat on his shoulder, held it by the crook of his arm, as if he didn't even need it, and mimicked a girl filing her nails.

I walked him again. Six pitches this time. The imaginary runner was forced home, and a new one took his place on third. Behind me arose a two-man chorus of complaint.

Did either of them notice that I had found the wheelbarrow twice? In Hangy's third at-bat, my first toss plunked it in the center.

"Steee-rike!" Quin and Adam yelled together from behind me.

Hangy, more attentive, gripped the bat with both hands and raised it above his shoulder. Uncurling from a severely closed stance, he shut his eyes at the last second with red-faced effort. He missed, as he often did.

"Steee-rike two!" Quin and Adam yelled, and took up a taunting chatter.

But the one after that Hangy did not miss. He spanked it. It hummed into the muggy atmosphere over the field. The ball, as we watched it leave, turned from a yellow sphere into dark speck well beyond the hedge, and gave a surprise brush-back to a limb of an overgrown pear tree before it thumped into a patch of briars.

Quin started toward the hedge, but soon stopped and came back onto the field of play. "I'll never find the ball way out there."

Hangy slowly hoofed it to third and then back to home, imaginary base runner scoring ahead of him. Two more runs. Three runs already off my pitching arm. Adam went to fetch a new ball from the shed.

"Might as well bring the whole bag out," Hangy said. "I'm not done yet."

He took off his shirt, beefy torso white in the sun. He forced it through an eyelet of the fence fabric.

In the lull, I walked around the mound kicking at dirt the way I'd seen pitchers in trouble do on television. I bent and swiped at the rubber with my glove, as if that would somehow improve my pitching. The rubber was a yellow 1954 Pennsylvania license plate, held in place by washers and spikes driven through the mounting holes. Sweat ran down my sides, so I took my shirt off too, and carried it to the backstop, where I stuck it in the fence near Hangy's. Adam and Quin came in from the field and did the same.

Through the lull in the action, Agnes May's voice prattled from the porch. In her summer dress, she bent and straightened, and worked down the pile of beans.

"Who do you suppose she's talking to now?" Hangy wagged his head and grinned. He leaned on his bat, just the way we'd seen in an old photograph of Lou Gehrig.

Adam gave a new ball to me as we all returned to the field. "I can't help it if my sister talks to herself sometimes," he muttered.

Agnes May, in her long, swishing cotton dress, came off the porch and stood by the shed. Adam grew quiet, and motioned to Quin to do the same.

"What do I care if she hears me?" Quin shrugged his shoulders.

"She'll tell on us for cussing."

"I'm not a kid!" Agnes May's cheeks flushed.

"She's got you there," Quin said, and smiled, showing lots of teeth toward Agnes May.

"Well, aren't you supposed to be snapping beans, little sister?"

"I'm done with the pile, and Mom is taking a nap. Well, aren't you supposed to be scraping and painting the church, big brother?"

Scrub resumed. I figured Hangy would keep on pulling hot line drives to left, or slam them into the ground at my feet so the ball spit grains of infield dirt into my face when I tried to make a play. Adam would have to back me up, hold my flubs to singles. Hangy reminded everybody of the mounting score, to which Quin, disgusted at my pitching and fielding, cussed loudly, Agnes May or not.

Off my next pitch, Hangy hit a low line drive, shin-high, so hot I knew I had no chance. I could catch a ball okay on a direct hop. A ball that came at my feet, or bounced close in front of me, would have me close my eyes, for just an instant: I'd never been able to get over being short-hopped in the mouth when I was nine. This time, dumb animal nerve put the glove down for me. My head stayed up, face turned out of the way, eyes closed. The glove came back up with the ball. Adam, as stunned as I was, hesitated, and was almost late covering third. I managed to get Hangy out with a perfect hard throw that slapped Adam's glove.

Hot mustard tingled my glove hand from fielding the line drive, but I trotted to the batter's box for my turn, pretending the play had been routine.

Ears red, Hangy took his time going to the last position in the field, where he refused to notice the excitement as Quin and Adam ran to their new positions and made a few tosses to each other. Once Hangy was all set out there, new pitcher Adam waited at the license-plate rubber for me to go through my own version of a Colavito warm-up. In deference to Agnes May's presence by the shed, I used a turn-away version of imaginary cup adjustment.

When I stepped in, Adam turned around to look over his defense, and sneered out to the others. "This won't take long." His defense laughed.

He turned back. "I knew it," he said, and threw his glove down. He kicked the glove...sent it flopping over the dirt, a blob of leather coughing dust. He walked in a circle around the rusty license plate. "I knew it!" He stopped and glared at his sister.

She had moved onto the field, and claimed third base with both feet. Hands on hips, she glared back at her brother: "What position do I play?"

## Chapter 12, New Catcher

You couldn't beat the wheelbarrow as an umpire. Propped up on its nose in the dirt behind home plate, open side of the pan facing the pitcher, each leg rested on the top slat of a wooden folding chair. Like the Pope, it was infallible: any pitch that plunked the metal and bounced forward into fair territory was a called strike. It made the zone much larger than regulation, but scrub — at least the way we played it — was anything but regulation. We weren't town kids, after all, coached in Little League by a dad, pack of menthols rolled up in his tee-shirt sleeve. Out here in the country, we were on our own, and the whole idea of playing ball was to put the ball in play.

But our faithful metal ump had one major flaw: In its other duty as catcher, it did a lousy job of throwing the ball back onto the field unless the pitch landed right on one of the bolt heads in the bottom of the pan, which tended to pop it back toward the mound. So, most of the time, it was the batter's responsibility to chase after the ball. That slowed the game down.

At first, Agnes May's demand to be included in our game met a unanimous, automatic response: "No!" Not because she was a girl. Oh, that would have weighed heavily against her all right, had it not been for Katie Ellen Stoops. A year ahead of us at Melody Falls, Katie Ellen had learned to play ball at home with seven brothers. She was hardly the kind of girl who was afraid of getting a stain on her white knee-socks. A raspberry bruise from a hard slide into second would only make her more determined as a base runner. On the playground at school, she had been as likely as any boy to be chosen first, never a cast-off to right field. Her playing days were over now, of course. Last year, when the time had come for her to move on to Steven Foster Junior High, her father, Ed Stoops had declared an end to baseball by sending her instead to the Catholic school, Saint Agatha in Wyotanda, where the nuns could enforce more lady like behavior on the playground. It was as if his only daughter had somehow been guilty of shifting his world on its axis, and it needed to be righted again.

So, we'd been around a girl who could play ball. But Agnes May was no Katie Ellen. As far as anybody knew, Agnes May had never played ball in her life. Now, here she was, demanding to play with us...not even asking, demanding.

"No!" Adam said again, and put an arm out stiffly, finger down, the way I'd seen him yell at the family dog, Happy, when he didn't want the mutt to follow us.

She folded her arms, stayed put with both feet planted directly on top of third base, and turned her face away.

"Get off the field," he hissed at her from the mound.

She stayed. He took one step toward her and stopped. She didn't flinch. He took another step, stopped, then another. She stayed put. She actually expected us to let her play. Adam's steps turned into strides, arms swinging, hands curled into fists.

So, this was it. Agnes May, the kid-brat who lived for getting others in trouble—especially her brother—was finally going to get hers.

No telling why it happened to me. It came from the way she stood on that base in her flowered dress, eyes closed, face turned away from her accuser, an icon sure to release from deep within any Catholic boy a fire-hose of feelings. Agnes May suddenly became the essence of all the virgin martyrs I'd ever learned about, whose images adorned the holy cards.

I threw down the bat and ran to the base. "ADAM!" My shriek sounded like it came from a woman. I said in a more-controlled voice, "Adam—no."

The action provoked Quin to yell, "Hey!" and Hangy, "Don't!"

Swift legs carried me there ahead of Adam. I got between him and his sister. He stopped, a bead of sweat running out of his hair and down his cheek, and huffed into my face. His sister did not move a muscle. I could hear her breathing.

Into his crazed stare, I said, "We need a catcher."

He broke off the stare to look at all three of us, one by one. Hangy shrugged. Quin chuckled. I stared back at Adam. He went from looking crazed to almost wanting to cry.

"She'll get hurt," he whined.

Agnes May finally released herself from a frozen posture, and put her hands on her hips. "So, now you're suddenly worried about me?"

Quin spoke softly to her, the way you'd see a male character on the movie screen try to reason with a female counterpart who just didn't understand how things are. "He's right, you know. One wrong foul tip and we're all in for it, if we let you play."

"There's catcher equipment in the shed," Hangy offered.

Adam wagged his head.

"Yes," she said, eyes bright, brow arched. "They use it for the men's Sunday church games."

Adam laughed hoarsely. "That equipment won't fit on a girl."

All eyes were on me. Quin and Hangy and Adam and Agnes May. Why had I thought up making her our catcher?

"And another thing," Adam said. "Who's going to call the strikes? Not her!"

She folded her arms and faced away, virgin martyr awaiting her destiny.

Borrowing my father's voice, I handed down my decision, poking index finger into opposite palm. "The wheelbarrow will continue to call the balls and strikes. It cannot make a bad call, and nobody can argue with it. Agnes May's only job is to throw the ball back to the pitcher...so, now the hitter doesn't have to."

I saw it in Quin's and Hangy's eyes: this was going to happen. I'd had a brilliant idea after all.

"The game will sure move along faster," Hangy agreed.

Appeals exhausted, Adam turned around and kicked dirt as he headed for the mound. We all went back to our positions. I picked up my glove and gave it to Agnes May, whose face bore a look of surprise. She stood behind the wheelbarrow and slapped her hand into the glove, the way she'd seen us do. "Ow."

I stepped to the plate. "Better get down. Keep out of the way of foul tips. Only come out when you're sure the pitch is finished."

I took a practice swing, pointed the bat at the outfield hedge. Hangy laughed, and Quin said, "It ain't gonna happen, man."

I brought it back, positioned the trade-mark, and held it high over my right shoulder as Adam went into his wind-up. My eyes left the field for an instant, just long enough to look back with a brief side-glance. Our new catcher hunched down, peering over the edge of the metal umpire, creek-pebble eyes wide and dazed.

Adam's pitch, too high, blazed over the edge of the wheel-barrow, forcing our catcher to duck down before it pinged into the backstop wire mesh. Agnes May's throw-back had a hitch and a jerk to it, and only went about half the distance before it fell to the ground and rolled the rest of the way.

Pitcher glared at catcher. "Hey! You have to get the ball back to me if you want to play."

I watched the second pitch all the way in. It was no better. She had to duck down again. Hangy, in deep field, slapped his glove. Quin, in short field, slapped his. "Better not get too far behind."

"What are you talking about?" Adam yelled. "This is Eugene."

She came out this time, threw from in front of the plate. Adam dug her second throw out of the dirt, eyes bulged and face flushed. "How 'bout throwing it to me instead of at me."

She hunched down behind the wheelbarrow, breathing hard with the exertion of a new experience.

The pitch came in a little more controlled, red stitches hissing, but still high. A downward tail at the end, it skimmed the top edge of the wheelbarrow this time, making her duck again, and fall backwards. She got up, red-faced and breathless, and brushed off the dirt from the rear of her dress.

Adam laughed. "Any time now," he glared at her as he held up his glove for the ball.

"Yeh," Hangy shouted. "And any time now, maybe the pitcher could throw a strike."

"You've run the count to three-and-oh," Quin reminded him.

I stopped Agnes May as she came around the wheelbar-row, her dress in a swirl around her, her motions magnified by not knowing what she was doing.

"I'll show you."

Allowing me the ball, she turned away from the field and wiped her eyes with her sleeve. I showed her a two-finger and thumb grip.

"What hand do you write with?"

"What?" she said, and blinked at me with glazed eyes.

"In school. I think you write left-handed, don't you?"

She nodded, sleeved her eyes again.

"Well, you gotta *throw* lefty too."

"But I thought I was supposed to catch with my left hand. How can I do both?"

Adam shouted into us, "Any time now!"

"After you catch the ball...well, actually, after you pick the ball up from the ground, pull the glove off and throw with the same hand."

She took the ball back and blurted a syllable of laughter. "You must think I'm so silly."

Adam shouted at us again. He turned to his fielders. "You see? This is what happens!"

She threw the ball, lefty this time. It was a mirror image of her tries as a righty: the ball fell to the ground and bobbled along in the dirt to the mound.

Quin yelled, "Better make it a good one, Adam, or ole Genie's likely to uncork one."

"Yeh, quit trying to hit your sister," Hangy snapped from deep field. "All you've done so far is make Genie into a cripple shooter."

Adam laughed with his mouth. His eyes were wide and round. He walked me on four pitches, the last one more like the first two, high and fast, and aimed at his little sister's head.

"Cripe'n-itey," Quin muttered. He leaned forward and spat.

"Runner on third," our catcher chirped.

So, she had been paying attention from her bean table on the porch.

When she came around to throw the ball back, I got behind her, held her arms, turning her so her right side was toward the pitcher. I reached for her left wrist, and brought the ball back. Arranging her fingers and thumb, I formed her hand into a grip on the ball.

Adam turned away again. "You see? This is what happens."

I held her from behind, and she relaxed just a bit against me. Heat came through her dress.

Hangy and Quin laughed. My ears burned. I didn't look out at them.

Beside her braid, into the curve of her neck, I said, "Do what I do." Together we took a step toward Adam and rotated as I guided her left arm in a three-quarter arc. She released the ball...the right distance this time, but it went toward Quin in short field.

Adam turned and put his hands out, "What was that?"

"Quit bellyaching." Quin tossed the ball to him. "Maybe you should concentrate on throwing strikes."

Adam walked around the mound, kicked up dirt, and then settled.

I eyed the pitch all the way in. I knew, by the way he re-leased it, this time he was determined to throw a strike. It came in straight down the middle. Just getting the bat on the ball was enough to mirror the pitch, a frozen rope straight back to Adam. Stuck in the end of his follow-through, he had no chance to make a play. The ball hit him on the hip and scooted to the left, out past third base. Quin, who had broken toward the middle, put on the brakes when he saw the hit ricochet off his pitcher, and sent a cloud of dust flying out ahead of his feet as he slid down on his butt. By the time Hangy hoofed it in from deep field to get the ball, I was already touching third, and racing for home. A long throw harmlessly pinged the backstop after I'd crossed the plate.

"Two runs in," our catcher, her face now pinked up, an-nounced to the defense.

"Yeh, yeh," Adam said. "Just do your job, Miss Catcher."

"The same goes for you, Mister Pitcher," Quin said.

Banter went back and forth among the three fielders. Adam, again, tried to get the others to see that allowing his sister to play had ruined everything.

"This time," I murmured to Agnes May, "imagine your brother's face in a window when you throw the ball back to him."

"A window?"

"Your job is to shatter the glass. Don't be content to bump it politely. Shatter it."

"Throw strikes," Quin and Adam yelled together, ending the field discussion.

Out front of the plate, she eyed the ball, adjusted her grip, looked out at Adam, stepped, brought arm over the top, and let go. Release of the ball turned her body like a dancer, and pulled the fabric of her dress against her shape. The ball snapped into her brother's glove. She smiled at me and breathed, let her small shoulders relax. Chest out, she put on the glove as she came back around to her position behind the wheelbarrow. She allowed a tiny laugh for just the two of us, and hunched down as she slapped her hand in the glove. This time, she didn't say, "Ow."

"Time," I said. Putting my left hand out at Adam, I crossed the plate.

Quin wagged his head. "This inning will soon be over."

"No doubt about it," Hangy agreed.

They'd seen my previous attempts at batting lefty: lots of foul balls, which would build the count against me, and then a strikeout every time. I had no reason to think this would be any different. No reason...but I did have a feeling. It seemed to come from Agnes May's sudden success at getting us to allow her to play in the first place, and then at learning how to make a good throw after just a few tries. And it came from her eyes looking at me, watching me, from just over the edge of the wheelbarrow.

The two fielders came in for a conference with Adam. Hangy did all the talking. He knew my weakness: low and inside. It tended to make me shy away a little before swinging the bat.

But that was right-handed. At some things I was a lot stronger as a lefty. When I carried water from the end of the hose to my father's transplanted lilacs, the buckets were uneven, one a five gallon, the other only three. I had always found it much easier to carry the heavy one left-handed.

Conference over, they went to their new positions, which were now shifted around to the right, making left field the new wasteland. First was now the active base. Adam threw the ball. I did what Quin had done: followed it all the way in, timed myself to it. The pitch started out like it would be up in the strike zone, then arced downward and crossed the plate a little tight, a little above the knees. Plunk from the umpire: a strike, which brought chatter from the two fielders, daring me to swing, already smelling a strikeout. I dug my feet in, held the bat high. The next pitch looked like the previous one, started out high, dropped down and in. I stopped thinking, stepped into the pitch, and brought the bat around with a snap.

"Crack!" And a new moment started that seemed to have its own existence, unconnected to all the others. I was an observer within my own body. I watched the ball go over the hedge, saw myself tag first base, and was already half way back to the plate before I remembered to go into a home run trot. Agnes May, eyes large and round, picked up my bat and handed it to me, her cheeks pink under tiny freckles, lips tight, as if my accomplishment partly belonged to her. I was not even aware of my feet digging in for the next at-bat, or of holding the bat over my shoulder. I heard Quin's voice as he chewed on Hangy to play me deeper, and Hangy jawed back that no way would I ever do that again.

But I did. It all happened just the same. The pitch was down and tight, the ball came off the bat the same, drove down the line the same, and cleared the hedge in the same place. It probably whisked the same leaves at the top as it went over. And Hangy, on those tree-trunk legs of his, again was way too late going back for it.

For the second homer, though, I did remember the trot. I took it easy this time heading to the plate. I went into a new-found power-hitter's jaunt, watching Agnes May watch me. Her eyes, not as round, not as large this time, settled on me — just me — like we were two people who knew a secret. She too seemed removed from the field, suspended out there in a single, simple moment of Eugene Ahern jolting home as Agnes May handed him his bat. Her lips relaxed, parted a little, showed her pretty teeth, and I wondered how I hadn't noticed them before.

Quin cupped his hands toward right field and cussed Hangy into playing deeper. Hangy continued to insist that I would never be able to repeat what I'd done — especially not after I'd managed to do it twice! But he did move back a step or two. Adam kicked the dirt. I dug in, and pawed a small hole with my back foot. I raised the bat, muscles in my arms and chest and shoulders hard and round. I felt her eyes on me, and tried to flex my jaw the way I'd seen actors do in the movies, ripple going across cheek. She took her position behind the wheelbarrow, plopped her small girl-fist into the pocket of her glove. We waited for Quin and Adam to finish a short, whispered conference at the mound.

I turned away from the field a little, trying to catch a sideways glimpse of her crouched behind the wheelbarrow, eyes level with its steel lip. I imagined how I looked to her, envisioned myself through her creek-pebble eyes, male shoulders squared for action, arms holding the bat up, cocked for a powerful swing. I must have looked stunning to her, an image of human form that asks you to let your eye linger, like that photograph of a Greek sculpture of Perseus that I'd seen in a book up in the library stacks. As the pitch came in — over the outer part of the plate this time — I observed myself through her eyes, imagined Perseus stepping in, bringing the bat around.

You can't hit a ball and think about it at the same time. And you certainly can't hit a ball and think about somebody else watching you do it. The bat did make contact, all right…the handle buzzed with it. The ball plopped off the end, bounced to the left and wobbled in an awkward dance out to the wasteland. The moment that had had its own existence now came to an end.

"See? I told you!" Hangy ran in to take up a new position. "No way he would ever do that again."

Quin, silent, wagged his head and walked to the pitcher's mound. Adam came home for his at-bat, threw his glove ahead of him into the weeds at the base of the backstop. I pulled my glove from Agnes May's hand. Eyes down, she seemed to not want to let me have it. I went out to retrieve the ball and dutifully take up the last position in the field.

"I told you," Hangy said again.

"Yeh, so you told me," Quin said as he took the mound.

Adam looked around for the bat. "Oh, no you don't!" he yelled at Agnes May.

From the field, we looked on as the two of them faced each other over home plate. The umpire, propped on the backs of folding chairs, stood mute.

## Chapter 14, Gotta Keep It Dry

"When do I get to bat?"

"You don't!"

Agnes May and Adam screamed at each other red-faced. She held onto the bat, both feet planted on home plate. He circled her, kicked dirt into a swirl of dust.

He was selfish.

She was a brat.

He was stupid.

She was ugly.

Quin and Hangy and I came in from the field and stood away from sister and brother. I'd already put a stop to one war between them today when I'd made her the catcher, and was fresh out of ideas.

Adam stopped circling and grabbed the bat. Agnes May held on. They pulled back and forth against each other. He muscled her off home plate and claimed it for himself. She refused to let go of the bat. His jerking had her hopping. The braid whipped around shoulders, skirt wrapping and unwrapping her legs.

For an odd instant yelling ceased. Then it resumed, each blazing away with bigger guns: She was the most unpopular, most hated girl at Melody Falls ever, and everybody knew it. He, don't anybody forget, had flunked a grade.

With so much ruckus, nobody saw Hughla Stippil come out of the house, off the porch and onto the ball field. We were first aware of her when a claw-like hand reached into the fray and grabbed a fistful of braid. Another hand grabbed an ear. Everything—jerks, hops, flying dust and screaming—came to an abrupt halt.

"Drop it!" their mother ordered, and Adam, who had wrestled the bat away at the last second, did so, face full of pain.

She marched them back to the house, up onto the porch, through a dark rectangle of doorway. The door shut with a bang.

Hangy said at me, "You had to go and make her the catcher."

"And showed her how to throw like one of us," Quin sneered. "What was that?"

I shrugged. It wasn't all *my* fault. The trouble started when we—when all of us—let a girl onto the field.

"None of you said anything then, so why is it my fault now?"

They didn't answer. The three of us looked away from each other for a while, silence doing all the shouting.

Hangy muttered, "Guess our game was just about over anyway. I expect the noon siren's about to blow." He went to the backstop and pulled his shirt out of the chain-link mesh.

Quin and I left our shirts jammed in the fence because, at my house, it would just be lunch, not dinner, and shirts would not be required. But Hangy took his because the noon meal at the Hobbes place was always a sit-down dinner, the main meal of the day. Not many people did that anymore, but Old Man Hobbes, though well-equipped with modern machinery, still farmed the way his old man and his old man before him had done. In summer, the day started at 4 o'clock. After first milking, as much of the hard work as possible—heavy chores, ongoing projects, the sweaty jobs it takes to run a dairy farm—was done in the cool of morning. That allowed afternoon to move at a slower pace, and time for the sun to burn off the dew ahead of haying and other harvesting of crops before the evening milking. And, right in the middle of doing things the old way was sitting down to dinner at noon.

The three of us headed through the short woods behind Fellowship Field, slid under barbed wire and crossed over a drainage ditch onto an access road that Old Man Hobbes had recently built up higher by adding a new layer of dirt, soft underfoot.

Hangy warned us not to walk through the oats. Once trampled, a crop with bent and broken stalks might not pass through the combine cleanly, causing jam-ups. "He would kill us all! Especially me!" So we went around the field to a lane at the bottom of the slope below the farm buildings.

Quin looked up the hill, eyed the milk house beyond the barn. "Got time to burn a quick one?"

We crossed into the pasture. But just as we started up the cattle path, the firehouse siren blew the noon hour, wailing through the valley below and up onto the mountain. It was too late to go for a smoke.

There was no holding him back from his dinner. Hangy hurried his pace. "After dinner, I'll bring painting tools back with me."

Quin and I, watching his powerful legs gain the incline up ahead, turned away and headed for my farm.

In our kitchen, Grandma Marja sliced bread for Quin and me from the loaf she took out of a steel box. We found plates and glasses, and poured iced tea for ourselves.

"Got something for you," Marja said, and winked a shiny blue eye at Quin. "Veronica went to the A&P this morning. I told her to see if they had this in yet."

She clunked a small can on the kitchen table. Quin's black eyes widened. He picked up the can and studied the label through his glasses: a blue sky emblazoned with red letters, CASTRO VALLEY, a flat field between two steep hills, rows and rows of green, leading away to the horizon where, in smaller letters of gold, ARTICHOKE HEARTS IN VINEGAR.

Quin licked his lips as he lathered bread with mayonnaise and laid down an artichoke bed on two slices of onion. I had crunchy peanut butter and grape jelly. Grandma stood by the table, watched us make our sandwiches as she nibbled cold oatmeal from a bowl left over from her breakfast, which she had fancied up with chopped nuts and raisins. We took our sandwiches and glasses of tea out to wicker chairs on the screened porch. The breeze licked at our sweaty skin.

"You going to watch fireworks from here this year?" Quin asked, then chomped down, mayonnaise and vinegar dribbling out from around bread slices.

From our porch, through a cleft in the ridge, we could see across the valley to where the fireworks would be shot off behind Melody Falls High School.

"Just like last year, I suppose."

Grandma came out to the doorway and watched us eat while she nibbled blobs of cereal off the end of her spoon. "You're always welcome to watch with us again, Quin," she said.

He spoke through his sandwich, "I'm kinda hoping my old man will take me this year."

She stayed in the doorway until we had finished our sandwiches, then Marja melted back into the house.

Quin said to me, "But I really can't depend on him to take me, you know. What about your parents? Why can't we go with them for once? Let's watch it up close and for real this year, instead of from three miles away."

"They go with political friends," I said. "Political people means no kids. We can watch with Grandma, here on the porch, like always."

"Could she drive us?"

I laughed. "Maybe on Grandpa Carroll's old tractor. I've seen her drive that thing, but only in low gear. I don't think she's ever driven a car, just the Massey Harris."

"Maybe you could teach her how to put it into road gear."

We both laughed as we imagined the three of us, Grandma Marja at the wheel, Quin and I on either side of her as we held onto the steel fenders, tire chains flinging dollops of dried mud into the air. Chugging over the country roads, we'd ride the Massey Harris all the way to the high school athletic field.

"We'd sure never live that one down."

"Doesn't your Grandma ever go anywhere? I've never even seen her at church."

Nobody had ever actually said it was a family secret. Nobody had ever said it wasn't either. All I knew for sure was that we didn't talk about it with outsiders, because it seemed to be something the family was quiet about, even within our own house. But Quin was always around, like a family member, and now he'd asked, and since nobody had ever said I couldn't tell...well, it just came out: "Marja won't set foot off this property."

His eyes widened. "Cripe'n-itey, Genie! Never?"

"Never. Not since her wedding day. And that was kind of a secret, for some reason."

"Not even for your Grandpa's funeral?"

"They had a wake here first. She wouldn't go to the church or cemetery."

"Well, hasn't she ever had to go somewhere...to the dentist, maybe?"

"Nope. That missing bottom tooth? She pulled it herself."

Quin laughed. "Nice try, but you aren't putting that whopper over on me."

I shrugged. It was true. With needle-nose pliers, she'd pulled that tooth herself, right in her kitchen. "That's a relief," she'd said, tears running down her face.

"For real?" he finally said.

"For real. She won't leave the farm. She's never said why. Like she's afraid somebody might recognize her, or something."

"That's it!" Quin's eyes widened. "She's one of the Boston Brinks gang. She's the secret leader of that caper. Nobody knows, because the rest of the gang is scared of her, afraid to rat her out, afraid to squeal to the fuzz that she's been hiding here ever since they pulled it off."

I imagined Grandma jumping off the running board of an old Packard, red-hot machine gun in hand, like a thug on the *Untouchables*. "Grandma is one suspicious character, all right."

"Yeh, it's all that oatmeal she eats. That would make you mean."

After a while I said, "She didn't even go to the hospital to have my old man or Uncle Dan, either. Had 'em right here, in the room that is now my father's office. Doc McNally came out."

Quin's eyes widened further. "The vet? She had the animal doctor deliver her babies?"

"No...not the one we have now. It was his old man. The first Doc McNally."

"But, the first Doc McNally was a vet too!"

We drank our tea and were quiet. Quin burped, making it into syllables. He was an expert at that.

On the way back to the ball field, we stopped at the Hobbes milk house to burn a Pall Mall with Hangy, then followed him into his old man's work room in the barn. From shelves in a wooden cabinet, he took down scrapers, a wire brush and old paint brushes, and laid them out on the work bench.

"Adam has thinner," I said. "Maybe we can work the stiffness out of the brushes."

Hangy, jerking his head toward me, grinned at Quin. "Better move outta the way. Genie's got a stiffness he needs to work out."

"Should we leave you alone?" Quin laughed.

"Don't say that in front of Adam," I said, "unless you want him telling us all about Hell and Jesus."

Hangy tossed one of the brushes into a trash barrel, and kept the ones that still had somewhat pliable bristles.

Quin opened the door to an old, wooden ice box, paint peeling off the sides. A sixty-watt bulb burned in a ceramic fixture mounted below the bottom shelf. Above it rested gray welding rod containers printed with blue lettering: Hobart E-6011. He reached in and touched one of the containers to feel its warmth, like someone petting a kitten. "My old man's been here," Quin said.

"A few months back," Hangy nodded. "My old man was cussing up a storm, thought something was wrong with his welder. He told your old man about it, and your old man told my old man it was on account of the rods picking up moisture, so your old man rigged this up."

Quin looked at the boxes of rod for a while, then closed the door. He borrowed Bert's voice: "Ya always gotta keep it dry."

Hangy chuckled. "That's exactly what he said."

"He did the same thing for Vern Rollheis," Quin said. "Used an old ice box with a light bulb. It's an old welder's trick."

I wondered if my old man—father—had ever done any welding.

When we arrived back at the Christian Fellowship Church, Adam sat cross-legged in the weeds, head hanging, scraping the clapboards. He glanced up at us, and looked away. Agnes May, on the porch, worked down a new pile of beans. She turned her back to us, round-shouldered.

Into the heavy quiet Quin said, "What d'ya say we all get some serious paint onto this old church!"

## CHAPTER 15, FORGET THE CHURCH

Quin insisted that he be up on the ladder. The three of us down below—Hangy and I armed with scrapers and Adam with a Sherwin-Williams can and brush—moved further along the siding to get out from under the paint-chip snow squall flying off Quin's scraper.

"Doing the work of three men up here," Quin announced.

He traded scraper for brush, which he lathered up with paint from an old Folgers Coffee can. The snow stopped and changed over to white droplets of paint.

Adam stepped back and looked up at what Quin was doing. "It has to be a good job, or he'll just make me do it all over."

"Not technically possible," Quin said. "Once it's scraped and painted, he can't make you scrape it again, not through the new paint."

"He'll find a way."

"If the Reverend doesn't like the job we're—I mean, you're—doing, all he can really do about it is have you slop more paint over what you've already done. No big deal."

"Oh, he can do more than that. I'm not talking about what he can do to the siding!"

Quin stopped. Free hand on his hip, he held the brush, bristles up and out in front of him, paint dripping down the handle and running onto his fingers. "Gentlemen—"

"Here we go," Hangy said to Adam and me.

Quin launched into one of his speeches: "My fellow Dumble-Doers, I stand before you atop this fine, splintery, and somewhat shaky ladder today, called upon not as artiste, a vocation that belongs to members of the leisure class, which certainly does not include the likes of me. No, my cause here arises from among the mere working folk, everyday kind of people, from whom it derives its much nobler purpose: get all of this here paint on this here wall as fast as possible."

Hangy grinned at us. "No way he can keep up. There're three of us, and we get to jump past the windows."

Quin, having painted as far as he could reach, scurried down, forcing the ladder to wobble back and forth to his steps. Grabbing the legs of the support frame, he lifted and dragged it to a new position as Folgers can, brush propped on its opening, teetered on the top step. He climbed again, and another snow squall began.

As we worked, the sound of Quin's short speech slowly faded away. A new quiet enveloped us. We had talked plenty during the scrub game, mostly baseball chatter with its endless taunts, the way we'd seen town kids do during their genuine little league games on David Wilmot Field, with its real bases and chalk lines that led all the way out to white-painted foul poles with flags on top that said SCHNITKER'S TEXACO. Our on-field jawing, especially between Quin and Hangy, who puffed their performances into exploits the rest of us were supposed to be amazed at, had worn out everybody's ears.

So, quiet had a welcome softness to it. As loose paint rhythmically flaked away in favor of a new coat of white to cover the clapboards, quiet allowed in sounds that lived beyond the harshness of our usual noise. In the distance, somebody chopped wood. Each stroke of steel ax head against fiber echoed off woods and hillsides and farm buildings in a diminishing repeat of echoes, so your ear couldn't quite pick out the direction it came from...most likely, from Old Man Hobbes, who seemed to never stop working, which was, according to my grandma, the source of his grumpiness. A crow cawed down by the tree line. Another answered, and yet another farther away. Two swallows, much discussion between them, attended a nest under the eaves of the Stippil's porch, where Agnes May—involved in a discussion all of her own making—worked her pile of beans.

So much quiet made it all the more obvious that nobody would mention my first homer...or my second. My sudden success on the field stood up like a Japanese-movie monster in a stormy lagoon. Both homers had cleared the hedge. Nobody could think up words to spoil what I had done. Maybe Hangy could have snagged either of my hits today from going over, if he'd been playing deep enough. But what could have been just didn't matter. I now had a real, new-found home run swing, no different than Quin's or Hangy's. And I'd done it as a lefty, which stung their hides all the more.

The longer we worked on the church without talking, the more the quiet demanded that somebody say something. They expected me to brag myself up, but I wouldn't do it. I'd make them say it. And the longer they delayed, the bigger it grew, drinking up all that quiet.

Adam couldn't stand it any longer. "It doesn't count, you know."

Quin stopped scraping. Hangy stopped painting. They both looked at me, and then at Adam. I kept on scraping.

"It doesn't count," Adam said again, eyes on me.

I shrugged.

The others, having stopped work, said nothing, waiting for Adam to say more.

"I never got a chance to bat," Adam complained.

"He's right," Hangy decided.

They wanted me to argue, but I wouldn't do it. I scraped more attentively than before.

Quin laughed. "Doesn't look like Genie's going to bite on that."

"Doesn't matter whether he bites on it or not," Adam decided.

"Yeh," Hangy said. "When Adam's kid-brat sister tried to take over the game, that ended everything. This one isn't going into the record books. It's like a rain-out."

I said, without stopping my work, "You going to stand around and flap-jaw? When the Reverend comes home, we won't have enough work done to make it look like Adam was at it all day."

"The Genie is right, as usual." Quin turned up his scraping to a ferocious pace, and the rest of us followed his example.

We worked late into the afternoon, glaring sun passing overhead, turning from white to yellow. To get some relief from an all-day burn, Quin and I went to retrieve our shirts from the fence. Mine was missing. A search of the weeds all around the base of the fence didn't turn it up.

"Maybe Happy took it to play with." But it didn't seem likely. Happy, the Stippil's hound, raised his head from under the table on the porch to acknowledge his name, then returned to his nap.

"Uh oh." Hangy froze, paint brush motionless in his hand.

A familiar '54 Chevy crunched along the church driveway and stopped by the yard just past the Stippil's house. While Hangy, with a worried look, stared at the car, the other three of us kept right on working, as if activity would somehow shield us from what was about to happen. But then, painting instruments froze in mid-air: our collective attention suddenly changed direction, like starlings in flight in the fall. It wasn't Hangy's old man at the wheel of the Chevy. It was Lucinda!

"Big sis drives now?" Quin said from the ladder.

"Not for real." Hangy put down his brush. "She just got her permit."

Lucinda yelled through the car window, "The old man is going to make hamburger out of you," and laughed with a wrinkled nose and crooked mouth.

Hangy looked more worried.

"What'd you do?" Adam said to Hangy.

"It's what I forgot to do," Hangy muttered. "Check fence. He told me to do it last night just as he was going up to bed. I was listening to the Yanks, and the radio started that *squack, squack, squack* it always does when the electric fence starts to short out."

Checking fence meant walking the full pasture perimeter, armed with a scythe, on the hunt for weeds that had grown up to touch the bare conductor. If you let it go for long, the electric pulse in the fence could grow weak enough to allow the herd to break out.

"Who won that game, anyway?" Quin said.

"Orioles."

She called again from the car. "He's going to make hamburger out of you. You're in trouble!"

Quin came down off the ladder, and the three of us stood around Hangy. Forget the church. This called for the Dumble-Doers to close ranks around one of their own yet again.

"How deep are you in it?" Adam said.

"Not sure," Hangy muttered, rubbing his chin.

I said, "How 'bout one of us fell and got hurt? I live the farthest, so maybe I fell and cut my head open, and you and Quin had to walk me back to my place."

"I helped walk you back too," Adam complained.

I touched Adam's arm. "Don't forget: you were busy painting the church the whole time."

Quin mussed my hair, "Good thinking, Genie. If the Reverend gets wind of the cut-open-head story, we don't want him to suspect Adam wasn't painting the Christian Fellowship Church. I mean, we wouldn't want him distracted by the need to help save somebody's life, especially the life of a Catholic."

Quin and I laughed. Adam stayed serious. Hangy finished rubbing his chin.

"I won't need it," he decided, eyes lighting. "If the old man was really bent on making hamburger out of me, sis wouldn't be so calm about it."

Adam handed Hangy some paint thinner and a rag. "But doesn't she hate you?"

"Not full-time." Hangy got busy cleaning his hands. "Sometimes she acts like she hates people, but she really doesn't. If she thought the old man was going to tan me, she'd be upset about it. She would be about to cry...you know, way ahead of anything actually happening, the way females do. She wouldn't be looking so happy with herself."

The three of us nodded as we absorbed this new information about Lucinda. She was impossible to understand, four years older than us, and a girl. None of us had ever seen a friendly side to her. It didn't seem right that such a snotty teenage brat would have those pale eyes and swirls of hair that teased the air when she turned her head in a way that made you look, and then made you hope she'd turn her head again and catch it at a little different angle this time; that a person who would make her brother think he was going to be ground up for hamburger could also fill your eye that way.

But you didn't dare let her see you looking. I'd made that mistake once, on a Sunday afternoon three winters ago in the Hobbes upstairs hallway. Hangy and I had been hard at work on assembly of his Lionel set. On the way to her room, Lucinda, in a big-sister huff, stepped over our town with plastic trees and rail yard in-progress. Her hand was wrapped around a coffee cup that she had brought from the kitchen, having adopted a love of coffee the moment Crystal suggested her step-daughter was too young for it. That afternoon, she was fleshy and fanciful, with a dimple on her left cheek, and freckles, and the breathless whisper of girl clothes narrating her movements. It had me supposing that there was so much I wanted to know about beyond my own world. The sheer surprise of it captured me, tied me the way you see a cowboy tie up a calf on Rodeo Day at the fair. A step or two from her bedroom door, Lucinda stopped and turned. The skirt swirling and hair swishing, she glared at me. In the tiniest of moments that held her blue eyes on the same trajectory with mine, another complete world spun into being, one without a four-year chasm between our ages. In that world, my insides stumbled like a toddler full of eagerness to take a step.

"What are you lookin' at, squirt?"

She looked down at me with one of those soon-to-be a-woman's amused expressions that so easily undoes a boy, a boy on the floor at her feet who, after all, still played with trains.

That, of course, was the end of the tiny moment, and the end of the world, real or imagined. Since then, I had never again let her catch me looking. But she seldom missed an opportunity to recall my sudden-death experience, always ready to plop that same, "What are you lookin' at, squirt?" into any chance meeting, savoring its red-face effect on me in the company of my friends.

So, as she arrived in the church yard behind the wheel of Old Man Hobbes's Chevy, I knew there was no looking directly at her. I wasn't asking for trouble.

But I was saved. I was saved by Agnes May. Abandoning her pile of beans, she came down off the porch. Lucinda shut off the engine, set the brake and got out, stood by the car in blue jeans and a yellow cotton top that wanted to fall off one shoulder. The girls eyed each other playfully, like two kittens in the hay, and then talked in short gasps of words. We were too far away to hear what they said. Lucinda, in that loose top, leaned back against the car, crossed one leg over the other, put her arms back and placed her hands out wide to either side on the fender behind her. Agnes May stood, bringing braid over shoulder to finger its weave while they talked.

Difference in age meant nothing. Lucinda and Agnes May did what girls always do when there are just two. They shared in a feast of female doings, a gabby feast, creating a spontaneous world that belonged only to them. It was not a world in a single glimpse, like the one that had popped in and out of existence for me up in the Hobbes hallway three years ago. It was a genuine world, ongoing as long as either nurtured it with words and gestures and laughter and eyebrows that went up and down. We four boys turned into observers. We got to watch as everything we had been doing today up until now was quickly erased from importance.

Hangy finished cleaning paint off himself the best he could. Smelling of thinner, he put down the rag, forearms shiny with it. "Let's go," he said to his sister.

The girls finished up their talk. Lucinda opened the car door, and Agnes May turned to go. But they suddenly stepped toward each other again, Lucinda reaching up to run fingers back through her blond hair, Agnes May still feeling the texture of her own braid. They put their heads together, spoke briefly in whispers that had Lucinda roll her head back to laugh into the air as Agnes May placed hand over mouth in a blush.

Hangy wagged his head and yelled over the top of the car from the passenger side. "Come on!"

She turned and looked at him, then at Agnes May. "He's suddenly in such a hurry."

Once they were both in the car, she started the engine. It stalled.

"You have to release the brake," Hangy said, turning his head away. His acid tone, rather than at his sister, came through the window toward us.

Restarting the engine, Lucinda succeeded in releasing the brake this time, and the Chevy shuddered to her shaky release of the clutch as she backed into the yard to turn around. She stopped and shifted into first, then let out the clutch again, this time more smoothly. As she swung the car into the driveway, from the driver's window, pale blue eyes latched onto me.

"What are you lookin' at, squirt?"

## Chapter 16, Baggie Hoy

"So, where you headed?" Baggie Hoy said.

"Up to home."

"Get in."

"No thanks. It isn't far."

The name Baggie had long ago attached itself to him thanks to his loud and often repeated claim to have bagged himself a thirteen-pointer within a minute of the opening of buck season back in 1948.

"Get in." It was a matter-of-fact command. He looked away as he said it, which ended all discussion. I could feel, through my grip on the comma-shaped door handle, unevenness in the truck's rhythm. One of the cylinders wasn't firing completely, or maybe not at all, engine muttering to itself.

He was the older of the Hoy brothers by half a dozen years. Baxter and Sheffield Hoy were the approximate ages of my father and uncle, and I'd heard many stories of the two sets of brothers, whenever they could get away from farm chores, pairing off to do the things kids did back then. I'd heard about it from Uncle Dan, never my father.

I climbed in, but Baggie's attention was focused on something other than putting the truck in gear, something seen far off in the undergrowth. We sat there a while as he studied it through bug-specked windshield, round head under a gray deputy hat that swiveled with each turn of a fleshy neck on bowling-ball shoulders. He was a puffed-out, sloppy version of his younger brother. After a time he gave up on whatever he'd been looking at, and once we started moving at a slow crawl along the rocky lane, he clicked his tongue.

"Yeah, I sure could tell you a thing or two about your old man," he said as he swirled his eyes in my direction, as if taking up a conversation we had left off sometime in the past. He let his words hang there, in the truck's up-front engine grumble and whir of gears from under the floor board.

The cab of the former telephone company vehicle smelled of male sweat from all the utility workers who had sat in it. Since acquiring the truck, Baggie had installed a homemade rack that allowed his over-under, a twenty-two/four-ten, to stand upright. The stock was fixed in a bracket that was bolted to the right-side of the drive-train hump, and barrel ends, clipped in a similar bracket, were jammed against the roof, where they'd left an oily skid mark in the fabric.

"The things I could tell you. And about your Uncle Dan, too," he wheezed through a laugh. "They didn't used to be so up-and-up and holy."

His speech drew a sensation on the back of my neck that wanted me to defend my father and uncle against...well, I didn't know what; against being laughed at, I guess.

"I knew them before they got all fancy, you know. We were all friends back then, in the tough times, before things got easy like they are now; easy for some people, leastways. Not for all of us, though. Not easy for me, that's for damn sure."

From what I'd heard of him, the grown-up Baggie was a man who had learned a lot about taking it easy. An occasional handyman job seemed to be just enough to keep him in cigarettes and Old Crow. He was also a volunteer deputy at the Sheriff's Department, and now he had this made-up job as a township animal control officer, thanks to his brother being a supervisor. Otherwise, nobody seemed to know what he actually did.

I couldn't think of how to defend my father and uncle against Baggie's smirky remarks, and maybe defend myself too. "I don't think anybody has it easy," I finally said. "It just looks that way from one person to another sometimes."

"Jesus, boy. Sounding like your old man. Gonna go into politics just like him, I expect."

I shrugged. How did he know about that? I only knew of my father's political plans from having listened to his end of a discussion on the phone with Ed Bath. Mister Bath was the Chairman of the Wilmot County Democratic Party.

Baggie swirled his eyes at me. "Or, maybe he hasn't let you in on his little secret just yet."

"Secret?"

"Word has it... "

Something again caught his attention in the undergrowth along the lane. He let his foot off the gas pedal. The truck's rumble and groan fell in pitch to where the idle just barely kept the vehicle moving in a series of jerks and shudders that had the tail pipe chirping against the frame.

"Guess not," he said, and nudged the pedal to bring the speed from almost-stop back up to a slow crawl. "There's been reports of a bobcat. I'm gonna get me that sucker, you mark my words."

"My dad told me about that. He said it was spotted down by Stonefall Bridge. Kind of a long way from here."

"No matter, long way or not. A bobcat don't care about distance. It's a varmint. It's got — you know — a criminal mind. Always looking for opportunity. Like the guy they called Specs, the one they caught right here, from the Boston Brinks caper."

The story had been in the *Clarion*. A guy named Specs, who had served a three-year sentence for a firearms violation in the overcrowded Wilmot County Jail, had suddenly spilled his guts to the cops about the Great Boston Brinks Robbery of 1950. One story was that he did it because he'd gotten word that other gang members planned to assassinate him.

"Now, Boston's a long way from here," Baggie instructed. "Must be five-hundred miles. But do you suppose, if a Wyotanda constable, one of our own, had figured Boston was too far to matter, he would have been able to do his duty and catch the guy? Nope, he kept his eyes open and nabbed the son of a bitch."

"That isn't what happened," I said, armed with information from every article ever written on the subject in the *Clarion*. Like my Grandma, I was an avid newspaper reader. "Specs had burglarized a hardware store over in Potter County, and somebody there got the license number. When he came this way, the Wyotanda constable was already on the lookout for him."

Baggie waved his hand to dismiss what I'd said. "Doesn't matter. The constable still got his man."

"But he only nabbed Specs for burglary," I insisted. "He had no idea at the time that his man was one of the Boston Brinks gang. Nobody knew that until long after the guy had been in jail, when he finally ratted out the gang."

Baggie swirl-eyed me again. "Doesn't matter," he said impatiently. "Just like your old man, you muddy up the whole thing with particulars that don't change the fact that a clever lawman did his job."

He slapped both hands on the wheel. "And I'm gonna do mine. Gonna nab me that bobcat," he hissed, sending a tiny glob of spit onto the windshield. "And nobody — not your old man or nobody else — will be able to say the Melody Falls Township animal control officer isn't needed around here."

I'd heard my father say that, all right...more than once.

He breathed heavily through his nose, moving snot around, which he presently snuffled in.

I stayed quiet in the wake of his heated insistence, despite wanting to defend my father.

After a while I said, "Are you considered a lawman?" It was an innocent question, merely to make conversation. I figured it would defuse some of his heat. I was wrong.

He looked at me. His eyes flashed fire. "What do you mean, 'considered a lawman?' What's this 'considered' bullshit? That's just like what your old man would say." He snorted through his nose and slapped the wheel again.

"Didn't mean nothing by it," I said quietly into the ozone.

"No 'considered' about it. I *am* law enforcement, goddamn it. Part of my position includes volunteer Sheriff's Deputy, for one, and Melody Falls Township Constable, for another. And if you and that bunch you run with — especially that Sloot from the house-trailer down the hill — if you all don't believe it, you just go ahead and break the law. Go ahead, and see how fast the toe of my boot goes so far up your ass it'll have your ear holes pooping out brain matter."

I stayed quiet. My ears burned at him calling Quin a "Sloot." It was a word I didn't really know the meaning of, but I knew some of the people — mostly the poor folks — hated being called that.

Baggie's voice settled a little. "That Sloot friend of yours — what's his name — that Gutierrez kid. He will be the first — you mark my words — to have his skinny little ass meet up with justice, Baxter Hoy style."

He had started with my father and uncle. And now it was my friends and me. He had called Quin a Sloot. I didn't know where to even begin to defend all of us. My stomach hurt.

"Going to the fair?" I said, as Baggie made the truck climb a short hill at the end of the lane, where he turned onto Belknap Road.

He shifted the gear box out of low, but gave it too little gas as he let out the clutch, stalling it out. Cussing, he pressed the starter button, but the truck was reluctant to respond, engine complaining unevenly, saying, "wuh-wuh-wuh-WEE-wuh-WEE, wuh-wuh-wuh-WEE-wuh-WEE." It sounded just like Mr. Rollheis's Oliver 66 Rowcropper, until Quin's old man had done a valve job on it for him. After another try, the truck sputtered and came back to life. Baggie punched the gas pedal as punishment, and made the engine roar.

"Yep, I'll be at the fair," he yelled above the engine noise and pinging of pebbles up inside a rear fender. "Like I said, among my many duties are those of a Sheriff's Deputy. I'm sure the good Sheriff Braddawl will be needing me."

We rode without talking for a while, owing to all the higher-speed noises the truck made as it rattled along. We slowed to make the curve at the switchback just before dropping down to where the road crossed the culvert over Hobbes Creek, which marked the border between Hobbes' place and mine.

"So, your old man hasn't told you the secret?" He swirl-eyed me, his face relaxed and friendly again.

"Not that I know of. What secret?"

"About him running for judge." Baggie looked at me with expectation.

I shrugged and remained quiet. I knew my father was planning to run for judge, all right, but I wasn't supposed to know. I'd heard about it through the cold air return. Up to this point, I'd never let on to anyone, because it would have compromised my source, exposing me as an eavesdropper, a sneak. But, if Baggie knew about it, or thought he did, maybe I could finally say I knew about it too because I'd heard it from him. And yet, maybe Baggie was fishing for information, trying to fill in something he only suspected. My father would not want anyone to actually know until he was good and ready to tell them himself, so I would still have to pretend I didn't know.

I was caught in it: the liar's labyrinth that Father Kearns had warned about. It was at the retreat for sixth grade boys, the purpose of which had been to recruit any of us who would aspire to be altar boys. It had started on a Friday night in April, went all the way until Saturday afternoon, with a sleepover on cots in the Saint Agatha Auditorium. It included a canned-ravioli dinner, powdered-eggs breakfast and baloney sandwich lunch, all served up by gray haired ladies — and one whose hair was bright yellow — from the Altar and Rosary Guild.

It wouldn't be enough — to any of us who would sign up — to just know the Latin responses and to be able to anticipate the priest's moves as he went through the rubrics of the Liturgy. A Saint Agatha boy, Father Kearns had insisted, who sought to serve the Lord in such a direct manner, had to be a cut above all other boys. An altar boy had to be pure in personal character. An altar boy, after all, would be inside the sanctuary, in close proximity to the body and blood of Jesus Himself, and to the tabernacle, where Jesus' father was watching one's every move from a flickering flame enclosed in red glass.

And one of those issues of character was honesty. Father had delved in great detail into describing how a liar can get snagged in his own web of lies. He called it, "the liar's labyrinth."

Things had been so much simpler when I was just a kid. That was before grownups had started referring to me as "young man," which was their way of putting demands on me, demands that had certain expectations connected to them. Lately, the demand for honesty was boxing me in. I supposed I had no choice: I'd have to reform.

But that could wait...for now. I pretended I didn't know what Baggie was talking about. When you're a liar, and you're not sure if you're going to get caught, your best strategy is to suddenly go stupid.

"Running for judge? What do you mean?"

Baggie laughed, savoring the thought that he would be the first to tell me.

"Yep, the word's around, boy. And the word is, he's running for judge."

"Huh."

"The way I see it," he went on, "four things are against him. First, he's a Catholic. Second, he's a Democrat, which most people aren't around here. And third—well, there's you, boy."

I looked at him hard.

"Yep, I mean you." He returned my look. "All the delinquent stuff you and your friends do that you think nobody knows about."

"What stuff?"

Baggie laughed over the steering wheel, adding more tiny globs of spit to a collection already on the glass.

I remembered the words I'd heard more than once through the cold air return as my father advised clients in trouble with the law. When an officer tells you he knows something, and then doesn't say what, he's fishing. He's hoping you'll get scared enough to jump right out of the water and into the boat for him. "Always make a cop do his job," my father would say to them. "Never tell him a thing. Wait for him to tell you what he might know instead."

That sounded like good advice for someone stuck in the liar's labyrinth.

I pointed across to Baggie's side window. "Hey, what's that moving in the woods?"

Gravel sprayed out ahead from under the truck as he jammed down the brake pedal and peered in the direction I was pointing. The engine died, causing us to sit in sudden quiet, except for our breathing.

"What do you see?" he demanded. "I don't see nothing! You sure you saw something?"

I pretended disappointment. "White tail," I said—or lied. "Gone now. It disappeared into the shadows. It would be a good idea to remember these woods come December, though."

"Forget deer season. Going to bag me a bobcat way before that," he muttered.

The truck said, "wuh-wuh-wuh-WEE-wuh-WEE, wuh-wuh-wuh-WEE-wuh-WEE."

Baggie cussed, which seemed to coax the engine to catch. He punched the pedal, punished the engine again by making it roar, and brought the clutch up, jerking us forward and around the last bend to the straight section of road in front of our house. When he stopped by the opening in the split rail fence to let me out, he kept his foot on the gas pedal, daring the engine to sputter or even hesitate.

"I guess you'll have to wait on number four," he said and swirled his eyes at me.

"Number four?"

"Number four. The fourth problem your old man's going to have when he runs for judge. Yep, I could tell you a few things."

I shrugged.

"But it'll have to wait, boy. I've got official duties to do right now."

I shrugged again.

"Hey, you want to have a little fun?" he asked as he watched me step out onto the gravel. "Just ask your old man what he did during the war."

Baggie laughed in a high pitch over the steering wheel. As he let out the clutch, the truck pulled away, spraying pebbles over my shoe-tops.

# PART TWO:

## COMMUNION OF SINNERS

## CHAPTER 17, DIDN'T MEAN ANYTHING BY IT

My father thought it was funny. He didn't know I'd heard him joke about it with my mother. With me, he'd only spoken of it in serious tones. My task was to patrol the vast expanse of our blue-grass lawn in search of dandelion blossoms. "You are to infer," my father had said, "that each bright yellow flower's presentation of itself to the world is a request for eradication."

To that purpose, he'd had Bert Gutierrez make up a special weeder out of three-quarter-inch steel rod, flattened and looped onto a handle on one end, and on the other, peened and curved and cloven into a blade for prying out those pests by their roots. A conventional weeder, shipped to us in the mail from Illinois by way of the Sears catalog, just didn't work in northeastern Pennsylvania dirt. Belknap Ridge, the ancient Appalachian mountain we lived on, had a bad habit of hiding a piece of shale right where you were trying to push in the tool. A manufactured weeder just didn't last long.

So, armed with the specially customized weapon, I carried out the program as instructed...at least, when I knew my father was looking. Every day I patrolled the entire battlefield in a systematic, circular route that began at the outer perimeter of the lawn and worked its way up-slope to the house at the center, the same pattern farmers use to make a windrow. I hated it: it took all my free time after school.

But then, the day after Memorial Day, school ended. I suddenly had extra time. At first, that only made the job harder. Evenings would have me wondering what I'd done all day. I'd find myself in a panic, and, after supper, would have to hurry to finish up before nightfall. My father, reading the *Clarion* on the porch, would occasionally glance over the top of the newspaper to watch my progress with a look of amusement.

Thankfully, as the summer got going, the dandelions lost enthusiasm for their annual uprising. By the middle of June, only a few stragglers bothered to show themselves, so my daily patrol grew much easier. Soon, I was able to spend a whole day following whatever path my twelve-year-old boy's nature would lead me down, then complete the yellow-head job quickly after supper before Dad could even get through the news section and into the sports.

One evening, after I'd dumped the weeds on the boxed-in humus pile behind Grandma's garden and hurriedly put away the bucket and weeder, I had plenty of sun left. I informed my parents over my shoulder that I was heading over to Hangy's place. I'd been using a new strategy on them: simply tell them I was on my way. No asking permission. It forced them to decide in an instant whether they would actually stop me, something I'd learned, once I turned twelve, they were growing less inclined to do.

"Be home before dusk," my mother said after a moment of hesitation.

"Done with the yellow heads already," my father said quietly.

Something in his comment was bothersome. Maybe his words were hiding a hatchery for some kind of plan. A new project for me?

But, down the hill through the hay field, under the barbed wire fence and into the woods, concern about his comment vaporized in cool evening shadows. I was pulled down, down the steep, slippery bank of the creek, and then up the other side to the edge of the woods, out into evening light and onto the Hobbes place. We'd all agreed—except Adam, of course, who was never allowed away from his family after supper—to a meeting of the Dumble-Doers at the milk house. We Dumble-Doers had plenty to do. We had big plans to make for later tonight, without Adam, who was probably better off not knowing the details anyway. They were plans that we would carry out after the rest of Melody Falls Township had gone to sleep...

The next morning, rickety outside stairs that my father said nobody was supposed to use anymore squeaked and creaked. By the time I made it to the bottom, the noise had drawn Grandma Marja to the kitchen window, looking out.

I had hoped to get away without breakfast. I was in a hurry. Quin and I would be hanging out down at the waterfall before we were to meet the rest of them over at the Christian Fellowship church. It was something we'd begun to do recently, by ourselves, just us. Where it entered the dark woods, Hobbes Creek dropped a good twenty feet over mossy layers of shale. He and I had been going down there more and more this summer, down into the coolness, drawn by the busy action of the falls. When the stream was running low, water prattled like children at play. After a thunderstorm, it roared like the stockcar crowd at the Wyotanda Raceway. We'd been daring each other to climb up the slimy rock face, but neither had yet gotten the courage to try it.

Today's mission was to get our stories straight: suppose word somehow got around about what we had done last night.

"What about your breakfast?" Marja called to me through the screen.

I lay my baseball glove on the bottom step, as if I'd planned to do that all along. "Just getting myself ready to go over to the field."

So I went inside and sat at the old drop-leaf kitchen table that she often reminded everybody had been her first piece of furniture, and that my mother often reminded everybody should be put away in the attic, replaced with a modern counter, like you'd see in *Ladies Home Journal.*

"You shouldn't use those old outside stairs," Grandma gave me a cross look. "I'll remind Owen about it again. He promised to tear them down long ago."

She tried to coax a fist-size lump of oatmeal from her ladle.

"Not oatmeal, Marja. We have plenty of other kinds of cereal."

When I slouched with disappointment, it reawakened the ache in my shoulders and back, so I made a point of sitting up straight. The ache was a leftover from last night's lugging of a heavy burlap sack. Quin and I had taken turns carrying it all the way down to Old Lady Hough's place and, once done with our mischief, all the way back again.

"Yes, oatmeal," she said. "The good kind."

"What kind is the good kind?"

She peered through the doorway into the rest of the house. "Not that stuff your mother makes out of a box," she said quietly. "We're all out of that until she remembers to put it on her list."

The brown, mottled lump, at her urgent shaking, succumbed to gravity, unstuck from the ladle and slumped into the bowl she'd placed before me.

"Yours does look a bit drier than hers." I pretended to compliment.

When she turned away toward her stove, I rolled my shoulders, loosening tired muscles without her seeing me do it. She would be sure to ask a lot of questions, eyebrows drawn down with concern.

Grandma had always preferred to prepare her own breakfast. She would soak oats overnight, and in the morning let them simmer on a back burner, stirring now and then until the cereal had the right feel. "Your mother buys those flattened oats in a box from the A&P. Nothing but gruel, invented for the army."

"The army? How do you know that, Marja?"

She didn't answer. Still facing away, she stirred the cereal.

My shoulder-rolling seemed to be help. The burlap sack, containing the battery out of the Jeep and my father's new set of Craftsman box wrenches wrapped in soft leather, hadn't seemed heavy at first. But time—a good half-hour each way, at least—had added weight to our burden.

"Must have been something I read about," Grandma said. "I don't remember when or where, but I do know that the oatmeal gruel your mother makes was invented for the army."

I hadn't seen her with any military history books. Lately, she'd been pestering Norman Johns to bring around material about the Middle Ages in his bookmobile.

"But you've read 'em all," he'd protested last month from the window of the cocoa brown van. "Missus Ahern, you've done cleaned me out!"

She'd looked at him under lowered eyebrows. "You mean to tell me, Mister Johns, we've exhausted every piece of information on the Middle Ages in the whole Wilmot County Library!"

"No. Not we. You!"

She seethed about it for days afterward, and met with silence the suggestion of anyone taking her down to the library to see for herself.

But then on his latest stop, this past Wednesday, Mr. Johns, wide-eyed, like somebody who'd struck gold again in thought-to-be panned-out hills, had come through for her. Before his van had even rolled to a stop in our driveway, he was already shouting to Grandma to come down off the porch and "take a look-see at my find!" As he helped her up into the bookmobile, he waved a hand over the green shelves that lined the inside walls, and confessed to having mistakenly assumed all such books resided in the history and literature sections.

"Just look what I found under art and architecture!" he exclaimed, and worked his lips over toothless gums.

She thumbed through book after book, about building cathedrals, about sculpture, painting, poetry, mathematics, and inventions. One book fell open to an illustration of a naked man who appeared to be doing calisthenics.

"I'll take this one," she said softly, and put it under her arm.

It didn't take long for her to add four more books to it, reaching the allowable number she could borrow at one turn.

None of those books on Wednesday had been about military history. "So, Grandma, when did you read about the army eating oatmeal?"

"Could have been before you were born, for all I know. I lose track of exactly when I read things." She turned around and watched me.

I stared at the cereal. Quin would be waiting. It wasn't that we needed alibis for last night. As far as my parents knew, I'd been asleep in my bed. Same with Quin's old man, whose evening drinking would have put him under for sure. Hangy would be the problem, if there was to be one. Suppose one of his family members—big sis, Lucinda, most likely—had heard him climb back in through the window just a little before it was time to get up for the morning milking. We needed to get to Hangy, find out if anyone had said anything. Hangy would be the one to need help with a good story: he was a terrible liar.

The rasp of a piece of furniture being moved on the hardwood floor somewhere in the house had Grandma peering through the doorway again. "Why must she keep rearranging?"

"Dad says it's because she's an artist, and artists can't be satisfied."

She shook her head and clucked her tongue.

"Are you sure the oatmeal my mother cooks was invented for the army?"

"The soldiers couldn't take time to fix a proper breakfast, you know. They had to hurry out of camp to kill the Johnny Rebels."

"So, they ate oatmeal?"

"Not real oatmeal...the stuff that comes out of a box. Aren't you listening?"

I teased the lumpy pile before me with my spoon: wet cement that didn't have quite enough water mixed into it. Grandma's eyebrows lowered. I loaded the tip of the spoon with a small, brown ball of the stuff.

I asked, "Did you have friends when you were growing up?"

She knew that I knew she loved to tell about her childhood. But this time, against my try at changing the subject, she stood her ground. She remained on watch, waiting for me to eat.

"I mean, other kids your age. What did you do that was fun, Grandma?"

She couldn't resist any longer the call back to her early days. Her eyes wandered away, away from her kitchen, away from Pennsylvania, all the way back to Finland. "I was the oldest of seven children. It was a lot of responsibility."

Her eyes quickly came back to our kitchen, and I had no choice. As my tongue flattened to cradle it, my teeth chewed away at gooey oat grains, processing them into something that could be swallowed.

In the Vanhala family—Grandma's family—four girls in a row had been followed by three boys.

"Without sons old enough to help, Papa depended on me. I was his farm hand, you might say. He worked me—I'm certain he didn't mean to—like a man. I was just a little girl."

She was quiet, eyes away from the kitchen again. "I did have this friend...Loviisa, a year older than me, beautiful flowing red hair. That girl never had to work a day in her life. Nothing would soil her lovely white hands. Once a month—except in winter, of course—she would come over to our place with her parents for Sunday Mass."

Grandma had previously told parts of the tale. Father Duda, a missionary from Poland who served the scattering of Catholics in that part of Finland, would arrive on his spotted mare the second Sunday of every month. The Vanhalas would set up for him in the grain room, making an altar out of the front door taken off its hinges and laid across sawhorses.

"My mother kept special white linen for the altar. The Father would bring the wine and bread, vestments, chalice, a big book, candlesticks. From the moment we lit the candles until the moment they were extinguished, Papa would be so nervous. He would normally allow no flame in that part of the barn. Only down in the milking parlor, where a single lantern hung from a beam."

I swallowed. She no longer eyed my progress. I put down the spoon softly. "Loviisa," I said. "She was your friend?"

"Oh, I had others, too, including my sisters. But, for a time at least, Loviisa was my special friend. We told each other everything."

"What things did you tell each other?"

Her face flushed and she turned to the stove.

"My three sisters were my friends too, Kaija, Elizabet and Onni. But I was the oldest, you see, and there was so much I couldn't talk about with them."

"I don't have any brothers or sisters," I said.

"Well, yes, but you have many friends. Do you value your friends, Eugene?"

What could I tell my grandma? I smoked Pall Malls with them, told dirty jokes, said "Jesus Christ"...except to Adam, of course. "They're okay."

"What about Quin?"

"Quin?"

"Quin. He's here just about every day. Does he mean more to you than the others? Can you talk with him about things you'd never talk with anyone else about?"

I thought a moment. "Sure."

"You see? Loviisa was that for me. Loviisa was my friend, like Quin is your friend. You are very lucky to have him as a friend."

"Dad says Quin is the lucky one. Without me, he wouldn't have any friends."

She turned from the stove to face me, forehead drawn. "Don't ever say that, Eugene."

"I didn't say it. Dad said it."

"Don't repeat it, then. Don't even think it."

"Why not, Grandma?"

She turned back to the stove. "I did not raise your father Owen to say such a thing. He should know better, that's all."

"Know better about what?"

She was quiet. Into the empty conversation I told her the chewy oatmeal was tasty.

She turned and came at me with another ladle-full, plopped its contents into my bowl. Hurt had taken over her face. "Imagine, thinking you are better than somebody else. No, not thinking, but believing it. I'm surprised Owen would say such a thing."

"Why is that so bad?"

She stood over me. "I am an immigrant. Your grandfather was second generation, but still just a crude Irishman. Owen, my own flesh and blood, knows better than to say such a thing. And you—my flesh and blood too—I wish for you to know better."

"But, Marja, Dad didn't mean anything by it. He was just—"

"He was just saying your friend Quin is something less than you, and you are something more than he is. And you, his best friend!"

"But, Grandma—"

"Not in my house, young man! No boy is better than any other in my house."

I'd always thought of it as our house. It hadn't occurred to me before that this was Marja's house. She turned back to the stove, clanked the ladle into a pan, and went to the sink. She washed dishes with furious movements that made the flesh on her arms quake.

"Grandma, please don't worry. I don't hold with such a notion."

She stopped and looked at me. Her blue eyes lit, and she smiled. "Of course you don't, dear." She took to washing at a slower pace.

While she worked, she talked about Loviisa Peltola's family. Loviisa's father, who was Lutheran, would stay outside during the Mass and watch over the horses. He had been a patron of the theater in Helsinki when Loviisa's mother met her future husband. People were astonished, Marja told me, that such a beautiful, glamorous woman would fall for a lum-

berman, the owner of a sawmill. And they were more astonished that a man of Protestant sensibilities would ask an actress, and especially a Catholic, to share his marriage bed.

"Their daughter, Loviisa, was everything I wished I could
be. An only child. The parents had money, which they were
not afraid to spend on her. She was the eye, the shining jewel,
of her family."

"You were jealous of her, Grandma?"

She laughed. "Oh, I wanted to be her."

"Why didn't she have any brothers or sisters?"

She stared at me a moment. "Well, I wouldn't know the
answer to that, lad."

"I wonder why I don't."

She was quiet.

I said, "You were jealous of your best friend?"

"Full of jealousy. But she was also the one person I could tell
anything to. And she needed me, being the only child. We needed
each other, don't you see. It was a time in life when nature
teases a girl toward womanhood, playing its tricks on us."

After Mass, Marja explained, she and her sisters would help
their mother serve a big breakfast to two dozen or so parishio-
ners, everyone famished from having honored the Catholic tradition of fasting since the evening meal the previous day. "We
couldn't let them all journey back to their homes with growling stomachs, now could we."

The special Mass linen was replaced with a common tablecloth, turning the makeshift altar into a head table for the priest.
Everyone else took their meals at the hewn benches they'd sat
on during Mass.

Afterward, Marja and Loviisa would go off by themselves.
In poor weather, they climbed a peg ladder to the cupola at
the top of the barn, where they wrapped themselves together
in a blanket, and peeked out through the slats in every direction, puffing into the cold air. In summer, they wandered the
farm hand in hand, Loviisa's soft, creamy hand in Marja's
strong, callused one. They would follow the brook path down
into the woods, duck into the brush, a hiding place from the
others, especially from boys. From there they could spy on the
ones who came past, watch with stifled giggles as pursuers
puzzled over where the two had gone.

"We would nestle together in the undergrowth, careful to
make no human noise above our own whispers."

I finished all the oatmeal. She came and took away the
bowl and spoon, and quickly washed them in the sink. "I'll
save the rest for tomorrow," she announced.

She stood in the middle of the kitchen and said, "Oh, Eugene, I so looked forward to those Sundays. No work beyond the daily chores. And best of all, I could be with Loviisa. I remember thinking, is this what heaven is like?"

"Heaven? Giggling with your friend in the bushes?"

She laughed. "I felt so at peace, yet so alive and tingling, so calm and excited at the same time. One of those rare, fine moments in a person's life."

"Do you and Loviisa still write letters to each other?"

"Never any letters. We stopped being friends." The glow left her face as she paused, and then began again. "When I was twelve, we'd had a severe winter, don't you see. When spring finally came, we had not been together for five months. In that time, we'd become so different. She was suddenly so much older. Nature had played another one of its tricks on us."

I got up from the kitchen table. The shininess of her eyes drew me to her. She hugged me tightly.

"Gotta go, Marja," I spoke into her unrelenting softness.

"Yes," she said, and let me go. "Now, you have a good day with your friend at the ball field."

"I'll be hanging out with Quin down at the falls for a while first."

She looked stern. "Don't you be climbing on those wet rocks, lad."

"Marja, don't tell Dad I told you."

"Oh, he knows you go down to the waterfall. He worries that you won't be careful on those wretched rocks."

"No, I mean, what he said about Quin being lucky to be my friend. Dad didn't mean anything by it."

She was quiet as I went out the door.

## Chapter 18, Box Wrench

At the Melody Falls Watchful Christian Fellowship Church, sunlight was yellowing toward four o'clock, which meant Hangy would soon leave for milking time. Two hours earlier, we had abandoned bats, gloves and baseball to the dirt around the rusty backstop, and took up in earnest the scraping and painting of the church building.

Out front, my father's Buick suddenly materialized at the side of the dirt road. He was a man ever careful when driving on dirt, worried that the treads of those big white-walls would hurl tiny stones into the car's finish. The special caution with which he'd arrived muffled the normally raspy sound of a car's approach. In one moment he was not there, and in the next he was. The shiny, light-green over dark-green vehicle had simply moved into position, like someone making a cheater's move at chess when you aren't looking.

We'd been late starting work on the church. The way we'd figured it, the Reverend Stippil, when he finally made it home, would never be able to suspect his only begotten son of any ill-gotten enjoyment, such as playing ball with us most of the day instead of doing his duty.

My father's car horn emitted an insistent toot. From the front seat, he motioned to me to go with him.

Throwing down a paint scraper, I cussed under my breath, but nowhere near as much as the others. Except for Adam, of course, they cussed my departure. With Hangy soon due back at his place, the frantic nature of the job, now cut to three people instead of four, increased all the more in intensity. Paint chips flew off the clapboards, and wet white paint was slopped on. Maybe the Reverend wouldn't inspect too closely today. Maybe the mischief we had done last night would have him back here late, too tired and frustrated to even bother checking up on Adam's work.

As soon as I pulled the car door open, my father put his hand up, palm out. He had me back away and turn around slowly, so he could make sure I had no paint on myself before getting into the Buick.

His briefcase, instead of its usual place in the left rear foot-well, rested on the seat between us, a sure sign he was in the middle of something important. It often meant somebody was in deep trouble, no doubt one of the thugs he sometimes represented.

Massive V8 mumbling, he carefully floated the Buick out onto the crown of the dirt road. I didn't dare look back to see the expressions on faces that watched me leave.

"So, where'd you go last night?" My father said without looking at me.

He knew?

"Went for a walk."

It wasn't a lie. It sure wasn't the whole truth, but at least could not be proven a lie. I stared straight ahead, at the remains of a large insect glued to the windshield in its own translucent innards, a piece of a two-tone wing jutting out of the mess, patterned like the dragon flies you'd see down at Stonefall Creek.

We drove out of the sun and into the shade where the road cut through the woods. He was quiet, which left my half-truth lingering in the air between us. The longer my words were left hanging by themselves, the more likely their survival as plausible—or so I hoped.

We came out of the woods and slowly rounded the switchback, and crossed the culvert over Hobbes Creek.

No way could he have known all of it. Had he heard me leaving last night through the attic over the garage, down those outside creaky stairs? He would have stopped me at the time, in that low baritone reserved for occasions when he caught me at something. "What the hell you think you're doing, champ?"

So, he must have gotten up in the middle of the night for some reason, and discovered that my bed was empty. How could he possibly know any more than that?

Our place came into view through the tinted windshield. His silence seemed to go on a bit too long: he was mulling it over. It was an awful silence, my half-true words yet suspended, naked. I suddenly had the urge to fix everything.

Tell him? That's it! Everything! No sense in holding any of it back. When you're caught, you're caught. You hold some little thing back, and it's likely to poop itself out later, and then you're in trouble all over again. Once you're caught in a lie, you might as well empty the whole shitload, and just let it stink for a while.

Tell him about how mean the Reverend was to Adam, how we'd figured a way to help Adam out. Tell him about removing the battery out of the old Jeep and putting it into Mrs. Hough's station wagon, which we'd hot-wired, but still had to push-start. How we'd driven without lights over to Stonefall Creek Road and back, Quin driving, Hangy and I in back with our heads out a window on each side to tell how close we were to the hedgerows in the dark. How we had tinkered with the engine on the township's Galion road grader, just to delay the Reverend a little, make him late getting back home today so we could have more time to play ball. My father would understand...wouldn't he? Uncle Dan had told me stories about them being kids, things they'd done.

For just a country moment, I noodled the insane idea of confessing.

But, what about borrowing the new Craftsman box wrench set, the one he'd specifically told me to never use without permission?

The moment didn't last long. Him understand? Not likely. Angry would not even be the word for it. He would be all red in the face, his mouth all teeth and spit. I couldn't imagine the punishment. A sentence of six years to life digging dandelions, chopping wood, shoveling manure, picking rocks from the fields. It would be six years before I'd be eighteen and could legally escape. The entire remainder of my childhood vanished before my eyes, just so Adam could play baseball with us. Maybe, instead of doing time, I could ask to be tied to a post in the barn and be horsewhipped. Whippings happened all the time on television westerns, and didn't seem to be all that hard to take, not for a real hero. Just recently, some bad guys did it to the *Rifleman*, and all he'd done was grunt and grimace and sigh. He'd hardly even flinched.

I could never tell all...maybe, everything except the part about my borrowing the box-wrench set, the Craftsman tools he kept lightly oiled and wrapped in a lambskin sheath, each shiny piece held in place by its own leather loop. Who was I kidding? My father wasn't a twelve-year-old boy. He was past forty, after all. Frozen by now into a grownup. Old man, frozen for all time in a fixed layer of grownup ways.

We both stared straight through the windshield.

"That dandelion project is just about over," he pronounced. "I've got something else in mind for you...a summer project."

I said nothing. Maybe he didn't know about last night. Just that I'd gone out in the night after I'd thought everybody was asleep. How could he possibly know any more than that? No, I was not going to tell him any of it. He'd have to pull my fingernails out first!

"We'll talk about it after supper," he said.

The Buick slowed almost to a stop before he turned the huge steering wheel to the right and eased it across a shallow depression that defined the edge of the road and the beginning of our driveway. As we crept around the driveway's sweeping curve, the massive V8 only whispered, speedometer almost lifeless, its needle softly twitching close to the zero peg.

We pulled up to the garage. All that silence no longer loomed so large. I continued to look forward through the windshield. Once you've turned twelve, you don't look directly at grownups much, and almost never right in the eye…unless it's your Grandma, maybe. My words, the ones not exactly containing the truth, which had been hanging out there between us for a long while, seemed to have finally dissipated, like a rain cloud fallen to earth, turned into runoff and, hopefully, were already far downstream and forgotten by now.

He shut off the engine and picked up his briefcase from the seat between us. Under it lay something silvery, something shiny. I stared straight ahead, focused on the bug splattered on the windshield, a dragon fly stuck awkwardly in its own goo.

My father said, "I stopped by Stonefall Creek Road on the way home. I checked on the Reverend's progress on that grading project. He had some problems today. He didn't get much accomplished."

I turned to look at him. He did not return my look. The shiny object, a box wrench, lay on the seat between us. A Craftsman box wrench.

"I think you forgot something last night," he said. He slowly got out of the car and closed the door. Shoulders hunched a little forward, he walked to the house.

## Chapter 19, Expectations

After supper, I sat in the plush chair on the other side of the desk from him. I tried to catch his eye, but my father wouldn't look at me. He was intent on rearranging some of the smaller piles on his desk, as if the need to do so had suddenly occurred to him at the same moment he had called me in there.

I should have felt honored to be seated before Himself in his private office, a space he had seldom invited me into. But a small matter filled the atmosphere of his office with something other than honor: that small matter of me having borrowed the battery out of the Jeep, so I could borrow Mrs. Hough's '49 Ford station wagon, so I could do a dirty deed to the Reverend Stippil, for which I used a wrench from my father's Craftsman set engraved with the letter A, for Ahern.

Many others had sat here in the visitors chair ahead of me, and their presence lingered in the leather. A few, simply to see my father at his home office for a chat...friends, neighbors, political peers. Most others, because they'd not wanted to be seen entering his office on Court Street for various reasons. They were the ones who sought a divorce, or looked for protection from what was being done to them, or wanted to get back at somebody else and still stay within the law, or had found themselves on the wrong side of the law. In the fine leather of the chair, a faint stew of all their odors, tobacco, human sweat, perfume, and a hint of something oily and pungent, like spilled brake fluid, most likely from Mr. Weller from the Esso station, who was in sales-tax trouble. My smell would be added to theirs.

"I'm sorry about the wrench," I offered.

My voice was feeble. It fell dead at the feet of busy desk-keeping. What had started as a token task soon turned into a real attempt to straighten things up. He moved stacks of paper in earnest, fingered through folders, filed pieces of paper here or there. His movements were brisk, folders landing on surfaces with a slap. His expression remained blank, and I wondered if he'd forgotten about me.

Fat chance. The smell—my smell—was fear. I didn't know how to read his face. What was he going to do to me? He'd only struck me once. I had deserved it. Or worse, he could commit me to Barry Town, where delinquents went for punishment for the really bad stuff. Technically, was borrowing Mrs. Hough's Ford grand theft auto? After I came back from a stretch at Barry Town, would I be like Eli Zorn? No longer the same person, silent about what they might have done to me down there.

I used to be able to read anybody's face, without thoughts to get in the way of it, but that skill was growing more difficult as I moved out of childhood. Except for Marja, grownups had begun to veil their faces, not willing to allow me easy access into their sense of the world, as if I had to pay some kind of dues first.

Lowdown, sleeping in the corner, raised an ear, then lifted her ancient beagle-basset head. Alert but not barking, she had heard the sound before, and waited. A crackly noise of tires over gravel in the driveway prodded the dog to get up and wag her crooked tail.

Following a knock at the porch door, my mother showed Sheffield Hoy to the office. He was a man in a hurry—always. No matter the concern that occupied him at any given moment, Hoy was an agitated blend of concern and excitement, like somebody responsible for laying down a squeeze bunt, or making the final basket at the buzzer. He was nothing like his older brother, Baggie.

"Which hat are you wearing tonight?" my father said.

"I try to avoid hats. That way my adversaries can't tell what to expect."

My father laughed. It was an ongoing current of humor that often flowed between them. Sheffield, an undertaker by trade, had somehow accumulated many responsibilities over the years, mostly ones that nobody else wanted, ones that paid meager stipends. He was the acting county coroner, Civil Defense coordinator, a township supervisor, volunteer fire chief, and constable. He even drove school bus Number 2 nine months out of the year for the Melody Falls district.

"You know," my father said, "you'll never find a woman that way. None of the good ones would put up with you never being home."

"Are there any good ones left?"

They laughed at each other. My father offered him my chair.

"I'll stand," he said.

I got up anyway and waited: you never know if a grownup means what he says. Sheffield, without looking at me, waved me back, and I slid into the soft leather again.

He shifted weight from one foot to the other slowly and evenly, back and forth, as he listened to my father launch into township business. Sheffield's eyes moved from side to side.

They could have been scanning a box score on the sports page of the *Clarion*.

"Don't know," he said to my father's question of which Melody Falls Township account the funds should actually come out of to pay Sheffield's older brother Baggie for expenses as the recently hired animal control officer.

"You guys—you and Art Snead—pulled this off while I was away," my father charged. "I never would've gone along with it."

"Even if you'd been here, Owen, we'd have done it. Two-to-one."

"No, it would've been two-to-one the other way with me here to talk some reason into Snead's little mind. You know, I saw him this morning coming out of the National Bank. When he saw me, ole Art suddenly remembered he had business in the opposite direction."

"You shoulda made sure you were here, then, for the regular meeting, instead of going off to—what was it—Indiana."

"My law school class reunion."

"Well, that's the breaks, Owen. Maybe a world traveler can't expect to have the time to also be a township supervisor."

"We can't have another full-time employee," my father insisted. "The Reverend Stippil, with all his dithering at the controls of the Galion road grader, is enough."

"Baxter's not full-time." Sheffield always called his brother by his given name rather than Baggie.

"And let's keep it that way. But I'm talking about Baggie's expenses. You seriously expect the township to pay for his time, his meals, and that used-up truck?"

"The man has expenses. What can I say?"

"Your big brother is driving up and down the back roads, just jacking—" He glanced at me and said no more.

"The man has expenses," Sheffield said again. "And there's been sightings of a bobcat, don't forget."

"There have always been sightings of bobcats around here. That's nothing new."

"And if somebody falls victim? Somebody's kid? What then, Owen?"

"None's ever been known to attack anybody's kid, Shef."

"Always a first time. We're supervisors for the township. The citizens have entrusted us."

"And as a supervisor, I'm not about to help Baggie pretend he is performing some kind of service. Maybe he could do his pretending just as a volunteer instead of charging it to the taxpayers."

"The man has expenses, Owen." Sheffield stiffened lips over teeth, hooked his hands in rear pockets and stood still. Most people who took on my father soon realized they'd lost, and gave up right away. But Sheffield Hoy was a stubborn man. My father sat back, folded his arms and stared back at him for a full minute. Then, his voice came out soft, surprising me as much as it surprised Sheffield. "The general fund, I suppose." He unclenched, leaned forward and looked down at his desk blotter. "For his time, I mean. Just for his time."

"And his meals and his truck," Sheffield tried to add.

"No meals. Nothing about this pseudo-job requires him to eat at the Red Rooster so he can reload his imagination every time Samantha spills out of her uniform." A quick glance at me.

Sheffield said, "He'll be putting some rough miles on that vehicle. Mostly in low gear. You know how that wears down a drive train."

"Standard rate. No more," my father said, hanging onto to a remnant of the strong resolve he'd shown earlier, when I had figured—mistakenly—he'd already won the argument.

They were quiet for a time.

"So, why did you come here, by the way?" my father said.

"Heard we had a problem down on Stonefall Road."

"Ah, you've got your constable hat on, then. What did you hear?"

"Our township grader," Sheffield said. "The Galion was vandalized overnight. The Reverend said you knew."

"I was down there earlier today. The Reverend had called me from somebody's house and said the engine would barely run, and when he checked it out he found the sparks had been loosened. Whoever did it left a wrench on the block."

"You took the wrench?"

"I've got it," my father said. "Nice tool. Craftsman. I wouldn't mind having a set of my own." He glanced at me.

"Shoulda left it alone, Owen. Now, your prints are all over it."

My father looked down at his desk blotter.

"Just one good print, and we mighta pinned it on the culprit," Sheffield said. "Shoulda left it for the professionals, Owen."

"You have to have a suspect first, Mister Constable."

"Oh, I know who did it."

I froze in the leather chair.

"You said professional, Shef. Not exactly professional to guess at it."

"Not for me to guess, Owen. I already know."

The soft leather would not sink down any lower for me. My father stared at Sheffield.

"That kid that lives down the hill, in the trailer at the Rollheis place," Sheffield said. "Gutierrez. The one they call Quin. Real name's Joe-a-quin. He's just the right age to start up with mischief, probably running with a bunch of troublemakers like himself."

I sensed the constable glance at me. My father made no reply.

"Quin's my friend!" I suddenly heard myself croak, and felt my face flush. "And his name is Quin, not Joe-a-quin."

The constable stared at me. I stared at him.

What was I doing? I looked away. I sat back in the chair to the pounding of my own heart. I should have kept my mouth shut. "Never tell them anything," I'd heard my father counsel other pitiful people who'd occupied this chair. From beyond my own heartbeat, I heard breathing, not just my own, but the two grownups and me.

Sheffield laughed toward my father. "The boy oughta consider some different friends."

"That Quin's okay," my father said. "He's had it rough, that's all."

"Rough? These kids shoulda grown up during the Great Depression, Owen, like you and I had to. A few less of them would end up at Barry Town, if they could just appreciate what rough really is. Instead, they have to learn it the hard way."

"Barry Town?" my father said. "For messing with the Galion? I don't think so, Shef. No harm done...just had to tighten up the sparks. Besides, you're only guessing about Quin Gutierrez."

Sheffield turned to leave. He'd made his point, and was not a man to be held up by courtesy or convention.

"Shef," my father said.

Already in the front hall, he turned back, and his face reappeared in the office doorway.

That soft voice again. "You going to back me, Shef?"

"You going to run, Owen?"

"Haven't decided. I have until next week to make up my mind." My father's voice grew stronger. "You backing me, or not?"

"Let me know if you decide to run, and I'll let you know if I decide to back you."

My father laughed, and Sheffield's face melted into an almost-smile.

"Shef, that's not the way it works, and you know it."

Sheffield thought a moment. "Okay," he laughed. "I'm in: Owen Ahern for Wilmot County Judge. That is...if you will back me, Owen."

"Back you?"

"Back me...for County Sheriff."

My father slapped his open hand down on the blotter and wagged his head. Sheffield did not wait for an answer and was out in the hall, on his way to the front door when my father yelled, "You'll never get a good woman that way!"

Sheffield yelled back, "I figure you got the last one, Owen," and stepped out onto the porch.

Lowdown scratched behind an ear for fleas, then settled on the floor. My father looked at his desk top a moment. Then, finally, he looked directly at me. "We're lucky. He forgot to ask for the wrench."

We? I sat forward a little in the leather visitor's chair. He'd been so careful to not rat me out to the crafty probing of Constable Hoy. To feel a sense of comradeship with my own fa-ther—up to now, shared only with other kids like me—was a new experience. It had me fantasizing for just a moment what other things we could conspire about, just my father and I.

Who was I kidding? It was not like he would be helping me lift cigarettes from the front display at Widmere's any time soon.

He said sternly, "I don't know your expectations."

Expectations...was I supposed to have some?

"So, here's the deal." He looked at me intently through the new valley he'd created by rearranging teetering stacks of fold-ers, papers and books on his desk. "That pump house down the slope behind the barn...other than to drain the tank, you ever go in there?"

"Once in a while," I said, casual, non-committal, not too defensive. What did he know?

"I used to worry about you going in there. That's why the first step in draining the tank has always been to throw the switch to OFF. But after we put in the submersible pump, it no longer posed the danger that it once did. No 220 lines hanging from the fuse box, no spinning flywheel anymore, and no drive belts that could pull somebody in. All that's in there is 110 wires, which are completely enclosed in armored cable."

I nodded. Last summer, along with Quin, I'd watched my father and Quin's old man replace the old mechanical lift-rod assembly with a new submersible, just like the one in the well beside the house.

"Secondly, you're not the curious little kid you once were. Well, just as curious, I'm sure—and maybe more adventurous — but I'd like to be confident you won't be doing anything foolish or dangerous."

It was not me he was talking about. It was a picture of me he painted to tell me what he expected, without saying so, a way to present a standard for me to reach for, one that put me in charge of myself, to not do foolish or dangerous things, like hot-wiring a car and vandalizing the township road grader.

"So, you've been in the pump house down behind the barn recently, or not?" His eyes sharpened.

My stack of secret notebooks...I'd bound them with a big rubber band, and hidden them under a floor board down there.

"A few days ago," I confessed.

The thought of him reading them had me flushed. Pieces of stories, pieces of poems, Mantle's batting average calculations... and those dirty doodles...what if he'd seen some of my drawings?

His eyes lightened. "I found the door open, that's all. Did you forget to latch it?"

"I don't think so."

"Well, you have to make sure the latch is down all the way. Don't want varmints making a home in there, droppings getting into the well through cracks between the floorboards. Contaminated well water could make the horses sick, you know."

That well was not the only source of water for the Percherons. What about the pond, when they were out to pasture? How many aquatic creatures of every kind, how many birds and animals left droppings in that pond? Not to mention, how many creatures, just passing by, might have peed in there, like my friends and me.

"This is what I have in mind." He passed a heavy book through the crooked valley.

*Grainger Catalog*, open to page 465 — "Electrical."

"Overhead wires, strung on three old, rotting poles from the barn down to the pump house need to come down," he explained, "and replaced with underground wires. Everything completely buried. We'll put down new pipe while we're at it."

Had I suddenly — and, by invitation — stepped into my father's world? A place of pumps and high voltage wires and hardware; a place of grownup gadgetry; a place of problems that made his forehead wrinkle; a place of technical drawings I'd seen him pouring over, and of strategy, of planning important things, the kinds of things he and Quin's old man knew about.

His eyes, as he looked at me, deepened. For an instant I saw Grandpa Carroll in that old photograph on Marja's dresser. Through my father's eyes, Carroll looked out at me and I looked back at him. Through his eyes I saw back, through the eyes of previous fathers and their fathers, back and further back, along an ancient string. A flame fired up within me—fanned by my father's eyes as he looked at me. A burning at my core, an expansion upward, outward, broke through the ceiling on which the sky of my world had been only a painted scene all this time. It broke into a new and vast world of grownups.

"How are we going to do this, Dad?" I said from the edge of the visitor's chair.

Quin shared with me the secret of his name one afternoon after we had trekked the three miles from Belknap Ridge down the mountain to the village of Melody Falls for cigarettes. Widmere's Five and Ten was still running the American Tobacco Company promotion that had a special stand-alone cardboard display filled with Pall Mall packs out front of the counter, topped with a red sign in white lettering that proclaimed: "OUTSTANDING...and they are MILD."

"Two sour lemon popsicles."

"We don't have sour lemon," the salesgirl said from behind the counter.

Quin said, "Could you look down in the freezer? We got sour lemon popsicles here last Thursday. They were down in the bottom, shoved way to the back."

"I was here last Thursday. I would remember." She cracked her gum.

"You couldn't have been here all day last Thursday," Quin said and smiled. "I would remember you for sure."

She didn't smile back. "I was here until five, then Mister Widmere came in to close."

"Well, that it explains it, then" Quin said, smile broadening. "We bought them from a guy. That must have been that Mister Wierdman. Look way down in the freezer."

She looked at us, first Quin, then me. "I've never seen any sour lemon ones," she said. She turned to the freezer behind her, bent at the waist and looked down inside, moving things around a bit. She came back up flushed. "Nope. Like I said, we don't have sour lemon. I've never heard of sour lemon. Not for popsicles. Cough drops, maybe."

"We'll come back at five, then," Quin said as we turned to leave. "Your Mister Wierdman knows right where they are."

"Mister Widmere," she corrected. "Maybe you mean lime," she called to us as we went out. "We do have lime."

Once outside and down the sidewalk past the plate glass window, we compared takes: one in each of my socks, one in each of his socks and another in a back pocket of his dungarees. Five packs in all: a pretty good haul.

On the way back we stopped at the edge of town at Melody Falls School. Big kids were not supposed to be on the kindergarten swings but, as often had happened between Quin and me lately, we were flooded by eagerness to do something we weren't supposed to do just because the chance was there. Besides, who was around to make us get off?

He suddenly said to me, "Wa-keen."

"Wa-what?"

"Wa-keen. That's my name."

"What're you talking about?"

Then he spelled it out. J-O-A-Q-U-I-N.

"Joe-uh-quin?"

"That's why I don't use it. You'd think it is Joe-uh-quin, but it's Wa-keen."

"Then why don't you call yourself Keen?"

"Because then everybody would ask me what my real name is, and probably make fun of me for being half Mexican. How many Mexicans do you see around here, besides my old man? None!"

His father, Roberto Gutierrez, or Bert, was from Pecos, Texas. He and Quin's mother Frances, a native of Wilmot County, had met at a bomber base in Texas, where he was a power house mechanic and she an Army nurse. After the war, they'd come back here, setting up a work-share arrangement with Vern Rollheis. Since the Rollheises had no children, the idea was that Roberto and Frances Gutierrez, if they could save up, would eventually buy their farm.

As we stood on the swings, we twisted the seats in circles with our feet, giving the suspension chains a workout they would never get from any kindergartener. He told me his mother had decided on Quin when he was a few months old. She'd even registered him as Quin Gutierrez when he started school. The name Quin was simple, recognizable, and even had some of the letters of his full name. He laughed as he told me the secret, but his black eyes behind the glasses did not flash the way they normally did when he would laugh about other things.

Up until that moment, it hadn't occurred to me that Quin was any different from me. "I didn't know your old man was a Mexican."

Quin eyes brightened. He reached over and mussed my hair. "You didn't know? You really didn't know? I'm half Mexican. My old man's family came from Guatemala first, where they were farmers, then Mexico, where they picked coffee, then Texas, where they picked cotton. That's where he was born — Guatemala. But people always figured he was Mexican, and he didn't see much need to explain any different. So, I'm half Mexican, you might as well say. Other half, Sloot."

"I didn't know you were half Sloot either."

He laughed hard at that. "I can't believe you really didn't know. I thought everybody knew that. My mother grew up in Slootville."

The unhappiness I'd seen in his eyes earlier returned, now froze down through the rest of his face. "I don't suppose she'll ever come back, so I won't be able to ask her about any of it." He looked directly at me. "She was Seneca, Sloot, and even some Negro, so they say."

"Negro, too?"

He laughed again. "Of course, they don't have that in any history book. According to my old man, Sloots have Negro in them. A long time ago, some French people came over here to build a secret hideaway for the king, who was being over-thrown. But he got his head cut off before he could make the trip, so the slaves that the French had brought with them to do the actual work decided to take off for the hills — the same hills where the Slootmaekers lived." He pumped up his swing.

We'd started out just standing on the swings, but then we got into twisting them, and later we pumped them up, bent our knees, pulled hard on the chains, and forced them to go higher and higher. And, as usual, Quin was way ahead of me. He took his to the upper limit of its arc in flight, where the chains would go slack, then jerk taught again, and make the old steel frame quake, its legs pulling part-way out of the dirt.

Quin was like that. Always way ahead of me. He was tall. He was strong. When we played sports, his movements were both smooth and quick, like a deer. He beat me at everything that mattered. Oh, I was maybe smarter than he, so I could beat him in history or geography or arithmetic, but that didn't matter. He did okay in school, but grades simply didn't matter to him at all, so they couldn't have importance to me either — not when I was with him, anyway.

## Chapter 21, Life All Its Own

Grandma Marja said, "Now, you think of it, Eugene. It is often things that seem unimportant that actually matter. Oh, big things take up our attention: crops coming in, babies being born, people graduating from school. But without little things to cement them together, big things would not survive by themselves."

She paused, lips pursed with resolve, and eyed the western horizon through the porch screen. Plenty of twilight was still glowing through the cleft in Belknap Ridge. It was too early for fireworks to start.

Quin elbowed me. Keeping his face turned toward me and away from her, he mimicked her facial expression, lips pushed out, which had us both suffocating a laugh.

"All those rocks that your grandfather pulled from the fields in the stone boat every spring after plowing. They became part of something important, used as foundation stones, or to make up the fireplace and chimney. They didn't seem like much until they went together to make up what they are all a part of. Don't you see?"

I nodded past Quin, who mouthed Grandma's words to me, "Don't you see?" and pouted his lips just like her. Grandma was too busy looking through the screen to notice.

She sighed. "Slower than molasses, the wait for darkness on the Fourth of July."

Unable to hold back any longer, Quin and I both relieved ourselves of laughter.

She gave us a suspicious eye. "Now, don't you think for a moment that I don't recognize silliness that gets a hold of a couple of boys. I raised two of them!"

We both nodded.

Field stones still on her mind, she told the story—the same one she had told many times before—of how my father and his father had set the stones while Uncle Dan dutifully mixed and supplied them with mortar.

"Now, think of it Eugene, and Quin; it won't hurt you to think of it too. Every last grain of sand that went into the mortar your uncle mixed up lent a tiny bit of importance to the larger importance of what they were doing. Small importances go together to make up big ones, don't you see, and big importances make the small ones more important..."

*       *       *

It took forever for darkness to finally pour itself out over the sky. Just as she had said, it was slower than molasses. The Fire Department could get to work now over at the Melody Falls High School athletic field. Across the valley to the west, my parents and their political friends would be watching fireworks soar overhead from a grassy slope.

A dandelion-puff of colored light appeared far off in the distance. Grandma said "Oh." More of them blossomed, one after the other. The distance was too great for us to hear the actual crackles and booms. Occasionally a sound like low thunder would roll through the cleft. We could not see the low ones that failed to clear the top of the near woods, but we knew when they were being set off by the glow they made in the underbelly of summer evening haze hanging in the air. Whether high or low, Grandma said, "Oh!" every time, as if each was a new surprise to her. Then she went silent.

I looked past Quin. Grandma, in the dim light from distant explosions, as she tilted her head forward, chin coming to rest on her collar bone.

"Grandma?"

Uncle Dan, as he got out of the car, looked at me with eyes that burned like embers. Crisp words spilled from his lips even before he came across the sunlit yard toward the house. "How did it happen?"

I nodded. "We were watching the fireworks—Quin too." Maybe if I added Quin, it would help spread out the anger I saw in his face.

His pale eyes searched mine. Then he placed a hand on my shoulder, and his face lightened a bit. "Must have been scary for you."

As we went up the porch steps together, he kept his hand on my shoulder, forearm hair grazing the back of my neck. The touch gave me the feeling that I was supposed to have done something to protect Grandma from whatever had happened to her. I sure could have done something other than making fun of her old-woman ways.

"She's up in her room?"

I nodded. "She's been sleeping a lot."

Two steps at a time, he went up to her. I stayed put.

My mother came into the hall from the kitchen, wiping her hands on an apron, and then my father's office door came open.

"Did I hear your uncle?" she said.

I nodded, and my father said, "It was his voice, all right...sounded like he's already gone up."

He turned to me, eyes searching, just as Dan had done. "What did he have to say, Eugene?"

"Was I supposed to...last night on the porch, when Grandma went to sleep like that, was I supposed to...was there something I should have done?"

My mother put her arms around me. My vision wrinkled up as she held me to her, my cheek touching hers. She hugged me, gathering me in a mixture of lilac perfume and her natural scent. I was about to step away, but she pulled me closer, held me tighter, arms and breasts soft and warm. She said into my ear, "You were with her for the fireworks. Marja has always loved doing things with you."

"That's right." My father allowed himself a grin. "You were her date for the evening."

She let go of me, and I stepped back, female touch staying on my skin an extra moment. I felt a flush in my face.

The interior of the '60 Studebaker Lark was unlike any other of this year's makes I'd seen. Most 1960 models had shiny steel and chrome curving around you in the front seats. This car's dashboard was upholstered in soft fabric.

Uncle Dan shaded the speedometer glass with his hand. "She has on her only...thirteen-hundred and forty-five miles."

"Is this yours?"

He laughed at that. "No, I don't own a car. In fact, don't own anything."

I thought he was joking. "Not even a pencil set, or a loose-leaf binder?"

He continued to grin, but held seriousness in his eyes. "No, I mean it, Eugene. We share everything. Simple supplies, like you are talking about, are in easy reach, but everything is shared...really."

Our conversation hesitated for chocolate ice cream we licked from our cones before it could drip onto our clothes — and onto new-car upholstery — in the summer heat.

"But you have money," I complained. "How can you say you share everything if you carry money?"

We both worked on our ice cream, licking the tops down to safe levels, observing other people who came in and out of the gravel lot at the Kinkaid custard stand, all of them, especially the men, eye-balling our shiny black sedan. You wouldn't often see a Studebaker around Wilmot County, especially not a new one.

"We share money, too. Our Superior is in charge of it, and if anybody needs some, he hands it over…usually. He would have to have the money on hand, of course, and there has to be a good reason why you need it. As soon as I told him about Grandma Marja, he handed me thirty dollars and the keys to one of the staff cars, and said 'Go'."

Having tongued my ice cream down to a plateau even with the top of the cone, I crunched through the edge of it. Pain shot up behind my eyes from too much too fast. I wrinkled my lips, trying to keep the cold away from the roof of my mouth.

Dan might have been a grownup and a biology professor and a priest, but as I sat there with him eating ice cream in the Studebaker in Kinkaid's parking lot, he was, for the moment, my uncle and my friend…and mine only. It was the kind of moment that we would get together to share for as long as I could remember.

He went on talking. In the small order of priests that he belonged to, the Holy Cross Fathers, everybody gave up owning anything individually. "That way each of us can be more worry-free to teach and do research, like me, or run a parish, or do mission work."

"Share everything? That's what the Communists do!" I suddenly recalled from one of Miss Hendershott's lessons.

Dan laughed hard. Tears came to his eyes as he swallowed too much ice cream at once. "Yes," he said, "in theory, it is very similar. I doubt that it is in practice, though." He wolfed down the last bite, the bottom section of his cone disappearing. "How come ice cream never gets down into the point of the cone? Your last bite is always too dry."

I shrugged, just as I would do with one of my friends. And just as one of them would do with me, he accepted my shrug as the answer to his question. Grownups normally wouldn't do that.

I said, "Do you think Grandma is going to be all right?"

He looked through the windshield into the distance. "No," he said, and sighed.

I didn't expect it, and didn't expect tears to erupt from me.

"I'm sorry, Eugene. But, no, she isn't going to be all right. Doc Willingham tried everything he could just to get her to go to the hospital, but she refuses to leave the farm. She's always been funny that way. And he's pretty sure that her heart actually must have stopped for a few minutes. Then it restarted, all by itself. And that's likely to happen again. And, well, one of these times…"

"Dan, she is my friend. Sometimes I think she might even be my best friend." I had to wipe my face in the crook of my elbow.

"I know, Eugene." He pulled a handkerchief from his pocket.

I didn't take it. I suddenly laughed through tears. "I'm not a girl, Uncle Dan." I wiped my face again with my shirt sleeve.

He laughed and put the handkerchief away. "Well, if you were, you'd make one ugly girl," he said, just like one of my friends.

I ate the bottom of the cone. He was right: no ice cream down in the point always seemed to make the last bite too dry.

He said, "I always thought Quin was your best friend."

"Well, he is. And when I'm with Grandma, she's my other best friend."

We both laughed at that. He started the car and pulled out onto the highway, heading back up the hill in the direction of home.

After a long quiet, I said, "Uncle Dan, who are the Sloots?"

He said nothing for a while. "Why do you ask?"

"People talk about the Sloots, but nobody ever says who they actually are. I even asked the lady at the Wyotanda Library how I could find out, and she told me to do something better with my curiosity."

"Who talks about them?"

"Baggie Hoy calls Quin a Sloot. What is that, exactly?"

"Baggie Hoy is an asshole," Dan said.

I'd never heard a priest say that before. I was quiet as we rode along, the Studebaker whining its way up the steep grade.

He gave me a light punch to my upper arm. "Pardon my factory French," he joked. "Let's just say Baggie's not very refined in his attitudes."

"But, what's a Sloot?"

"It's a term that refers to the Slootmaekers. I'm sure you know of lots of people around here by that name. They are descendants of Hendrik Slootmaeker, who came here from Holland. He and his sons cleared much of the best bottom land around here, and became wealthy farmers. Then, the Revolutionary War broke out. He tried to get rich by brokering weapons to the British. In those days, the Dutch were renowned as weapons dealers. After the war, the Slootmaekers lost everything. They scattered up into the hills to keep from being hanged, I suppose, at least in Hendrik's case."

"But Quin's name is Gutierrez."

"That's right," Dan said. "And his mother, through her father, is from the tribe of Seneca who still live out near Kinzua. It was her mother, whose name was White, who was related to the Slootmaekers. You don't have to have the name, you know, to still be considered one of them. Even if she's just distantly related, some people might still think of her as a Sloot."

On the dirt road stones were pinging inside the fenders of the shiny new staff car. I wondered what the superior back at Notre Dame would think if he knew.

"Uncle Dan, why didn't the Library lady just tell me that?"

"Maybe she didn't know. Or, could be that she did know but her thoughts were clouded. Meanness—especially meanness that a lot of people share in—has a life all its own, Eugene. It can just go on and on, often without any thought at all, and even long after the reason for its existence has long been forgotten."

At home, we got out of the Studebaker and stepped up onto the porch together. We went through the front door into the house, and our shared moment came to a gentle close.

A week after Dan went back to Notre Dame, satisfied that Grandma was doing much better, Quin stayed overnight. The idea was we'd watch TV as late as we wanted, expecting to switch back and forth between Channel 12 out of Binghamton and snowy Channel 22 out of Scranton for old movies, once the regular programming was over. But both carried the political convention from California far into the morning hours.

I soon fell asleep on the living room floor, but Quin, ever fascinated with speech-making, stayed up to watch the whole thing, along with Marja, who had watched it from the very beginning, but was disappointed at not catching a glimpse of my father among the Pennsylvania delegates. My mother had given up and gone to bed early.

When it was finally over—my father never did appear beneath all the signs bristling from humanity on the convention floor—I woke up long enough to go out onto the porch hammock, where Quin and I fell asleep in mid-July mugginess. The last thing I heard was Quin cussing mosquitoes.

The next day was hot and sweaty, sunless air clinging to your skin. Rain was in the forecast, so the plan was to have a basketball game in the barn. But before Hangy and Adam could come over, the sky suddenly opened up, wrung itself out, roaring onto the barn roof. Once the downpour started, Hangy and Adam never showed up.

Quin and I played a game of one-on-one. But it wasn't long before he was beating me badly, too badly for me to keep going. With the score already 38 to 8, he insisted on trying to goad me into playing more, just so he could keep on using me to hotdog himself.

"What's the matter, Genie? Tired of getting kicked all over the court?"

I wanted to say, "I'm quitting this game, Joe-uh-quin." That would have hurt him good, would have stopped him in his tracks. But, just as I was about to say it, when I looked into his laughing face, I couldn't do it. His taunting of me was not something that made him happy. It was more something he needed to do. In that flash of an instant before I was about to make him my enemy instead of my friend, I knew, to be his friend, I just had to take it. I put the ball away in the wooden box and said nothing.

I couldn't look at him. He followed me out of the barn. He stopped laughing after a while, and I could feel his eyes on me as we crossed the muddy yard to the house, where my mother was painting on the porch—it was too hot up in her studio—while Marja, in her usual spot, read the *Clarion*.

I asked my mother to give Quin a ride home. We couldn't expect him to walk down the hill a half-mile to his old man's trailer in the rain. Since we'd come from the barn sweaty, she insisted we put on new shirts before we would be allowed to sit back in the plush rear seat of her '53 Mercury. The car had become hers when my father bought the new Buick. From a pile of folded laundry, I put on a clean tee shirt, and handed Quin one of my father's, which fell over him loosely but stuck to his sweaty skin in a way that made the fabric form to his muscled torso.

She made us put down cardboard in the foot wells and then drove us down to the road that went past the Rollheis Farm, turning up a rutted lane to the trailer. My mother opened her side to allow Quin to hop out. He took off the shirt and gave it to her. He held up his arms to the sky, luxuriating in the rain. My mother eyed him. She craned her neck to follow his saunter up to the door, where water cascading off the trailer roof made a waterfall.

As I changed from the back seat to the front—I was sure to move the foot-well cardboard up there too—she watched Quin. I sat in the front and closed the door, but she held hers open, foot on the brake pedal, and gazed at him. Quin, eyeglasses in one hand, stretched his arms up and turned round and round in tumbling water that made a sliding sheen over his shoulders and down his chest. He looked like a picture I'd seen in an art book. The guy's hands were tied above his head, and he was pierced with arrows. He was downright beautiful. Not something I would ever want to tell anyone, of course.

"Quite a young man," she said.

"Aren't we going home?"

"Yes...yes, dear," she said, and glanced at me.

Pulling the door closed, she sniffed the tee shirt he had handed to her—like Grandma would do to our clothes when she loaded the washer—and laid it on the seat. She put the Mercury in reverse and backed down the rutted lane.

"I'll put a rump roast in the oven," she said as she headed the car back uphill toward home. "You have plenty of time for a shower, young man."

"What really happened to Quin's mother?" I said.

"Oh, that's tragic. She—a few years ago—simply disappeared."

"Disappeared? What does that mean? She stood at the stove in her kitchen, frying eggs, then went 'poof?'"

"Oh, you know what I mean. She left home one evening to drive over to Kinzua, but never made it there. Never seen again. She and the car simply vanished. For days, they looked all along Route 6, but never found anything."

"What kind of a car did she have?"

"Now, what difference does that make, Eugene?"

"I'd just like to know, so I can picture it. Was she in a Studebaker? An Oldsmobile? A Ford? And what year was it, what color?"

"A Ford, I think. No, it was a Dodge. A gray Dodge. You know, an old fashioned one, with rounded fenders and a pointy hood."

"Why was she going there, all the way to Kinzua? Isn't that a hundred miles?"

"At least a hundred. She was on her way to visit relatives. At least, that's the story. We kinda think she was actually going there to—you know—to make trouble."

"Trouble about what?"

"The new dam. The Seneca in Kinzua were all upset about it, and still are. The whole town will have to be moved before the project is finished, even the graveyard. The bones of ancestors, or something."

"They're moving the cemetery?"

"The whole cemetery, bones and all. The town of Corydon, too. Ask your father, dear, when he gets home from California. He's much better with details."

"Kind of a warm day for a rump roast," I said.

Just as we arrived home, she changed her mind. "You're right, Eugene. Too hot and humid to go steaming up the kitchen. I'll find something quick to make."

Sandwiches again? Cooking was something Marja had always done for us, but my Grandma's illness had put the responsibility onto my mother, at least for a while.

In the shower, I shampooed my hair, then used the extra suds to lather all over. The curtain moved, lightly tugged by motion of air from the bathroom door being opened.

My mother's voice. "I won't peek."

Over my shoulder I saw her shadow on the curtain, fingers to chin in thought.

"Eugene," she said after a while, "have your friends been breaking off the weathered stumps?"

When a grownup asks you if your friends have done something, they're actually half-asking if you did it, suggesting that by blaming them you can make a sideways confession.

"Weathered stumps?" Always best to stay stupid until you find out what it's really all about.

"Those beautiful weathered stumps. You know, the ones your Grandfather Carroll tipped onto their sides and jammed together to make a fence when he first cleared the farm."

"The ones down in the pasture?"

"Yes, the ones down in the pasture. What other weathered stumps would I be talking about, dear?"

I told her I didn't know of anybody doing anything to them, which was the truth. I had no idea what she was getting at.

"I'd been planning a series of still-lifes. Did you ever look closely at the stumps? Gray wood, swirls of grain, roots up-turned in the weather for half a century. So strong, almost muscular, straining under the gravity of time."

So she was working herself into doing more paintings. If she was thinking of painting stumps, maybe she wouldn't be asking me to sit for her. Whenever she would want me to do that, I'd not been able to tell her no. I would strain under the gravity of time, all right, while she scratched with her pencils onto rough canvass, and later would come more sessions when she actually brushed on the oils. In summer, even with the skylights open, beads of sweat would tickle, unseen critters of itchiness wandering over flesh, having their way with me, like fleas on a dog, while I tried to hold still in the heat.

"Aren't they still there?" I said. "The stumps?"

"Yes, of course they are. They'll be there another hundred years, they're so massive. I went down there yesterday to sketch. So many have been damaged: pieces broken off. Beauty has been ruined forever, that's all. Your friends didn't do it?"

"No, not us. Maybe the horses, you know, rubbing against them."

"But, it doesn't seem random. It's the points...the points left over from where smaller roots have been weathered away. The delicate points are broken off, and just gone, like some-body took them on purpose."

I felt the shower curtains part, a tiny slit up at the top. I faced away.

"You're peeking!" I said. I wasn't afraid of her seeing me naked. But this was my shower, after all.

The slit at the top of the curtains closed back up.

"I don't mean to embarrass you. I'm sorry, dear. How sad it is—that's what I'm thinking."

"Sad?"

"We were talking earlier about Quin, and Frances Gutierrez, Quin's mother. How sad it is. How sad for her, wherever she is, and it must be terribly lonely for Quin. He was only five when she left."

Was that why she was peeking? Something to do with Quin?

After a time of quiet, she said, "I suddenly needed to look at you, that's all, Gene." She only called me Gene when she was feeling affectionate.

Another long quiet. Was I ever going to get to finish my shower with her standing out there?

"You are growing up." She laughed to herself. "Naturally, I do want you to grow up."

It was sad that Quin didn't have a mother, all right. But at least he didn't have to put up with anything like this. He could take a shower—no, there was only a tub in that trailer. He could take a bath by himself in peace.

She said, "But at times I wish you wouldn't, dear. Grow up, I mean."

## CHAPTER 23, STARTERS

High pasture grass, thick, uneven, and clumped around milkweed, burdock and thistle, pulled at my dungaree pant-legs. When I arrived down by the pump house, I heard singing. A female voice. Around the corner, in front, a small pile of wood had been left on the ground, tied in a bundle. I approached the small building out of sight of the door.

So, I wasn't the one who'd left the door unlatched, after all. Somebody else had been going in there, and was in there now.

Her song was not loud enough for me to distinguish the words, only the tune, as if she were singing quietly to herself. And then I saw that her bundle, neatly wrapped in an old leather belt fastened with a brass buckle, was made up of bro-ken-off pieces of weathered pine stumps.

So, it wasn't my friends who had done the damage my mother complained about. A thief had been stealing firewood, a singing thief.

The last few steps, I planted my feet carefully in the tall grass and knelt down by the uphill side of the pump house, just under a knothole. I was slow to put my eye up to it because, from inside, the knothole might wink out, and alert the singing wood-stealer that I was outside. But listening a while, my ear conjured her position, that the singer within faced away. I could chance a brief, one-eye glimpse. I looked and, as I ducked back down, my mind's eye registered what I'd seen—bare flesh.

A second, longer look confirmed it. Flesh moved away from the knothole, then back to it again, pushing a small puff of air. Movement continued back and forth in front of the knothole, slow and rhythmic, in time to song. Curve—delicate curve of a shoulder—a slight, bare shoulder, so close to my eye the skin fuzz on it was lit by daylight that fell in through the doorway on the other side. A small, left shoulder—not a full-round woman's shoulder, like in those photographs hidden in my father's of-fice—more like what you'd see in the Sears Catalog on the girl's underwear page, or that advertisement in Life, featuring a young woman in an evening gown that almost fell off her shoulders as she was about to step into "The Finest Lincoln in Forty Years."

It was a female shoulder with subtle, girlish roundness. Her shift of position brought into view brown hair, long and rippled, flowing down a naked female back.

I sat against the pump house, listened to the song. No vehicle, so she had to have walked here. Somebody close by. A neighbor? I went through my memory's images of slender, brown-haired women who lived nearby. Some slender ones, all right, but older. There was no one like this, shoulder delicate and fair. None I could think of had such beautiful hair flowing like a waterfall, waving with small curls. It was somebody who had been coming back here more than once to steal wood, who had damaged the weathered stumps, had left the door unlatched, had gotten me into trouble.

I crawled away with caution, crawled uphill for a distance until I felt it was safe to stand, and walked up the slope to the barn. I had gone down there to fetch my notebooks from their hiding place under the floorboard, and suddenly there's a young woman with a soft singing voice, a firewood thief, whose curls fell in waves down a naked female back.

Around the barn, across the yard, along the porch...and I knew I just had to go back down there.

She didn't know I'd seen her, that I knew of her presence in the pump house, and that I'd received a hint of her scent. She thought she was safe and secure all by herself in that little house, doing whatever she was doing, girlish shoulder exposed, hair falling down.

On the top porch step, Lowdown, without lifting her ancient beagle-basset head, eyed me. Lowdown was arthritic and no longer eager to follow me around in my wanderings of Cloven Hill Farm and beyond. Her eyes, low-burning coals that melded into my mood, looked at me with expectation.

"I have to go back down there."

Plop. Plop. Old, crooked tail rose and fell against the step. Lowdown looked away, then quickly back again, then away, and breathed out a sigh through her nose.

"You come too."

Her head rose up, ears alert. She stood slowly, and I wrapped my arms around her bow-legs, and picked her up against my chest. A noise came from deep inside her, a hound-sound of simple delight.

By the time I reached the pump house again, I was sweating and my shoulders ached. I heard no singing now. A basket now lay beside the bundle of wood, a small woven basket like you'd see on a picnic. Lowdown's tail wiggled suddenly, so I let her down. Ears flat against her head, she parted the high grass and limped her way around the corner to the doorway.

"Oh, puppy," a voice came from within, the same voice I'd heard in song, but now in the lower pitch of speech...now familiar to me.

Fingers came from the doorway and scratched Lowdown's ear, exciting her crooked tail to draw circles in the air. Then a hand, wrist covered by the sleeve of a dress I'd seen often enough. I went around to the doorway. No naked woman. No bare shoulder, as she hurriedly did something with the top button at the back. No woman at all.

Agnes May, from where she sat against the inside of the pump house wall, looked at me sharply. "It isn't polite to sneak up."

"Sneak up? This is our pump house, Agnes May."

When Lowdown climbed up through the doorway, her hands came around and engulfed the dog's ears, hands that were every bit hers, not the hands of some strange woman. I'd seen often enough one of those hands up on the end of her bent-backwards arm in school, drawing the teacher to call on her, to rat on us, or ask a question just for attention. But, in her fussing over Lowdown, her hands did not look so much like a kid-brat's hands. They moved with confident gentleness you'd see from a grownup, like Crystal Hobbes tying her daughter's shoe, or Grandma Marja kneading bread dough.

Agnes May in that same long dress, one of the few she always wore, ankle-length, long sleeves, delicate violets—some of her dresses had tiny clovers—in a repeating pattern on cotton fabric. Hair—free of its braid and bonnet for the first time ever—fell down her back.

High-top brown shoes, socks tucked into them, were off to the side. My looking at her bare feet had her tucking them under as she shifted herself to sit at a sideways slant, which pushed out a hip and pulled fabric tight over the roundness of it. She looked at me with distant eyes; not really at me, more like she saw something far away that I didn't know about, and she was not about to tell me.

"What're you doing here?" I said.

At my question, she looked down, her eyes going into hiding. Her face flushed, erasing her freckles. "Resting…can't you see that?"

"Yes, I can see that. Did you notice that round section of flooring with a pipe coming through it?"

She rolled her eyes. "Of course, I see it."

"That's the well cover. If you're going to be in here, you don't want to be putting your weight on it."

Her eyes flashed. "You mean somebody would actually make a well cover that a person could fall through?"

"No. But if you ever did fall through, it's a long way down, so don't chance it—that's all I'm saying."

She clucked her tongue and turned her head away.

"So, what are you doing here?" I reached for the basket. "Having a picnic?"

She lurched forward and grabbed the handle before I could. Her motion exposed a dot of daylight: the knothole I'd been looking through earlier. Leaning back again, she rested in the space between two wall studs, and the dot of daylight disappeared.

"Don't worry, Agnes May, I won't steal your lunch."

My saying her name seemed to lighten the color of her face, and freckles returned. Daylight falling in on her through the doorway shone in her brown eyes.

She said, "You remember, don't you?"

"Remember?"

"What I told you down in the school basement, that day Miss Hendershott made you stay after."

"I remember. It was about a secret person. I've never told anybody, just like I said."

"Not just a person, but a child. Philip," she said, looking down at her basket. "Our Philip."

The tone in her voice had me glance at her, but I quickly looked away again. Knowing about her secret, her imaginary person—or child—didn't mean I had to pretend Philip was my imaginary person too.

"So, what're you doing with this wood that you bundled up?"

At that, she unfolded herself in jerky motions, pulled on her socks and shoes, then rapidly laced them up. No longer was there a confident gentleness to her hands. She was the kid-brat again, who seemed in a hurry.

"We were talking about Philip." Her lips and tongue and teeth snapped out the words. "And you suddenly accuse me of stealing wood. Doesn't Philip matter to you?"

"Just wondering, that's all."

"You Aherns...just because God gave you this wood, it's not all yours. Nobody else can have any of it?"

"Well, it is our wood, Agnes May."

"Not if you let it go to waste, just rot away into the ground from which He hath raised it up. Not when real people could make use of it, as I'm sure He intendeth."

She finished with her shoes, put her hands behind her head, arms up with pointy elbows, and started to rebraid her hair. Fingers moved like a high-speed mechanical device.

She'd made her speech sound biblical, as if she was cursing me for not wanting her to steal from us. The words, "you Aherns" singled me out me and my family from other people.

"I meant nothing by it, Agnes May."

Lowdown stretched herself out on the ground and sighed.

Agnes May's face softened a little. Her position, elbows up as she wove the braid, pulled the dress tight around her, and formed it to her shape. Agnes May with a shape…my mind's image of her had to rearrange itself. She was not just the kid-brat two rows over and one seat up in Miss Hendershott's sixth grade. She was a girl with wavy hair and soft, round contours. And I'd seen her naked back.

She looked at me, eyes like brown pebbles in Hobbes Creek, the same eyes that had flashed when she handed me the bat after my second home run.

"Why come all the way over here for firewood?" I said. "What's wrong with gathering it over by your place, those woods there? That's all I'm saying, Agnes May. It's got to be a half-mile trek each way."

Fingers slowed in the task. Her face relaxed, turning away in thought. "Mostly, I gather from our own woods, but I've pretty much taken all the small pieces. I would try to glean the Hobbes Woods out, but Old Man Hobbes is forever working around his farm, and the Reverend says he's a wicked man, so I wouldn't want to run into him."

I laughed. "Old Man Hobbes? He's not wicked. He might like you to think so. He does enjoy yelling at people."

"This dried-up wood, from your stumps, lights up quickly. It makes good starters."

Grandpa Carroll had placed uprooted stumps in a row to make a fence for his first pasture over fifty years ago. The once-craggy, spiny roots had been rendered by time into lumpy gray swirls, tapered points woven together in soft abandon, the way new-born puppies lump themselves together. She had broken off some of the points to make up her bundle. I lifted it by the leather belt she'd bound it with: easy to carry.

"You don't even need paper, most of the time," she said, eyebrows arched, brown eyes pulling me into her explanation. "Just hold a match to it, as long as it hasn't been rained on in the last day or so."

"My mother's an artist, you know. She asked me who is breaking off the wood. She was hoping to paint these stumps."

Agnes May laughed, put her hand over her mouth and looked away. "She wants to paint these?"

"No, not paint the wood. Paint a picture. The stumps would be in the picture. Or, maybe lots of pictures. But, if the points are broken off, she says it ruins their beauty."

Agnes May turned to me and smiled. "I've no artists in my family. My father—the Reverend—was once in a barbershop quartet, until he was twenty-two, and then was redeemed in the Lord, and so he stopped doing it."

"My mother just does the painting for herself," I said. "She's not well-known for it. She's no Grandma Moses, or Georgia what's-er-name."

With laughter, her face had softened a little more. "Is she a good artist?"

I shrugged. Spurred by her interest, by the curiosity in her eyes, I wanted to tell her that sometimes I sat for my mother, that sometimes she painted me too. Talk of art and beauty was not something I could do with any of my real fiends. That day in the basement of Melody Falls School had somehow turned Agnes May, as much as I hated her, into a friend, maybe a pretend-friend. Her probing eyes, the way she looked into me as she asked about my mother's art, had me wanting all those hours of trying to stay absolutely still in one position to take on a new feeling, as if I'd actually enjoyed doing it.

But I kept quiet. I would never live it down if people—especially my real friends—ever found out that I posed for my mother. What if Agnes May told everybody?

She said, "How does she have the time? I mean, with all the cooking and washing and taking care of that big Ahern house, and all."

"She has lots of help. My grandma does most of the work. It's her house."

Finished with the braid, she fastened it with a brown rubber band and tied on the bonnet. She rested her hands in her lap, and looked past me. "My mother was a writer, but just briefly. She joined a school-by mail, run by Mr. Bennett Cerf. Ever hear of him?"

"That short guy with glasses on *What's My Line*? My parents watch that, and my grandma, too."

"I don't know. We don't have a television. My mother saw an advertisement in the *Clarion*, and wrote to him, sent him a sample, and he wrote back and invited her to enroll."

"So, your mother is pretty good?"

She mirrored my shrug. "She only sent one story in. Mr. Cerf sent it back, but my father saw it in the mail. Not something a Christian housewife should be taking up her time with."

We were both quiet, having come to a moment when conversation stopped on its own. She looked at me and I looked at her. I wished, as happened between Grandma Marja and me when conversation stopped, Agnes May and I could just look at each other, take a vacation from what you're supposed to do. But we couldn't look at each other for long. We both looked away, and only glanced back and forth across the silence, as if afraid we'd be caught at something.

"Agnes May," I said. "This row of stumps runs from here all the way down to the end of the pasture. If you take wood from down there—you know, at the end—instead of up here, it would be a lot closer for you in your trek back home."

I didn't mention that it would also help me out. My mother would never notice any damage so far down the line.

Agnes May said, "How thoughtful, Eugene."

"Of course, you might run into that loony run-away from Rollheis' herd. She's been hanging around down there."

"Oh, she's not loony. I was afraid of her at first, the way she comes up to me all big-eyed whenever she sees me. We've gotten to know each other now. She's curious, that's all."

"A dried up old milker," I said. "Not much good for anything. If Rollheis ever catches her, he might get a few bucks out of her for dog food, maybe."

"Oh, don't say such a thing, Eugene. She's seems very happy to no longer be a milker, wandering the pasture, happy to just have you scratch the underside of her neck."

"Nothing but a grass burner," I said in the same voice I'd heard Vern Rollheis use to say it. "Her name is Oriane-Florisse."

"What a fancy name for a cow."

"That's Missus Rollheis, for you. She insists on naming all the cows, and I guess Vern lets her do it. They all have names like that: she's the French teacher down at Wyotanda High."

"Oriane-Florisse," Agnes May said softly. "When we get to high school, Eugene, I think I'll take French. Do they have that at Melody Falls High?"

She stood, came out of the pump house into full daylight, basket in hand, and picked up the wood by its leather belt.

Lowdown raised an ear, then put it back down and sighed.

"The reason I come all the way up to this end for the wood is because—well, because of Philip, you know."

"Philip? The one in the radiator? What does Philip have to do with kindling?"

Her face pinked up. "Philip. Our Philip. He is yours too, you know."

I looked at her without saying anything.

She put both burdens down again, opened the basket, and carefully removed a bundle of rolled up white fabric. Placing it in the crook of her left arm, she slowly cradle-rocked back and forth, and stroked it with her fingers. "My chore conflicts with his feeding time." Her eyes gleamed. "I come up here to use the pump house." She leaned and whispered, "You know—for privacy."

In time to gentle rocking, she hummed the tune I'd heard earlier through the wall.

"Agnes May."

She looked at me.

"You know Philip isn't real."

The moment lasted a long time. Then, tears poured out and slid over freckles. The object in her arms flew at me, unrolled in the space between us, opened onto my face and shoulder.

"Take it," she spit. "Take the smelly thing and leave me alone."

Lowdown rose up and looked at me, hound eyes asking what I'd done.

Agnes May grabbed her things. High top shoes in rapid steps quickly parted clumps of pasture grass that swiped at tiny violet blossoms in the fabric of her long dress.

The unwrapped white bundle had crimson letters—SAINT AGATHA. It was my tee shirt, the one that had come up missing at the ball field. Why did she call it smelly? Maybe it smelled a little like me. But it also smelled like her—I sniffed it and, sure enough, it had the scent that had puffed at me through the knothole. My tee shirt smelled like Agnes May.

## Chapter 24, Real Work Boots

I rounded the corner of the barn, and stopped short.

It was the nature of my father's work as an attorney to have no set schedule for when he would be home from work each day. It was usually late. Today, it was early. Not that I didn't want him to be home. Not that I did, either. It was something about being twelve years old. I'd passed an unmarked milestone. It was unmarked by everyone else, that is, but me. Twelve changed from a number to a feeling, a feeling of motion, of going from a kid toward becoming a grownup, a feeling in my stomach that, once it took root, sprouted a sprig of alertness that demanded keener observation of surroundings. And what could be more important to observe than whether your father was in or out of range? At twelve, you realize you're just about done being a kid. But your old man still owns your behavior...but only your behavior, not you. When he's out of range, well, then you own yourself.

So, just as I was getting home from a day of baseball and helping Adam Stippil paint his old man's church, I stopped short. The Buick was not there, but a different vehicle was in its place, front wheels turned a little left just like always. A shiny red Jeep panel wagon, like the one advertised Sunday evenings on the *Maverick* TV show, a fully enclosed, all metal vehicle—fancy cousin to a regular Jeep.

Something was up: my father would not have easily surrendered his light-green over dark-green '56 Buick Special. The tail gate of the Jeep wagon was open, a bundle of gray pipe sticking out the back, red flag attached to the end.

"Where's the Buick?" I asked right away at the supper table.

I'd learned that if I was quick to start conversation, I could stall him from questioning me about what I'd done all day with my friends. He already knew anyway that we were helping Adam Stippil paint his old man's church, that we were trying to fool the Reverend into believing his only begotten son was putting in a full day's work, so Adam could steal some time to play ball with us. But my father knowing about it, and his asking detailed questions, were two different things. It would be like Father Kearns knowing we hung out under the Third Street Bridge after altar boy meetings, and him asking what girls we talked about, or which cuss words we used.

"I traded," he said. "You know Mister Pollard, the RFD mailman? That's his new vehicle. He let me trade with him after he finished his route today, so I could haul some pipe home."

"What's it for?" my mother asked, and touched napkin to lips.

He looked at me. "Our summer project," he said, and grinned.

I did not grin back. Our summer project? We'd been talking about it, doing lots of planning, and at first I'd been excited about being engaged in it with my dad, entering his world to take part in grownup importance. But now it was going to happen—for real. Now I saw that it could invade my life, take it over, and possibly ruin my time with friends for much of the summer.

"After supper, we'll get started."

After supper? Tonight?

Grandma's eyes looked back and forth between my father and me.

My mother and Grandma looked at each other. My mother said, "Owen. Can't it wait until morning? Evenings are for relaxation, after all." She and Grandma looked at each other again.

He shrugged away the comment. "Except, I'll have to get Pollard's wagon back to him in time for his mail route by first light."

So, after supper it was. He changed into dungarees and a blue work shirt. Sitting on the bench in the mud room to lace up his old army boots, he eyed my Keds. "Can't have you doing any real work in those."

"The only other shoes I have are for school and church."

"Tomorrow—after we take Pollard's vehicle back to him— we're going down to Tomkins Shoes. It's time you had some decent footwear to work in."

He backed the wagon away from the garage and drove it over to the pasture fence near the barn, where I unlatched the gate for him. Once he passed through, I closed and relatched it, and climbed into the passenger seat.

The only other Jeep I'd been in was Old Rusty, the patched-together vehicle my father had purchased from Rooney's junk yard for use around the farm, a '46 CJ2A, flat-fender. He kept it under the overhang behind the barn, its primary purpose a farm tow-motor, mostly to pull the horse-manure spreader out to the fields. Its left side was dented in and creased, wind-shield missing from a rectangular frame that had been bent into a trapezoid, and front bumper bowed in a permanent frown. Dark voids had taken the place of its headlights.

Mr. Pollard's red Jeep panel wagon was a new, upscale model. The seats were soft, and its overhead-cam engine purred under a pointed hood crowned with a strip of chrome down the center. Cream-color dials fancied up the dashboard. It had a chrome ash tray and lighter, and even a clock. As we moved through the barnyard, we took the bumps evenly — none of the squeaky jerks and lurches Old Rusty would have treated us to. It was a Jeep, though. The gear shifter — cream-color knob instead of black — came up through a rubber boot in the floor, and beside it, a pair of smaller levers. Riveted to the glove box, a label showed an array of gear patterns.

At the end of the barnyard, my father flipped levers to new positions. When he let out the clutch, the transfer case came to life under the floor with a whir, and low-range gears began to sing. Through the windshield, the fancy hood dropped from the horizon as we went over the bump-edge where barnyard and pasture met, and crawled a steep incline nose-down on the grassy slope.

In a short distance, he stopped and had me get out. "Pull one section at a time off the back end as I go along. Careful — don't drop one on your foot." He eyed my Keds again.

Untwisting a wire, I removed the red flag from the end of the pipe bundle. A paper tag was attached, "Van Shoor Hardware" printed on it. The ends of each length had been wrapped in brown paper, blots of oil ghosting a pipe-thread pattern. A cardboard box lay in the corner, also spotted with oil. It was full of threaded couplings.

"What about these fittings?" I called through the back.

Eyes in the rear-view mirror, he told me to leave them. As the Jeep inched down the hill in the direction of the pump house, I slid lengths off the tail gate and laid them end to end.

"Won't the pipes rust, lying on the ground like this before we get them buried?"

"They're galvanized," eyes finding me in the mirror again, his tone instructional. "Where they cut the threads — you're right, you could have rust after long exposure, but we won't be leaving them in the open that long."

This project wasn't so bad, maybe. It had my father talking to me like I was just another man doing what men did, and talking it over as we went. But then, what was it going to do to baseball with my friends?

At the back of the pump house, I pulled off the last one. He shut down the engine and got out. Peering up along the line of pipe I had laid, he decided it was not straight enough, and had me walk back up the hill. He called out how I was to reposition each of the lengths. When I finished at the top of the hill, he motioned me back down.

With a grunt he slid the box of couplings off the tail gate. "Get the pump house door," he said, and carried it against his belly around to the front of the building. Setting it inside, he was careful to get all of his fingers out from under it as he let the box drop the final inch with a thump. When he straightened up, he placed hands on hips and breathed heavily as he went back around the building. "Look up the hill, Eugene."

The sections of pipe, after my repositioning, drew a perfectly straight silver line in the grass all the way to the barn. It brought a smile out of me that I couldn't hold back, and he winked at me just like Uncle Dan would do.

"Now, as you dig, measure for the edge like this," he said, and demonstrated by touching heel to pipe, his army boot perpendicular to it. "Where your toe comes down, that marks the edge of the ditch. Do that all the way up the hill, and we will have a nice, straight excavation."

We? But only I would be manning the pick and shovel.

"How deep?"

"Below the frost line...let's see..." He scratched over his right ear and peered into the distance. "Two feet ought to do it. Cut yourself a two-foot stick, and another at eighteen inches. Use the two-footer for depth, the other to set your width." He toed the grass with his army boot. "Once we get this in the ground, we'll have Van Shoor cut and thread the final connection pieces to be fit up."

He talked like it was our shared project. It was shared, all right: instructions shared by him on how I would do the work. How would I have any time to help Adam Stippil, and time to play ball with my friends?

As he looked around and studied the soon-to-be excavation site, he reached down and pulled a head of timothy from pasture grass, and drew it out of its sheath. Biting off the tender end, he chewed on the stem. Here he was, one moment, my father, successful lawyer, Democratic candidate for County Judge and, suddenly, the next moment, a farm boy chewing a piece of hay. He had probably been a lot like me, once...a long time ago. Would I ever be like him?

An idea came to me. "Doesn't the existing pipe run right along here too?"

His eyes lit at the excitement in my voice. "A couple of feet over this way," he said, indicating by a swing of arm. "Runs parallel to where we'll be putting in the new pipe."

"We could reuse the old pipe," I said. "Just feed the new wires down through it."

His eyes darted back and forth. The piece of hay fell from his mouth. He smiled at me. "Might work...good thinking, Eugene, except, we don't know what kind of failure could be lurking in that old pipe. It's been underground for years."

I felt my idea drain away, and along with it, my chances of ever playing ball again for the rest of the summer.

Eyes settling, he said, "We sure don't want an unseen glitch to have its way with us later, maybe a month from now, or in the middle of the winter."

Walking around to the front of the pump house, he peered inside. "Not sure what we're going to do about the old pipe, yet," he said, my idea having inspired him to think about it aloud. "Leave it for now, I suppose. The horses need water up in the barn while we're working on this, anyway."

My father was a man educated in the law, skilled in politics and at handling people's important business...how did he know about pipe?

He grinned. "But that could be your next project, once we finish this one: digging up the old line."

I did not grin back.

Latching the pump house door, he climbed into the driver's seat. He had me shut the tail gate, and said, "Let's go. We'll get you started on this in the morning, after we find you some real work boots."

We...again.

I got in and stared through the windshield as he started the engine, turned the vehicle around, and pointed the nose up toward the barn. The drive train groaned at being made to climb the steep hill, gravity pulling us against the backs of our seats.

I realized he'd been glancing at my hands, marked with paint residue in the creases and under fingernails. He said, "So, how's the paint job going over at Stippil's church?"

Another thing about turning twelve: my father, instead of talking down at me from the top of the wall between our two worlds, would occasionally ask a question about what was going on in mine, almost asking permission to climb over and talk with me down on my ground, like we were neighbors talking about the weather or the price of seed.

"Moving along," I said. "But none of the others ever want to start early enough, so we always end up rushing, just to make it look like Adam got plenty of work done by the time the Reverend gets home."

It brought a neighborly chuckle from him. "Sounds like you're working at cross-purposes. When you told me you guys were trying to play ball, and also help Adam pull a fast one on his father, I had my doubts."

He shifted into lower gear to negotiate the last steep angle of the grade. We were quiet the rest of the way up, the vehicle giving off a truck-mix of machinery noises. At the gate, I got out and let him through, and he parked in front of the garage.

As I walked across the yard toward him, he looked at me. "Four hours," he said.

I stopped, meeting his eyes.

"Four hours," he said again, hands on hips. "I expect you to give your project a full four hours every day, Eugene. Understand?"

I nodded.

As we headed to the back door, his hand touched my shoulder, voice gentle over my ear. "That should leave you a little time to paint the church and play ball...and whatever else you guys might be up to."

## Chapter 25, Not Just Anybody

The leather of my real work boots creaking with newness, I opened the door to the pump house. A 50-gallon water tank stood in the corner, sweating in the muggy summer heat. I filled my jar at the tank's drain valve. As I drank it down, I let cold water slop past my mouth onto neck and chest, cooling me down.

Way back when I was in first grade, draining this tank was the first chore my father had assigned to me. He had brought me down here and showed me what to do: flip the control box lever to OFF, close the valve to the barn, open a valve at the bottom of the tank, and when the pressure gauge went to zero, climb a stool to open a valve at the top. The tank would empty itself of water as it sucked in new air. When it was all finished burbling and hissing, I would close the two tank valves — making sure they were both tight — open the one that went up to the barn, and flip the lever to ON. The massive Westinghouse pump that used to be in here would come to life, fly wheel whirring, rods clanging.

It was an important job because, over time, the air pocket would shrink. If it shrank too much, the tank could no longer supply the horse trough up in the stable. The automatic switch could go into a start-stop-start-stop spasm, throwing the whole assembly — switch, motor, pump, well rods and pipe — into an ongoing rattle of convulsions. To keep this from happening, you had to occasionally drain the tank and create a new air pocket.

At the age of six, I was suddenly somebody.

I was reminded to do this on the first of each month by another assigned task: flip the page on the calendar that hung on a nail over the work bench in the cellar.

So, there was no excuse for the first and only time I failed to do my job. I was eight when that happened. The snow was deep, the wind cold. The calendar's February illustration was of a girl in purple underwear holding a red pipe wrench. She had curly hair and rosy cheeks. Large brown eyes invited me to stand by the warm furnace and pretend I was the one she was handing the red pipe wrench to.

"You're just lucky!" my father yelled at me, tears running down my face. "If you'd ruined the motor, you'd be saying good-bye to your allowance for...for the rest of your life!"

"Oh, come on," my mother said to him.

"The rest of his life!" he assured her. Then, to me, "As it is, young man, it'll take a good six months for you to pay for the pressure switch you burned out."

Six months, when I was eight, had loomed as a massive bite out of the rest of my life. I realized why my mother didn't approve of those calendar girls. They were dangerous.

And then he had pointed at me, like God at Adam from the Garden gate. "Just how do you think the horses enjoyed going without water for a few days? Those poor critters were down to eating snow just to get some moisture!"

I never forgot again.

Now, the water tank looked lonely, standing in the corner all by itself. The middle of the floor still bore the scars and bolt holes left by the old Westinghouse that, last year, my father and Bert had removed. A modern submersible rested out of sight at the bottom of the well, where it would quietly hum whenever called into action.

Refilling the jar, I went outside and set it in the shade on the back side of the pump house, closer to where I was working. I had a couple of feet to go to finish up the length of trench my father had marked out for me for the first day of the project.

"This ought to be about four hours' work," he had said in the morning before leaving for town.

He'd been right. I'd be finished soon, just about lunch time, judging by the location of sun that had been beating on me. I knew enough to keep my shirt on most of the time, but left it off now to let the air cool my sweat and the water I'd slopped on myself.

Back down in the trench, I raised the pick overhead and brought the point down hard. Prying on the handle broke the sod. A few more strokes with the point, and then I turned the pick over to the chisel side to leverage loosened dirt—rocks mixed in as always—down into the space around my feet. I put the pick aside, rested, hands on hips, arm and shoulder muscles quivering, not used to this.

No, not used to it, but I found in the ache of it something new...a kind of discomfort I wanted, and needed to savor. Tiredness, sweat, grunts that accompanied each motion, pungent odor of opened-up earth, the smell coming off my own flesh...it all had me feeling more like a man than a boy. I was twelve, a boy no doubt in the collective eye of everybody else. But I was ready to pretend.

So I ignored the whisper of grass behind me, not up to allowing another person's approach to interfere. Besides, Quin would be taking his shirt off too, and there we would be, side by side, one of us tall and slim and sinewy and muscled, and that wouldn't be me. Was he about to say something smart-ass?

I bent at the waist and pulled rocks out of the dirt, and flung them aside. It was never just a matter of picking rocks up, most of them flat and irregular pieces of shale, some the size of dinner plates. They stubbornly clung to Pennsylvania dirt no matter how well you thought you'd pried them loose.

The grass stopped whispering. I turned to retrieve the shovel. Not Quin...it was Agnes May, sitting on the ground beside my water jar in the shade of the pump house, knees folded up to her chest under that long dress, her back against the siding. When she looked at me, her eyes turned from serious to gentle. Her lips parted a little.

I said, "Digging a trench all the way up to the barn."

"Yes. I can see that. You're working real hard at it."

I shoveled dirt, added to the long pile parallel to the excavation. "You back for more kindling?"

"It's a never-ending chore," she said. "Thank you for suggesting that I gather starters from down there. It is much closer to my place, so I don't have to carry them as far."

Maybe she had forgotten how angry it made her right after that when I tried to tell her Philip wasn't real.

"I've already tied up a bundle," she said, "and left it there when I saw you were here."

"So you're done for the day?"

"With that chore, but, of course, I have others to do."

"I'm almost finished with what I have to do today."

"I'm just resting for a moment." She opened a book that she'd brought with her and, as she studied its pages, scribbled into a pad. Knowing she was there erased the need to think about what I was doing. I swung the pick, pulled rocks and shoveled dirt without thought, and without another stop to rest. I quickly made my way to the end of today's assigned length of trench, she looking over at me from time to time as I worked.

Finally, I moved the last shovelful. "What are you studying?"

"Stenography."

I'd heard of it, but knew nothing about it other than the girls in high school took classes. Maybe she was getting a head start. Wouldn't that be like her? Determined to be out front of all the other girls by the time she started ninth grade, a whole two years yet.

I climbed out of the trench, breathing hard, and sat beside her against the pump house, forearms on bent knees. "Want some water?"

"Sure." She took a sip and handed me the jar. "Thank you."

I drank after her, drained the jar, and spilled it all over myself again.

She laughed. Her pencil danced nervously as she copied marks from the book into the pad...indecipherable marks.

"Cripe'n-itey, Agnes May. What is all that?"

She turned and peered from under drawn eyebrows and said nothing.

"That's instead of Christ Almighty," I explained, "My mother yelled at me once for saying that."

"Did she give you a good whipping?" Agnes May emphasized the h and double-p sounds, and I remembered someone saying that her family had come here from Arkansas.

I laughed, but she did not laugh along.

"No. She made me promise to tell the priest about it in Confession. She even drove me down there that Saturday to make sure I did. It was his idea to change it to another word."

"Oh, I forgot. You Catholics may do whatever they want all week and then ask a priest for forgiveness at the end."

"It doesn't exactly work that way."

"So, how does it work, then?"

I had to think about it. "Confession is more like—you know—when you empty the vacuum cleaner bag."

"We don't have a vacuum cleaner." She looked away.

"We have one, just for the rug in the living room. My grandma has me empty it for her once in a while."

Agnes May said gravely, eyes dark, "Your mother should have whipped you good."

I tried to laugh at her seriousness, but she would have none of it.

"My mother would never do that," I said. "Maybe my father would, if he got good and mad, but so far he hasn't ever done anything like that. He spanked me once, but that's all."

"They've never whipped you? Well, this time they should have. They should have whipped you soundly for being so loose-tongued with His sacred name."

There was nothing left for me to say. I had to accept her anger at me, not for anything I had done to her, but for something I'd done all by myself that had somehow violated her understanding. In that moment I was grateful to not be a part of her church, where your wrongdoing would be the business of others. For us Catholics, no matter what you did, it was all between you and the priest and God, and once you owned up to it, it was all over. A Catholic got to walk around with a collection of secrets that could be emptied right into the priest's lap in the confessional.

I said, "Is that what they do when you do something wrong?"

She looked up from her stenography practice. "What are you talking about, Eugene?"

"Whipping," I said, emphasizing the h and double-p sounds as she had done.

She turned a little red. "Oh, I'd thought we were done talking about that, since you went silent."

My mind's eye brought back all those angry bruises we'd all seen at the pond on Adam's bare flesh. "Is that what they do to you, Agnes May?"

The color came back, this time scarlet, but she said nothing, looking at her work.

"I'm just asking. You seem to be informed on it."

She glanced at me, and looked away. "Once," she said softly.

"Once?"

"Once! Yes, I said once! Didn't you hear me?"

Then she exhaled loudly. "Eugene," she said, and resumed scribbling. "Once, when I was talking to the Reverend, I tried to be a little too fancy, that's all."

"And they whipped you for it?"

She looked up from her work. "Not my Mom. My daddy — I mean, the Reverend. I deserved it."

"For being fancy? Whatever does that mean, Agnes May?"

She looked away. "It's what the Reverend calls it. You're not a member of our church, so you don't know. He talks, in his sermons, about how people sometimes get the notion of being fancy, and it gets in the way of grace, and in the way of accepting and embracing the Higher Being, our Heavenly Father."

"But, what does that mean? The notion of being fancy?"

"Well, you're Catholic, so maybe you can't understand because you haven't received the grace that allows you to accept and embrace."

"Cripe'n-itey, Agnes May."

Her face reddened. "Don't say that. Just because it isn't an actual curse, it takes the place of one you would actually like to say, so it's the same thing."

"I mean, what could possibly be so evil about being fancy that earns a whipping, and makes the person who gets it say she deserves it?"

"Well, you can't understand. You're Catholic."

"So what?"

"You haven't received the grace."

"Oh, bullshit!" My face flushed and felt as scarlet as hers looked.

She returned to her pad, jaw set, eyes darting back and forth.

After a while she spoke softly. "It's just that you don't accept and embrace the Higher Being, that's all."

"We have a Supreme Being."

She looked at me, eyes wide, and smiled. "There, you see? You do accept and embrace Him, only you just call it—I mean Him—by a different name!"

"I suppose so."

"Although," she said, looking away, "I don't know how real it is if you've never testified."

Now, that was a term I understood. "I've seen people testify in court for my father."

"Not that," she laughed. "You Catholics don't ever testify before the communion of sinners. About your conversion, I mean."

I had no idea what she meant. This talk was giving me a headache.

"It's not for real if you don't testify. It only stays in your own mind, and then it's meaningless, until you testify before the whole community."

"So, you testified before the whole church, that you had fancy notions?"

"Well, I did testify that I'm a sinner and in need of redemption, and that I accept and embrace His having died to save me."

We were both quiet. I stood up. Her eyes moved back and forth between the notebook in her lap and me, and then settled on watching me as I put my shirt on, her shiny, creek-pebble eyes brushing lightly over me, then she looked away.

"Agnes May."

She looked up again.

"I didn't mean to pry. I mean, about your fancy notions. I have secrets, too, that I don't admit, not to just anybody."

She said softly, "Well, I'm sure everybody does."

"You know, the one time my father spanked me?" I suddenly wanted to tell her. "It was because I let the horses run out of water. They were down to eating snow, just to keep from dying of thirst." Voice quivered, "I was eight. I've never talked about it before."

She looked away.

I took the pick and shovel to the pump house. The grass whispered behind me as she followed from where we'd been sitting together behind the structure.

The sun lightened her, painted wisps of braid. "Eugene—"

"Agnes May," I interrupted, "I shouldn't have asked you about it." I finished leaning the tools just inside the door. "Nobody wants to blab their secrets to just anybody."

"Eugene Ahern." She looked straight at me, hands on hips like a scolding adult. "Didn't you know? You are not just anybody."

I shrugged.

## Chapter 26, Adam's Idea

Nothing was wrong with Adam's idea when it first came up. I mean, Baggie had it coming. What harm could have come of it if everything had stayed as planned?

Baggie showed up at the Christian Fellowship Church in his dog-catcher truck and volunteer-deputy outfit to question Quin about a break-in at Old Lady Hough's place. Someone had stolen two dollars and seventy-six cents from her kitchen drawer and swiped her AM/FM radio right off the shelf above the stove, ripping the wallpaper where the antenna wire was taped. They'd also opened a new can of frozen juice—the one her daughter had just bought for her it at the A&P yesterday—gouged some out with a fork and then just left it on the table to melt into a blob of orange slurry. They didn't even bother to put what was left of the can back into the freezer.

When Baggie showed up, we had just finished playing ball for the day and were starting in on painting and scraping.

"Where were you last night?"

"Where were YOU last night," Quin responded from the ladder and just kept on scraping.

Baggie, hands on hips, swirl-eyed Quin, face growing red, and in a sudden movement stepped toward the ladder. He pulled his nightstick and poked Quin in the back of the knee with the end of it. Quin buckled, sending the ladder into a shaky dance as he grabbed onto the top step with both hands, which sent the Folgers coffee can tumbling, along with the brush, splattering paint onto the window. He hobble-hopped down the ladder.

"Lucky for you I didn't get you where it would really hurt," Baggie snorted.

Quin sat down on the ground hard against the stone foundation, knees up to his chest, tears running down his face.

Baggie pushed the nightstick into Quin's chest. "I won't be quite so nice if I have to ask you again," he said, then raised Quin's head up, nightstick under chin.

Hangy took a step on his tree-trunk legs toward Baggie. "Leave him be."

Baggie eyed him. "Think you won't be next? When I'm done interrogating the Sloot bastard here, don't you go thinking you might not be in for some of the ole Baggie treatment your *own* self."

Hangy took a longer step toward Baggie. "Leave him be," he said, steady eyed, one hand on hip, the other curling at his side. He turned to Adam. "Go in and get your ma to call Eugene's old man."

Adam wrinkled up his face and looked at me. The Stippil family didn't have a phone...it had been disconnected a few months back. I turned away from Baggie so he wouldn't see me wink, which sent Adam on his way toward the house.

"Now, hold on," Baggie said, his voice finding a higher pitch. He took the stick away from Quin's throat and fastened it to the loop on his belt. "Doing my job, that's all. Doing my duty." He flicked the edge of the constable badge pinned to his shirt.

Adam stopped and turned back to us.

Hangy said evenly, "None of us know anything about the break-in. So, there you go...Deputy."

Baggie gave a hollow laugh, eyes narrowing. "You little shits," he muttered and walked away.

As the dog-catcher truck backed out of the church drive-way, reverse gear whining and tires spitting stones, Hangy and I helped Quin up. He winced and rubbed the back of his leg.

That was when Adam suddenly came up with his idea.

Before I made the call I made sure my mother was up in the attic over the garage working on her art. Grandma Marja was already snoozing in her wicker rocker on the porch.

"Hello." A woman's voice in the earpiece.

I thought I knew everyone who worked for the township, and they were all men. I said, "Is this the township?"

When Quin and Hangy and Adam heard my best female voice, they had to hold back their laughter. Then Quin advised in a whisper, "Put some more air into it."

The voice said, "This is the answering service. There's no-body available right now. Do you have an emergency?"

"Well," I breathed, "you might say that."

"What is the nature?"

"Nature?"

"Please state what your emergency is. A fire? Disturbance?"

"I see. Yes, it's a disturbance, you might say." My female voice was settling in. Quin was right: put lots of air into it, like Marilyn Monroe.

The woman said, "Do you require the constable?"

"I need to report that my daughter and I were chased by a cow."

Trying to stifle a laugh, Quin whinnied through his nose. I waved at all three of them to get out of the living room so the woman at the answering service wouldn't hear them.

The woman clucked her tongue. "Chased by a cow? A cow? Are you sure?"

I was too busy swallowing a laugh to answer.

The woman said, "Your name, please."

I hadn't expected that, but quickly conjured a story. "Missus Burns. With me is my daughter, Lydia. From Utica—that's in New York"

"Yes, I know where Utica is," the woman rasped.

I suddenly recalled some of Miss Hendershott's Pennsylvania geography. "We're on our way down to Lewisburg. My husband is painting a bridge down there. That's what he does. He paints bridges. He's painting the Lewisburg bridge right now, the one that crosses over the Susquehanna."

"You don't say."

"Yes, and when he gets through for the day, won't he be surprised that his wife and daughter are knocking on his motel door."

Quin and Hangy and Adam roiled in the dining room, wide-eyed, faces tortured.

"When and where did this happen?" the woman said.

"It was just before we got back onto the highway and found this Esso station to call from. You see, we followed a lovely country road to have a picnic and, well, a cow, this crazy cow, chased us. It was all I could do to pick up Lydia in one arm and throw stones at the cow with the other. We managed to get away. But something should be done!"

"Missus Burns, in the first place, you shouldn't be going onto someone's property. And in the second place, are you sure it wasn't a bull? Cows don't normally attack people."

"Oh, no! I may be a city girl, but I'm sure it was a cow. It even had one of those—you know—udders. I certainly know the difference between an udder and...well, those other things that..." I fell to a raspy whisper, "...you know, a bull would have."

More stifled laughter spilled out of the dining room, like bubbling water from under a pot cover.

"And she attacked us, a black and white spotted cow," I said. "She was crazy. We were lucky to get away with our picnic basket! Now, I suppose we'll have to stop at one of those disgusting roadside tables to eat our lunch. They're always covered with bird droppings. Not very sanitary, if I may say so."

"And where did this happen, Missus Burns?"

"In a meadow along some woods. As we got away, I saw a mail box nearby that said—now what was that?—Ahern."

"Ahern...you mean the Ahern place?"

"Yes, that was it. The mail box said, Owen Ahern."

"It just so happens that we've recently hired an animal control officer, Missus Burns. He may want to check it out. And I'm sorry that you had to—"

I hung up. My friends couldn't hold off any longer. A burst of laughter sent them into contortions that shoved a dining room chair into the table.

Grandma Marja called out from her nap on the porch. "Eugene? Is that you?"

"On my way out, Grandma," I answered in my normal voice. "I'll see you later."

I herded my friends through the kitchen and out the back door, a little sad that I had to leave Marilyn's voice behind.

It didn't take Baggie long. We were passing around a Pall Mall in the undergrowth behind the barbed-wire fence when, from up the hill, a cloud of dust rose on the dirt road in front of our house. He slowed and turned onto the weedy field-access road that paralleled the fence, MELODY FALLS TOWNSHIP ANIMAL CONTROL in yellow letters clearly visible on a side panel.

Just opposite our hiding place, we had removed a section of stone-pack placed there by Grandpa Carroll many decades ago: the roadbed had a hole about knee deep. High growth in the road should have hidden it, or so we thought. Somehow Baggie saw it, and stopped a few feet short. He got out of the truck. As he came close to the ditch, looking over the pile of stones we'd thrown down there, we flattened ourselves, submerged into the musty smell of the forest floor on our side of the fence. He spit and got back into the truck. Rising up, we watched him steer around the hole, his face flushed with determination to go after the mad cow that a trespassing picnicker from Utica had reported.

The truck groaned away from us in low gear to where the road dipped downhill toward a low corner of the farm. Hobbes Creek came under the fence from their farm onto ours, broadening out to a bowl-shaped bog that slowed the water to a wide crawl. There, the stream moved along in a lazy seepage before slipping over a gray shale shelf, where it gathered itself again into a torrent and started a deep cut through a walnut grove. In the bog, Oriane-Florisse, Rollheis's dried-up runaway, had taken a liking to the lush grass that was plentiful there, standing in quiet shade of a massive willow, chewing cud and looking at the world with big round eyes.

The truck went into second gear and lurched off the stone-pack, engine groaning. Oriane-Florisse turned her head to the noise and, freezing in mid-chew, widened her ears out. Her eyes flashed in the last instant before she bolted out of the way. Baggie, his truck ka-humping over willow roots, passed the tree and turned in a wide arc, rear tires throwing cake-slices of turf into the air. The cow eyed him lining up the truck again as growling engine hurled the vehicle forward. She jerked and ran away in a zigzag lunge, tail curled up on her rump. Baggie, closing on her, shifted to high gear to gain speed…too high of a gear, suddenly throwing the engine into a spasm of coughs and sputters. He worked gas-pedal and clutch to keep it going, then downshifted. But the truck had already lost too much momentum to maintain traction on the soggy ground. Front wheels first, then the drive wheels, slowly sank into the turf up to the hubs.

The frantic cow stopped at the fence, where she turned around and glared at the mechanical ogre that had been chasing her. The truck was no longer moving, but its engine let out a ferocious roar. A long squeal came from its rear, and then a cloud of blue smoke rose into the air. The cow took off again, ran along the fence until she found a place where she figured she could make it over. Just a stone's throw from where we hid, she leapt across the ditch and almost cleared the barbed wire…catching a rear hoof on the top strand as she went over. The trip-up threw her to the ground on the other side. Eyes glazed, she struggled to stand, to a noise like cracking knuckles. She hobbled away on three legs, right rear leg flopping along, and soon disappeared among the trees and undergrowth.

For a long time, sleep would not fall out of the night for me. Eerie bawling from down in Hobbes Woods haunted the darkness. It was from a long way off, and at first I wasn't sure if it was real or came out of my imagination as a result of what had happened. And then, once I accepted it as real, a part of my mind that I couldn't control grew more attentive to it. The sad bawling of a lone animal traveled about the woods and slopes and farm building over the distance, gathering all the echoes into what sounded like haunting pleas of a whole herd. Sometime during the night, she must have quieted. I suddenly awoke to lavender morning light and singing of birds from the trees across the road.

At breakfast my father rattled the *Clarion* over his eggs and toast, and mumbled that as far as he was concerned Baggie's dog-catcher truck could rot until the winter freeze would allow our Massey Harris tractor onto the bog to pull it out. "The damned vehicle better not be leaking anything into the soil, or he's in for a lawsuit," he said, snapping the paper for emphasis. He turned the page, but soon gave up on finding anything else worth reading, and placed it on the table.

My mother said, "Please don't say 'damned' at the breakfast table."

Lowdown raised her head up off the floor. Somebody was approaching the house. A few quick wiggles of her tail told us it was somebody she favored, and then we heard the rumble of an engine. She managed to get herself up on arthritic legs and waddle to the door.

"Come on in, Vern," my father yelled in answer to the knock.

The dog's tail went into a blur as Vern Rollheis came in holding a brown paper bag filled with dusted jelly doughnuts. "From the missus," he said. Lowdown got the first one. My parents invited him to sit down, and Grandma automatically got up and brought him a cup of black coffee.

They talked about the hay crop this year, and how far along the corn was and, of course, the fair coming up. They did not talk about politics. The Rollheises were Republicans, or at least Vern was, and everybody assumed his wife—she would never actually say—dutifully went along with her husband.

After a pause in conversation, Vern said, "The missus told me about your phone call this morning. I was still finishing up in the barn...Bert never showed up for work. Musta been sleeping one off."

"That dried-up milker was bawling half the night," my father said, then licked away a sugar mustache. "I thought you should know."

"So, how is Elvira?" my mother said.

Vern merely nodded in response to her query, moving on with men-talk. "Sorry if it was an inconvenience for you all. I should have come and collected that old bag a long time ago."

"Not a problem," my father said. "I know how busy you must be trying to milk forty head."

"I'll bring the International stake-body and a ramp back here this afternoon. I'll have her off your place in no time, if I can get some help."

My father looked at me. "I'm in court today. How about, after lunch, before you play ball, you and your friends give Vern a hand."

Itching with adventure the four of us followed Vern inside Hobbes Woods. He looked up through the tree canopy at two buzzards circling. "Doesn't look good for her."

We turned and went with him back beyond the fence on the access road, where he'd parked the International. From behind the bench seat he pulled out a long green canvass bag. He un-strapped it and pulled out a rifle.

"Thirty-thirty?" Hangy said.

"Thirty-oh-six," Vern said. "My old man bought it from World War One surplus." Sliding open the breach to an oily smell, he pushed in three shiny brass shells with gray pointed tips.

Guided by the buzzards—now a half-dozen of them—we found Oriane-Florisse in a ravine. Having slid down onto moss-covered shale outcropping, she lay on her side, nostrils twitching with shallow breath, pink tongue hanging part-way from her mouth. Her eye, blinking at flies buzzing around it, moved as we approached, followed Vern as he walked around her. She muttered a sound from deep in her throat.

Vern made a clicking noise in the back of his throat, the one some farmers use when talking to livestock. "Yeh, I know," he said softly, and knelt down on one knee to wave the flies away and pat her flank. "Gonna take care of you, girl. It'll all be okay." He slowly worked the bolt action, stood and put the muzzle against the side of her head.

The big eye looking up at him relaxed a little. The thirty oh-six went off. Oriane-Florisse jerked. It was the beginning of a jerk, but never got a chance to finish. It just stopped in the middle of itself. The eye slowly widened out as it deepened into a blackness that wanted to pull us all in.

## CHAPTER 27, LAKE MARGARET

It had been dubbed the Saint Agatha Retreat for Young Crusaders, but we knew better.

Under the Third Street Bridge, Al Cousineau, with new sideburns and the first makings of a mustache, had told us, "Don't let the name fool you for a minute. It's got nothing to do with knights from olden times chasing down Mohammed's followers."

He had attended the first one back when Father Kearns had just arrived as our new pastor, and had recently leaked it to us in a smoky, mellow baritone: "It's about sex. And let this be a warning to you innocents. After the retreat, sex won't ever be the same again. Say good-bye to your peckers until your wedding nights, you sorry sons-a-bitches."

The retreat was intended for 12-year-olds from St. Agatha Parochial about to enter junior high. This year, for the first time, two of us "publics" from Saturday catechism were included. And, of course, it was limited to males. The girls, we understood, other than attending a half-hour lecture from Doctor Willingham about their periods, would be expected to be told about sex from their mothers, their education on the subject to be finalized by husbands only on their wedding nights. It was further limited to those boys handpicked by the nuns at Saint Agatha, and by Father Kearns himself, a selection process that was careful to exclude the "not readies," for whom a one-hour remedial lecture would be mandatory in the Saint Agatha Gym.

Quin, according to my father, had initially been rejected by the nuns. They had known him from grades one through five in Saturday catechism. But Father Kearns, who taught us sixth grade catechism, reinstated Quin to the "ready" category because, according to what my father said over Sunday breakfast, "He knows you've been such a good influence on him, Eugene."

Quin and I sat in the back seat of the '56 Buick Special in the same clothes we'd worn to Sunday Mass, white shirts, dark slacks and good shoes. Quin's shirt was a bit yellowed from too many well-water washings, and his slacks showing shiny patches of wear. Our belongings, mine in a brown canvas gym bag, his in a cardboard box that said, "Westinghouse 4-

pack, 40 watts, seventy-two count," rested between us on the seat under two sleeping rolls tied with twine.

The back of my father's head, beneath his fedora, was salted with gray where the barber had shaved a perfect edge. His lined neck disappeared into a starched collar. A dark blue suit showed flecks of dandruff on the shoulders, which my mother, had she been riding with us, would have readily whisked away. The Buick cradled us in tufts of upholstery and chrome trim, and surrounded us with a gentle whir of machinery from up front and under the center hump.

Quin was quiet. It was not like him. Nor was it like me to let him stay that way, to not take a poke at him there in the back seat to get him going again. But I knew this retreat bothered him ever since that day under the Third Street Bridge, where Al Cousineau, a soon-to-be Junior at Saint Agatha, had proclaimed through broken cigarette puffs, "You two innocents will be one sorry pair," and then popped out a series of neatly formed smoke rings. I had kept quiet.

"What d'ya mean, Al?" Quin had said, which yielded another set of smoke rings to hang lazily around our heads. Cousineau stretched his neck out, which revealed a lone whisker by his Adam's apple. His sideburns had those narrow shadows under them of a man who'd recently tried shaving, and light fuzz above his lip nurtured a collection of darkened strands.

"So, you want to know what I mean," he finally said. "Well, I'll tell you what I mean." But then he went silent again, took another drag on his Winston — Al would never smoke any other brand — and snickered a blue cloud at us.

"Ole Kearnsy will tell you, all right," Cousineau finally spoke to us after a long wait. "You sorry sons-a-bitches..."

"Come on, Al. What d'ya mean? What's he going to tell us, exactly?"

Cousineau used the burned-down butt of his Winston to light up another. "Well, now, I'm not allowed to tell."

"Not allowed?"

"Under pain of mortal sin."

"Mortal sin!" Quin yelled. "Cripe'n-itey! Just for telling us what he said?"

"Don't blame me, Quin, my boy. That's the hex ole Kearnsy is famous for putting onto everybody right at the end a retreat. The pain of mortal sin: we dare not tell anybody younger than us exactly what was said."

"But you've told us some already," I said. "And once you tell part of it, doesn't that make you obliged to tell us the rest?"

Quin looked at me, grinned, and then mussed my hair. "That's right," he said to Al. "You can't get past old Genie, here. He's got his old man's lawyer-mind. You're already in the land of mortal sin, Mister Cousineau, and so now you are committed to telling everything you know."

Cousineau took a long drag on the new Winston, and through puffs of smoke said, "Kearnsy only told us not to tell. It's nowhere close to mortal sin territory to just tell you inno-cents that I can't tell you." He looked at me and snarled, "I don't care if Genie's the only begotten son of the Pope himself."

"So what is it you are actually going to tell us?" Quin's voice crackled.

"Well, that's easy. All I'm saying is that by the time you've heard all the good stuff Kearnsy has to offer, then you'll know for sure that you won't be able to use any of what you've learned, not until your wedding nights, under pain of mortal sin, you sorry sons-a-bitches!"

The way I figured it, Cousineau was no better off than we were. He was five years ahead of us. Big deal: a five-year head start at being one of the sorry sons-a-bitches himself.

The Buick's Dynaflow transmission jerked, and went into a high-pitched whine. Route 6 wavered on steep curves that had been cut into a rock face on our left as we climbed high above the Susquehanna, which dropped off rapidly over the edge to the right. We came up behind a semi-trailer flatbed loaded with bundles of pipe, inching up the grade, its engine in a throaty roar, tractor billowing black smoke into the muggy August sky. The snaking concrete road refused my father any opportunity to pass. The Buick, its high-performance machin-ery held to a crawl, jerked back and forth between first and second gear, trapped in a purgatory of indecision. Half-way up the mountain, the incline surrendered to a brief level area, where the widened shoulder allowed the tractor-trailer to pull off. We passed by, and soon resumed the steep grade, climbing again, Dynaflow singing now, until we reached the summit.

Our car nosed downhill through more twists and turns, now at a fast whisper. We swung around the curves, and swished past labored vehicles coming up from the opposite direction. It didn't take long to make it down to river level again. My father braked almost to a stop, and slowly swung a sharp left onto a shady dirt road. With manual shift into low gear, he kept our speed to a crawl—he hated hearing pebbles hit the bottom of the vehicle—as we began to climb inland away from the river.

For a few miles of billowy dust, the tree-shaded road clung to the side of a steep slope, until it finally made a right turn and cut through a narrow cataract, then dipped. We drove down into a natural bowl, surrounded by white pines and hemlocks.

A barn-like structure stood beside a still pond that reflected the sky. White letters on a sheet of dark brown plywood proclaimed, MOUNT HENRY, and below it, DIOCESE OF SCRANTON, and below that, PRIVATE — KEEP OUT! Father Kearns's black '60 Mercury was against the building.

We parked in the gravel yard and got out with our gym bag, cardboard box, and sleeping rolls. My father made a move, like he was about to hug me. I stiffened against it. Was he really going to do that with Quin standing there? He changed his mind, made a fist instead, and gave me a soft tap on the shoulder.

"Now, you — both of you — listen carefully to what Father Kearns has to say," his voice a little wavy. "It's important to the rest of your lives," he said, and looked away. "I'll give your love to your mother. And to Marja too, of course," he added

Quin and I both nodded. It was one of those times when Quin was allowed to be Marja's grandson too.

We watched my father get back into the car, do a slow, gravel-crunch turn around, and head out of the yard in low gear. The shadowy dirt road swallowed the murmuring Buick back through the cataract.

Quin spoke quietly, "First order of business: once Kearnsy lets us out of these duds, we gotta find a place where we can burn one."

I felt the pack of Pall Malls in my side pocket. They didn't seem too badly crushed, maybe flattened a little.

Jim Gorski, bug-eyed and saintly, stepped toward us along a flagstone walk. "I didn't think they'd allow publics to attend."

"Oh, yeah?" I said. "Remember, you didn't think they'd allow us to become altar boys, either."

Quin laughed. "Genie's got you there, Gorski."

"You're the second and third ones here," Gorski reported. "I was first. You can decide between yourselves who was second and who was third."

Quin and I looked at each other. Gorski had ridden up here with Father Kearns. They'd been doing things together lately, Gorski following Kearnsy around like a puppy. Most of the kids now called him "the Shadow" — which had replaced "Bugsy" — behind his back.

The Shadow, with us in tow, strolled back toward the building along the flagstones like a man on official church business.

"Rutherford Henry's vacation lodge," he announced as he led us through double screen doors.

"Rutherford who?" I said.

"Henry. Rutherford Henry, the former heir to Wallenpaupack Anthracite." Whenever the Shadow told you something, he would process it with teeth and lips that formed the words precisely, the way Old Man Hobbes's pull-behind baler scarfed up a windrow and pooped out perfect rectangular hay bales.

"Oh, *that* Rutherford Henry," Quin said at me and grinned.

The lodge was like a barn from the outside, with a high gambrel roof and board siding. But it had been finished off inside more like a house for the first ten feet up, walls plastered, whitewashed, and trimmed in pine. Higher, the beams and rafters were left exposed, though, unlike any barn, they were smooth, and covered in coats of varnish. You didn't see any knotholes winking daylight at you, or gaps between the boards either.

"Mr. and Mrs. Henry abandoned it after the death of Margaret, their only child," the human hay baler informed us. "She drowned in the lake in 1939. The lake today bears her name."

Quin said, "The lake? What lake?"

"Maybe he means that pond we saw," I said.

"Lake Margaret," the Shadow assured us.

Quin laughed and poked me.

Our guide pointed to the end wall at a cabinet structure, made of open square sections. "You have your pick of spaces — they're called cubbyholes — for your stuff, except mine, of course. I was here first."

Neatly folded clothes occupied the uppermost center cubbyhole, sleeping roll on top. Quin and I picked out two of our own, far away from the Shadow's, down at eye level so we wouldn't have to reach. We unpacked and stowed our clothes — hand-over-hand method of folding made it quick and easy — and neatly placed our sleeping rolls.

The lodge — now a retreat house — was divided into two sections. The north side, where we had come in, was a wide-open space with large windows and, up high, dormers built into the roof.

"This is the assembly room," the Shadow said. "We'll gather here for our sessions. At night, we'll spread out cots. They're presently stored in the shed out back."

Next, he showed us the other half of the building, the south side, a closed-in structure of two stories: on the ground floor, a kitchen, tiled and stainless-steel shiny, like you'd see in a school cafeteria, then, a bathroom under a staircase. Through a pair of full-length louvered swing-doors, we entered the dining room, with a long, fancy oak table surrounded by carved wooden chairs, and a brass chandelier overhead. In the corner, a door was open. Father Kearns sat at a desk, reading intently. I recognized the book: the same breviary my Uncle Dan used. Kearnsy didn't look up, his lips moving in silence through the Latin.

Gesturing to a staircase, the Shadow solemnly whispered, "We're not allowed up there. The second floor has private rooms, reserved for married-couple retreats." Then he inhaled to pump more air to his hushed speech, "I sneaked up there when Father first got busy reading his divine office." His eyes grew even buggier. "Down quilts, lace curtains, and just one bed to a room."

Quin and I looked at each other: were married couples allowed to "do it" during a religious retreat?

At a crunch of gravel from the yard, the Shadow cocked his head, and found his official voice again. "Gotta go, fellows. More new arrivals. Help yourselves to looking around outside." He hoofed away through the double screen doors.

We went out to the water. The dock, a few replaced planks yellow with newness, led out from a grass bank. Off to one side, a beach had been built up from spread-out loads of brown gravel-pit sand, where tractor tires had left herring-bone impressions. A red Massey Harris 55, blade attached to the front, was parked under a tree, upside-down rusty tin can protecting the open end of the exhaust pipe.

"Sorry excuse for a lake," I said.

Quin widened his eyes. He puffed out his chest, and bellowed, using the Shadow's voice: "It still bears her name. Lake Mar-ga-ret."

"More like Pond Margaret," I said, and we shared a laugh.

"Wasn't that Peggy Murphy's real name...Margaret?"

"Peggy Murphy," I said her name like I hadn't thought of her for a long time. That freckle-faced redhead with a pony tail I'd wasted much of third and fourth grades trying to corral into being my friend. I had once offered to push her on the swing so I could accidentally touch her, but her pony tail swished my face every time the swing came back. She had stubbornly refused to have anything to do with me after that. The summer before fifth grade, her old man had moved the family — and his dental practice — down to Carbondale.

"Yep," I said. "She was Margaret, all right. Everybody called her Peggy."

Quin, turning himself into a parade official, marched to the end of the dock, where he adopted a low, somber tone, "I hereby proclaim thee: Pond Peggy!"

## Chapter 28, Catholic Sex

In the next quarter-hour, the rest of the retreat-goers arrived, a few in rapid succession, which had the Shadow quick-stepping to perform his self-appointed duties. There were thirteen of us in all.

At exactly 2 o'clock, the Shadow, beads of sweat running down flushed cheeks, white shirt stained at the arm pits, came out to stand on a rotted stump and ring a brass bell in all directions, eyes bright, and jaw working side to side in time to the motion of his arm. We gathered inside, where folding chairs—no wonder the Shadow was sweating—had been hastily set up in the assembly room. The arrangement was a crooked half-circle with a lectern as its focus, brass reading lamp plugged in and lit.

Quin and I took two seats together at the far left. Empty seats filled in. The Shadow was quick to sit directly in front, bell centered on his lap. Its shiny brass skirt tapered upward, narrowing into a polished handle.

Papers at the ready, Father Kearns came out to the lectern. He looked us over. Gray eyes seemed to rest on each of us, and call down a silence whose hush teased our eardrums into aching for the sound of his baritone to finally get going.

He made us wait. Straightening a layer of papers, he plopped their edges against the top of the lectern, looked through them without hurry, clicked his pen from time to time, and dashed notes to himself in the margins. In August swelter, the requirement for thirteen boys to maintain silence soon fell into syllables of fidgeting, coughs, shuffle of shoe soles, rusty squeaks among the ancient folding chairs...

On a winter afternoon last January, I was supposed to be putting away Christmas ornaments, as light spilled through the window of an attic dormer, painting a parallelogram of lavender on rough floor boards. A red-and-white checkered oilcloth invited me to look under it. I moved it, exciting a puff of dust particles, and found cardboard boxes. They had all come from a big box mountain at the front of the A&P where Zachary Goldman—Wyotanda High's star point guard—manned the end of the check-out registers.

As the cashiers rang them up, with perfect timing he would move from one customer to the next, his rapid choosing of boxes from the mountain tuned to highly honed knowledge of just what sizes would put order to any jumble of groceries.

When he completed one order, swift steps would carry him with ease of a dancer over to the next position, his athletic upper body settling into a momentary calm. As he finished with each customer, Zachary's pale blue eyes would come to rest, Adam's apple bobbing with soft baritone: "Thank you, ma'am, for shopping at the Wyotanda A&P today."

When he said that, my mother would look him up and down and say, "Oh, you're quite welcome," in a quiet, somber tone that echoed his. She didn't know that once I saw her wink at him, which almost cracked his workman face.

She also didn't know, nor did my father, that I had found what was hiding in frigid attic boxes under checkered oilcloth in the attic: books. As little as six months earlier, I never would have suspected that grownups had a hiding place for the purpose of secreting books away from me. But now, I was twelve. I was finding out different.

I was finding out different about lots of things, about grownups and what they'd been up to all along, especially once they had taken to calling me "young man." From deep inside me had sprouted a restless offshoot, a yearning to learn what they'd been up to all these years, a fast-growing tentacle winding its way toward a source of light that I was certain I was not supposed to draw energy from.

I was no longer just a kid. I had grown. It used to be that I never knew I was growing until somebody said so. Well, now I knew about it without being told, and I yearned to reach a level where I could glimpse what they thought was still out of my reach. My chest, my stomach, and my groin twinged with desire. I felt myself stretching in a heightened reach of curiosity, more agile than before, certainly more determined—the way Zachary Goldman's jump-shot had so much improved in the summer between his junior and senior seasons.

So I put my hand into one of the boxes, and tugged a book out of its place. It did not come easily. I had to force the other books apart to release the tight hold they had on it, and make the space it came from inhale a puff of air.

Old-book smell teased my nostrils. A hint of something foreign, exotic, had me open it, which the binding responded to with a noise like a boy cracking his knuckles. The print was smaller than I was used to, a sign that these words had been put there for eyes more grownup than mine.

My mother didn't know I'd seen her wink at the box boy. My father didn't know that, on one of my forays into his office,

I'd seen the photos of a woman he kept in a file at the bottom of the stack on the floor by the window. And neither of them knew that I had secreted the book from the attic into my bedroom. The grownup world didn't know that, over the next few days and nights, little else would matter as a forbidden narrative carried me like driftwood floating in a stream...

"Are you with us, Mr. Ahern?" Father Kearns, gray eyes on me like two spear points, brought me back to August swelter.

"Yes, Father."

Those two grays held onto me, had me wriggle a moment, before letting me off.

Kearnsy had put down the papers, ready to begin. He removed his Roman collar, placed it on the seat of the chair, and then took off his black shirt and hung it over the back. We had never seen Kearnsy this undressed before. Tufts of male hair poked out of a tee shirt stretched and lumpy with physique of the former football star, like a sack filled with squash and melons, ham-like upper arms forced through tortured sleeves.

Al Cousineau had told a few of us this would happen. The written instructions to our parents had said we were to show up in Sunday dress that, according to Cousineau, we would only be required to wear for Mass in the morning. So, we'd been sitting here, sweaty, just waiting for Kearnsy's first order of business.

"The good Lord invites us to be casual." he finally said, just as Cousineau had said he would. He gestured toward the open windows. "No need to be quite so formal, not in this heat. We are at the retreat cottage, not in church." He smiled upon us.

He had not even finished saying it when we followed his example in a flurry. Then the smile melted into a stare, at each one of us individually, cementing us into a quiet that concealed our quivers.

In a brief moment, while Kearnsy was eying somebody on the other side of the room, Quin and I glanced at each other. So, this was going to be it: the great mystery, the secret ever so-skillfully hidden all these years in a thicket of odd adult language, words whispered, left half-spoken, or only hinted at with cocked eyebrow and facial tick; words that had to be contained in books hidden under dusty oilcloth in the attic with tiny print, buried in sentences that took up three-quarters of a page. Here we were, at last: Saint Agatha's Young Crusaders, on the edge of a cliff, eager and ready to charge over that edge into enlightenment, our parents having turned us over to our Jesuit-trained pastor. Finally, they were going to let us in on it: Catholic sex.

## CHAPTER 29, LIME KOOL-AID

"The thing to do with a sin once you know you've committed it—and all of us are capable of sin because of our fallen nature—is to seek forgiveness right away. There are two important reasons for haste, gentlemen. Reason number one, is to close up the wound you've inflicted on your own soul by your actions, or in the case of a mortal sin, to immediately bring back to life the soul's opportunity to be reunited with God at death, which could happen at any moment. This is done, of course, through Confession."

Father Kearns stopped and looked around the room.

"Reason number two, is that each sin cuts a channel for every other sin to follow, and the longer you allow your own evil-doing to linger on the surface of your soul, the wider and deeper a swath it cuts there."

When his gaze reached me, it lingered.

"Suppose you tell a lie, for example. A lie is easier the next time because your resistance to it has already been compromised. On a surface already eroded by the first lie, the second one has a ready route to follow. The longer you delay in seeking forgiveness the deeper and wider that imperfection."

His eyes had a tight grip on me, and my liar's eyes had nowhere to look. In the barn, I'd once heard a rustling behind the horses' feed bin, and when I'd pulled the bin out from the wall, a black snake had a rat by the snout. The rat struggled to get away, but the snake would not let go, its jaws firm. When the rat, in a struggle to breathe, tried to back up, the snake moved forward. When the rat tried to twist away, the snake turned it back upright. The last thing the rat ever saw of its own miserable life on earth was a pair of snake eyes glaring into its own eyes. And now, sweat ran down my ribs. I picked out a spot, a tiny mole on the bridge of our pastor's nose to focus on. Only then, did he move on to someone else.

"No doubt you all are aware of this, for as children, haven't we committed sins common to childhood? And isn't lying one of the most common? But we are no longer children. You—yes, every one of you—is a young man, whether you've begun to think of yourself as one or not."

He relaxed at the lectern, and everybody moved a little.

"Follow Saint Paul, and put away the things of a child. Take on the things of a man. Being a grownup means you take on the potential for achieving many new things. But maturity also brings with it the potential to commit a new multitude of grownup sins."

He looked angry. Not angry at us, angry at sin. But, since we were in front of him, it might as well have been us.

"The types of sin and the marks they leave behind could be so many and so varied as to make your soul into a crosshatch record of evil-doing, a series of trails cut into the once-pristine ground that would allow future sins of every type to find easier going. Temptations arrive to a growing young man like invading Russian paratroopers in the night. Failure to seek immediate forgiveness presents to them a landscape whose surface has already been thoroughly crisscrossed by predecessor sins on earlier visits. With so many scars, the surface of your soul is turned into a road map."

His voice quieted. "I put it to you, gentlemen, do you want your soul to be a road map for the invaders?"

We sat in silence.

"DO YOU WANT YOUR SOUL TO BE THE ROADMAP OF SIN?"

The outburst sounded like the Reverend Stippil one Sunday night when Quin and I had hid out in a secret space in the bell tower of the Watchful Christian Fellowship Church, waiting for Adam to get free. But unlike the Reverend, whose sudden hollering had unleashed an avalanche of responses—"yea brother, amen"— Kearnsy's roar had the opposite effect. We were Catholic boys, after all, and when a Catholic priest raises his voice, you keep quiet.

Someone breathed. Someone coughed. Someone shifted, causing his chair to yield a tiny frightened squeak.

"Satan's desire is to take over your soul. He sends out his phalanx of temptations with instructions to prepare the way for him to ultimately lay siege to you for all eternity. Satan's grand plan has always been to use God's most favored creation—mankind—against Him."

He paused, drank half of a glass of water—the Shadow had left it on the lectern for him—in one gulp, and wiped his arm across his forehead.

"Just as with childhood, so too are there sins common to manhood, and specifically to young manhood. Who will venture a guess: what sin is most common to a young man?"

Mickey Hollingsworth suggested fighting.

"Very common among young men, yes, but the one I'm asking about is far more hideous."

"Murder?" Cas Kaminski offered. No surprise, not the way Cas was always talking up the latest episode of *Naked City*, which no other parents would allow us to watch.

"Most grievous, all right. But how many murderers do you know?"

Quin shot his hand up. "Pride, anger, greed, envy, lust, gluttony, sloth!"

Kearnsy grinned, and that made everyone laugh. "Good try," he said, "but in your eagerness to answer, you didn't listen to the question." Then to all of us, "Well, we've danced around it, haven't we. It's now time to be men, time to stop lying to ourselves, time to own up."

In silence, he gave us that stare of his: a rooster looking over the chicken-house yard.

We sweated in place. Ears turned red.

"It is the sin of impurity...sexual pleasuring...abuse of the male means endowed by our Heavenly Father for extending his creation; the turning of that wondrous potential into a hideous instrument of gratification."

It was one thing to know it within yourself, or to have joked about it with your friends, but another for Kearnsy to invite it right into our midst; to lift the trap door down into a shadowy dungeon underlying twelve-tear-old lives where built-in, obscene evil had been residing in secret...until now. He had drawn it up, forced it out, and brought it into the sunlight for everybody to stare at.

But the prospect of shame that had reddened our ears and sent rivulets of sweat running, when it actually fell, came with a gentle surprise. It was like finding a better tune on the flip side of anguish, which induced a strange calm. Not one of us had to utter a word on our own, while Kearnsy, using his priestly skills, forced the troll out into daylight where, at no cost to us, we could each silently admit to its existence at last, and agree on its ugliness.

No wonder it took years and years to train a priest. I'd heard my parents say that Uncle Dan's training, starting with his first year of college, had lasted nine years. I imagined him pouring over ancient books with pages that crackled when you turned them; memorizing in Latin the secret rubrics and rituals, potential solutions to every possible human folly; what prayers to pray for what occasion, how to wave that incense thurible just so, and make it "click, click, click," sending up those billows of sweet smoke. How long a wait it must have seemed for the moment when somebody would finally come down the hall, knock on the door and whisper through the crack, "Okay, Daniel Ahern: we're ready for you now." What a day for him.

What a day that same experience must have been for Father Kearns, especially after being a star football player in college, and after fighting in World War II. Forget the tiny mole on his nose. In awe of my pastor, I allowed him a moment to gaze directly into me.

We concluded the session with a series of prayers. When he finally allowed us outside, we burst through the doors. An excursion through the woods had us picking up pieces of forest debris, which Kearnsy inspected for size and burnability. We carried it all back to the barbeque grill, where he chopped the thicker branches. One overhead swing of the ax in his beefy hands was enough to send sections flying. We broke up the lesser twigs by hand. The grill was made from a steel barrel resting on its side on angle-iron legs. It had been cut horizontally in half, the sections hinged together, and each fixed with sliding doors for venting. Welded steel rods formed the grate.

Just a small portion of what we'd gathered proved to be enough to heap up the bottom half with wood on top of a layer of balled newspapers. Once a match was put to it, orange flames licked through the pile, roared and crackled. Tending with a poker, Kearnsy soon tamed the initial inferno down to a heap of shivering white-hot embers into which he placed foil-wrapped sweet potatoes, covered them over, and waited. When they began to hiss and sing to his liking, he swung down the grate and tossed on steaks, positioning and turning them with a long-handled fork. Smoke and sizzle roused our hunger.

Quin poked me, and pointed at the barbeque grill. "You know, my old man made that."

The Shadow stopped behind us to oversee our progress on the basket of corn we'd been assigned to. He said, over Quin's shoulder, "So what."

Quin, face flushed, shifted into double-time, husks and silk flying as he plopped denuded ears into a cauldron of water. It didn't take long for us—mostly Quin—to strip two dozen ears and surprise Kearnsy with need to make a space for it on the grate.

We ate in the retreat house dining room. Our pastor said grace-before-meal at the head of the table, the rest of us six to a side, and the Shadow at the other end. Making swales in mounds of soft butter with hot ears of corn, we nibbled down to bare cobs. More melted butter formed yellow ponds inside potato halves that disappeared, Kearnsy insisting that we eat the skins too. Our steaks we dribbled with Worcestershire and devoured. The meal started out with slurping, smacking, clicks and scrapes of silverware but, as our bellies filled, conversation grew to claim any quiet spaces. When everybody had finished—he made each of us show him a clean plate—we slowly allowed talk to give way to expectation of him invoking a final grace.

"At this retreat house," he intoned, "we have a tradition. A tradition now fallen to you, who are charged with seeing it carried forth."

His eyes made the rounds, forced each of us to acknowledge some new responsibility. Cousineau hadn't told us about this one. "At Sunday dinner, every last one of you, without exception," his fist came down hard on the table, rattling unused silverware, "is required to eat a dish of chocolate ice cream...whether you feel like it or not!"

Quiet collapsed in on itself, displaced by laughter. From the kitchen, our pastor retrieved a huge brown cardboard tub, from which he scooped out and passed around mounds of dessert in bowls.

When everybody was served, the Shadow suddenly stood and raised his glass. "To Father Kearns, for preparing for us such a wonderful meal. Let's all stand and raise our glasses to our pastor and our chef."

Father Kearns shook his head and waved off the toast. The Shadow beamed and smiled with lots of teeth. When a ball is tossed at you unexpectedly, instinct has you reaching out to make the catch, and with sudden scraping of chairs we stood, raised our glasses to Kearnsy and took a swallow. But after you catch the ball, time has a way of pausing enough to allow some thought about what just happened. And it was during just such a pause that I thought about how the Shadow had surprised a dozen of us into doing what he wanted; how he had managed to multiply his personal need by a factor of twelve. In the background of my thoughts lay the still-raw memory of him saying to Quin, "So what."

Everybody sat down with more floor-scraping of chairs... except me. I was thinking too hard to notice that I was still standing. The entire table turned its eyes. Kearnsy stared, tilted his head a little one way and then a little the other. My thoughts came together, released me from stupor, and lit me with realization that all those staring eyes expected me to do something.

I raised my glass. "To Mister Gutierrez. With a torch and a welder he crafted that fine grill out back."

Nothing but silence as time, again, paused, and suggested that it might just leave me there, all by myself. But sudden-ball-toss surprise kicked in once more and, with more scraping of chairs, the retreat group rose as one. Father Kearns raised his glass and boomed, "To Mister Gutierrez!" in the direction of Quin, prompting all of us to a man to drain the last of our lime Kool-Aid.

After grace, we cleaned up under our pastor's direction in a communal washing of plates, glasses, bowls and silverware at the massive stainless kitchen sink; the scrubbing of cauldron, pans and kitchen implements at the spigot out back; and scraping of burnt grease from the grate with balled pieces of aluminum foil. "A good lesson in teamwork," he said.

In the assembly room, we folded and put away the chairs and opened up the cots for our sleeping rolls, and arranged them in rows as instructed by Kearnsy, who set up a cot for himself by the door.

"Gentlemen, when you leave this retreat you will have learned the Kearns methods of personal maintenance. Maintenance applies to both body and soul," he said, and handed out small packets, each containing a tooth brush, tooth paste, soap and a washcloth. "In the infantry, they teach you how to take a bath in your helmet."

We stood in disbelief, motionless. Cousineau hadn't mentioned taking a bath in a helmet.

"But this isn't the Army, so grab your towels and follow me."

We all laughed, and followed him down to the shore of Pond Peggy.

"Last one in is a rotten egg," he said, and stripped, putting his clothes and shoes on the dock. Before anybody had a chance to think about it, we all stripped along with him and followed him into the water. Knee deep, we brushed our teeth first, dipped our faces to rinse, then left our brushes and paste alongside our clothes on the dock. Lathering every surface of that massive beefy body of his, he demonstrated the Kearns technique of using soap and washcloth, then went further into the water to his waist and submerged himself for a rinse. Thirteen boys followed suit, a half circle, in and out of the water like ducklings.

Cousineau had told us, "You boys best not be shy 'cause you'll be bare-assing it, you know."

It didn't seem like much to Quin and me, who had been bare-assing it since we first knew each other. But you could tell a few were surprised, all right, at being naked together. Along the route of Kearnsy's wake, in waist-deep water, the surprise wore off for Tommy Tanager. He suddenly didn't want to be seen naked, and he froze up, tears running down his face. Cas Kaminski had a different problem: he came up out of the water with a strange look in his eye, and a hard-on. He splashed his way over to the dock for his towel. Kearnsey told us to grab our clothes and head back up to the retreat house, and to not be gawking. In a gentle voice, he slowly talked Tommy back to shore.

## CHAPTER 30, THE STRIPPER

A two-mile Monday morning trek took us through the woods to a mission chapel at The Pines, a rich folks' resort on a bluff overlooking the Susquehanna. We attended mass there, celebrated by Father Kearns, the Shadow serving as altar boy. Nobody else was in the chapel. It was Monday, and anybody who was up this early was out on the resort's nine-hole golf course.

By the time we'd made the return trek, we readily wolfed down eggs and bacon and flapjacks with syrup, Kearnsy making up as much as we could eat. When everything was cleaned up, we took down the cots and put back the folding chairs...

Father Kearns looked us over from the lectern. "You boys — you young men — are going to see and hear things here today that you've never seen or heard before. And I must warn you, under pain of mortal sin, you are not to disclose to boys in lower grades what transpires here."

He paused and looked at papers, cleared his throat, looked up and spoke again. "I hesitate to refer to you as young men. Men are strong. Are you strong? Or, are you weak? If you are weak, you will take what you learn here and find it something to make light of, a basis for disrespect, even disrespect for your own mothers. Worse, you will allow knowledge imparted to you here today to lead you into the most despicable kinds of behavior, actions and attitudes and fantasies that you allow straight from Hell; straight from where they are fabricated by Satan himself."

He was quiet. The room was quiet. Sounds of nature did not come through the walls from outside...they seemed to know better.

"ARE YOU JUST A BUNCH OF WEAKLINGS?" he shouted.

Our chairs moved back on their own.

He put his hand to his ear, turned his ear toward us. "No, Father," Our weak voices responded in a jumble of syllables.

He leaned over the lectern toward us, hand still at his ear.

"NO, FATHER," This time a single, clear voice.

He left the lectern and went past us to the back of the room. The Shadow jumped up, turned off the lectern light, throwing us into darkness but for small glows coming around the shades. He pulled a portable screen into place in front of the lectern, and set it up. In the back, Kearnsy removed covers from an ancient phonograph and a film-strip projector.

So that's what Al Cousineau had joked about. "When he starts the sex talk, the first thing he will do is bring out the stripper," he'd said, and then laughed in our faces.

The stripper whined to life. White block letters appeared on the screen, fuzzy at first, but soon brought into focus: THE MIRACLE OF PROCREATION. A scratchy noise came from the phonograph, followed by a deep, familiar voice.

It was the same voice that had narrated a short movie for a special assembly of all the kids at Melody Falls last year. Sheffield Hoy, in his fireman's jacket and Civil Defense hard hat, sweat dripping down his face from so much gear, had spoken about how many times the firehouse siren would blow if the Russians were about to drop an atom bomb on us. In the film, a woman wearing a round, cake-like hat and pearl earrings, said good-bye to her two kids as they boarded the school bus. In the next scene, she had dropped her bag of groceries, cans of corn and tuna rolling around on the sidewalk, as she ran for a shelter marked with yellow triangles. Then her son and daughter and their classmates at school crawled under desks and covered their eyes. The man's voice had been both matter-of-fact and excited.

That identical voice, coming off Kearnsy's record, had the same mixture of matter-of-factness and excitement. It had that familiar instructional tone, belonging to a man to whom other grownups had imparted grave responsibility.

The voice: "Procreation. Sounds like a big word, doesn't it. It comes from Creation, and means the magnificent process by which God's original act of creation remains ongoing in the lives of all his faithful children."

"BEEP."

The white letters slid sideways off the left side of the screen, displaced by a picture that slid on from the right: Adam and Eve, a familiar depiction of our first parents that was near the front of first-communion prayer books. Among the boys, it had soon suffered from wear and dog-eared corners and accumulated smudges. Here they were, in their natural state, prior to committing the Original Sin. Flora from the Garden of Eden modestly positioned itself in the way, and Eve was posed by the artist with one arm across her breasts, just like my mother would do when she first took her clothes off to step into the pond.

"The first humans," the voice reminded us, "loved by God so much that he prepared a special place where they could have dwelt with him in living splendor for all eternity."

"BEEP."

Exit Adam and Eve. Enter Eve alone, arm about to drop from its protective pose as she looked dreamily over her shoulder at the you-know-who snake, whose split tongue hissed temptations at her in the form of S's that float in the air.

"The divine purpose for which God has wrought Eve out of Adam's rib is to provide him with a suitable mate, so he will not be lonely. But, is she content to serve her true purpose? Will she instead choose to listen to the Devil? Become an instrument of evil?"

"BEEP."

Adam back again with Eve in a new illustration, flora still strategically in place except that Eve's breasts were uncovered, out in the open. We'd never seen this one in any prayer book. You'd have to go up into the stacks at the Wyotanda Public Library, in the art section. The snake coiled around Eve's feet. They were under a tree, where she held fruit out to Adam, who had acquired the same dreamy look as his mate.

"Instead of his helpmate, Eve becomes Adam's temptress. Under the Tree of Knowledge of Good and Evil, serpent at her feet, she offers him the forbidden fruit: man tempted by woman, who acts on behalf of the Devil."

"BEEP."

God was angry. He stood, white locks askew, robes disheveled by gestures, one arm waving at the garden, the other extended, finger pointing at the gate and all that lies beyond it. The two sinners, eyes wide, wrapping themselves in skins to cover their shame. They look back at what they have done, and at what they have forsaken for a worldly life that only ends in death.

"Man, once basking in glorious innocence, is now guilty of disobedience before God. He must henceforth earn his way by the sweat of his brow, must now travel the earth in shadow of sin. Woman, too proud to accept her role as his helpmate, has fallen, and must know suffering, must endure the pain of bearing children, not only for herself, but for all the women to come after her until the end of time."

"BEEP."

A woman, naked, sideways, all the flesh from just below the neck down to mid-thigh stripped away to expose fat and muscle and innards that looked like the goulash they serve on Wednesdays for the school hot lunch program; nothing at all like the woman in my father's secret folder.

"You have all heard it, no doubt. Snickers, jokes, disrespectful remarks about a woman's body. Such are the product of minds ready to lean in the direction of evil choices. But a young man who chooses a life of virtue respects women, because he respects her Creator who, to provide her with the means to carry out her worldly destiny, has designed a reproductive mechanism most magnificent."

"BEEP."

A closer view of the same illustration, female apparatus enlarged, a solid line that leads from an arrowhead in a small shadowy hollow out to block letters at the picture's border: WOMB.

"This is where a man's seed finds its intended place. The act of love, if it is God's will, inspires another human soul to come down from Heaven, take up residence where the woman's body prepares it for life on earth."

"BEEP."

The same woman. But now her belly protrudes out and, thanks to the special view of her insides provided by the artist, we see a baby upside down in her belly, eyes closed, arms and legs curled, head against an inner knob that seems to hold everything in place until the big day. Wording at the end of the arrow: FULLY DEVELOPED BABY.

"Woman about to fulfill her divine purpose, about to present to her husband his offspring, about to bring into the world a new soul that will be in need of redemption."

"BEEP."

A photograph of a sleeping baby in a blue hat, wrapped in a blue and white blanket.

"A child with his entire future before him. What will the future bring to this picture of innocence? No one can predict what happiness will come to him, or sadness. With proper upbringing, and especially by the grace of God, he will learn to choose wisely. He will, in the face of evil throughout his life, choose good, and when he recognizes his failure to do so, will seek forgiveness through the Church and the Sanctifying Grace of her Sacraments."

"BEEP."

Two kids, sandy haired, a boy and a girl, walking with their parents, mom in coat and hat with a veil, dad in a suit, the whole family dressed in clothes like you'd see in a ten-year old Sears Catalog, as they headed toward a church. They have just emerged from the blue '51 Ford Custom with whitewalls, parked at the curb.

"To grow in his faith, a boy requires proper guidance from his parents. If it is God's plan for him, he may even be called into the priesthood someday. His younger sister may be called into the sisterhood. Or, they may be called by God into parenthood, where they will have to be made ready for the responsibilities of bringing new souls down from Heaven."

"BEEP."

The photo slid away to blackness.

Kearnsy had a long pole with a brass fitting on the end of it that he used to grab the rings at the ends of the shade cords of the higher windows, so he could release them from their ratchets and let them roll back up. Following behind Kearnsy, the Shadow released the lower shades. The two of them half circled the room until the job was done. The only other sound was the whir of the stripper's cooling fan, whose lamp had been turned off.

So, that was it? When I looked around at the others, I saw eyes blink against the return of light from the windows. Was I the only one wondering, "What about mating?"

When one of Hangy Hobbes' old man's Holsteins was in heat, the others would bump and jostle, snort at her slime trail, climb on her back, as if trying to mount her, female on female, until she would grow big-eyed and bawl, wailing for the bull who was kept in a distant field, her memory flooded out by desire, eager to forgive the stumbling ferocity of their last encounter.

I'd seen the Percheron stallion and mare running together in the pasture. It was a race without rules, made of shoves, kicks and biting of ears;, Beethoven in pursuit of Sweetpea, she teasing him to a frenzy, he on a wide-eyed chase. It had gone on all day in fits and starts. Sometime toward evening, when she finally allowed him to mount her, all the exhaustive doings came to an end in a single brief moment. Then pasture dust began to settle back into the grass, ears ceased their twitching, two horses stood side by side under a mulberry tree, nickering to each other.

Was God really present everywhere? Around the farm, He seemed to want to stay out of the way, careful not to interfere with what wanted to happen. On the farm, no arrow on a film strip pointed out where new life nudged itself into existence.

Looking around me at the others, I could not catch anybody's eye. Nobody wanted to look up, each of the boys being held back by his own thoughts.

## Chapter 31, Impure Thoughts

After lunch, we all pitched in to give the place a thorough cleaning, and then packed up to go. Throughout the afternoon, parents came to pick up their sons. My father, who would not be here until four, would be one of the last, so Quin and I went into the woods for a smoke.

We got down and crawled into a chapel formed by the interlacing of bramble, where we sat on ground softened by layers of old leaves. Quin was fidgety. He was quiet. He lit up a Pall Mall, which we passed back and forth, as we kept an eye toward the retreat house in case somebody came our way. I figured he was just as disgusted with the sex talk as I was.

But that wasn't it.

"A few days ago." he said in a soft voice, "an old army buddy came by to see my dad."

I'd never heard him call him his dad. I'd almost always called my father my father and he'd almost always called his father his old man. Quin's eyes brightened through his glasses when I looked at him.

"He might have a job for him," he said. "A real job, I mean. Welder."

"Your old—I mean, your dad can certainly do that."

"Not just sticking things together, Genie, like he does for farmers around here. I'm talking about real welding, the kind you have to pass a test to do: pressure pipeline welding, all the way across Texas and up to Illinois."

"Texas? Illinois?"

His eyes darkened. "It means I'd have to move."

We were quiet, not able to look at each other. He wiped his nose with the back of his hand, quickly, like it wasn't really necessary.

His eyes lightened again. "But it would be a real job, Genie. None of this handyman stuff."

"No more shoeing my father's horses," I said, "or building barbeques," and we both laughed, and we both wiped our noses quickly.

"But my dad looked kind of serious after the guy left."

"You think he'll take it?"

Quin shrugged, and tears fell down his face. "I figure he's thinking, maybe, that my mother still might come home someday." His voice quivered. He wiped his nose for real with his fingers and wiped them on his dungarees.

I looked away.

"I used to have a simple want," he said, "when I was a little kid."

I looked at him, but he did not look at me as he talked. He told me he wanted things he couldn't have. He wanted a mom, or even just a grandma. He said that whenever he came to my house my Grandma fussed over him. Heat wafted off hot-water radiators in winter. Clothes were folded in my dresser drawers...more clothes than I, or any other one kid, could possibly need. And, at breakfast, I had the choice from a big selection of packaged cereals, or hot oatmeal, and at supper, slices of roast beef with potatoes, and afterward, cake or pie or some kind of fruit, just because my Grandma felt like preparing it. But more recently, he said, his hunger went way past wanting the same things I had.

"I don't want to be a poor kid anymore, the half-breed kid of a Mexican and a Sloot. And I'm tired of wondering why my mother ran off." He drew the back of his hand over his eyes. "I'm tired of being the kid who can't be like you and most everybody else." He teared up again, and his eyes came at me through the wet gleam. "I'm a person, too."

I'd never said any different, so he had no call to be mad at me about it.

He looked long and hard into my face. "Sometimes, I don't know how I'd make it without you, Genie."

His eyes teared again, running down his face, and he looked away without bothering to wipe them away.

My face was hot from the way he was acting. He wasn't a crier, unless he was really hurt, and I'd never seen him so hurt like this: from inside himself, not from outside.

He said through cigarette smoke, "It's no longer just a pup, or a kit, yipping or nipping at me. Lately, Genie, it has turned into a grown animal that comes to me in the night with a serious look in its yellow eye."

"What animal? What are you talking about?" My own voice sounded far away, betraying that I wanted, if I'd had a choice, to be far away from him right now.

The animal would wake up, he told me, just as the lights and noises of the day were dimming. The animal would wake up and hold him back from the edge of sleep. It would pester him, stir inside him, rouse him, hunch its back inside his chest and stomach, and writhe in his groin.

"It takes over my thoughts, Genie. Remember Baggie Hoy said those things about me being a Sloot? That night, when you were probably asleep at your house, I was in my bed at home, thinking about things I'd do to him. I imagined his face turn purple while I strangled him with a wire. As I turned a knife under the middle of his rib cage, I watched his eyes turn hazy...you know, like when my old man is about to slaughter a steer for somebody, and he ball-peens it right behind the ear."

I'd seen that once. My father had hired Quin's old man to slaughter Willys, whom I'd raised from a calf. I'd gotten the name from raised letters in the side of the hood of our old Jeep. "Nothing like grass-fed beef," he'd said, and snapped the hammer into Willys' skull. I'd watched the life go out of his eyes, and then my steer was no longer who he used to be, quickly nothing more than a form trussed up by its hind hooves, gutted, skinned and its backbone sawed down its length clean in half. Quin's old man cut off what used to be his head, and cut out what used to be Willys' tongue. And even his brain. "I'll take it if you don't want it," he'd said to my father, and later my father had told me Bert and Quin would most likely eat Willys' brain for dinner.

Quin looked at me with eyes that asked me to do something for him, but I had no idea what to do. He looked away.

"The hungry animal takes over my dick, too," he said.

We laughed in the direction of each other, and I was glad he finally said something funny. Now we were back on ground we could share. It felt okay again to be beside him in the underbrush.

I joined the conversation. "My old man warned me about that. My dick would pretend to be a separate creature, and try to take me over. I don't think he expected that I already knew. Our parents always think we're kind of stupid."

He laughed and was quiet again, looking away.

I told him, "That happens to everybody, Quin. My old man didn't know that I wake up at night with a surprise hard-on. I can't believe he didn't think I already knew all about that, as if I'd never had one."

Quin smiled. "Well, I know that." He reached out and mussed my hair. "And I didn't need my old man to tell me."

It felt good to have Quin back to himself, not saying things that made my face hot.

"In their day, people didn't have hard-ons much," he said. "I figure, maybe not until they were older, eighteen or twenty. In those olden days, they had a bad enough time just keeping shoes without holes and finding enough to eat, with the Great Depression going on...and with my old man being Mexican. You know how men from those times always talk about the

Depression, how bad it was back then. I figure talking about hard-ons is more recent, more modern…like Polio vaccine."

I nodded, and wondered how Quin always knew so much more than I did. I wished I knew where he got his information, so I could get it first once in a while, and be out front of him on something. I was better than him at figuring, but he was always first at knowing real things.

Quin suddenly decided, "That's why Kearnsy has this retreat once a year. Hard-ons used to be restricted to married men. Hard-ons for kids, well, that's completely new, just like Communist spies living right in the middle of us is something new. The grownups caught onto us having hard-ons, so now they have to warn a new batch of kids every year."

"But, why do they act like it's such a big secret?" I said. "They just hint about it, and then send us on a retreat to have Father Kearns fill in some of the details. They don't do that when it comes to warning us about the Communists."

"Because of girls," Quin explained, "they have to be extra careful. They can't exactly put it in newsreels, the way they do about the Communists, because girls are delicate and aren't supposed to know. They have to hide that kind of stuff from girls."

I tried to claim credit for some of Quin's wisdom: "That would be my guess, too. The grownups have to be careful giving out information: a little from my grandma, a little more from the old man, and then a little more from Kearnsy. They warn us boys just in case we would be too surprised when it happens."

"Your grandma? She told you about it?" Quin suddenly laughed.

I nodded, pretending I hadn't heard how stupid I sounded.

"How could she know anything?" he said. "She's a woman, and an old one at that. Cripe'n-itey, Genie, she was born in the last century. And she's not even American."

"She is too American!"

"Well, I didn't mean that. I meant, not originally."

Did he think Marja shouldn't know things just because she was born in the 1800s, or was not an original American? The way I figured it, people in Finland knew just as much as people in America. That's how Marja had learned about America in the first place, and decided to come over here.

Quin studied me, looking for something. I could feel it on my face. "I can tell you things, Genie. You keep secrets. And you can tell me things too…if you want to."

He mussed my hair again. "We have a secret club, just you and me, and the first secret of the club is: we don't rat each other out."

Our eyes connected for a moment.

My voice wavered from too much smoke. "Well, we *are* best friends, Quin."

He took the butt, dragged on it, and spoke through the smoke smoothly. "Most kids think feelings are their own private secret."

"Exactly," I said, as if he had just said some wisdom I'd already known about.

"We can always keep secrets between us," he said, looking into me.

I nodded. My face grew hot, and I looked away. I'd felt hunger inside, too. But I'd never been inclined to actually say so. The animal inside him was much more eager to find its way out than the one inside me.

He said, "That night we slept on your porch, after we watched that political convention in California on your grandma's TV."

Not much of a memory for me: Quin had never tired of the speeches and floor demonstrations and favorite-son signs bouncing up and down. I'd fallen asleep on the living room floor. He'd stayed up and watched, fascinated. And throughout the next day, he had repeated political words and phrases he'd heard, and in succeeding days, drove me crazy trying to mimic the speeches, and trying to sound like Kennedy.

"Afterwards, we slept in the hammock on the porch," he said.

Happy the boredom was finally over, I'd groggily moved from the living room to the porch. It had been the only thing four nights in a row on either TV channel, Channel 22, the snowy one from Scranton, or Channel 12, the clear one from Binghamton.

"That night," he said. "That night, while we were in the hammock, the animal..." He swallowed. "It was alive." His voice was uneven. "I wanted to go to sleep, but I also wanted to...I mean, the animal wanted me to...hold onto you, hold onto you real tight."

My face grew hot. My ears burned. I didn't look at him. I could feel his eyes on my face, wanting me to look. But I couldn't.

"It surprised me, Genie." His voice cracked.

I finally looked at him. I expected to see the yellow eyes of the animal, but only his brown eyes looked back, reddened, with unashamed tears gushing out of them onto his face.

I looked away. He looked away. We were quiet for a long time, passing the butt back and forth as it burned down. Quin crushed it out in damp earth under the leaves. He sniffled, and wiped a forearm across his snotty nose. My face and ears were hot...burning hot.

"It scared me," he said. "I mean, what does that make me?" And he suddenly laughed as he cried, which pumped out more tears.

I laughed along with him. It felt so much better for us to be laughing at each other.

He said, "Remember Agnes May played baseball with us...her dress swishing around her legs? And, that time Hangy's older sister Lucinda came over to fetch her brother home for milking time? Lucinda had that yellow top on, and she and Agnes May in that swishing dress talked women talk while they waited for Hangy to get going. Their eyes flashed at each other, and they fingered their hair while they talked. That's when I realized how hungry the animal inside me really is."

"Lucinda," I laughed, "in that yellow top, leaning back on the fender of the Chevy—yellow top falling off one shoulder: now, that was a real boner maker."

We both laughed again, and my ears started to cool.

He said, "and Agnes May," and wagged his head.

"But—Cripe'n-itey, Quin—Lucinda *and* Agnes May?"

"That's what I mean: even the kid-brat of Melody Falls. The animal only knows that it's hungry."

He laughed again, just with his mouth. His eyes searched my face.

"But, even Agnes May?" I said.

"That's what I mean, Genie. The animal gets so hungry."

"But, Agnes May?" I said again. "The kid-brat?""

"When she decided to play baseball with us, well, that night, the animal was restless. That night while I was trying to sleep, Genie, Agnes May's dress kept swishing all around my face."

A shadow came over him. "But Kearnsy's ruined it. Why does he have to go and ruin it? With all his talk about impurity, he's ruined it."

"Impurity."

"Impure thoughts." He shoved my shoulder, as if to awaken me. "Mortal sin, Genie...mortal sin! I'm going to hell for sure. How am I not going to have impure thoughts with Agnes May's dress swishing all around my face when I'm trying to sleep, thinking about her legs? How am I not going to hell?"

"Cripe'n-itey, Quin. The kid-brat's dress swishing around your face?"

"Kearnsy ruined it for sure. Impure thoughts...mortal sin! Well, you're so smart about everything, Genie. So, you tell me.

Tonight, what if I die right after the hungry animal visits, before I get a chance to go to Confession?"

I shrugged. "It's something you could ask Kearnsy about this afternoon...you know, before we leave."

"Ask him about it? In front of whoever is still here?"

"Not everybody...just the Shadow," I laughed. "Kearnsy might need some assistance with a problem this big."

Quin punched my shoulder. "It isn't funny. We're talking about Hell here, dipshit."

No, it wasn't funny. But it felt good to turn it into something funny, even for just a moment.

Quin wiped residual snot from his face. "Do you remember anything from catechism that covers it? I've tried, but I just can't think of anything."

I thought about it. "Act of Contrition, maybe?"

Quin thought about it too. His eyes suddenly lit. "That's it!" He punched my arm hard. "Genie, that's it! Recite the Act of Contrition. Once you do that, it holds a place for you in case you die before you go to Confession...don't you remember?"

"That's right," I said. "We had the answer all along...good ole Kearnsy's catechism."

He punched my arm again, even harder, then mussed my hair, a wide grin taking over his face. "You did it again, Genie. You came through for me." His eyes glistened.

I rubbed my shoulder.

"Genie," Quin said, "do you have impure thoughts? About the kid-brat, I mean."

I shrugged.

## CHAPTER 32, EVER AGAIN

On Saturday, Old Man Hobbes did not show up for dinner. Due to all the work that had to be done each day between sunup and sundown, breakfast and supper could be eaten on the run. But dinner, always precisely at twelve o'clock, was the big meal of the day, the one nobody ever missed, especially in the busy summer. The family would all wash up and sit down together at the dining room table to silverware and china, tall glasses of lemonade, serving dishes steaming with meat and potatoes, at least two kinds of vegetables from the garden, and a pot of coffee.

So, when the old man didn't come in from the field where he'd spent the morning cultivating corn, Crystal sent Hangy down there to fetch him. "Ask him if he needs to hear out of both sides of his head to notice the noon siren blaring away from the firehouse."

Hangy went out the door without answering. Why make light of the old man being deaf on one side?

Up at the top of the field, between the first dozen rows, weeds had been neatly upturned. But the next pass had gone only a third of the way before something didn't look right. A trail of toppled corn drew a map telling where the Allis-Chalmers tractor, cultivators mounted front and back, had veered off course, swinging in a wide arc without regard to contour. Gravity had taken over the steering, headed it downhill, cross-wise against the rows all the way to the bottom of the field. He spotted the old Allis at a nose-down stop in the ditch, and hurried down there. Engine still droning at the proper throttle setting for cultivating corn, still in gear, ribbed rear tires methodically tossed out bits of soil from the two deep trenches they had already scalloped into the earth. Climbing onto the draw bar, he reached from behind around his father and shut off the ignition switch. Sudden quiet was pierced by a hiss from the radiator.

As soon as Crystal called to tell us about it, we went right over to their place. My mother sat with Crystal at the kitchen table. Twins Elsie and Elise, wide-eyed, hung onto their mother, clutching the material of her house dress.

My ears now burned at the memory: one afternoon a few months ago, Crystal had fed me fig bars and a glass of lemonade, and then, right before my eyes, the person who had always been just Hangy's step-mother turned into someone in whose wonderful female arms I suddenly wanted to be. And, that night, in the tumble of my mind toward sleep, she had clung to me, holding me in womanly round softness.

My imagination had gathered her beauty and fashioned it for myself, like stealing the plume from a magnificent bird to make an adornment. Crystal, the woman whose face had brightened that day, her cheek wicking light from the window as fingers swiftly tied a tiny shoe, now sat at her kitchen table, staring at my mother, not looking, just peering through her, a stunned look on her face.

"He still had one good ear. Didn't he hear the noon siren?" and then tears.

My mother said she was sorry, and held her hand and rubbed her forearm.

My father and I stood by, two males not knowing what to do with our hands, until we finally left for other parts of the house. He found a tiny desk in the parlor that his long legs barely fit under, and soon started going through the old man's papers in an effort to help arrange things.

After searching through the house for Hangy, I gave up, figuring he must have gone outside, that he wanted to be by himself. His older sister, Lucinda, sat out on the front porch, index finger planted against her cheek, chin held up by her thumb, three fingers wrapped in a half-circle over her mouth. The swing seat, suspended by chains from the porch ceiling, remained perfectly still.

I stepped out to say, "I'm sorry," the same way I'd heard my mother say over and over to Crystal, but Lucinda didn't hear me. Silence seemed to have been tossed over her like a blanket. A wisp of blond hair that had escaped the wide barrette holding every other hair in place formed itself into a lone, upside-down question mark by her ear. Her chest slowly rose and fell. Pale blue eyes were frozen into the distance.

The twins were waiting for me when I stepped back in, big eyes asking me to read the *Clarion* to them. Putting one on each knee, my arms around their small, fleshy shoulders, I opened the newspaper to an article about a man whose hunting cabin on Craddock Creek had teetered part-way down an embankment, caused by the digging activity of woodchucks. They looked at me with big, round eyes. I finished the article and moved on to *Beetle Bailey*, then *Curly Kayo*. By the first frame of *Steve Canyon*, the twins started to squirm. I let them down, and they went to their mother in the kitchen.

My father had paused in his work at the desk to quietly listen to my reading. When the girls left, he said just above a whisper, "It's going to be tough for them...tough for all of them." And then he went back to his task. "Typical of old Harold. So meticulous about crop rotation schedules, equipment maintenance, milk production, vaccinations, breeding cycles on the cows...all in perfect order," he said, closing and tapping the front cover of a soiled, dog-eared, spiral notebook. "Last entry was just this morning." He placed it in a side drawer. From the desktop, he lifted a tangled mound of papers. "Personal business? A total mess," he said, and let it plop back down.

I went outside to escape the thick hush that filled the house, stepping past Lucinda without looking at her, down onto the gravel walk. In the distance, the Wilmot County Coroner's panel truck groaned, crawled up from the field onto the road, Sheffield Hoy at the wheel, a helper in the passenger seat. They drove slowly away, heading down to Melody Falls, where he had an examining table in his undertaker facility.

Searching the farm buildings, I found Hangy in the milk house. He sat on a three-legged stool, smoking a Pall Mall. He didn't look up when I came in. I pulled out another stool and sat down beside him. He'd already crushed out a number of butts on the floor. Without looking, he passed the cigarette to me. We sat in clouds of smoke, passing it back and forth between us.

"I should have wondered about it while I was painting the corn crib, this morning," he said. "It didn't sound right."

"What didn't?"

"Him cultivating: it should have changed—you know?— because the field changes as you move along, making the tractor work harder in one place than another. The last couple of hours, the sound never changed. I just didn't think hard enough to wonder about it."

When the cigarette was down to almost nothing, he tossed it on the floor with the others and crushed it with his heel.

Finally he looked at me. "You think you could handle the Farmall M, Eugene?"

"I've never driven a tractor by myself."

"You've driven your old man's Jeep, though. So you know how to clutch."

"Yes."

"Not that different, driving a tractor. No gas pedal. A throttle, two brake pedals, lots more gears. I'll show you. You'll do fine."

"What are we going to do?"

He stood up, hooking thumbs in back pockets just like the old man would have done. "Gonna have to pull Old Allis out of the ditch. There's no way she'll ever back her own way out of there, not after she dug herself in, and her wearing all those cultivators to get hung up."

He slid the crushed butts out the door with his foot. "Shouldn't be smoking in here," he decided, and looked at me. "I'm not going to allow it in here ever again."

## CHAPTER 33, EVE WAS TO BLAME

I threw the last shovelful of dirt and climbed out of the trench, pleased with how well I had stuck to this project each day, sweat dripping off my hands and every other part of me as I cussed shards of gray shale packed so tightly with stubborn earth. I had already completed three-quarters of the distance from the pump house to the barn. I was pleased with myself, a pleasure that quivered in my chest and shoulders and arms and hands.

Tonight after supper, like we'd been doing every night, my father and I would ride down here in the old flat-fender Jeep, two large pipe wrenches and a length of chain in the back. He would stand over the excavation and inspect my work, and would say something like, "We gotta keep the bottom all the same pitch," talking to me like I was a grown man, standing there with him.

Together we would connect two ten foot lengths. Then, it would be my job to feed electrical conductors into one end as he pulled them through. When that was finished, after lowering it into the trench, I would hold the far end of the twenty foot assembly in a chain sling and follow his instructions to raise, or lower, or swing to one side or the other, as he hand twisted it into place, threads oozing pipe dope. Once it was started, I'd slide out the chain. Each of us would man one of the pipe wrenches, and turn them against each other until he said, "Uh!," a sound that would come from deep inside him.

That had become our evening routine. This morning, as I stooped to gather pick and shovel to put them away, my having finished the day's work opened a space inside of me, a smoothed-out recess where calm quiet resided, and awaited that moment after supper. I'd come to look forward to that "Uh!" at the end of each day.

I leaned the tools inside the pump house and went around to the back. Agnes May, as she had been doing every day now, sat against the structure, basket beside her. Out from under burning sun, I took my shirt off to the cool air of the shade and sat down with her. I shared my water, and she gave me half of her biscuit.

I pretended to lose my balance and nudged her with my shoulder. "Sorry."

She laughed. "That was not an accident. My mother did warn me, you know: watch out for boys."

"Watch out for boys?"

"Because boys get funny ideas."

"They do?"

"That's what she says. Do you, Eugene? Get funny ideas?"

I was quiet for a while. "I guess I don't know."

"What kind of an answer is that?"

"I guess I don't know," I said again, and touched my forehead to hers, which made her eyes cross for the last inch or so.

She pulled away. "My mother has been giving me lots of warnings lately."

"About what?"

She thought a moment, furrowing her brow. "Every woman since Eve has had to be very careful. Do you think that's true, Eugene?"

She looked into me with eyes that expected an answer.

I said, "I've heard that too," and then I added, "somewhere," sounding like a man of experience.

She continued to look into me for another moment, then turned away, and curled her lip.

From her basket she pulled out a green booklet. I had seen it before. It was the one that Miss Hendershott had given to both Agnes May and me to work on during arithmetic period; something to keep us busy, to discourage Agnes May from incessantly raising her hand to ask hard questions, and me from disturbing my neighbors with idle misbehavior.

Block letters proclaimed, *SOLVING FOR X,* by Theodore H. Ulbricht, PhD, University of Akron. For the last four weeks of the school year, Agnes May and I, having gotten too far ahead, had been expected to sit quietly and solve for x under Professor Ulbricht's tutelage while Miss Hendershott continued to explain multiplication of fractions and long division to everybody else.

And it had worked. The professor's word problems had doused any need I might have felt for causing mischief. I was too occupied with trying to uncover the secret values of x. As I had progressed through the book, the situations got more complicated, but if I followed the examples, x didn't have a chance. Agnes May sat two seats up and one row over from me, where I could see pink tongue curling out of the corner of her mouth, a sure sign that she was determined to beat me at this game.

On Tuesday of the last week of school—it was the last day of regular lessons before final exams—I had noticed that the pink tongue was not out. Instead, her whole face had pinked up, judging by the side of her cheek visible from where I sat. And then I heard a sniffle, and soon after that, blubbering.

Miss Hendershott had seen it too and, without missing a beat in her review of normal-kid arithmetic for tomorrow's exam, had slid down the aisle and took away our special workbooks, leaving Agnes May with her head down as she tried not to cry into her forearm, and me with pencil poised above the space where the very last x had been suddenly swiped out of existence before it could be solved for.

"You've both done exceedingly well," our teacher had interrupted her lesson just long enough to say, as she dropped the two workbooks into her desk drawer for the last time.

And now? It had reappeared, here in my father's pasture behind the pump house. But only Agnes May's workbook. What had happened to mine?

Agnes May saw me looking at her, and said quietly, "Miss Hendershott said I could finish it over the summer."

I moved away, and lay down in the grass.

"You must have finished yours," she said.

"No. I was still on the last problem. She should have given mine back too, so I could have finished it, like she did you."

Agnes May opened the book. "But I was way behind," she confessed. "I didn't do any of the problems in the final lesson. I just couldn't make any sense of them."

I lay on my back, hands behind my head. I didn't have to look directly at her to see her eyes dart back and forth on the page, her lips contort into grimaces that displayed her mind at work on the problems.

"Eugene, how do you know this stuff?"

"I don't know. That's just the way it is. It's like Deb Cook being able to play the piano."

Agnes May stuck out her tongue. She hated Deb Cook.

I said, "Deb probably wonders why the rest of us can't play—who is that guy she always plays?—Chopin, in front of the whole school."

Agnes May stuck out her tongue again, and then came and stretched out in the grass beside me, book between us. She turned on her side and looked at me with her eyebrows drawn.

"Why don't I have anything like that?" she said. "Everybody's supposed to have something. Aren't they?" She looked at me for an answer.

"You're very exact, Agnes May. You raise your hand more than anybody else I know. When the teacher tells us about something, you're not satisfied. You make her give out details."

I didn't mention that she had ended up with a higher overall average than I did, which was special enough, although that was helped by a 99 in Conduct to my 76. Was Conduct a real subject?

Her jaw relaxed. "Would you help me with it, Eugene...the last lesson?"

So, here she was, the kid-brat herself, asking me for help.

"The last lesson is just solving for what x is greater than or less than instead of solving for an actual value."

"But that makes no sense!" she exclaimed. "How can it be called solving for x, if you don't ever find out what x is?" Tears came to her eyes, angry tears, not the kind that run down.

"It's the same thing as solving for x, Agnes May. Only you find out what x can't be on the one hand and what its possibilities are on the other."

She stared at me for a long time, creek-pebble eyes unblinking. "I don't want your help."

"But I don't mind—"

"No. I'll do it by myself!"

"Why does it matter anymore? The year is long over, and the grades have been in for two months now." I didn't mention I had gotten a 97 in Arithmetic to her 93.

"It still matters to me!"

"Well, stenographers don't ever have to solve for x anyway."

"I'm not going to be a stenographer," she said matter-of-factly.

"Since when?"

"Since my mother has been buying eggs from that lady who sets up a table behind the courthouse on Fridays. She knows all about chicken breeds."

"That old egg lady? Why does she care if you study stenography? But, then, it does look a lot like chicken scratch."

Agnes May looked up at the sky until I stopped grinning at myself.

"While she and my mother jabber about things, I go inside the back door. I'd never been there before. So beautiful. So...magnificent! Your father must be happy to spend so much time in the courthouse, all that woodwork, all those pillars and arches, all the paintings on the ceiling. But the Indians should have more clothes on."

"Plenty of stenographers work in there," I reminded her.

"Like I said—weren't you listening?—I'm not going to be a stenographer after all."

"There is one lady lawyer, Mrs. Bowman. She does title searches. Maybe when she dies off, you could take her place."

"Oh, I'd never be a lawyer!" Her lip curled.

"So, what are you talking about, Agnes May? What do you want to be? A chicken-breeder lady, selling eggs?"

She hesitated before looking at me. "Architect," she said just above a whisper, "designing buildings," and looked away.

We were both quiet. I looked up at the sky and could feel Agnes May, on her side, her eyes still on me.

I slid sideways and nudged her with my elbow, pretending it was by accident. I moved a little away from her. Maybe she would nudge me back.

"I haven't told my parents," she said. "I'm a little afraid to. They won't look kindly on a girl wanting to do a man's job. Eugene, did you know that it was the first woman who tempted the first man six thousand years ago? But I'm not inclined to believe that I am wicked underneath just because of something Eve did."

Another quiet grew between us, and within it I continued to hear her words, her tone, and the way her teeth and tongue made sounds, consonants more explicit than most people's. Agnes May was ever so precise in her speech.

She poked me in the side. "Well, Eugene, what do you say? Did you miss the most important part of what I said? I said, Eve was to blame."

I shrugged, and she touched the side of my chin, coaxed me to turn my head toward her. Her eyes moved back and forth as they searched mine. Her breath tickled my face, and I knew she wanted me to answer.

"Women can be very tempting," I pronounced. It sounded to me like the answer.

Her eyes abruptly stopped their search. She thought about what I said for just a moment, then pushed my chin away.

"Not all, of course," I softened. "But some."

She pulled my face back toward her. "Such as...such as, who? Name one. Who do you know like that?"

"Not exactly anybody I know well. But I mean you see it in women, in the way they act, the way they look. They give off a feeling in the air that makes a man feel...things."

Agnes May—more gently this time—put my chin back to where my face was straight up again. She shifted onto her back with hands behind her head and stared up at the sky. My pronouncements slowly melted into the natural whispers and twitters of the pasture.

She asked quietly, "Am I like that, Eugene?"

"Like what?"

"Giving off something in the air—you know—that would make a man feel things?"

"Of course not, Agnes May. You're not like that at all. I wasn't talking about you. Is that what you thought? Cripe'n-itey, Agnes May."

## Chapter 34, A Slice of Moon

The day I finished the project, my father looked at me across the table after supper. "What do you say we finally get 'er all buttoned up?"

Once again he had borrowed the Jeep panel wagon from our mailman, Mister Pollard. It was parked in the yard, odd configurations and lengths of new pipe from Van Shoor Hardware protruding from the open tailgate.

Shutting off the power at the fuse box in the barn, we rode down the hill, drained the system and dismantled the last of the old pipe at that end. One connection stubbornly fought us. Adding extensions to the handles of our wrenches, we gained some leverage to break free fittings that had rust-welded themselves solid. We turned the tools against each other, he much stronger than I, but my wrench with a longer extension, which pretty much evened things out. Sweat soon ran down both our faces as we applied increasing force with each try.

Flushed with effort, he huffed, "Might have to put a torch to the bastard." But an instant later the connection squeaked and, with a raspy sigh, the old threads just gave up. My father saying "Uh," grimy pieces clanked onto the floor of the pump house. With me applying dope to the new threads, he fit up the new line to the tank, and the two of us together finished it off with wrenches and male grunts.

Up at the other end of the line in the barn, each of our roles in the process already once-learned, we dismantled old, assembled new, and carried it out in half the time, as we wiped our faces on shirt sleeves. He made the final wire connections in the fuse box, threw the switch, and from down in the pasture the pump hummed up through the pipe, soon followed by hiss and gurgle of the system filling. A couple of burps, and water splashed into the horse trough. We sat down on the manger, then, two tired and sweaty farm boys side by side, my father and I. We looked at each other, and shared a grin. Before long the trough was full, and a float-activation switch automatically shut the system down.

Into the quiet he said, "You know, I've wanted to get this new line done for a year now."

It had been that long since he and Quin's old man had replaced the clanging push-rod pump with a smooth-running submersible. Last summer, they had done that part of the job in a single day.

"Dad, why didn't you just hire Bert to finish it up? He would have done it a lot faster than me."

"No doubt."

"You wanted me to do it?"

Leaning back against the stable wall, he said, "I could have had Bert do it. Now, that is one capable man for just about anything you've a mind to hire him to do."

I nodded. "Remember how he overhauled the engine on Vern Rollheis' Oliver 66?"

My father chuckled. "Poured a little gas down the carbure-tor, hit the starter button, and in two or three cranks that in-line six fired right up. Vern mentioned it just the other day: that tractor's been running smooth as a sewing machine ever since."

So, if he *had* hired Quin's old man, the project would have been done much better, and certainly much sooner. And I could have spent every morning playing ball at the Fellowship Field instead of over here in the pasture, swinging a pick, shoveling dirt, and pulling out the rocks. But, then I would have missed out on having time with Agnes May. Would have missed out on having her always nearby, sitting against the pump house in the shade with her books; on the way she would steal glances at me when she thought I didn't know, and then, when I tried to catch her eye, she would suddenly think of something to say.

"Why didn't you just hire Bert to do it?"

"Don't you remember, Eugene? We discussed it that evening in my office: this was your project."

I nodded. I did remember. But I wanted to hear it again. I wanted another surge of that moment in his office when my father had invited me into his world of tools and know-how and just plain taking care of important things on the farm. But, also, I could not forget that he had told me about it right after discovering that my friends and I had vandalized the township's Galion road grader; to think about that now made my ears burn.

Leaning forward, he pulled his wallet, opened it and fin-gered something out. "You did a hell of a job, son. Put this away for yourself."

It smelled new. Andrew Jackson…twenty dollars! No kid I knew would have expected to be paid for doing work on his own farm. I laughed, "I didn't know I would get paid!"

"I didn't either," he grinned. "Just put it away. It's a lot less than I'd have paid Bert."

I smelled the twenty once more and tucked it into my sock.

"Eugene, you know what I am most proud of? No Quin. No Adam. No Harold Hobbes in on this one. It was all you."

My throat clamped, kept me from speaking. Yep...I had done this all by myself. Oh, Agnes May had kept me company much of the time, all right, but that was something...well, something not the same as if my real friends had been in on it. Besides, I would not have wanted my father to know about Agnes May. We sat there in quiet for a while and, like two grownup men would do, looked at everything but each other.

He said. "You're going to keep the money folded in your sock?"

"Just for now."

"Well, don't forget about it. You wouldn't want it to end up in Grandma's washing machine."

"No, I won't. I'll find a safe place...until the fair."

We got up, gathered our tools into the back of the panel wagon and rode around the side of the barn, through the gate to the garage. While I put things away, he tied the old fittings together with twine so they wouldn't bang around in the back of Mister Pollard's new Jeep, and then wiped around them with a rag. Tomorrow, before he returned the vehicle, he would drop off the scrap at Rooney's junk yard.

Closing up the panel wagon, we headed for the house. On the front porch he sat in the bench swing and tapped the seat beside him, inviting me to sit. "Let's cool off a bit." Whenever I had sat here before, his leaning back had not allowed me to plant my feet firmly on the floor. But now we nudged the swing back and forth together, and within the gentle motion of it I realized that I must have grown a bit this summer. To the west, twilight poured through the cleft in Belknap Ridge, illuminating a blue haze that had settled over the valley between us and the next rise, a few miles off.

His face broke into a grin. "Did I ever tell you? I had to miss the fair one summer. I was about your age." Grin softened into momentary quiet as his eyes looked out at the haze. "I had this over-under, a twenty-two over a four-ten shotgun. I borrowed—I took—a few muskmelons from your grandmother's garden and used them for target practice." His pleasure slowly melted away. "I thought it would be funny." Eyes came back from his boyhood and rested on me. "It turned out to not be funny at all. Well, I had it coming...the punishment, I mean. No fair for me that year." He wagged his head, and then enjoyed a one-syllable laugh at himself.

"Baggie Hoy has an over-under," I said.

"Could be the same one. I sold mine to him." His voice dropped as he talked to the porch floor as much as to me. "Your grandfather made me sell it. I had to give the money to Marja for what I'd done to her melons."

He looked out at the distant horizon, and found his voice again. "That twenty I gave you ought to buy you some fun at the fair, all right."

I nodded.

He said, "You'll be spending some of it on Quin, I suppose."

"Sure. Quin's my best friend."

"Yes, I know he is." He was quiet for a while. "But don't forget to think about yourself now and then, Eugene."

"I do think about myself, Dad. Twenty is more than enough for two of us at the fair."

"Oh, I'm not meaning just at the fair. I'm talking about long term."

I didn't answer. What was he getting at?

He said, "Quin's a good boy. Bert does a fine job raising him, considering. And we've all tried to help out." He turned to me. "I mean, haven't we always included Quin? Like one of our own family." He turned away. "Now, don't get me wrong..." When a grownup said that, you know something's coming. And it was. "I just think it's time for you to move on," he said. "Nothing wrong with a few farts and giggles with your friends. At a certain point, you have to look a bit beyond that."

I was quiet: I knew there had to be more.

"There's nothing wrong with public school," he said. "A studious young man can do fine there. But you are always surrounded by people who—let's just say—generally have somewhat lower goals." He stopped the swing and turned toward me. "Your mother and I have been talking it over. You're about to start seventh grade. It marks a step into your future, and a chance at opportunity; a perfect time to move on to Saint Agatha."

I looked at him. I had that feeling you get sometimes in the back seat of a car when it takes a dip in the road too fast. "Will Quin be going there too?"

He looked away. After a while he said, "Well, I don't see how."

He started the swing again...by himself. It went catawampus at first, until I remembered I was now tall enough to follow along. We sat together in the soft motion of the swing while darkness settled. A slice of moon, and Venus bright enough to be seen through summer evening haze, appeared in the cleft. Overhead, stars waited a long while for the twilight to steal away before taking up the sky. We watched Venus set, and then the slice of the moon followed. We sat in quiet and let the dark of night come on, let it have its way, fill itself up with tree-toad peeps and cricket rhythm.

Through the living room window screen we heard a click, and a blue light flickered out onto the porch as my mother turned on the Channel 12 late news from Binghamton... "but first, a word from the Genesee Brewing Company."

She called, "It's about to start, Owen."

They seldom missed watching the news together.

We got up from the swing to go inside.

"But, Dad," I said. "Quin is my friend."

"I know he is, Eugene. I know he is."

# PART THREE:

# TWELVE AND THREE-QUARTERS

## Chapter 35, Peep Hole

"Gonna let you in on something." Baggie Hoy clucked his tongue. He pulled his gun belt higher on his hips, touching fingertips to the worn grip of the Colt .38 Special that the Sheriff's Department had issued to him as an event-volunteer deputy.

I'd found him standing there when I came out of the fair's equine barn, having helped my father stable our Percherons among the other draft horses. Baggie had been waiting for me in the shade of the building, out of the mid-morning sun. With a jerk of his beefy head he motioned me to go along.

We walked side by side around the barn into weeds between buildings. When we reached the stony hard-pack of the service alley at the rear, he looked around us, searching, and then we moved along to the next building, which housed shower facilities for exhibitors and people working the fair.

Baggie slowed, and I almost bumped into him.

"What are we doing?" I asked.

He didn't answer. He looked up and down the alley. The fair would not officially open until tomorrow, so few people were around this part of the grounds.

With a sudden, tight grip on my arm, I was tugged off the hard-pack surface into elderberry overgrowth that covered the old bricks of the shower facility's back wall. We were quickly covered in shadows. He clenched my arm and peered through the elderberry out into the open daylight.

"Hey. What are we doing?" I was against the wall, shoulder blade reading the roughness of bricks, grown man's massive hand gripping my elbow.

He squeezed himself into a space between the elderberry and the wall, tight against me, continued to search, his round head on fleshy neck making half-turns in either direction, eyes doing a sweep. Heat wafted from his body. He smelled of sweat.

My balls drew up. *Go for his eyes:* advice I'd once heard my father give to my mother if she were ever to get into a situation. My hands ready to form into claws.

"Okay," Baggie said. "We're clear."

He let go of me and jingled a wad of keys. I started breathing. He popped a dirt-black padlock off a rectangle of plywood, and the rectangle gave way into darkness, rusty hasp flapping from its edge.

"We're in." His voice breathy, smelled like bratwurst. "You're the only one on the face of the earth 'cept me who knows about this."

"What are we doing in here?"

A crooked grin crept to his face. He pushed me aside. The bottom of the warped door rasped against the dirt floor as he forced it back into its frame, closing off daylight. Then, I lost him to musty blackness. My stomach quivered. I tightened my claw-hands. Whatever else happened, I'd make sure he lost an eye. How would he explain that?

"Rear of the old administration building," he whispered. "The utility room. Nobody's been in here—'cept me, of course, and now you—since we had them low-lifes from the jail fix the place into shower rooms."

I located him by voice. He moved away as he talked in a hushed tone. "Back in '56, the 4H Committee asked the Sheriff to appoint yours truly as the supervising guard." He clucked his tongue.

I could see his movements against a pale backdrop. He slid away from me. I turned to get out of there, to where I remembered the door to be. But in that direction, I saw only blackness.

"Come on," he hoarsed at me, farther away still.

As my eyes adjusted, pale light beyond him revealed the brim of his deputy hat, the bowling-ball roundness of his shoulders. Now that he'd stopped gripping my arm, and no longer pushed me, my quivering let up. As I moved in his direction, slow progress taught me the way through a narrow, dirt-floor area between outer brick wall and interior structure. I could feel plumbing and wiring attached to studs, and the backside of lath which had dribbles of hardened plaster in the gaps.

"Shhh," as he moved closer to the source of light, which softly illuminated his face. He bent down to put his eye up to a hole in the backside of the plaster, almost closing it off. "We're okay," he said aloud, voice suddenly booming off the surfaces. "It's not likely anybody would be around this time of day, but you never know till you look. Sometimes, one of them will come in at an odd hour."

He backed away from the hole and grabbed my arm again. "Have a look-see."

Pale light came from the hole. Looking through, I saw a wall on the opposite side of a room lined with tan-colored tiles.

"Don't be shy." He pushed me closer to the hole, his breath flitting on my neck.

Up close, the view widened out. Across the room, four shower heads with brass faucet handles and shiny soap dishes were mounted on the wall. It was the ladies shower room, mirror image of the gents. I was looking through a hole in the near wall under the last shower head on this side. But, unlike the gents, where all eight showers were in the open, one of them here was enclosed, a stall for women who wanted more privacy.

I backed away from the hole. As my eyes adjusted to the dimness, I now saw the rough plumbing on my side of the wall and two anchor screws coming through, close together, just above the peep hole. So that was it: a hole out of sight, a peep hole hidden under the soap dish.

"What are we doing in here?" I asked.

Baggie chuckled. "Nice view, don't you think? Nothing to look at now, but wait till evening: the ones that camp here all week come in then, most of 'em young. A few saggy ones, now and then, but plenty of prime rib, you might say, to balance out the uglies."

He pushed me away from the hole, took another look for himself, a long look, wrapped in his own breath and heat and sweat.

He said, "Of course, I'll know."

"Know what?"

"If you ever tell anyone, I'll know right away it was you." He switched to the other eye. "Cause there just ain't anybody else on earth who knows about this...besides me, it's only you."

"Why are you letting me in on it?"

He turned to me with a chuckle. "Just like your old man, aren't you? Always wanting to figure the reasons for things." He turned back to the hole. "Old times' sake, I guess. Was a kid myself, once, just like you, just like your old man was. I guess he and I went different ways, though. He went the smart way, fancied himself up and all. I'm the more clever, you might say. Well, someday, we'll see which one wins out: smart or clever."

And then he herded me back along the wall, back into the darkness we had come from. He knew, by feel, right where the door was located, and cracked it open to peer out. He rasped it all the way open and pushed me out, then closed the door quickly and padlocked it. We stepped through elderberry overgrowth, out into full daylight, onto the hard-pack.

Tipping the brim of his hat up, he hooked thumbs in his belt and looked around, searching again for anyone who might have seen us. "You aren't a blabber," he said quietly, as if others might be listening. "That's why I let you in on it. You're one of those thinkers. A lot like your old man...a thinker. Thinkers always mull things over. Of course, should you ever mull your way into being a blabber, I'll know. You can count on it. I'll know it was you right away."

He pulled the brim of his hat down. "You see that?"

I followed his eyes to a cluster of Rose of Sharon down and across the alley at the rear door of the barn where the steers were stabled: swatches of color. The eye could have mistaken them for blossoms among the leaves.

He shouted in that direction. "Come on out! You think I haven't been watching you?"

Something moved the shrubbery: white blouse; patch of denim; purple kerchief and brown slacks shaped in feminine legs. The Rose of Sharon parted slowly, and Lucinda Hobbes emerged from cover, another girl close behind. They stood at the edge of the alley, eyes round, staring at Baggie. He motioned them closer. They hesitated, each expecting the other to go first.

"I ain't gonna bite ya," he said, then turned to me and whispered through a grin, "not yet, anyway."

Lucinda came along first, just a few steps.

"Right here," he commanded, and pointed to a spot before him in the middle of the alley.

Lucinda's eyes narrowed the instant she noticed me, then widened again as Baggie made a slow inspection of the two girls. The other girl was... I suddenly recognized Enid Neudecker, a year ahead of me in school. I hadn't seen her since last year when she'd moved on to Stephen Foster Junior High. Taller now, and rounded out, almost a different person altogether. She stood still, eyes glazed in dumbness, like you'd see on a heifer the first time she's locked into a stanchion.

He pulled up his gun belt, hooked both thumbs into the front of it and drummed his fingers on the hard, black leather. He glared at Enid. "You ain't old enough to be smoking, now are ya, girl."

Lucinda stepped in front of her and spoke up, "Well, I am. I'm sixteen." She looked him in the eye, while Enid looked down at the ground.

"Oh, is that so." He nodded and looked pleased. "Well, then, if you're old enough to smoke, maybe you're old enough to explain why you're hiding in the bushes just to burn one. Or, maybe that's not all you were up to, eh?"

"We weren't hiding." Lucinda's face pinked up. "We just didn't want to stand in the alley, that's all."

Enid, behind her, remained silent.

He laughed. "Afraid of blocking traffic? How many vehicles do you see coming through here?"

Baggie looked them over as he spoke in my direction, as if I was working with him. "A sweltering summer day...and who's hiding in the bushes? Two little hot bitches....hmmmm.... "

Lucinda noticed me. Her eyes narrowed at the recognition, pupils black and deepening. I wished I wasn't her brother's friend. Enid jerked, suddenly hid her mouth with her hand. An auburn curl escaped from behind her ear.

Baggie stepped around Lucinda and yelled. "Feeling a little shame, are we?"

Enid covered her face with both hands.

My stomach tightened. "Let's leave her be. She hasn't done anything."

I sounded like I *was* somehow working with Baggie, assisting him...an event-volunteer deputy's deputy. Lucinda glared at me. I was afraid she might try to embarrass me the way she would do in front of my friends, maybe call me "squirt" in front of Baggie and Enid.

Baggie rolled his head on his neck as he let out a bellowing laugh and then gazed down into Enid's crying face. "Should I go down to the weigh station and tell Farley Neudecker that I found his little girl—what are you, all of thirteen?—hiding in the bushes with an older girl, a sixteen-year-old bitch in heat? Wonder what he'd think of that!"

Enid bent at the waist and bawled like a calf.

Lucinda's face reddened. "Big deal! We were smoking! I'm old enough, but she isn't. So take us to jail—Dick Tracy!"

He raised the back of his hand. "Watch your mouth, Sassy."

She stood straight, hands on hips. "Go ahead, big man. Slap a girl. Or, better yet, shoot me with your great big gun. Do you even know how to use it?"

Baggie glared, face red.

Enid straightened up, eyes puffy, sniffled, and stared at Lucinda.

"Hey, we gotta go," I said to Baggie.

He turned to me, mouth open.

"It's a hot day," Lucinda said in a tone as if she was merely explaining something, and looked to me as if I *was* the event-volunteer deputy's deputy. "We have to get back to our steers, now."

Enid wiped her hand across her nose and sniffled again.

Baggie pushed his hat back, and watched as the girls turned and went down the alley. He yelled after them, "Yeh, give each of them steers a drink of water, on me. Then you try doing something useful. Go home and bake some pies. Make 'em *cherry* pies, my favorite."

Lucinda cupped her hands and yelled out to the fairgrounds, "What's the matter, Deputy Hoy...that big gun of yours loaded with blanks?"

He made a move in their direction.

"Let's go," I said, my stomach tight.

He stopped after one step. A rivulet of sweat ran from his side burn. He was all breath and sweat alongside me, heat and the sourness radiating through his uniform.

I changed the subject. "Won't somebody see that hole in the shower wall?" Here I was, talking about it like I was in on that peep hole...like he and I were board members of the peep-hole committee.

His breathing slowed. He grinned at me, put an arm around my shoulder. "There you go, worrying, just like your old man would do."

I shrugged.

"Young Mister Ahern, right where that hole is, at the base of a soap dish, well, that's in a shadow on account of where I had them jailbirds mount the light fixture when I was supervising them back in '56. I *told* you I was clever. Don't you worry: the ladies won't see it. And they won't see us."

See *us*?

He took his arm off me as he rolled his head back and laughed. His face widened and pinked up, eyes bulging. We came out of the weedy space between the buildings. As he looked around he spoke softly, savoring his words, "The shy ones, they tend to shower in the stall, the ones that don't like others looking at 'em. Just makes it all the more fun for us, them trying to hide themselves, not knowing they're right up close to our special viewing station." He poked my shoulder. "You'll see what I mean."

I turned back toward the barn.

Before I could leave him he pawed my sleeve. "Hey, kid," he breathed. "Do you suppose that neighbor of yours, the sassy Hobbes bitch, is in love with me?" He let out another rolling laugh, and left me at the door.

Out of the sun, dripping sweat cooled under my shirt as I sat on a green hay bale in the sweet pungency of feed and fresh manure. Stabled horses nickered to each other from their stalls.

## CHAPTER 36, SO TELL HIM

How was I going to tell Quin about me changing schools? We'd been together always. I remembered all the way back to the day Bert Gutierrez had first brought his son by our place: we were three years old. We had soon gotten lost in high pasture grass while his old man and mine were busy reshoeing the Percherons. When they had finished the job and found us, I'd been the one crying, Quin the one reassuring me. And, he reassured the grownups, "He's okay...just scared."

After lugging the decision around with me for a few days now, I had made up my mind to tell him at the fair today: "We won't be in school together anymore." Just plop it out there between us at the right moment when the fun we were having would — well, maybe — dull the effect.

Today, Tuesday, the first day the fair officially opened, we had planned to meet at the maintenance gate at noon. That's when I would tell him, while we were both excited.

Quin didn't show. By quarter after, I could wait for him no longer. My father wanted me at his walking-plow demonstration, where I would step in from time to time to portray how a boy back in the olden days would have been expected to work like a man. So, I left the gate and went down the cinder midway, past the Ferris wheel giving its first rides to people with open mouths and flushed cheeks; past the merry-go-round, bumper cars, the kids' ponies, and the haunted house that would not open till evening. The cinder path turned to stony hard-pack and split in two, the left walkway heading back to the large-animal area.

Up on the slope behind the livestock barns, I would not have recognized the man as my father, except he had been doing the same thing year after year. In a field of timothy that had grown up since last time, he cut into the earth on a first pass that threw dirt uphill off to the right of the moldboard. Light-blue work shirt — sleeves rolled up hairy forearms — reflected the brilliance of high summer sun under a wide straw hat, frayed red-rail hawk feather sticking up from the weave. Patched jeans hung from brown suspenders, and favorite old army boots were double-knotted with rawhide laces.

Pointed ears of the two bays turned and twitched, anticipating a new command as they approached the tree line of the half-acre plot. A single tongue cluck told them to slow, and he lifted plow out of the ground. "Whoa."

With more commands, he got the team — identical-twin Percheron geldings — turned around, faced in the opposite direction. Jupiter was on the left, down in the furrow's fresh-cut trench, and Saturn up in the grass on firm ground. Reaching a claw tool from where it hung by a wire on the handle, he pulled a pin that allowed him to swivel the plow over on its frame.

"Never once had to do that," an onlooker commented, a leathery gray-eyed man in checkered shirt and ancient hat with a misshapen brim. "My place is mostly bottom land. I could always plow in two directions without a changeover."

My father nodded. "You look familiar. The Horn place… down along Quarrel Creek?"

"Cecil Horn," the man said, and they shook hands. "You Carroll Ahern's boy…the one running for judge?"

"Guilty."

Mr. Horn let his face crack a smile, then returned to a stony set.

"You're lucky," my father said. "Never did anything but hill plowing. When I was a kid, I'd have done anything to work some of that soft bottom land."

The man nodded and said, "Eh-up."

"Where've you been?" my father said to me, and did not wait for an answer. He handed me the reins.

Jupiter and Saturn, ears twitching, knew from the feel of it that I had them now. A double-cluck of tongue against my back teeth put them in motion.

My father and Mr. Horn walked alongside, talked about what it used to be like to farm. Mr. Horn said "Eh-up" again when my father told him about all the rocks the plow would turn up that he and my uncle would have to load onto a stoneboat.

"Don't let 'em forget who's driving," my father reminded me.

Folks gathered along the furrow. Children held onto their mothers and stared wide-eyed, having seldom seen anybody plow with horses, especially not a kid. The older people looked on quietly and nodded to one another. I felt all those eyes on me as I held the handle, gripped the reins, slogged along behind the implement, a boy looking like he was doing a man's work. I knew the secret, of course: my father was an expert at setting up the assembly, so it pretty much took care of itself while making a furrow. Once in motion, the front disc made a clean vertical cut, like slicing into cake, and right behind it the plow point and share lifted out a perfectly sized portion of sod. The moldboard turned it over, folded it on itself, and pushed it aside into the trench left by the previous pass. At the rear, just ahead of my feet, the follower-pan scoured out a new trench. So, the walking plow did its job of making a furrow.

My job was to correct when it tried to veer off course, which meant leaning the handle. I gave the reins an occasional jostle to let the team know I was back there. Jupiter and Saturn did the real work, hooves plop-plopping against earth at an even cadence as they pulled draft. Polished steel surfaces cut and lifted and scoured — almost kissing sounds — which you'd never get to hear from the seat of a noisy tractor.

When we approached the end, ears began to twitch again. A single cluck slowed the team as I brought the plow out of the ground. "Whoa." They stopped on a dime, ears pointing skyward. I dragged the plow off to the right. "Haw. Haw." The team swung to the left, and I managed to get the whole assembly turned around and faced back the other way. "Gee," I said — using a hard g — and they obeyed with a clop-clop to the right, Saturn down into the trench we had just scoured out, leaving Jupiter to have a turn upside.

My father handed me the tool.

"What's he doing?" a small voice from the onlookers.

"Just watch. You'll see."

They were silent as I pulled the pin and swiveled the assembly back over to a right-side discharge. Jupiter and Saturn held still, each nibbling a handful of grain brought out from one of my father's bulging pockets. When I'd reseated the pin, he took the tool from me and hung it back in its place on the implement. As I handed the reins back to him, he looked at me with soft eyes. "You done good," he said quietly. Ever at the ready to correct my English, he had broken the rules in favor of using farm talk to tell me that.

Two tongue-clucks, my father driving again, had the team in motion on a third furrow.

"I'm going to find Quin," I said.

A brief raise of the hand without looking back told me it was okay for me to go.

Mr. Horn stood still, resting at the end of the furrow I'd made. Looking me over, he tipped up his ancient hat brim. "Eh-up," he said, hooking thumbs in back pockets, elbows pointed out, the way old farmers like to do.

I knew I'd done good, all right.

Back down at the maintenance gate, still no sign of Quin. Out at the grove of trees, past where the carnival drivers had lined up their transports for the week, was a '49 Studebaker, the car Bert Gutierrez had rescued from Rooney's Junk Yard. He had mechanically resurrected it into a working vehicle, painting THE GRAY BULLET in red letters along the right front fender. Movement took my eye to an open back door: Quin was there, leaning inside the car. He slammed the door and ran hunched over like a running back, clutching a bundle rolled up in a towel. Near the gate, he saw me—and stopped, froze, as if somebody had turned off a movie projector but had left the lamp on so the last frame remained on the screen.

"That time already?" he said, breathless.

"Way past. We were supposed to meet at noon."

He came through the gate and looked at me, eyes clouding. "I was hoping I was early." He threw the bundle against the bottom of the fence and suddenly sat down there. "Didn't want you to see me...not like this."

His clothes were sodden with some kind of gray mud, especially his shoes and pant-legs, which were caked with it. The same stain was on his hands and splattered his tee shirt and arms.

I said, "What happened to you?"

He sat back against the wire mesh, arms resting on bent-up knees, face turned away. He didn't want to answer. "I tried to get to the showers before you saw me."

He looked up at me with the same eyes I'd seen at Lake Margaret in the bramble that afternoon we had stolen away at the conclusion of the retreat to share a Pall Mall. "I'm covered in it," he said shakily, and held out his hands. "Didn't want *anybody* to see."

"I'm not anybody, Quin."

"Just once, I'd like my best friend to not know me like I am right now: the kid who just finished helping his old man clean out the septic tank that everybody else shits in."

I remembered hearing my father on the phone with another 4H Committee member, wondering aloud who they could hire to service the fairgrounds septic tank; it would need to be cleaned out for sure before the fair opened and then again after it closed at the end of the week.

"What did you have to do?"

Quin just wagged his head without saying anything. But he knew that I really did want to know. It wasn't like I would be making fun of him about it. After a while his eyes lightened, and he started telling me.

"After my old man pulled the bolts on the access lid, he used a crow bar. Prying on one side and then the other, he walked it off. Then, we lowered the washtub down inside, him in the cab of the Pettibone boom-lift, me using a two-by four to force the tub under the muck. The old man kept warning me not to get too close to the opening. If I fell in, no getting me out before I would have died of the fumes in there!"

The way he brightened with the telling of it, I started to feel like I'd missed out on an adventure.

"Imagine suffocating in a place like that, Eugene."

I couldn't.

He said, "You ever see that old truck the 4H Committee bought last year?"

I'd seen it: a six-wheel-drive Army surplus. I remembered they had hired Quin's old man to remove the bed and fabricate a steel trough on the back.

"Well, when he raised the washtub over it, I'd have to climb up there and tip the tub by hand, turning it over to dump the sludge into the back of the truck." His face darkened again. "No way I could keep it from getting all over me, the way it splattered. And it must have taken fifty scoops before we got the tank emptied, down to all except the last foot or so."

I wasn't sorry that I had missed out on this one after all.

"Quin, what did you do with all the shit?"

"They have a trench opened up out at the dump just for that, way down at the end where nobody else goes."

We were both quiet for a while, he reliving the job, while I pictured what it must have been like.

Quin grabbed the roll and stood. We walked the hard-pack lane together, septic-tank smell lingering along with us like it wanted to be our friend, and headed to the shower facility.

With the fair having just opened, we were lucky that nobody else was around this part of the grounds. We entered the foyer and then the gents section, where Quin unrolled the towel on a bench. He had a clean pair of jeans and a tee shirt inside, neatly wrapped around his good sneakers, one stuffed with socks, the other with Ivory soap in a plastic bag. He stripped, turned on the water and got under the shower head enough to get himself wet, then stepped away to soap up.

I stripped and got under the one next to him.

"What are you doing?" he said.

"Seemed kind of funny to just stand here watching you take a shower."

Laughter erupted from him. "But didn't you forget something, Genie?"

He handed me his soap.

So, he didn't want me to know him as he really was. But this was how he really was: the kid who laughed, tall and lean, ropy with muscle, soapy water sliding over him the way your eye wants to slide over a naked form in one of those art books up in the stacks of the Wyotanda Public Library. I wished I was him. I wished I, like him, could cry one minute, and then be excited the next minute, and then laugh at things the minute after that. People often told me I was a thinker, as if it was a compliment. I wished I was less of a thinker and more the kid who always knew how he felt, and that it showed on my face — like Quin.

Soon, we would not be together anymore. And I had not yet been able to tell him. After sixth grade, I was now finished with public school, was already enrolled at Saint Agatha for seventh. He would be going on to Stephen Foster Junior High, something we had both been looking forward to. We had been in school together since kindergarten. Bus Number 2, now on its early run for the higher grades, would be passing my house with Quin on it, but not stopping for me anymore.

I finished soaping up, set the bar in the plastic bag on the bench, and got under the spray. He turned off his shower and, as he dried himself, watched me rinse off.

He suddenly grinned at me. "Forgot something else, didn't you, Genie."

I turned off my shower.

"Here you go. Use my towel," he said.

No. I could not tell him today.

## Chapter 37, Kid Stuff, Mostly

My mother nibbled a breakfast roll. "Just don't let him talk you into helping him."

"Talk me into helping him?" My voice rose in pitch. "Is *that* what you think about it?"

The *Clarion* rattled, top corner tilted, made way for a scowl from my father. I wasn't supposed to talk to her that way. I said no more, and the corner of the paper rose back up. My mother put the roll down, adjusted the position of her fork, leaned on her elbows and joined her hands above her plate, fingers interlaced, and hazel eyes on me. But I kept mine to myself.

"People do tell you things sometimes," she said, "to get you to help them. That's all I'm saying. I'm not saying Quin did that. But that's what people do, Gene."

She called me Gene instead of Eugene, turning affectionate.

"That's not what Quin was doing," I said evenly.

The *Clarion* rattled again. "Forecast calls for hot and humid, no rain." The corner of the paper tilted, and my father looked at my mother. "Expect a good turnout for your performance." He winked, and she quickly smiled.

"It's just that...well, who knows what could be in that sludge," she said gently. "And Quin could still have some of it on him even after he showers."

Grandma looked sternly at her plate; would not look at me, and I knew she agreed with my mother. And my father gave me a quick look over the edge of the paper before it rose up again to hide his eyes. I never should have told them.

My father and I were at the fairgrounds by late morning, he in a clean set of farmer-plow clothes. Grandma had put yesterday's clothes in the wash. Other than the appointed times when I was to show up to help him, I would be free for the day.

Quin and I roamed, he with a dollar his old man had given him for helping with the septic tank, but unsure of where to spend it. My mother's voice—"could still have some of it on him"— remained sharp in my ear at first, and even had me keeping a stiff extra inch or two between him and me. But, hadn't I used his towel yesterday? Too late to be careful now. That realization was a big relief, and my mother's words soon melted away.

I still had the earnings my father had given me last week for the trench project. So I told Quin not to worry, keep his dollar. Yesterday's fair expenses for both of us had hardly made a dent, even after Quin had lost fifty cents of it at the Tubs 'o Fun—fifteen cents a throw, four for a half-dollar—where he'd been certain to win the stuffed replica of a genuine Pennsylvania white-tail. Two of the balls that had gone into a bucket had somehow managed to bounce right back out. Today my pockets still jingled with coins, a pair of ones smoldered in my wallet, and a cool ten was folded in my sock.

We hit all the rides that we'd missed the first day, kid stuff, mostly. Little cars made to look like Model T's, hooked together and evenly spaced by lengths of chain, took a slow, deliberate trip on a track through a fake town. Quin, long legs doing the splits to ride atop the car ahead of me, wildly motioned with all his limbs and yahooed at everybody he saw. He soon had the little kids pointing and their mothers scowling. The carny— a tan, skinny man with one droopy eyelid—stopped the ride, and told us to get off and get out.

Baggie Hoy, attracted by Quin's yelling about a refund, appeared in his deputy uniform with gun belt. His round eyes avoided Quin. He looked only at me. "Think you and your Sloot buddy might be a little big for this ride?" Not waiting for an answer, he motioned with thumb over his shoulder like an umpire calling us out.

As we left, the carny suddenly seemed to grow an inch or two. "And don't come back. You two are banned from Yester-Town...banned for life!"

We moved on, Quin allowing me to nudge him along until we were out of earshot where he could call them both assholes. The cinder midway ended, and we took the right-hand split onto stony hard-pack that we'd not explored yesterday, where just a scattering of people wandered. A twine-haired woman in a man's fedora, checkered shirt and striped overalls had clay pots, bowls, urns and vases for sale, and a second display of colored items that were labeled, KENTUCKY ART GLASS.

"You break it, you bought it," she grumbled through corn-like bottom teeth, blinking through lenses that made her look like an owl, "and I doubt you can afford it," she added, looking Quin up and down.

So we passed her by for another tent where the sign MOD-ERN WOODMEN drew us in. We figured a sign like that showed promise of outdoorsy information on hunting or fishing. But as we approached, a balding gentleman in a blue suit and gold tie stared at us blandly, and just before we arrived within reach, he managed to slide a dish filled with lollipops away from the edge of the card table and surround it with a bulwark of colorful leaflets. From glossy literature, a picture of a fair-haired woman and three fair-haired children—man of the house was missing—projected piece of mind that nothing but adequate life insurance could have provided.

While I read a leaflet, Quin asked the man, "Who's the candy for?"

"Prospective clients." He looked at us like a cat guarding kill. A pocket name-tag identified him as Harry.

"So, Harry, who's the extra chair for?" Quin said.

Harry turned and eyed the empty canvass chair beside him, as if he'd seen it for the first time. He blushed pink. "It was intended for the new agent I've been training. He failed to show up, today. I guess he changed his mind."

"Well, I'm not surprised. They've needed a good man to clean the fairground septic tank," Quin suggested. "No doubt he jumped at the chance."

I tried not to laugh as I nudged Quin's arm.

"Oh, I doubt it." Harry's frown transformed into a sneer. "He might be in the tank all right. Not one that would require any work, though."

Quin, with the swiftness of a jay snatching grain from a horse trough, reached over the leaflets and took two lollipops from the dish: purple for him, orange for me. Harry glared at us.

Further along, we spotted the tent that was manned, as always, by Kyle and Cedric Horan, whose ancient father owned a small equipment business in East Wyotanda. Among new pumps and generators and various low-horsepower Briggs & Stratton and Cummins engines, we spotted a used two-man chain saw. It was a McCulloch 99, the kind used by loggers, bicycle-like handle bars on either side of its engine and a single handle down at the other end of a long chain bar. Quin grabbed onto the double handles, I the single, and together we felled an imaginary massive oak or maple or walnut, constricting our throats to mimic engine whine and wail as cutter-bits on the chain ripped through imaginary fiber and rake-teeth spewed sawdust chips from the notch.

Kyle Horan wagged his head at us, and spat tobacco juice through brown lips into a coffee can. "Between the two of you I doubt there's enough ass to handle that for real."

Cedric laughed along with his twin. "No, this one ain't for little boys. See you fellows in four or five years, maybe."

We left, slurping our lollipops, for a large tan tent whose open flaps revealed a row of picnic tables with yellow and white checkered tablecloths. Over the entrance, a sign proclaimed, VICTORY TENT, in green block letters.

Adam Stippil in a clean blue shirt and creased dark pants appeared by one of the flaps. "Jesus is Lord over all of Wyotanda!" he shouted, and then saw that it was us. He looked away for a moment.

Quin and I both laughed. "Amen, Adam."

But Adam's face was firmly set. Gray eyes rose up, looked right past us. The Reverend, dressed the same as Adam, appeared by the other flap, eyes afire. He held a small Bible high in one hand and boomed, "And over all of Wilmot County!"

"Let there be no other before Him!" Adam responded.

Quin and I looked at each other.

Agnes May appeared between her father and brother in a fresh tiny flower print dress, one I hadn't seen before. The print was miniature brilliant butter cups sprouting from bright green stems. It must have been a recent production off her mother's sewing machine, not yet dulled by washing, and it fit her more loosely, didn't seem to hug her, not shaping itself to her nipples the way often-worn ones had started to do. She had a gray bonnet and, instead of the usual rubber band, a purple ribbon held the end of her braid.

"Are you here for some nourishment?" she asked, forced to come close under continued hollering from her father and brother, who now were proclaiming that Jesus was Lord over the entire earth.

"You mean, you serve food here?" I said.

"We of the Christian Fellowship are here today to nurture both body and soul," she managed to recite with a flushed face, and handed each of us a paper. Mimeographed blue type offered hamburger, shredded chicken or pulled pork on a bun for twenty cents; coffee for ten, milk for seven—but crossed out with a pencil—and lemonade for five. The other side of the paper was professionally printed with a Bible passage surrounded by black border. An ink-stamping at the bottom told the times of services at the Melody Falls Watchful Christian Fellowship Church on Belknap Road.

Quin glanced at me, and I said, "Why not."

She led us past the two others—they were proclaiming that Jesus was Lord over all of Wyotanda once again—to a table at the rear. Mrs. Stippil, dressed exactly like Agnes May, even down to purple braid ribbon, manned a smoky grill just beyond an opening at the side of the tent. With nobody else in the vicinity on the hard-pack gravel, the evangelists turned toward us again, and continued to yell their litany of praises.

I felt Agnes May's breath, soft on my ear. "Take as much time as you like, Eugene. As you can see, we have no other customers."

She straightened up and went away, sudden coolness of air taking her place. Scent lingered...had me suddenly down in the pasture, she watching me swing the pick and shovel, eyes looking away briefly when I took my shirt off.

Quin said through cupped hands, "Maybe this was not such a good idea. Let's get outta here," he said. "Too noisy, with them yelling. I'm not *this* hungry."

I cupped my hands. "We leave now, we abandon Adam, and Agnes May too. Who knows what the Reverend might do to them just because we left. He'll blame it on them somehow."

I didn't really think that, but said it so we could stay.

Quin thought for a moment. "Cripe'n-itey," he muttered, and looked away.

She returned with napkins and plastic forks and paper cups, and placed a set by Quin, then by me. Her motions were quick, dress material hugging and then letting go of her roundness, long skirt swishing about. Someone's gravel-crunch arrival on the path drew the evangelists' attention. They went outside. It grew quieter in the tent.

"May I take your order?" She had found her normal voice, and stood by with a small pad and pencil.

We chose pulled pork and lemonade. Quin smiled at her. She went away, then came back with ketchup, mustard, diced onions and relish, and then went away again. Her coming and going teased the air with a mix of smells that had me realizing that I'd missed my chance. I hadn't even known the chance existed through the summer, and now, the trench project over, it was gone. My mind suddenly filled with all those discussions in the pasture about arithmetic and stenography and architecture and the temptress-nature of Eve, Agnes May's teeth and lips pronouncing precise words. I'd missed my chance during the trench project. If I'd been more like Quin, I could have smiled...maybe put my arm around her, just once. I could have nuzzled behind her ear; held her, let her smell mingle with my breathing. I imagined kissing the swoop of her neck, that perfect hollow there. Would she have made me stop?

CHAPTER 38, YELLOW-WHEELED RIG

Through the day, Quin would go with me when I had to report back to my father to plow a furrow, and then we would be on our own again. At two-thirty, we carried full buckets up there and watered the bays at the side of the field in the hedgerow's shade, while my father went down to the fairgrounds for a lunch break. We stayed near the horses, sitting on mossy rocks to share a Pall Mall. The pulled pork we'd eaten at the Victory Tent had us both burping.

Quin mentioned that Agnes May was the only girl he'd ever seen wear a full-length dress in the summer.

"She never wears anything *but* a full length dress," I said, "same as her mother. It's something about being in the Reverend's family. That's why Adam wears those old clothes, too."

He wagged his head at that. "Makes you wonder what her legs look like."

I shrugged...as if it didn't matter to me.

"Well, you're always thinking, Genie. Don't you ever think about Agnes May's legs? I mean, bein' as how they're always hidden under a long dress."

"The kid-brat?" My ears grew hot. "Why would I want to think about the kid-brat's legs?"

Quin went quiet and looked away. He had said something about her legs in the woods that day at the retreat, too.

My father came back, and I plowed my furrow. Quin and I went down to the fairgrounds again, where I bought each of us an elephant ear and a bottle of Nehi Orange.

"This ought to put a little pressure on that pulled pork we ate, maybe push it further down," I decided, and bought four more elephant ears.

Quin burped. "Maybe stifle it from talking back to us," he agreed.

But it didn't. So, through the afternoon, we tried corn dogs, more bottles of Nehi, cotton candy with Nehi, and finally sugar-dusted brownies baked by the Republican Auxiliary, and still more Nehi to flush it down. No matter what we piled on top of it, Hughla Stippil's pulled pork stubbornly burped its way back up through.

I did another furrow at five o'clock, just as burps seemed to ease up and change over to farts, which had us both laughing.

Then, at six, Quin and I went to get the horses. We unhitched and led them down to the barn for a full hour's rest and plenty of water and alfalfa. We stayed with them, brushed dirt and grass out of their coats and straightened up their manes and tails, which had been braided and bobbed for the evening's event. Two of our stalls were empty. My father had taken Beethoven and Sweatpea around back of the barn to get them ready.

By seven we had the geldings back on the field, plow hitched up to the harness and positioned for more work. A crowd had gathered, women, children, men and old folks, whole families trampling the narrow strip of timothy along the final stretch of ground yet to be turned. It would take two more passes with the plow to finish the field.

We did it every year on the second evening of the fair — the last furrow. And every year it drew a larger crowd. Some folks had even begun to dress up for it, men in cowboy hats and vests and chaps, women in full billowy dresses and flowered hats, all for this. It was the final night of my father's old-time walking plow demonstration. Tomorrow the fair's serious judging would begin on the grounds. Everything imaginable would be entered into some competition, from bush beans to beef steers. But these past two days of the plowing had led up to the present moment. Jupiter and Saturn, sensing excitement, did not want to hold still, so I had to keep talking to them. People milled and bunched up with jumpiness like a brook after a downpour. Women talked in clusters, men swapped tales that met with loud remarks and guffaws, bigger kids ran weaves in and out of grownups, while the littlest ones held tight to their mothers.

At the sounds of an approaching rig from the lower corner of the field, it all paused, turned itself to that direction. A shiny, black runabout, four bright yellow wheels rolling at a whir around crimson hubs, burst onto the field's access road, pulled by a team of grays, a stallion and a mare. Beethoven and Sweetpea, in perfect step with each other, pounded the earth in a flurry of mud-dollops. The rig came up along the hedgerow, driver in western finery: black Stetson, string tie, salmon shirt and indigo vest. The woman beside him in the purple-tufted spindle seat sat erect, blond hair pinned in a tight bun. She wore a felt bowler gray hat trimmed in red piping and a side bow. A matching cape covered her white blouse, and a three-quarter skirt fell to fancy stitch western boots.

"Whoa." The man pulled back on the reins, and the team, heads high, eyes afire and nostrils flared, came to a halt. The rig continued to roll a bit to and fro from the team's nervousness until the driver talked to them, calmed them with his voice.

When they were settled, my father alighted from the runabout and offered his arm to my mother, who stepped down to the ground, drawing polite applause. Smiling, with lowered eyes — I'd seen her smile that way at my father once or twice — she unpinned the bowler and set it up on the seat. Releasing a top red button, she loosened the cape. Exposure of bare shoulders stilled the air, opened a silence in which you could hear the fabric swish as it fell away, a silence that had the horses' ears standing straight. Gathered respectability of everyday folks found a momentary recess, a place to quietly savor just a bit of nakedness as my mother reached up to put her cape beside the hat, lithe feminine arms in August evening light.

At home, a moment of casual undress would not be like this. Down at the pond for a family evening swim, entering the water in twilight would have her reach down with one hand and lightly splash as she sought to somewhat cover herself with the other. My father would suddenly slap a wave to douse her, or maybe say something that would break her shyness so she would raise her eyes and laugh. No, this was a different kind of moment, one in which she presented herself boldly while all of Wilmot County looked on. The quiet concluded in a rustling, then murmurs, then a rise in chatter. The moment seemed to have slipped out of place from time a little, but now caught up again.

My father offered his arm. He led her as if onto a dance floor, elegant, petite blond woman in sleeveless white blouse, gray skirt and stitch-patterned boots that had everyone looking — Quin too — with big eyes. My father handed her a snap-whip and brought her to the plow. She turned and, with a grin, swished the rawhide loop in his direction, raising a chuckle from the crowd, a few catcalls from males. The geldings jerked in harness. "Whoa," I said, before handing over the reins. Her hands went from feminine, soft, and supple to the gristle and tendon of a tight grip on rough leather. One hand still holding the whip, she took up the plow handles.

"Yah!" and a double tongue cluck put the geldings in motion, pulling the plow point under. Disk sliced new earth, moldboard turned sod over, and follower pan scoured out a fresh trench.

My father retreated back to the runabout team to hold steady Beethoven and Sweetpea, as he watched my mother in evening finery operate the plow behind the bay geldings; watched my mother stride in fancy clothes, her fancy boots skitter the dirt, the crowd on the sod up ahead spreading apart, out of her way as she worked the first pass. Syllables arose, and soon sprouted into male hollering and whistles, and above that came female yells of encouragement. The children were quiet.

Then it caught my attention: there, in the crowd, Baggie's deputy hat; that beefy neck; bowling-ball shoulders; those round eyes. I froze solid. In another instant, searing fire turned my insides to liquid — boiling liquid.

"Where you going?" Quin said.

Over my shoulder I glimpsed Quin open-mouthed as started down the hill.

"Hey," he rasped to me, "if you gotta piss so bad, just go over in the hedgerow."

"Must be that pulled pork," I said back to him, surprised at how instinctively I could lie, even to my best friend.

"But I feel okay now," he complained, voice waning as I jumped the corduroy rows of earth left by all of our plowing from the past two days.

I headed into the barn. It had to be here: the quart can of brown spar paint my father had used for the Masonite name-signs above our assigned stalls. I found it in a supply bin. But, no brush. The brush would have dried up by now anyway. I searched other supply bins for something else I might use, lockers that belonged to other people, people who no doubt trusted me to not be looking through their things. In one of them — assigned to the McKees — among the equine tools and supplies was a blue gym bag. Inside it, a woman's toiletries: powder, hairbrush, barrettes. I turned my face away from a half-dozen Kotex napkins in paper wrappers banded together. Then, nail polish, and two round mirrors, one regular and one close-up. Nail brushes were too small. I looked for a makeup brush, like my mother would have had...nothing. I searched the length of the barn, rapidly opening every bin and locker. Still, nothing I could use. Back to the McKee's' supply bin — I looked around first to make sure I was alone — and from the banded package, I loosened a paper-covered Kotex napkin.

Opening the can of paint, I dipped in a finger wrapped with napkin and painted a sign on a left-over blank Masonite board, careful to space the letters so I would have enough room for all the words. When I was finished, the paint can went back into my parents' supply bin. Shoving the napkin back in its paper wrapper, I buried it in the trash barrel, deep down so it was covered by food containers, soda cans, and an empty Sloan's Liniment bottle.

Not a soul stood in the space between the barn and the shower building. The ladies door opened into darkness. Snap of light switch revealed showers, and there it was, that lone private shower stall back in the rear corner. A divider between common showers and the private one cast a shadow over the soap dish, but bending down brought into view the dark, round peep hole. I propped my sign across the hot and cold water faucet stems, and leaned it back on the tiles. The faucet handles held its bottom edge, and kept it from sliding forward. Letters smeared in brown paint, read: SORRY, THIS SHOWER IS OUT OF ORDER. I hurried from the building to a whoop of the crowd from the field above...

When I got back up there, the noise had fallen back to loud conversation. My mother, having finished the second pass, had completed the last furrow. She handed the reins to my father; it should have been to me. Over by the hedgerow, Quin had been conscripted to holding steady the runabout's team. My mother's face was flushed, glistened from exertion. She smiled at the folks swirling around her, women laughing, men nodding and talking to her.

My father saw me, took my shoulders and turned me aside. "Where've you been?" his brow knitted.

I used the same lie, told him that something I'd eaten had sent me to the gents room. He gave me the reins to the geldings without comment, and then fished something from his pocket; he put a coin in Quin's hand. Turning to my mother, he helped her up to the seat of the runabout, and climbed up after her. With a snap of reins, the rig lurched forward, made a circle on the field, and headed back down along the access road.

Quin looked at me. "You okay now?"

"False alarm: nothing but farts."

We laughed. He showed me a Liberty Head and Eagle silver dollar, dated 1923.

Children shouted and poured from the edges onto the plowed field. Their excitement, driven by knowing they no longer had to stay off, had them running atop the soft new dirt underfoot. My mother, sitting erect as she rode, swung the cape onto her shoulders and, buttoning the top red button, raised her arms to carefully pin the bowler.

Deputy Baggie Hoy stepped over the furrows. He moved down the slope toward the shower facility. His head turned under his deputy hat as he big-eyed the yellow-wheeled rig with the stallion and mare out front of it, prancing...

"Genie, what I said about Agnes May's legs...I didn't mean anything by it."

Having finished brushing Beethoven and Sweetpea first, we were now in the other stall, the one shared by the twin bay geldings. I looked back over my shoulder into Quin's deepened eyes looking at me through his glasses.

He was talking about her legs again. My face felt hot. "It doesn't matter to me one way or the other," I lied, turning away. I tried to concentrate on brushing Jupiter, but couldn't stand to leave silence between us. "Say whatever you want to about her legs. Why would it matter to me?"

Quin was quiet for a while as he worked on Saturn. Then he said, "I don't want anything to change."

"So, what is changing?"

"I can tell you things. And you can tell me things. It should stay that way, that's all...like we've always done, just you and me."

I turned around. "You can say whatever you want to say, Quin, like always."

"No." He looked down, avoiding my eyes. "Some things I can't say."

I shrugged and turned back to Jupiter. "Why would you worry? I'd never rat you out on anything you told me that was a secret."

He finished with Saturn and left the stall to put the brush away. "Not that. If I say anything about Agnes May, your look tells me I shouldn't have said it."

Heat in my face radiated, had me feel like I was a cartoon character: steam wanted to whistle out through my ear holes. All I could say was, "Cripe'n-itey, Quin."

From over by the supply bin, he tried to catch my glance, but I wouldn't look.

He said, "I want it to go back to the way it always was: I say whatever I feel, and you can too, and neither of us has to be so careful about it."

I continued to brush Jupiter. Quin walked away.

"Where you going?"

He didn't look back. "Be by myself," he said, voice choked. He walked the aisle to the doorway and out into the night.

He was right. His talk about Agnes May would stir me up inside. It was like what he had described in the woods at Lake Margaret, that wild animal he had told me was within him. Well, one was within me too: a wild animal of my own. Hearing Quin speak of Agnes May would awaken my animal, prod it out of sleep the way a poker provokes embers to flame up. My animal did not like being disturbed; did not like the dream interrupted, a dream in which Agnes May would look up, eyes searching. Tiny flower fabric of her dress would gently rise and fall as she turned to me to form words with teeth and lips and tip of tongue, and her breath mingle with mine. Whenever I was away from her, ordinary things would come along to tease. Just the swish of walking through high grass, or burst of breeze along the porch, would seem to put her right at my ear. She would speak to me in that Arkansas way of hers, those drawn-out tones, and plain, flat vowels turned into swales of talk: Agnes May. If I stepped into the barn filled with new hay, or scooped silage into the feed cart, or picked a sprig of rosemary for Grandma from her window box, the air would suddenly not be air anymore: Agnes May.

Jupiter bent his neck around. I'd been brushing the same place over and over. He looked at me to ask if I would wear a hole through his hide. With a pat on each of the gelding's shoulders, I moved out from between them.

A few sections of a bale went into the mangers. As I refreshed and placed water buckets, my parents came into the barn hand in hand, having changed from their western finery back into everyday clothes, hair shower-damp. As they approached they let go of each other, like I was not supposed to know. At home last Sunday, during lunch, my mother had stood beside my father's chair in the dining room, looking over his shoulder as they read the *Clarion* together. Twice she had forced his hand away from where he touched her, placing it at her waist instead, with a glance toward me and my peanut butter and jelly sandwich.

"All the horses bedded for the night, I see," my father said. "We'll trailer them back home first thing tomorrow. Ready to head out?"

"Quin is somewhere out on the grounds. Can we give him a ride?"

"We'll wait here for you, then."

They sat down together on what remained of the loose bale. As I left the barn they took each other's hands again.

I found Quin at a coining vendor. When he turned to me, orange lights whose rapid on-off pattern chased itself around the booth, reflected in his glasses.

"So, what's up with you?" I said.

"Having something made here."

A short old man with thick glasses came out to the front of the booth, a soiled blue and white pin-striped cap crooked atop his gray head. "One and sixty-four," he said in a European accent.

"What about the pendant?" Quin said.

"You pay up, you get it: one and sixty-four first."

Quin handed him the crumpled bill he'd earned from his old man and the silver dollar my father had given him tonight, and the vendor counted out change, his voice turning gentle. "Always, from working of metal, you have some heat." He lowered a shiny pendant into Quin's palm, chain slowly curling itself on top. "Molecules move around, you see, and get hot. But not so much that you cannot touch."

"Thanks," Quin said.

"Thanks to you also." The man peered at him. "You good boy, I can tell. You learn Latin."

Quin laughed at that and poked my arm. "See? Good boy. He can tell."

"Doesn't know you, then. Let's go."

We were okay with each other again.

Quin stopped on the hard-pack. "Not before I give this to someone."

"My parents are waiting to go. You can't take long, you know—"

He handed me the copper disk, chain connected to it by a link that went through a tiny hole, words pressed into its surface.

"I had him coin it upside down. You can pick it up to read it right-side-up while you're wearing it."

I put it over my head, let the medal, warm through my shirt, fall onto my chest, and then looked at the inscription.

*In hoc Signo Vinces.* "In this sign shall you conquer."

"Our secret saying, from the Pall Mall pack. But you spent all your money—on this! On me."

"Not all: I still have thirty six cents." He laughed. "How much of your money did you spend on *me* the last two days?"

I put the pendant down inside my shirt. It was warm against my skin. "Dipshit," I said.

"Dipshit," he said, and mussed my hair.

## Chapter 39, In All Things

When I knocked at the porch screen door, Mrs. Stippil called to me, "He's out behind the church." She appeared as a silhouette against curtained daylight from a window at the back of the house. She wore her bonnet, even inside.

I wasn't here to see Adam. As I had come up the slope, he was out there chopping wood, but I had kept the crown of the hill between him and me, not wanting to deal with him talking at me about the Lord.

When I hesitated on the porch, she came forward. "He's out behind the church," Hughla Stippil said again through the screen.

"Thank you, Mrs. Stippil, but I was checking on Agnes May."

Her eyebrows drew together. "Agnes May? What do you mean, check on her?"

"Just to see if she needed any more starters for your stove. We have some old stumps over at our place."

"Yes, I know about that. Agnes May told me about the stumps, and that you were very cordial, allowing her to take pieces of them." She looked at me with sharpened eyes. "Come in, Eugene," she said, and opened the screen door.

I hadn't expected that. As a Catholic I'd never entered a Protestant church, not all the way. I'd always figured the rule applied to a Protestant preacher's dwellings also. But she opened the door wider, her brow relaxing and eyes lighting up in a way that warmly invited me in. With a quick check to be sure the Reverend's Power Wagon was not in the driveway, I decided it would be okay. I followed her to the kitchen, where she took a tin cup down from a hook and dipped water out of a pan.

"It's good water, not that sour stuff that comes from the well."

The pan was under a pitcher pump mounted on the edge of the kitchen's wooden sink, with a pipe through the floor down to a cistern. I'd been told that cistern water could make you sick, but before I could refuse, she placed the cup in my hands. The Stippils had always seemed healthy enough.

She moved a stool near the doorway to a windowless room off the kitchen, a converted pantry. A sewing machine and a small wooden chair had been crammed into it. "Sit here," she said, motioning to the stool as she squeezed herself into the chair.

I faced into the tiny cubicle. It was lit by a single light hanging from the center of the ceiling, bulb in a screw-in receptacle that the sewing machine cord was plugged into. I waited, sipped water as she took up a garment of bright green silky material and began to work on it, picking at stitches with a small, double-hooked tool. I'd never seen the Stipples wear any material like that.

She seemed in no hurry to tell me why she had asked me in. Was Agnes May home? Maybe in another room, or upstairs. Except for the little fluffing noises coming from the fancy fabric as she worked on it, the house seemed silent. I'd never been this close to Mrs. Stippil before. I saw her daughter's eyes in her eyes, although a bit darker. Agnes May had her mother's cocoa-brown irises, with extra milk.

After a long silence, shifting my weight on the hard stool, I said, "We've got plenty more of those stumps. I just came by to let her know she can break off more pieces for starters."

"Why, thank you." Mrs. Stippil smiled, exposing her teeth, which I'd never seen her do before. One of them had a small chip out of it. "She mentioned that you are the most considerate of the boys, and I see what she means."

Agnes May had talked with her mother about me.

"Very kind of you," I said and, my lie about the starters having gone over so well, decided to sit still for a while longer.

"And polite." She smiled again, even broader, like a woman in a TV commercial using a new dish soap. "We're wanting for politeness around here at times." Her eyebrows drew together again as she focused on her work. "Please excuse my busy doings. I must finish taking this dress out for Elvira. She's coming by around noon to fetch it. You know Elvira? Elvira Rollheis."

"My folks know her. I've seen her husband, Vern. He comes by now and then, and talks with my father."

"Your father," she said, mostly to herself. "He's become quite the leading citizen."

She turned quiet, attentive to her task. Having finished removing stitches, she pinned the seam and started re-sewing it with needle and thread, fingers moving rapidly, the way Agnes May's fingers had moved that day at the pump house when I'd seen her braid her hair.

"Are you sweet on her, Eugene?" She said quietly, eyes on her work.

"Ma'am?"

"My Agnes May." She stopped to look up, peering into me. My voice choked a little. "We're friends at school."

She smiled again and went back to sewing. It wasn't a friendly smile. More a smile that said she knew: knew why I was here, knew that I'd only pretended it was to talk about starters. She'd figured out pretty quickly what a liar I was. It made the stool — the top of it a flat circle of rough-cut wood — harder through the seat of my dungarees, my flesh reading the grain.

"She is only twelve, you know." Her fingers picked up speed. "A girl — a girl of twelve — doesn't know what's truly in her heart. Her heart has not yet had the chance to grow to the full size of all those things that are suddenly trying to occupy it."

She was quiet for a while, till I said, "Yes, Ma'am."

She stopped and peered into me again. "I look at Agnes May and see me — age twelve. You suddenly feel yourself under an avalanche, you know, of so many sensations at once, and ideas and fanciful longings, all jumbled together, all very confusing."

Agnes May had talked about being whipped once by her father for having fancy notions. What did her mother think of that?

She went back to her sewing, eyebrows drawn tight, push and pull of needle and thread having slowed. Then it stopped altogether. She looked up at me, eyes clouding. "Will you promise me, Eugene?"

"Promise you? Promise you what, Mrs. Stippil?"

"To be...just her friend. Be her *true* friend. She is so good natured, you see...so vulnerable. Promise to never hurt her, Eugene. Never hurt her in the ways a boy can hurt a girl in that dreamy state. You know what I mean. A boy can get funny ideas, after all."

Laying the work over the sewing machine, she placed her hands in her lap, and looked at me as she chewed her lip. "I'm so afraid for her in times ahead, as I'm certain your parents are for you."

I shrugged.

"You are at that age too, Eugene...as the Reverend says, the age when parents must begin to put grownup demands on a young one. At times, it may seem he is a bit strict with Adam. But Adam is tough as nails. Not so, Agnes May."

She twisted her hands together, twined her fingers. "Her little life is sure to become more difficult now: she is at that age." She breathed a short laugh. "I'm sure you can see we are not as refined as you Aherns. Poor simple people, that's what we are, who have little more than our faith in the Lord to see us through tough times."

I nodded, and took a sip of water.

"This is a tough time in a girl's life," she said, "a girl's sensitive, youthful life, and we must now be in earnest about imparting old-time values. We must — not that the Reverend isn't understanding of natural human struggles, Lord knows—but we parents must be intent on strictly forging and sharpening a righteous blade to separate what is heavenly and what are just fanciful notions."

The angry bruises I'd seen swirled into Adam's flesh that day. And Agnes May had already told me of being whipped too. The Reverend had even made her think she *deserved* it. It suddenly made my face hot.

"Mrs. Stippil."

She looked up.

"Yes," I said. "I intend to be a true friend. I promise. I won't get funny ideas around her."

Her face melted into a smile—this time a friendly smile—and her hands let go of the grip they had on each other, rose up, palms brushing back errant hair at the edges of her bonnet. "I don't know your parents well. They must be fine people, Eugene." Her eyes flashed.

"Mrs. Stippil," I said as something rushed from deep inside me. "Will you also promise me?"

Smile brightened further. "Of course, Eugene."

"Don't let the Reverend put a hand to her. Not ever."

She stared at her lap, eyes rounding out. I waited for a long time while the seat of the stool grew harder, grain of the wood rougher. I waited, but Mrs. Stippil lost the light from her face and did not look at me anymore.

I waited a long while, then got up from the stool, put it back in its place in the kitchen, and put the tin cup in the wooden sink, the noises of my motions loud against the silence. Outside, as I stepped down from the porch, she called through the screen, "Young man!"

I turned around.

In a strong, even voice she said, "'Now, as the Church submits to Christ, so also should wives submit to their husbands in all things.'"

Long dress swirling, braid whipping around, she went back into the house to her sewing. The sound of Adam's chopping briefly came to a halt behind the church, then resumed.

I was well on my way toward home, all the way to the tree line at the bottom of the hill, before I realized that I'd never learned where Agnes May was that morning.

CHAPTER 40, NEWNESS OF IT

I was about to turn and head up the hill to the house when I spotted a speck of color. There, far down in the lower pasture, in the walnut grove: a light speck of color that moved, and when I focused on it, Agnes May, tiny in the distance, stooped over something, straightened up and stooped again.

Spreading two strands of barbed wire, I went into what my father told me had long ago been the summer pasture. In his later years, Grandpa Carroll, grown too weak to farm anymore, had closed down the dairy and sold off the herd, and nature ever since had been slowly turning this piece of steep land back to her own purposes. Among clusters of shrubs and a scattering of pine and hardwood saplings, I made my way through a tangle of grasses and wild flowers, a waist-high thatch flourishing over the years on ground that was no longer being grazed. My father's horses were not allowed down here because of walnut toxins, which had never seemed to bother cattle.

She was down at the far end, where the high trees were rooted in slanted ground just above where Hobbes Creek ran through the east end of the farm. Agnes May, alerted by the swish of undergrowth, stood and turned. She was wearing her everyday clothes again, faded with washings, dress shaping itself to her much more closely than the new dress she'd worn last week at the Victory Tent.

Her cheeks pinked up. "I suppose you're going to say something smart, Eugene."

She had filled three bushel baskets with fallen walnuts, and was working on a fourth, cotton gloves black and sticky with residue from the husks.

"You need any help?"

"Just as I thought: something smart."

"Agnes May, do you or don't you want my help?"

She straightened up again, hands out away from her dress to keep from staining it. "Do you see a pair of gloves for *you* anywhere?" She stooped and went back to gathering.

She was right. If I tried to help her, I'd be wearing it on my hands into next week. Not a good way to start seventh grade, especially at Saint Agatha, which had mostly town kids.

"I can help you carry the baskets, then. Where are you taking them?"

She rolled her eyes at me. I already knew that her family came over in the evenings without asking to take walnuts from this grove. They'd been doing it for years. And I knew that my father pretended he didn't know, and I suspected that the Reverend Stippil pretended he didn't know that my father knew. I decided to pretend, for Agnes May's sake, that I didn't know either.

"I'm just glad somebody is putting all these walnuts to good use," I said.

She stopped working, turned to me. "Why doesn't your family ever do anything with these? You Aherns think nothing of wasting such plenty." She spoke in a scolding tone, but without looking at me, her face and neck flushed.

I shrugged. "They actually belong to some candy company."

She studied the baskets, her brow knitted. No doubt she had assumed the walnuts belonged to us: that the Stippils had been stealing from the Aherns all along, not from a company.

Looking up at me, she spoke above a whisper, worry constricting her voice. "Do you suppose the candy company notices they are missing a few?"

"Not likely." Hooking thumbs in my back pockets the way my father would do, I rocked up on my toes and back on my heels. "Wesley Confectionery went belly up some thirty years ago." It was what I'd heard my father say to the man who had come from Michigan to talk with him about the walnut trees.

Placing a few walnuts atop the last basket, her eyes lit up. "Then, these don't really belong to anybody, do they?"

"Technically, they belong to..." I had to stop and remember who the man had said he represented "Grand Rapids Elegant Fine Furniture. So, I doubt you need to worry. A furniture company wouldn't give a hoot about any nuts; only about the trees they fall out of, which they claim are actually theirs."

"The trees are not your family's?" She looked up into the canopies high overhead, the pale stretch of her throat drawing my eye to her.

"What I heard is that a candy company paid my grandfather to let them plant the trees back in 1911. Later on, somehow, a furniture company got the rights to them."

She looked at me, eyes glistening, cheeks red. She showed me a face I'd never seen before. "Why do they do that?" she said, arms spreading from her sides.

"Who? Do what?"

"Oh—the grownups, I guess," she said, her mouth wet with spit, eyes glaring. "Somebody can own a grove of trees who's never even seen it? Or own walnuts they don't even know fall to the ground every year, and then would just rot away unless people came along and stole them? And tell me this, Eugene: just how can your family own all those old weathered upturned stumps that have rotted away into the ground for fifty years, instead of letting people use them for firewood?"

I shrugged. "Don't yell at *me*, Agnes May. I didn't do any of it."

Pulling her gloves off, she threw them onto one of the baskets, then sat down on the grass, pulling her legs up to herself, dress stretched over her knees. I sat down too. My hip lightly touched hers, feeling heat from her.

We were both quiet. The air filled with syllables from water flowing over stones down in the creek. On the bleached end of an old limb that was partially embedded in the creek bed, two box turtles, motionless, took in the sun.

Turning to me, she said, "I get tired of it sometimes, that's all…the way grownups have to boss every little corner of everything, and then make it all so complicated."

We both suddenly laughed at that. In just an instant it occurred to the two of us at the same time that you can get real tired of grownups. Just like getting tired of a long winter, or the last hour of a school day, or chores you have to do. Maybe grownups had no higher standing than anything else that could bog down your life.

"It used to seem like they were always right," I decided, "but now, more and more, it seems like you just have to keep quiet and pretend to go along."

"But why does somebody always have to own everything?" She leaned against me. "I mean, do those turtles belong to anybody?"

I laughed. "Maybe somebody from somewhere, like New Jersey, or Delaware, or some state out west, will suddenly tell us we aren't allowed to look at them sleeping on a log."

She smiled and wiggled against me. I reached—was I supposed to put my arm over or under her braid? I decided, under—across her back and found her shoulder, surprised at how small it was, at its softness. She tucked her other shoulder by my ribs.

She turned to me, her braid swinging away, tickling as it brushed the back of my hand. "Did you ever think we would be friends, Eugene?" her lips and teeth forming words so close to me.

"No."

She laughed, rested her head on my shoulder. The smell of her hair drew me to new hay, to fresh silage, to Grandma's window box thriving with spices. It was like a mixture of all those favorite smells, and yet it was not those same smells at all...just in the way it drew me in, had me wanting to sit even closer to Agnes May.

She said, "You're my only friend, you know."

"What about Lucinda Hobbes? I've seen you talking with her plenty."

She straightened up, shifted away a little. "Oh, my parents don't approve of the Hobbeses, especially Lucinda. Besides, she is so much older than me that I don't understand her much of the time. And, well, now she's gone anyway."

"Gone?"

"Didn't you know?"

"Know what?"

"She ran away. She ran away with some Catholic boy from Wyotanda. Al something... Cousineau?"

"Al Cousineau? She ran away with him? What does that mean: she ran away with him? To where?"

"Nobody seems to know. They both disappeared that night the fair closed, disappeared in that boy's old gray Ford."

"I wonder how they even knew each other, Al and Lucinda."

"At the fair...haven't you been listening? They somehow met at the fair. They were together the whole week. They even came into the Victory Tent one evening, Lucinda's face so full and eyes so shiny and blue. They ordered lemonade. They stayed only a few minutes on account of the Reverend staring, and then he questioned how old they were."

The moment that had seemed to pop in and out of existence three years ago up in the Hobbes hallway, the moment when Lucinda and I had looked at each other: I had been imagining all along that it was somehow still going, still going in its own secret world. Now it was gone for good...a world that suddenly went poof!

"Huh," I said. "Al Cousineau and Lucinda."

Agnes May stood, sliding my hand off her shoulder. "Well, I have to be getting home. They'll be sending my brother after me before long."

I stood too, my arm warm from having been around her. "Are you going to leave the baskets here, then?"

She blushed, and spoke with hesitation in her words. "We'll be coming over later, after supper, in the truck."

The turtles moved. We watched them climb off the bleached wood and slide into the water. Just their heads emerged a moment later. Walking up the hill together, we helped each other through the barbed wire.

"I certainly know my own way home," she said as I continued to walk along with her.

I paid her remark no mind, and she said no more about it.

When you walk the contour of a hill with a girl, should you be upside or downside? It had never mattered before because I had never done it. Grandma had told me that a gentleman always walked on the traffic side of a sidewalk because, in the olden days, he would protect her with his body from mud and water splashing off carriage wheels. So, on the side of a hill, how would I be protective? Maybe on the downhill side, in case she stumbled, so I could protect her from falling further down the hill and hurting herself. But, why would she stumble? Agnes May walked by herself through fields and woods all the time. I tried it anyway, for a while. It put her head above mine, so I soon switched. And now, shorter than me, she was so much lower that she had to bend her neck back to look up as she spoke more about Lucinda, telling me how she would miss the talks between two of them. So, I switched again.

She stopped and put both hands on her hips. "What are you doing? Why are you moving back and forth?"

My skill for lying suddenly awoke to save me: "Snakes."

Soft brown eyes turned hard. "Snakes?"

"Mostly black snakes, but you never can tell. Copperheads are known to be around here too, you know."

She frowned at that. "Oh, I don't think so, Eugene. Did you miss school that day? Poisonous snakes are seldom seen in Melody Falls Township. Across the river, now, that's a different story. Those people have to be careful over there. And they are said to be plentiful over in Susquehanna County."

I should have figured: Agnes May would never have forgotten any bit of knowledge passed on to her from the lips of Miss Hendershott.

My face flushed. "I knew that," I said. "But it only takes one copperhead to kill a man, you know — or a woman — I mean, a girl. I'm just keeping my eye out."

Her eyes softened. "You could walk out ahead of me…scout them out." She smiled.

I didn't return her smile. I was the male, after all, and knew instinctively the seriousness of the situation…a situation that I'd made up.

Now, this was more like it. This is just how Quin and I would walk the contour of a slope together: single file. But then it grew awkward that she wasn't talking any more. Another boy and I would have easily talked without looking at each other as we walked along. Behind me, there was nothing but breathing and swishing of grass. I stopped, turned and took her hand.

She pulled away. "You really shouldn't, you know."

"Shouldn't what?"

"If you were truly Christian, you would already know what. If you came to our church, you could learn about virtuous resolve."

"Never heard of it."

"That doesn't surprise me. It's what you can lose if you get too close to someone before you're old enough to marry. That must be what happened to Lucinda."

I stood and looked at her. Her eyes slowly lost the brightness of being so certain, and she had to look away.

She said, "Are we just going to stand here? I have to get home."

"I'm thinking."

"What's there to think about?" she said. "It's all very simple, really."

"Is it something you can feel?"

She peered at me. "Is *what* something you can feel?"

"Losing your—what did you call it?"

"Virtuous resolve. The Reverend has preached many sermons on it. You wouldn't be asking so many questions if you were a member of the Melody Falls Watchful Christian Fellowship."

"Agnes May, all I'm asking is what it feels like to lose it. I mean, is it like getting a flat tire on your bicycle, or what?"

She flushed. "It is not a joke, Eugene."

"I'm not joking." I took her left hand with my right. Her eyes sharpened. Her lips opened a little as she peered at me.

"What do you feel?" I said.

"Your hand. It's very rough compared to mine."

"Well, it figures. I was digging that trench for half the summer."

She smiled. "Yes, I watched you almost every day. Remember?"

I lightly squeezed her soft hand. "Agnes May, do you feel any virtuous resolve leaking out?"

She laughed, her breath puffing my face.

I took the downhill side. Holding hands as we walked had us much closer together, which almost put us at the same height. I found myself glancing at her face so near mine. We didn't talk, but it was not the awkward silence that had earlier shrouded us while walking single file. Side by side so close, bumping each other now and then, breaths at the same cadence…the newness of it just didn't need our voices.

## Chapter 41, First Time

The night before my start as a seventh grader, Grandma Marja had another bout of feeling poorly. She fell silent on the sofa, and then pushed away our attempts to help her up. My parents gave her bedding and let her stay there for the night. I heard them talk about moving her bedroom downstairs soon, the way they had done for Grandpa many years ago.

So, my mother, in place of Grandma, got up early to fix breakfast. She stood across the table from me, yawned and watched me slurp oatmeal.

This wasn't Marja's oatmeal. No, this breakfast had come out of a round box, the stuff that Grandma had told me was invented as gruel for Civil War soldiers. And my mother had cooked it way too long and with too much water. It was like a lump of paste, and in spite of smatterings of sugar and cinnamon, it had turned into slime. A plentiful dousing of milk made it easier to swallow, but also sent it sliding down cold.

Lowdown, stretched out below the window, plopped her tail once.

"Eugene, is something the matter?" my mother said.

I had stopped eating, and looked at the dog. Lowdown knew: Bus Number 2 was on its way. Still some distance off, out of human ear-shot, it was just beginning a steep climb up the side road along the narrow wooded gulley that would bring it up here to Belknap Road.

"You have to eat more than that, mister."

Lowdown, a slight shift of her head, one-eyed me. She must have thought it strange that I was up so early for school at an hour when the bus made its first pass, after all these years of being picked up on the second pass. No way the dog would know that becoming a seventh grader would change my schedule. Well, this pass wouldn't be for me either. From now on, I'd be riding with my father to school in Wyotanda, to Saint Agatha.

"You don't like my oatmeal. I know it's not your grandmother's, but, really, I tried my best for you."

"Oh, no. It's fine." I put the spoon back in motion. "Pretty good, Mom."

She looked at me with suspicion. "I would ask whose is better, but it's not a fair question, is it." She headed for the stairs. "I'd better make sure your father's up. It's going to take him some time to get used to leaving so early."

Lowdown raised her head. Ears perking, she looked at me. And I heard it too: the whining of low gear as Bus Number 2 left the Rollheis farm. It had made a stop at Quin's trailer. It would be filling up with all the kids I knew, those public school kids, the ones who "generally have somewhat lower goals," my father had said. But hadn't my father gone all the way through twelve grades at Melody Falls? Hadn't Uncle Dan?

I put the spoon down, grabbed the new loose-leaf binder, pen, pencil and eraser we had purchased yesterday at Widmere's Five-and-Ten, and ran through the living room to the front door. I ran across wet grass to the break in the split-rail fence. I needed to see Quin. Suddenly that was all that mattered: to see him look at me through his glasses, and me look back at him, the way we could just about have a whole conversation together with only our expressions, the way we'd always been. He had told me in the barn at the fair that he didn't ever want things to change between us. Now, I felt it too, gnawing deep.

Down the hill the bus made the turn onto our road. From there it crept up the last steep incline, headlights appearing in the morning twilight. As the road leveled off, the transmission dropped in pitch to second gear and the bus started to pick up speed. It passed me in a whoosh, Quin looking at me through the window and yelling at the driver. An instant later, brakes screeching, it came to a stop, with gravel flying. Red lights flashed on its roof as I ran along the right side to the opening door.

I jumped up the steps. Sheffield Hoy pulled a clipboard from a space beside the driver's seat. Quin grinned at me from same old pair of seats we'd been riding in since first grade, from where we would mimic Sheffield going through the gear shift pattern and turning the wheel one-handed, tight grip on the spin-knob.

"Hold on, Eugene." Sheffield touched my arm, held me back from going to my seat. "You're not here...not on the list."

"Must be a mistake." I glanced at Quin.

"Well, I'm not supposed to take you. Didn't I hear that you were headed to Saint Agatha? Or did that get changed?"

Quin's eyes deepened. I had to look away.

A thump on the side of the bus, and Sheffield slid back the small vent window.

"What are you doing?" my father demanded, glaring at me from down in the road, face puffy, red tie loose around his neck.

I turned, stepped down and out the door, and walked around the front of the bus to the side of the road, keeping my back to Quin's window. Bus Number 2 farted from its brakes, and took off again.

My father put hands on hips. "What was *that* all about?"

"I forgot," I lied. "Sleepy, I guess."

We took the long walk back to the house without a word. He didn't believe me. It took him two tries to knot his tie as he huffed early morning air. My ears burned with embarrassment at such a stupid act. Suppose he hadn't come out to the bus to get me: how long could I have possibly carried on the charade of pretending I'd suddenly forgotten all about transferring to Saint Agatha? I could still hear the bus groaning in the distance as it wound its way along the road, heading south to pick up more of the kids who "generally have somewhat lower goals." I wondered what Quin was thinking, now...

In the house, my mother had gone back to bed. Lowdown was looking at us. She came to me, wagged her crooked tail, sniffed my crotch, and licked my fingers. My father, car keys at the ready on the table, hurriedly spooned cold cereal into his mouth from a bowl. Across the front of the Wheaties box, former pole vaulter Bob Richards calmly rode his bicycle, a broad smile on his face.

At lunch in the Saint Agatha basement cafeteria, there was plenty of space around Tommy Tanager, so I sat down. His face in a book, he was at the end of one of the ancient wooden lunch tables yellowed in varnish. I smelled tobacco on him, and having forgotten to put a cigarette in my shirt pocket, quietly asked him what brand he smoked.

Looking up from *The Foundation Trilogy*, he said, "Luckies."

"Can I bum one? I'll give you a Pall Mall tomorrow."

"No. Don't like them. But we can share one of mine," he said, "as long as you agree not to join the tease."

"Tease? What would I tease you about?"

His face reddened. "You know: when I couldn't come out of the water at Lake Margaret. They just won't leave me alone about it. They even told the girls." His face reddened some more. "They told everybody about Kaminski's boner too."

So, first thing after school found Tanager and me down under the Third Street Bridge passing a Lucky back and forth in a cloud of smoke. Pebbles skittered down the earthen embankment from the edge of the concrete abutment, followed by a pair of long legs in school-dress slacks, and then Cas Kaminski came down, ducking his head to clear an overhead steel girder.

"Thought so," he said through his nose. Kaminski spoke with a grown man's low voice that sometimes, without warning, would jump to a high falsetto. It turned his nasal tone into a tractor-trailer horn operating without enough air pressure.

Taking a drag, I handed the cigarette back to Tanager.

"I just don't believe it," Kaminski warbled at us: "Two queer-baits under one bridge."

"Hey, gaper," Tanager laughed and handed him the cigarette.

"Hey, gaper." Kaminski nodded, took a drag and handed it to me while he coughed. "Jesus, Tommy, how can you smoke these things?"

"What's gaper mean?" I asked, which had them both laughing at me.

Tanager said, "People are always making up new words around here. Gotta keep up, so better get used to it. You're not one of the Publics anymore."

Kaminski expelled enough air to warble, "Gaper...short for 'gaping ass hole.'"

They both laughed again, and I laughed along. So maybe I was making new friends.

More stones skittered down. Kaminski grabbed my shirt at the shoulder and he and Tanager and I scampered up the opposite embankment and hid behind rough concrete.

"What're we doing?" I whispered.

"Spying," Tanager whispered back. "Irene Meagher and Bev Timmons smoke down here too. Things can get real interesting."

Kaminski remained silent. Maybe he didn't know how to whisper without warbling. He raised his eyebrows at me and grinned instead.

Click of a lighter came from under the bridge, but no voices, which had Tanager peeking around the corner.

"Holy Mackerel," he shouted down into the shadows, "when did you get back?"

We followed Tanager down under the bridge. Al Cousineau, a Winston hanging from his lips, eyed the three of us. Cousineau, who would now have been a Saint Agatha Junior if he hadn't run off with Lucinda Hobbes, blew smoke over us lowly seventh graders. It hardly made sense that, almost a grownup, he would be hiding under the bridge to smoke. He could do whatever he wanted, couldn't he?

"Where've you been, Al?" Tanager said. "They said you'd taken off with some hayseed dairy maid from up on the ridge."

"What's the difference?" he said, and looked away. "I'm back."

Kaminski honked, "Back to Saint Agatha?"

He sneered at that. "Back for the day. And I'd appreciate you chumps forgetting you even saw me. Don't need anybody coming around my old lady's house to ask about me. I'll be gone in the morning anyway, but no sense in her being bothered."

I said, "Where you off to?"

He looked at us again, eyes lighting a bit. "The old lady signed papers for the recruiter last night. 5 tomorrow morning, it's the bus station for me, and I'm off to see the world...compliments of the US Navy."

"But, what happened?" Tanager demanded.

He turned sideways, eyes glistening. He spoke through smoky syllables, "Made it to North Carolina, all right. Figured we'd eventually find some backwoods preacher to marry us, you know, just to make it legal. Thought we'd nest up there, me with a meat-packing job maybe, and she learning to do hair."

"But you were only gone a week," Tanager said.

Cousineau swallowed, turned away and wiped his face in the crook of his arm. "First time...well, it just didn't work out."

## Chapter 42, Incense

Just the way Al Cousineau had shown me two years ago during my training in the Saint Agatha church basement, I folded my hands prayer-like, pushed them into the neck hole of the garment like a diver going into water, then spread them apart again before letting the surplice fall from above onto my shoulders. From inside the envelope of fabric my hands found arm holes and I pushed out. The altar boy looking back at me from the mirror had not suffered one hair out of place.

Candle lighter aflame, I left the tiny servers' sacristy for the sanctuary at Immaculate Conception Mission Church, where I immediately ran into trouble. None of the six candles would light. People noises from the scattering of worshipers — scuffs, coughs, banging down of kneelers they were not used to — turned my ears hot with embarrassment. I mean, what else did they have to look at other than a lone altar boy up there, fumbling his shiny telescopic pole fixed with a lighter on one side and a snuffer on the other? I tried everything I knew: extended the wick, bent it down at a steeper angle, moved from one stubborn candle to another, in the futile attempt to get one of them started, as if that would encourage the rest of them to go along. Finally, a finger snap turned my attention to the priest's sacristy, where Father Kearns, in the midst of putting on black vestments, motioned to me.

When I got in there, he spoke in a hoarse whisper, "It's probably been decades since a High Mass was sung in this church. You'll have to take them down one by one and light them in the sacristy by hand."

He was right. Placing the first one on the floor out of sight of the onlookers brought the top of it to eye level, where it exposed at least a quarter-inch of dust. I blew it off, finger-nailed the wick upright and lit it with a match, then repeated the process for the remaining five candles before carefully carrying each of them to the altar.

By the time I finished the job, Kearnsy was giving me that thin-lip stare from his sacristy doorway that said he was not at all pleased. But I gathered some hope that maybe he wasn't really mad at *me*. This was a funeral, after all, at which the priest was not exactly expected to appear happy. Besides, he had met us with that same dour expression yesterday in the rectory office as he accepted twenty dollars from my father in response to the words, "How about making it a High Mass for her, Father."

Father Kearns was not used to having people suggest to him what to do. He was more comfortable telling *them* what to do. But my father had, as my mother would say, "some pull around here." Two years ago, Kearnsy, looking over the parish books, had suddenly grown eager to close our mission church, which was down to serving just a handful of Catholics in the Melody Falls area...close it, save some money, maybe even sell it off to the Protestants. "Not gonna happen," my father had said at the dinner table. "No Protestants will be getting a hold of the little church where my parents were married." The next day he had confronted the pastor, which had led to a deal: keep the church open in exchange for ensuring that the cellar would be filled with firewood each fall, and that heat would be pouring out of the single cast iron floor register on cold mornings well before the start of weekly Mass. Oh, and my father would provide designated altar boys—that would be Quin and me, although today it was only me—so Kearnsy wouldn't have to find anybody to bring with him from Wyotanda.

So, when I finally finished lighting the High Mass candles, he stared me out of my sacristy and over to his—genuflection midway—where he handed me a gold container. "You ever been the boat man?"

"No, Father."

His lips grew thinner. "Put the incense boat out with the wine and water crucibles. When Mass if over, you spoon a little incense into the thurible for me."

I nodded. I'd seen Cousineau do it at Rebecca O'Sullivan's funeral, the third grader who had died of a liver blockage. "Yes, Father."

Things went smoothly after that. I'd never served a High Mass before, but it turned out to be not so different from a Low Mass. Nor had I ever served a Black Mass, but it too was not so different from a regular one...not for the server, anyway.

For the High Mass, Father Kearns chanted many of the prayers instead of the usual mumbling, which seemed to loosen him up a little. As time wore on he started looking a little more pleasant. The biggest difference, though, was the presence of three sisters up in the creaky balcony at the back, whom he had brought with him to Melody Falls from their convent in Wyotanda to sing, in clear female voices, responses to his gravelly incantations. Latin song filled the little church with sound that was both beautiful and haunting. It had you supposing that God would never refuse such full, womanly wailing that begged for mercy on behalf of the departed soul:

"*Kyrie eleison...*"

The charcoal at the bottom of the thurible had just about gone out by the time Mass was over.

"We'll fake it," Kearnsy whispered as he opened it up and had me spoon in some incense anyway.

I stood by at the front edge of the sanctuary while he went around the casket clinking the thurible against its gold chain, the noise distracting anyone who might have noticed that no smoke was coming out of it. Just as we returned to the sacristy, the charcoal hissed and restarted itself. By the time he was out of the vestments, we were in the midst of billowing, sweet clouds of smoke.

At the grave, out back of the church, the Sisters and a handful of mourners stood around the casket poised above its black, rectangular hole. Mister Rollheis was there...a Lutheran, and so he stood a little away from us. But Miss Hendershott, an Episcopalian, stood right there among us Catholics, eyes red, dabbing her round cheeks with a tissue. Kearnsy, with violent shaking of the aspergillum, spoke more Latin prayers as he threw holy water at the casket.

When it was all over, as most everybody headed for their cars, Father Kearns assured those of us still close by: "She's most likely in heaven, rejoicing with the angels."

I went to Quin and, like the adults were doing, shook his hand. I'd never seen him in a suit before. The handshake lasted only a moment. He broke it off and suddenly hugged me, like he would have done when we were three years old.

"I only wish I could have seen her," he said, tearful. "I don't really remember what she looked like. You know, if I coulda just had a glimpse, one glimpse, before they locked her in there forever."

On the way home, the Buick whined at having to climb the steep grade to Cloven Hill Farm. I told my parents from the back seat what Quin had said. They looked at each other briefly.

My father said, wagging his head. "She'd been in that vehicle for seven years. Not much left of her, I'm told. Certainly not anything for her son to look at."

They'd found her in Blacksmith Run, the article in the *Clarion* had said, a few miles west of Smethport, on Route 59. A highway worker, part of a crew that was busily applying a new coat of zinc-rich paint to the guard rail, had spotted it in the underbrush down in the ravine: rusting carcass of a '47

Dodge. On a frigid, foggy night in 1953, on her way to visit Seneca relatives, Frances Gutierrez had apparently taken the right fork in Smethport, turned off Route 6 in favor of a less traveled road over the mountain to Kinzua.

So now, seven years later, Quin's mom was finally back home.

## CHAPTER 43, THE MAN FROM BRANTFORD

Sister Aloysius Gonzaga appeared at the top of the stairs. She lowered her head and, through upper sections of rimless lenses, peered down at me on the bottom landing, where I'd been waiting just inside the door to the school pick-up area.

Through firm lips, "You're wanted on the phone."

I went upstairs, and when I entered the principal's office, she motioned me to the telephone on a small side table. The contents of a yellow folder—the lone item on an immaculate blotter—occupied her stony attention as she sat at her massive desk.

"Please forgive me," my mother's voice squeezed in over an electric hum. "I'm finally working on that weathered-stump series this afternoon, and lost all track of time. Have you been waiting long, Gene?"

"Half an hour."

"Oh, please forgive me—I can't believe I did this. I'm leaving right now."

"I'll get a ride. Don't worry about it."

Sister Aloysius glanced up from her work.

My mother said, "Oh, if you could, that would be just delicious, dear. I do so want to apply a tinge of burnt sienna while the gray is still wet—give it a more natural look. I'll make it up to you—we'll have peaches for desert, your favorite. How does that sound?"

"Sounds good," I said. Pears were my favorite, but I didn't correct her.

"It's all set then? You're sure you can get a ride? You can always go down to the courthouse and come home with your father. I'm sure he won't mind."

My father did not work set hours, like a banker. No telling how long he could be in court. "The judge is God," my father was fond of saying, "and if the judge decides to go past five o'clock, we go past five o'clock, because God said so."

"I can catch a ride with somebody here," I assured my mother as Sister looked over her glasses at me.

A man in a new canary yellow Pontiac picked me up near Wyotanda's traffic light on the corner of Bridge and Main. As we rode out of town and up the highway, he informed me that he worked for the Blue Bird School Bus Company. At the end of a ten-day sales trip, he was finally on his way home.

"That's too long to be away from the missus," he said, and grinned. "I expect to be home by nightfall, depending on traffic at the bridge. On the phone this morning she promised me — my sweet Marilee — pot roast with potatoes, carrots and onions. She knows just how much oregano."

"What bridge is that?"

"Peace Bridge, from Buffalo over to Niagara Falls. I'm from Brantford, a little ways into Ontario."

I'd never met anyone from Canada before. Here I was talking to a real foreigner…a foreigner who, by nightfall, would already be back in his own country.

At the top of the long hill, a half mile before the cut through the mountain, he stopped to let me out at my dirt-road turnoff. "Sorry I can't take you all the way. But they're callin' to me, my sweet Marilee and her pot roast," he laughed.

"Thanks," I said, closing the door on the new-car-interior smell.

Not long after I'd started hoofing it toward home, I heard the sigh from behind of an approaching car, and then shoulder gravel crunched. I turned around to a dust-covered green '52 Coronet coming to a stop.

So Baggie Hoy had gotten his old hit-or-miss Dodge going again. The broken-down dog-catcher truck was still down in our field, awaiting the township's decision on what to do with it.

We traded small talk as we drove the winding road north along the eastern contour of Belknap Ridge. When we passed the Stippil house, Baggie leaned toward me, grinned and spoke in a quiet tone. "That Stippil girl ever let you play with her puppies?"

What puppies?

Agnes May's dog Happy was an old male who had shown up at the Stippil house last turkey season, or just at the end of it, a tired-out pointer, so old that half his coat was made up gray hairs. He had a sore hind leg, sad eyes, cockle-burred ears and a crook at the end of his tail from an old break. After a few days without a lost-dog ad in the *Clarion,* the Reverend had been about to take that used-up animal down to the woods and "administer the Lord's mercy with a sudden case of lead poisoning."

Agnes May, sensing what he was about to do, had pleaded, cried and begged, promised that she would look after the mongrel. As he'd tied a rope around its neck to drag it to the truck, she had dropped to the ground and wrapped herself around her father's legs. She would not let go, even after the Reverend drew his belt from the loops of his pants and cracked her across the shoulders. It had been effective in the past against similar acts of insolence on Agnes May's part. Not this time. Her embrace had only tightened, and then she'd scissored his work boots with her legs, not letting him drag the dog off the porch. He had brought leather down on his daughter again...not just with wrist this time, but with full arm force.

When she had told me about it, she said the *crack!* surprised her at how loud it was, that the sound didn't just come to her ears but traveled through her body, and she'd heard herself scream like a wild animal. And the pointer had growled. Through tears, she'd seen murder in the dog's eyes. The lips had curled back, yellow fangs showing.

"NO!" She'd cried. "Happy, NO!"

The dog had stopped short of going after the Reverend. With sorry eyes Happy had looked at Agnes May and wiggled its crooked tail as if the name she'd suddenly given him turned out to be the right one.

The Reverend had done nothing more, feeding his belt back through loops. He'd handed the end of the rope to his daughter with a warning that she'd "just better take care of your new responsibility — or else!"

Baggie was still looking sideways at me as he drove. "Well?"

"She doesn't have any puppies."

He rolled his head back and laughed hard.

He said, "Don't forget, in my official capacity, I had reason over the summer to park down along the old side road...you know, watch for peculiarities. Now, I saw you two, saw you in the grass together. Those old-fashioned clothes of hers can't hide those new little puppies, not from department-issue binoculars. No, you ain't fooling ole Baggie."

"You were watching Agnes May and me?" My voice wavered. My hands wanted to form into claws, like they'd done the day he'd taken me into the darkness behind the showers at the fairgrounds to show me that secret peep hole of his.

"Aw, now don't you come jumping up at me right outta your jockstrap, size small. I didn't see nothing, as if there woulda been very much to see anyway. Give her another year, and those pups will be young hounds looking for attention."

My stomach quivered.

"Well, a piece of advice, young Ahern: you keep at it. Don't give up. You know that Hobbes gal, the one that screamed at us in the alley at the fair?"

She hadn't screamed at *us*. She'd screamed at Baggie. Lucky for me, Lucinda was too angry with him to remember to say, "What are *you* lookin at, squirt?" like she normally would have done. Had she said that to me in front of Baggie, all of Wilmot County would have heard about it.

"Lucinda?"

"Yeh, Lucinda." Baggie licked his lips. "Hard to believe that such a prime piece could have come from Old Man Hobbes. Makes you kinda wonder if his first old lady—Angela, the one that died of the titty cancer—makes you wonder if maybe she'd served up something to somebody else on the side."

"Hangy's real mom? I didn't know her," I said. "She was always sick. She died when I was in first grade."

We rode along in silence until we rounded the curve at Hobbes Woods and stopped in front my house.

"Well," Baggie said, "you just keep on trying. Like me with Lucinda. I'd been turning on the ole Baggie charm whenever I saw her, anticipatin' it wouldn't be too long, she'd be of age, you know..." he rolled his eyes at me and spoke more quietly, "where it wouldn't come back on me if I did get to play in the hay some fine day with those full-grown lovelies of hers. And now, after all my priming, she up and ran off with that Cousineau kid."

As I moved to get out of the car, he poked me in the arm and laughed. "But now she's back! Back and lookin' for a *real* man. Won't be long: yours truly can expect to pay a visit to the little doghouse."

"Thanks for the ride," I lied.

Maybe it was because I had successfully made it through elementary school with only one mark against me in my mother's mind, my only crime having been to finish second in the class instead of first. Or, now attending the Catholic school, maybe it was that I was under the strict tutelage of seventh grade teacher, Sister Miriam. Word had it "Big Miriam" had grown up on the mean streets of Brooklyn, New York, and just because she wore rosary beads on her belt, was not above, "jerking you to the principal's office by the ear." Whatever it was, my mother must have figured I had finally arrived, had attained a new level of maturity, one that rendered her previous homework-policing activity unnecessary. In the two weeks since the opening of the school year, she had not once insisted on inspecting my papers.

Nor was I required to sit at the dining room table after supper to complete my assignments, the way I'd done for the first six years of my academic life. I was free to be a mature "young man;" free to lie in luxury across my bed in my own room if I felt like it...and I did feel like it quite a lot; across my bed where long division might have been at the mercy of a sudden impulse to sketch the North American Racing Team's Ferrari 250, where assigned chapters in the American History textbook could have readily surrendered to batting-average calculations. I mean, so close to season's end, the batting title on the line, who wanted to wait for the Sunday sports page? And sentence diagrams that Big Miriam from Brooklyn was obsessed with making us do could have easily wandered off the page as — clock ticking to zero — I made a stretched-out fingertip catch in the corner of the end zone, or blasted a German oil refinery from above and flew right on through the aftermath, plume of orange flame unfolding hundreds of feet into the atmosphere.

But distraction was not limited to imagination. Just as easily, tractor drone and pungent smells from Oswald Tull's end-of-summer plowing drew me from my bed to the window screen. As I looked into soft light of evening, my ride with Baggie this afternoon was still fresh with sadness. It was a sadness not composed of sights and sounds and smells, but sadness that came from its own world, which I knew nothing about. And my stark ignorance of that world allowed it to expand into my own world, where it wanted to take over. The things Baggie Hoy had said — his words, gestures, tone of voice — had tried to spoil feelings that were sprouting, feelings I had thought of as clean and new. It was as if crude hands had grabbed one of Marja's lace curtains, ripped it from the window, and wiped up filth from the floor.

Through my window, I looked far into the distance. Up on a rise formed by one of the mountain's eastern folds, white-tail deer were out of the woods to graze. You never saw them come out. By some kind of magic, one moment just turned into another and they were suddenly there, tan specks in a far hay field.

Closer by, down in the lower pasture, yellow pond grass parted. A red fox carefully eyed her surroundings, ears alert, and then lapped up a drink of water. She soon disappeared the way she had come.

Suddenly something moved along the side road. I kept looking until a gap in the hedgerow revealed what had drawn my eye down there: a dark shape…the nose of Reverend Stippil's truck.

I left my bedroom and went out into the cricket-filled evening, figuring to spy on the Stippils stealing walnuts. As I made my way down the side road, I kept to the ditch, careful to not be seen by them, careful to not spoil the silent pretending that had gone on for years. As I moved closer, I went into a crouch, inching along in the stony ditch, allowing the ancient dark Power Wagon to lure me, as if it knew of my weakness for investigating things mechanical.

The tailgate hung almost to the ground, a large impression of DODGE reversed and upside-down in the steel panel. The cargo box yawned unabashedly, exposing gaps, gouges and creases in the bed and sides, where a few scratchy remnants of original black paint clung to terraces of rust. Dented, round fenders scantily covered the wheels, whose military style scallop-treads were armored with tire chain, flattened links harboring small bread crusts of dry earth. The headlights, attached atop the fenders as if an afterthought many years ago at the Dodge factory, had long since lost the will to share a common aim. Out of a rippled weld on the front bumper, a C-channel structure rose up to a winch pulley that dangled a rusty hook, like the beak of a great iron snapping turtle.

I squatted down, hand resting on the warm radiator grille, and peered at the beast's underbelly: grimy gear boxes cowered behind skid plates, shafts poked from massive bell housings, all arranged in a dark, mysterious congregation that, in a state of rest, quietly dripped oil.

"Away from the truck!"

Only then was I aware of the sliding sounds of their approach in pasture grass. I half-turned…froze, the way a rabbit would. From under the bill of his brown hat, Reverend Stippil looked at me with large, round, gray eyes, and I re-envisioned the elderberry stain crosshatch I had seen crafted in Adam's flesh. The missus, Hughla Stippil, gray bonnet tied below her chin, stared at me. So did Adam. So did Agnes May. The closer to the truck the family of round eyes came, the closer I came to bolting. In my mind's ear, my father was already yelling at me for being the cause of a great unravel of all the pretending.

Muscles strained the sleeves and shoulders and buttons of the Reverend's blue shirt. He carried two full baskets, one against the belt buckle of his dungarees, the other atop it, against his chest. Mrs. Stippil's basket stretched her arms out, so the burden bobbed against the pinned-up skirt of a full-length tiny flower dress with each step. Adam and Agnes May managed one basket between them. As always, they were dressed in a manner so similar to their parents that they seemed like miniature versions of them, even to the same brown hat for Adam and Agnes May's bonnet and full-length dress.

From somewhere beyond the primitive need to bolt, my voice sounded small, "Do you folks need help?"

"How thoughtful of the boy," Hughla Stippil whispered toward her husband, who offered no reply as he lifted his burden onto the back of the cargo box. The truck shivered on its suspension, and from somewhere down under, the chassis chirped. Attentive to his task, his round, gray eyes finally let me go. Mrs. Stippil smiled at the ground. Adam looked toward me, his head at an odd angle, as if to ask why I couldn't just disappear. Agnes May looked away.

When I stepped toward Mrs. Stippil and grasped one of the handles from her stretched-out grip, her cocoa eyes left the ground and alighted on me. Together we swung the basket up onto the cargo box. The motion caused her long braid to swish around her torso, revealing a blue wad of rubber band that held it fast near the end. We both quickly got out of the way for the Reverend to reposition the basket along the bed with a raspy shove.

I stepped close to Agnes May, close to her braid, with the same blue rubber band holding it at the end, and attempted to take her place as Adam's partner in their struggle. She resisted, refused to look at me, at first refused to give the wire handle to me...until her mother frowned at her. She finally let go, and rubbed her hands together as if to erase the red lines left in her palms. Adam and I swung up the last basket. The Reverend shoved it along the bed and raised the squeaky tailgate. With a clang and rattling of chain, he fastened it shut.

Adam stood with his father for a moment, their heads down so hat bills concealed lowered eyes, the two of them examining the ground. Adam, with the toe of his shoe, loosened dry mud and tiny pebbles from the rear bumper. The Reverend, pulling a soiled rag from his back pocket, attended to the lone taillight, which had suddenly developed a need for removal of years of grime.

Mrs. Stippil smiled with all of herself. And then, Agnes May smiled too. Up close, they both radiated flushed cheeks and faint womanly smells. As mother and daughter moved toward the Power Wagon's passenger door, daughter briefly sidled close to me. In the last of evening light, she looked at me, eyes turning from solid light-brown to sand, and her breath touched my face.

"Let's go," the Reverend said, and they all climbed in, Adam in back, sitting atop one of the baskets.

With complaint from the starter, the old Power Wagon coughed to life. He backed it out and turned around. The Stippils headed back up the side road, tire chains singing to the whir and whine from various underbelly shafts and gear boxes.

It was almost nightfall. The man from Brantford would be arriving home now; home after ten days of missing his pot roast with potatoes, carrots and onions with just the right amount of oregano; home to sweet Marilee.

## Chapter 44, The Color of Grapes

Daylight filled the window. In my grogginess, a flash of fear — was I late for school? No — today was Saturday.

I threw off the sheet and swung my feet onto the floor, which brought me to full wakefulness. Part of me wanted to lie back down and return to the dream, which rapidly faded away...return to it before it was gone for good. But I knew I shouldn't. Even as I stood to dress, the dream's sweetness, running in rivulets out from under it as it melted away, stayed with me.

Would I have to go to Confession again? Father Kearns would be in his dark cubicle in the rear corner of the church from 4 to 6 this evening. If I asked my parents for a ride to Wyotanda, they would be suspicious, wondering what I'd done that had me going to Confession for a second Saturday in a row. It would be a bit obvious — wouldn't it? I could hitchhike down there, maybe.

But, why would I have to go to Confession, just for a dream? To be a sin, there had to be a choice, Kearnsy had told us in catechism, and then again at the retreat. While asleep I hadn't *chosen* the dream. No way it could have been a sin, then. I hadn't *chosen* that the woman in my father's secret folder come to me — again.

Al Cousineau had been right, though, that day under the Third Street Bridge when he warned us that Father Kearns's retreat would ruin us. Thanks to Kearnsy, I now knew it was a sin to even *think* about sex. Of course, the woman was only a picture, a black and white photo tucked in a folder at the bottom of a stack of old, musty legal papers. She wasn't real. But her pestering — my thinking about her, dreaming about her, even knowing about her — was my own fault, having come from being a sneak, from nosing in my father's things. And it came from having secreted a grown-up novel out of the attic last winter, the one I had covered like a school book, printed ARITHMETIC on it so my mother wouldn't ever look in there. In the scene where Philip, the ruler of Macedon, was being entertained in a tent after dinner, the nakedness of women was so delicious; the author used the word succulence, which even *sounded* delicious. So, I had looked it up in our dining room dictionary, and later, in the process of deeper probing its meanings in the thesaurus in my father's office, *succulence* found a place to curl up under my breath, a place to doze off until the next time I thought of that woman in his photo folder. *Succulence*.

New yearnings had been rising in me: it seemed like being twelve was behind it, although it must have started well before that. When I was a little kid, maybe, when Grandma Marja had cut out and given to me a potato eye, telling me to put it into a flower pot in some dirt on the sill and "watch what happens." I'd soon grown weary of watching, soon forgot all about it. Now that I was twelve, what was arising and stirring inside of me gave off the same feeling from that day when I was a little kid and came home from school to Marja's crooked finger pointing to the flower pot, to a sprout that reached for the window out of nothing but dirt. What now sprouted out of me, from nothing but a sliver of myself, from a tiny eye of the larger kid I'd become, reached for light from the window, its brightness bathing me in fresh awareness. I just knew that grownups were up to something, had been up to something all along—up to a lot of things—that I was starting to catch on to, and I was pretty sure I wasn't supposed to know about them. The grownups, my parents and Father Kearns and Grandma Marja, didn't know that I knew about succulence.

And yet, in Confession last week, Kearnsy had not seemed surprised at all at the things my twelve-year-old mind had been conjuring up, things that—thanks to his retreat—I now knew to be a sin just to be *thinking* about.

"Avoid the occasion of sin," he had droned from the darkness beyond the screen, and then had gone on to explain that nobody can just *not think* of something. "What you have to do, as soon as the occasion of sin appears on the horizon, is immediately look away at something else. Replace it with something pure to focus on." I'd stayed silent, to which he had said, "Our Blessed Mother is a big help under such circumstances. When the gang of impure thoughts starts riding toward you, focus all of your attention on the purity of the Virgin."

I'd tried it, but it hadn't worked at all. She was okay for crowning with blossoms and singing a hymn to. But just what was she, other than a statue with upturned, unmoving eyes? Yet Kearnsy—according to what people said—had been trained by the Jesuits, which they seemed to think made him more than just any old priest, so I figured there had to be something to his advice. In the past week, faced with those occasions of sin, I had tossed out the Blessed Virgin, and replaced her with Agnes May instead. Agnes May was real. Her eyes flashed when she spoke to me, her dress swished around her legs when she threw a baseball. The Blessed Mother smelled like candle wax. The succulent woman in the photo smelled like old paper. Agnes May smelled like a girl, like womanhood.

Once, as we sat against the back of the pump house, she had suddenly pointed and said, "Look there, over past the hill," just in time for me to see the tip of a disappearing fox's tail. Her words had come out, "Looky thar, over paste the heel," in that song-like Arkansas way of hers, all fidgety beside me, and her face bright in the moment. Now, that memory was something I could chase off an impure thought with. And there was that afternoon down in the lower pasture, warmth trading back and forth between our palms, breath falling between us like feathers as we walked together from our place over to hers.

But I knew it wouldn't last. The sighting of the fox, and that walk in the lower pasture, had both happened too long ago, and time was ever moving further away. I was afraid of being like the old Jeep parked under the overhang next to the manure spreader, which sometimes wouldn't start, its battery having slowly lost power from going too long without use. I needed to touch her...yes, touch her, before my purity drained away; maybe touch her for its own sake. I just needed to. My insides—my stomach, my heart, my lungs, and whatever else makes a person alive—had continued to go along and do whatever they do. But, while I was awake, such awareness of myself would fall asleep and, with eyes open, I would be dreaming of Agnes May...

My father had me help him fill the wood bins, planning way ahead so we could have a fire in the fireplace during the Thanksgiving and Christmas holidays. He had always done the splitting and I the carrying. But this year, he decided I was big enough to learn how to handle the axe. At first I had nothing but trouble.

"Few things in life are easy when you first try them," he intoned, as he watched me struggle.

My problem was that I kept getting the axe head stuck. I would have to pry it out, or use a chisel and sledge hammer to open up the fibers. I wanted to go back to carrying—a job I had always hated before this—but he wouldn't let me.

"Step into it," he said, "and just as the head is about to meet the wood, snap your wrists."

That helped, and I slowly got better at it, stepping with left foot and swinging from over right shoulder...a lot like swinging a pick, and maybe like hitting a baseball. And when I tried it as a lefty, I could develop more power, just as I had discovered on the ball field in the summer. Before long, I was no longer getting the axe head stuck at all. The motion of it allowed me to think less and less about what I was doing, took over on its own, sending a jolt of power up my legs into my back, through my shoulders and down to my wrists; ending in just a touch of the sharpened-steel edge onto upturned flat surface of the log that sent pieces flying apart with a clatter. I built up a sweat in my jacket, and took it off, smelling like a man. As we neared the end of the chore, I was splitting wood faster than he could carry, and so I helped him take the last of it into the house.

"You know," he huffed as he stood up from the wood bin, "the Protestants have it easy."

They did? Most of the neighbors, the farmers around us, were Protestants, and most of them heated their houses with firewood. Our fireplace wasn't really used for heating the place anymore. We had a new propane-fired hot-water system. We even had a thermostat on the wall to control it, whereas their only form of control was to throw another log on or change the damper settings. Then, by the look in his eye, I knew he was talking about something else. He sat down on the sofa.

"Are you starting to make friends at Saint Agatha School?"

"I think so." If you could call Tanager and Kaminski friends.

"I know it's been tough for you. But it's important that you learn what it is to be a Catholic."

"You didn't go to Saint Agatha, Dad. Neither did Uncle Dan, and he's even a priest. And besides, we go to church every Sunday."

"It's not the same anymore. In the public school, you are surrounded by kids of today, kids with different values than I'd like you to have, especially now that you're growing up."

"What values?"

"Protestant values, or no values." He looked past me. "They're taught to only worry about what they think of each other." His eyes came back to mine. "You're a Catholic. That means learning how to worry about what you think of yourself...a much tougher row to hoe, Eugene."

His face was set, the way it would be whenever he made a point he was sure of.

But the Hobbes family didn't go to church at all, didn't even believe in God as far as I could tell—except for saying a blessing at meal time, when maybe hunger made them think about it a little—and they seemed like nice enough folks. And what about Agnes May? She was the daughter of a preacher, about as Protestant as you could get, and she was a nice person too, once you got to know her.

"But Dad," I said. "Quin is a Catholic, and he goes to public school."

He shrugged, sighed and looked into the cold fireplace. "Well, at least we got the wood bins stocked up way ahead of the snow this year."

I didn't mention that we used propane to heat our house; using the fireplace was just something he did for fun these days.

Somebody was checking fence behind Rollheis' barn, and at first I thought maybe Vern had taken on another hired man. But after banging on the door to Quin's trailer and getting no response, I went over by the barn and saw that it was no man at all, just Quin in a man-size jacket and a brown cap.

"What're you doing?" I said as I came up on him.

"What's it look like—dipshit?" He didn't smile when he said it.

"Looks like you're checking fence, I guess." I was just trying to get some talk up between us. "I thought you hated hats," I said.

"I do." He stopped just long enough to take it off and wipe his forehead. It was a new cap, no smudges on the bill. "Vern said I have to wear it while I'm helping with the milking, so I just wear it all the time."

"You're helping Vern?"

"Yep."

"Alongside your old man, I guess."

"Nope. He's gone away. Cashed in my old—my mom's insurance policy, and headed south to meet up with someone who has a welding job for him."

"Quin...you mean, you're all by yourself?"

He shrugged. "Rollheis is looking after me, you might say. I'm in the trailer, but he and his old lady make sure I'm okay. He hired me for chores around the farm. They don't have any kids, you know, and now that my old man is gone, they need help."

"For money?"

He smiled with his mouth, but not his eyes. "Seventy-five cents an hour."

His face went back to a stony set as he moved along the fence, scythe rasping at the grass that had built up under the electric wire. I went with him as he moved around the pasture's edge, neither of us saying much.

"Sorry about your mother, Quin," I said after a while.

He stopped swinging the scythe. "Thanks." And then went back to work.

Where the fence finished circling around the bottom of the pasture and headed back uphill to the other side of the barn, he started to sweat.

"You want to take a breather?" I said, and was about to take off my jacket to help.

He stopped, thought about it for a moment, then said, "No," and went back at it. After a while he took off his cap and wiped his forehead. He took off his jacket and hung it on a fencepost, and put the cap on top of it.

I reached for them. "I'll carry these. You won't have to come back for them."

"Leave them there," he said without looking at me.

I stood still. He went on with the scythe, working his way up the hill. My thinking stopped. The part of my brain where thoughts come together suddenly boiled away: "Dipshit!"

He looked at me.

I looked up at him. "You got a corn cob up your ass, or what? Dipshit!"

In the next moment the space between us vanished. He was down the hill, face against mine, his eyes two black holes. He still held the scythe. I grabbed its handle with both hands. He yanked it away, and threw it aside. A hard thump on the chest, and I suddenly fell away, as sky and weeds and my own limbs tumbled through my vision, over and over, down the incline. I finally stopped, lying on my stomach, the ground seeming to spin under me. The tops of Quin's shoes appeared in front of my eyes. I grabbed his legs. He was bigger, stronger, much more savvy, and I'd never been able to get the best of him at anything. But thought was just not in the making of that moment. The moment was consumed with fire and a roar in my ears and a smell in my nostrils like burnt match-heads. I grabbed his legs, and held on as tightly as I could. My knees slipping on the grass, I tried to bring my feet under me. Fists fell against my back, an avalanche of boulders. The roar in my ears lessened a little, and words came out of him to the drumbeat of his pounding away at me.

"...damned trench of yours...don't want to hear about it...all she ever talks about...the school bus every day...all she ever says anymore...you and her and that trench...don't want to HEAR it!"

I managed to get a foot under me. I rose up—lifted him off the ground. He fell back, arms windmilling until he plopped squarely on his back, and said, "Ugh." He blinked, looking at me with round eyes. His face turned the color of grapes. He opened his mouth, but no sound came out.

The heat inside of me burst its bubble, and my chest heaved for some air. But my stomach sucked itself inward, and everything that was in it rushed past my throat and onto the ground…a puddle of curds.

Words came out of him, then, as he lay on the ground, his face coming back to its normal color; words I could barely hear because his breath was not yet ready to fully return to him:

"Leave me alone. Just get outta here and leave me alone."

Two experiences came together to spawn a notion that was, well, all wrong.

One was from a movie, *Spartacus*, a new release that wouldn't have been at the Susquehannock in downtown Wyotanda for months yet. But Tommy Tanager's older brother, Edwin, a Saint Agatha Senior, had driven Tommy and Cas Kaminski and me all the way to the Capitol Theater in Elmira to see it. The four of us had managed to squeeze into the narrow front seat of his '41 Dodge, which had no back seat. We three seventh graders paid for a fill-up at the Texaco station in Wyotanda and provided him with three packs of Winstons and, of course, had to swear not to tell anyone that he had actually taken the likes of us to a movie.

"They say it's of great historical value," we'd all told our parents, enough of an adult-sounding review to leap past their objections. Still, my mother had rattled through the Scranton Catholic diocesan paper just to check on it, only to realize that the movie was too new to have met up with the Church's official decency rating.

Jean Simmons, naked, bathed in a pond as Kirk Douglas stood at the edge, watching. I, along with the other patrons of the Capitol, had a sudden intake of breath, which we held onto as one. The theater was taken over by a vast, hollow silence that stayed in place as she came out of the water. He raised up the end of his gray tunic and lowered it down with her inside, the two of them in the same neck hole. And then breathing started up again.

The other experience was Quin's pummeling down in Rollheis's field. I'd pissed pink about an hour after we'd fought, which had had me worrying over whether to tell someone or not. Later that day my pee was back to normal, but the bruises had stayed with me for a few more days, stabbing pain slow to lose its sharpness, whenever I turned or twisted or coughed or laughed… not that I'd been laughing much.

You'd hardly think that such different experiences could possibly join together, like pieces from two separate puzzle boxes that somehow were made to fit. But on a warm evening after supper, I spotted Agnes May crossing our lower pasture, and I started down the hill. As I went around the pond, Jean

Simmons rose up out of the water to dry off, and Kirk Douglas welcomed her, wet and slippery, into his tunic. And as I stepped off the bank of the pond a twinge of pain came out of hiding from a muscle in my back, where Quin's fist had landed so many times.

The moment I had arrived at the spot where Agnes May was gathering walnuts, I saw her look at me. I saw those eyes, brown with tiny crystals of other colors, glistening like creek pebbles. I saw those eyes, the way she glanced at me, but my own eyes, my whole mind was captive to Kirk Douglas and Jean Simmons clinging to each other, slippery and wet, and Quin's fists coming down from above. Agnes May looked at me, and then her brow wrinkled just a bit, and she looked away.

Those two unrelated experiences joined, roiled up, displaced my thoughts, and spawned a notion without form. So, I did not see what was in her eyes, did not feel what was behind a brief look. Instead, the notion took over: we were male and female, alone in the walnut grove. Her dress shaped itself to roundness and little hollow places, formed itself to a shoulder, to sweep of thigh; fabric fitted itself around ripening plum of breast, and followed a hip's curve. The female stooped as she gathered walnuts, then stood straight again, belly flattening. The notion lasted only a moment. I did not see what was in her eyes because, in that whisper of time, a man inside of me, beaten and aroused into a raw state, saw himself grab the female by her long braid, drag her away...maybe to the same dark cavern in which he kept alive a naked woman from the photo file.

I knew that it made no sense, that it was all wrong. It had come to me in an instant, and then vanished. Had she seen what was in my eyes? She had turned away and did not look back, did not say anything, gave no further sign that she even cared if I was there. In her resin-stained, sticky gloves, she was fully taken with the effort of her task, filling a basket with walnuts. Sound was taken up with lapping of water in the creek, breeze rasping the trees, evening song-chatter of birds on the meadow near and far.

I picked up the full basket and carried it up to level ground. She said, "thanks," the way you might say to a box boy at the A&P. When I returned to the grove, she had started another basket. She did finally speak to me, then, looking past me at the woods, her eyes darting along with a narrative about algebra, which she was doing very well at: best in the seventh grade at Stephen Foster. And she'd been reading a biography from the Bookmobile about a mathematician, a woman from Europe who had known Albert Einstein. She asked me about Saint

Agatha, and I told her about Tommy Tanager and Cas Kaminski, and the nuns being more strict than public school teachers, the classes more difficult.

The orange evening sun lowered, outlining in red the tops of distant thunderheads. I realized that the look I had seen in her eyes earlier was not about to return. I had missed its tiny wisp. My eagerness to be with Agnes May, to see the light in her eyes, to feel her touch again, so much yearning, now sought a hollow place inside of me, a place to curl up, exhausted.

"Must be about time for your family to come along in the power wagon," I said. "I ought to go."

She nodded, a slight frown showing that we shared the same discomfort about them finding us together. She raised her eyes and looked at me—a flash of a look—then, lowered them. In that flash, and in the little sadness that her face took on the moment afterward, my yearning quivered back to wakefulness. I knew that I would likely have another chance.

"Be seeing you," she said with a little wave of sticky glove, sadness in her face turning to a crooked smile.

The next time I saw her I would be sure to look into her eyes first thing. Next time, I would look to see what she was seeing. I would not miss out again, not let the moment pass by.

I trekked back up to the house, did my homework, and went to bed. When I turned out the light I saw her shiny creek-pebble eyes. The yearning inside of me remained curled up in the hollow place it had found for itself…not sleeping soundly, but at peace where it rested.

I'd not quite fallen into slumber when Lowdown, from her favorite spot in the downstairs hallway, spoke up in her way that said she was unsure of who was approaching the house. Bark—pause. Bark—pause. My parents were still up, watching the 11 o'clock news on WNBF. Voices came from the hallway, men talking, one of them my father. The voices moved into his office below me. I slid closer to the register.

"According to the family, she was last known to be heading this way around six-thirty." The voice belonged to one of Sheriff Braddawl's deputies. It sounded like DeVerl Holland. "She takes walks now and again along Hobbes Creek where it runs down through your pasture."

"Not really walks," my father said. "The Reverend sends his kids over here to gather walnuts down there. He didn't want to admit that to you. His usual MO is to bring his truck over around dusk, when they load it up."

"Stealing? The Reverend?"

"Well, he knows I look the other way. More like helping himself than stealing."

"Huh."

"But it doesn't sound good." My father lowered his voice, which had me pressing an ear to the grate. "This is not like a normal disappearance, DeVerl."

Holland lowered his voice too. "What're you saying, Owen?"

"What I'm saying…well, it's not like some townie is wandering in the woods. From what I know of that girl, she'd be pretty savvy. It's doubtful that she just went and got herself lost."

"Huh."

"DeVerl, what is Braddawl doing about it so far?"

"Well, not much he *can* do, not tonight. Once I report your concern, he'll likely dust off the list of perverts. He's borrowed a team of sniffers from over in Potter County to start looking at first light. If anybody can find the girl, those hounds will do the job."

As the deputy left through the front door, Lowdown spoke one low bark to complain that the man didn't belong here anyway. Rustling came from the trees across the road, and then my window pane began to ping with rain.

I lay on the bed, eyes open, staring at darkness.

## Chapter 46, Trading Card

I heard it before I saw it. Just after feeding the horses, as I closed the barn door and crossed the yard toward the house, radio calls crackled through a half-rolled-up window of a dark brown '59 Plymouth in the driveway. The vehicle was nose-out toward the road, having been turned around before it was parked beside the house. Chrome antenna, too tall and whippy to stand by itself, arced forward from the rear bumper and was tied to the rooftop siren.

Any of his four deputies would have brought one of the older vehicles, with a conventional antenna adequate to pick up the lone department signal from atop the County Jail. But, for his own patrol car—always the newest of the fleet—Sheriff Dolan Braddawl insisted on access to the low-wattage radio chatter from every township jurisdiction within his domain.

I stepped up onto the porch to the clinking noises of engine cool-down. Inside the house, kitchen clatter and the smell of thyme told of Grandma Marja's dinner preparations. The sheriff's gravel laugh came through the closed office door as I passed it on the way to the stairs, and my father responded with rolling laughter of his own.

I lay across my bed, aroma from one of the sheriff's Tennessee River Rum cigar wafting up through the wall register from the office below.

"You're joking," I heard my father say. "A clairvoyant? You must be talking about the leader of those bird watchers from down at Crooked Stone. Consulting her could make you look...just a bit silly."

"Owen, ole boy, I'm kinda hoping you can help me out in that department. Maybe a little trade? Just between you and me."

"What do you have in mind?"

"You want to be the next county judge. I want to keep on being sheriff," Dolan Braddawl intoned.

"The fact that we are from opposing parties notwithstanding."

"Bull-feathers, Owen. It's just you and me talking a little trade here; two boys stealing a look at each other's baseball cards."

"Like I said, Doley: what do you have in mind?"

"We can each help the other."

"How so?"

~ 278 ~

A quiet moment followed. It ended with a soft, wet kiss the sheriff gave to his cigar as he puffed on it. "I should have no trouble at all whipping Sheffield Hoy this election, but it does help to have some insurance. Now, we honorable Republicans could let word drop in just the right places that my worthy opponent is a closet fag...as if you didn't know. But I'd like to avoid going down *that* low."

"I don't know any such thing about Shef Hoy."

More gravel laughter. "Oh, sure you don't. Even Baggie will admit to it, if you ply him with enough Old Crow. Yep, Baggie's ears turn mighty red when he says it, but get enough in him and he'll open up about his little brother liking boys."

My father was quiet. I heard the click of his lighter, and soon the smell of Prince Albert do-si-doed up through the register with the Tennessee River Rum. "So, tell me exactly what are you asking me to do? More to the point, why? You claim you'll have no trouble whipping Shef."

"Under normal circumstances."

"What's not normal?" my father said.

"This case. Disappearance of the Stippil girl."

"Got you stumped?"

"That ain't so bad, Owen. I've been stumped before. What's different here? Well, it's a little white girl, the daughter of the Reverend, with all his churchy followers, and it's drawing attention from national papers that can't wait to paint the local law enforcer—that would be me—as a dumb dick. And word is, if I don't hurry and solve it, the State Police are sending detectives from Harrisburg to move in on my damn investigation."

"That last item could help you, Doley. You just say you're calling in the big guns because this case is so important to you. Make it your idea."

"You'd be right, Owen, if the election were tomorrow. But it's two weeks away. Two weeks! Suppose that girl stays disappeared: two weeks is too much time to allow the notion to fester that maybe I'm not up to doing the job anymore."

"Sheffield Hoy would sure feed into that, all right," my father said. "And you can't underestimate Shef's popularity. People still talk about him as the hero of the '58 President's Day Blizzard."

"He stole it right out from under me," the sheriff huffed. "That mealy mouthed Civil Defense Coordinator went right around me, called the Governor, and next thing you know he's riding in a National Guard helicopter out of Tobyhanna Depot."

Conversation stalled, displaced by the raspy sound of my father drawing on his pipe. Then he said quietly, "Doley, what you've really got to watch out for is that Christian Fellowship group. No doubt, you've heard the nest of lies they've stirred up against Bert Gutierrez?"

"I don't miss much, Owen. I've heard the poison tongue-wagging, all right. They have poor Bert tied in with an imaginary gang that kidnaps girls and hauls them off to—where did Gutierrez come from?—Texas?"

My father said, "You never know where that herd might stampede to next with Reverend Stippil heading them up. It's *his* daughter that's missing. He might decide Sheriff Braddawl is in on it too."

"Exactly. I trust you won't mention that last observation to your honorable Democratic cohort. I don't need my opponent noodling around *that* idea."

"Like you said, Doley, it's just you and me talking here. So, what's the trade you're after? A Herb Score for a Whitey Ford?"

Sheriff Braddawl laughed, started coughing, and tried to speak through more wet coughs.

"You okay, Doley?" my father asked.

He coughed some more, then cleared his throat. "Ain't that a shame what happened to Herb Score? Lost the mustard after McDougald tattooed him in the face."

"McDougald's not the same either," my father said. "Seems like it did something to him, too: word is, he's done. The Yanks'll have the new guy at short next season—you watch. A Polish kid from Milwaukee."

They were quiet again, and let the office settle into more soft cigar and pipe noises.

"You want to see my card, Owen? Here it is for you. You ain't gonna win no how, not all by yourself. You already have two strikes, and I happen to know what the next pitch is gonna be from Bill MacKenzie, my Republican friend and your worthy opponent."

"Two strikes?"

"Two strikes. You're a Democrat—strike one. A Catholic—strike two."

"Doesn't seem to be hurting Kennedy," my father said. "The polls give him a pretty good chance against a Protestant Republican."

"But this here ain't New York or Chicago or Saint Louis—unwashed hordes of Micks, Spics, Dagos and Pollacks eager to do the Papacy's bidding."

My father laughed. "'In the Pope We Hope,' soon to be stamped on every coin in the land."

"This *is* Wilmot County, Owen. You can't be our next judge without some Protestant Republican votes...period."

"Don't even say it, Doley. You can deliver them for me."

"I can deliver them for you, and a whole lot of them. What's the word? Discreetly. I can deliver them for you very discreetly."

"In exchange for?"

"Your son."

"Eugene?"

Hearing my name, I slid closer to the register, black metal cool against my ear.

My father laughed a hollow laugh, the kind that falls from the front of the mouth. "What is it, Doley? You want to recruit him to be one of your highly skilled deputies?"

"I need the kid, Owen, just for an interview. One interview. And I need his silence about it. Nobody—and I mean *nobody*—needs to know."

"Sorry, Doley. I just don't recognize the trading card you're showing me, nor what you're asking for. What could Eugene possibly have to do with any of this?"

Quiet was broken by the scratchy sound of a match being struck. Soon came the smell of sulfur, and a new waft of rum aroma from another crook.

"As you know, I interviewed your kid yesterday. Him and the kids he runs with. Hobbes, that Gutierrez whelp, and the missing girl's brother. I've been at this for a lot of years, and your kid knows something, Owen. Now, he might not even know he knows. But he definitely knows something."

I realized my breathing was hard and fast. What if they could hear me? I moved a little away.

"So, interview all of them again," my father said. "Why does it have to be a secret?"

"Because, I want Dolores Kettering to do the interview. Yes, the bird-watching lady from down at Crooked Stone. Just her and your kid. Nobody else."

"So, you *do* think there's something to the clairvoyant. Doesn't sound like you, Doley."

"No. Not exactly. I did watch her at the fair, though. Have to hand it to her: a real artist. She can get things out of people they don't even know they know."

"Why the secrecy?"

"Just what do you suppose my opponent will say to the voters of Wilmot County about a sheriff who consulted a clairvoyant? He couldn't figure out the case for himself, that's what—had to get help from a psycho—from a psycho bird watcher, of all things." He went into another coughing fit. "You get the idea," he said among spasms.

When he had recovered, my father said, "You mean a psychic."

"Yeh, that too. I doubt she's for real, though. They say that some are and some ain't."

"But why Eugene? You interviewed him yesterday. You think he knows anything that any of the other kids don't know?"

The sheriff kissed his new cigar with a loud smack. "The difference between him and the other kids — well, first of all, I judge he's the kind who will keep quiet when his old man tells him to. Second, word is he'd been seeing a lot of the subject, our Miss Agnes May Stippil."

"Word? Whose word?"

"Baggie's."

My father laughed hard. "You're putting credence in anything Baggie Hoy says? Your reelection campaign must be in the drop, all right."

"Just hear me out, Owen. A little help from Old Crow, and Baggie's word is good, generally."

"No, you hear me out." My father cleared his throat. "Eugene is friends with her brother, Adam. He went over there a lot to play ball during the summer, and help paint their holy roller church. That's all."

"Not talking about playing ball over there at Fellowship Field. Let's talk about the hole you had your kid dig half way to China on the back forty."

"The trench? A new water line for the Percherons. Jesus H. Christ, Doley. What's this about?"

The sheriff laughed. "Too cheap to hire a backhoe for one afternoon, you paddy tightwad. Make your kid work his ass off all summer long."

"It was good for him," my father said more calmly. "Educational."

"According to Baggie, our now-missing lass was over here, down in your pasture day after day, helping your son...with his education."

"How much Old Crow did it take to loosen *that* dirt out of Baggie?"

"The point is, your kid seems to know the girl better than anybody. Our friendly bird watcher just might uncover something I can use for a lead; like, where she goes and what she does. I'd be way out in front of those State Police stiff suits from Harrisburg...maybe figure out whose abandoned cistern the young thing might have fallen into. Suppose I pull this case right from under their frosty noses: local dumb dick makes the front page of the *Daily Planet*."

They were quiet for a while. I smelled new mingling of smoke as it rose up through the register.

"So tell me, Doley—just for flops and jiggles—why would I allow my son to be party to this scheme?"

"Because, Owen ole boy, like I said, you're going to need Protestant Republican votes if you have any hope of getting on base. And don't forget the strike-out pitch. I know what MacKenzie's got in mind."

"You think he's got something on me."

"Not exactly. Not on you. On your kid."

"On Eugene? What are you holding back?"

I slid close again, and held my ear tight to the register.

"Well, your kid is best friends with the Gutierrez kid—what's his name?—Joe-uh-quin. That's all it takes. Your opponent just needs to mix it into the stew. Folks can be counted on to add in their own spices. You know: young, innocent girl hauled off by a Mexican, kicking and screaming, down to Texas, where sweaty oil riggers bid top dollar for a virgin, possibly a real one for a change. Many a pious voter will imagine filthy hands pawing over that innocent, soft, white flesh…still hairless, maybe."

"Jesus Christ, Dolan," My father muttered.

"Yeh, I hear you. Pardon my crudity. Spend a day in my chair, some time, and you'll find yourself seeing into some of the darker corners."

After a moment, my father said, "Your chair is not all that far away from mine."

The sheriff laughed. "You don't have to tell me. I'm the man who's arrested every one of the low-lifes that you keep getting off."

The squeak of leather was followed by a grunt and a breathy change in the sheriff's voice from the effort of standing up. "I'll leave you to your thoughts, Owen."

"Promise me one thing, Sheriff: you won't ever ply Baggie Hoy with any of the good stuff. I'd hate to imagine a bottle of Jameson disappearing down *that* stinking hole."

"I'll throw that into the deal," he said, and coughed. "I can see it's mighty important to you, counselor…I mean, Your Honor."

## Chapter 47, Within the Shadow

It was only a weekday, but my mother had made a fuss about preparing dinner all by herself, refusing to allow Grandma into the kitchen.

We sat around the dining room table to Grandma's grumbling. "It's not my birthday, you know."

My mother said, her tone soft, "You've always done so much, all these years, Marja."

My father and I were quiet, both busy cutting away at our pork chops and forking mashed potatoes and peas.

"I hope you're not saying you don't need my help anymore, Veronica." Grandma's eyebrows lowered. "It's a job, seeing after men folk."

My mother smiled. "It's time I took on more responsibility, that's all."

My father forked the last lump of his mashed potatoes into his mouth. Switching the fork to his left hand, he stabbed and slid his pork chop around in slurry of left-over gravy.

"I so appreciate it, Marja." She smiled again. "And it's time for you to stop working so hard, now, to enjoy yourself more."

Grandma inflated her lips. "Pooh," she said, looking away.

My father placed his silverware at the top of his plate and rested his hands on the table on either side of it. He swallowed. He sat back in his chair, which drew our attention.

"*Kulta*," he said. "Veronica has something to tell you. Something important." His eyes shifted to me. "Something to tell both of you."

As he went back to his fork and knife and pork chop, we looked at my mother, who sat back, hands in her lap, eyes down. Her face suddenly flushed, and she looked up at Grandma, then me, then steadily at my father until he put the silverware down again.

"We're going to..." She smiled as her breath caught, eyes blinking rapidly. Then a tear fell, which she quickly wiped away. Taking a breath, she started again. "This morning, I saw Doctor Willingham." She looked at me, hazel eyes deepening. "I'm carrying."

"Carrying?" I whispered into the silence of the dining room. Grandma's fork clanked onto her plate.

More tears rolled down her smiling face, one of them suddenly taken in by the corner of her mouth. "God is sending you a brother or a sister, Eugene."

Going down the stairs to the lower section of the barn, I was filled with a new world. A brother! A sister! What would that be like? I would be thirteen when it happened. Thirteen— I pulled the light chain—and for the rest of my life, I would be somebody's big brother. I could be a kid's favorite person, just like Uncle Dan was mine.

Something moved in the shadows—hair suddenly stood up on my neck. Over there, behind a support beam. I backed up and, not letting my eyes off the beam, felt in the corner for the handle of the wide broom. Had I forgotten to put the lid all the way down on the feed bin? I held the broom out in front of me, took a step toward the bin, eying back and forth between the bin and the beam. I would be ready for them this time—when I swung the lid up, ready for the furry mass of movement, those tails and scurrying feet, the beady eyes. But a fast glance at the bin, and the lid was all the way down. I focused on the beam, and held the broom up.

"Genie?" More of a squeak than a voice.

From behind the beam he came into the light from the hanging bulb.

"What the hell," I said.

A red, coma-shaped gash under his left eye, a smear from where he had wiped blood away. His jacket, ripped at the seam where sleeve joined shoulder, bulged with a fluff of cotton lining.

Quin put his palms up at me, and I realized that I still held the broom out front of me like a weapon. I put it down.

"Genie," he said, more in his own voice but still out of a tightened throat. "I need help, Genie."

"What happened?"

I threw the broom away, and the space between us closed up. His eye, above the gash, was reddened, swollen. His hair was matted with mud and seeds and a small cockle-burr.

His voice went back to a squeak. "I got away." Breathing hard, he looked around the old milking parlor. "You think they'll search here?"

I grabbed his arms. "Who?"

Eyes widened. "Baggie! Baggie and some other deputy."

Standing close to me, his breathing slowed a little. His eyes narrowed back to normal. Voice lowered to more like his. "When I got home from school, they were there. They were throwing everything out of the trailer, like none of it meant anything. I yelled at them to stop. They waved a piece of paper that said they could do it." His eyes teared up. We moved over to the feed bin, where he sat down. "Baggie…" shoulders jerked as he gasped through a bout of crying. "Baggie slammed me around. The other one, he just laughed, but then told Baggie to leave me alone 'cause they were after my old man, not me."

I remembered what Sheriff Braddawl had said. Not about to tell Quin what I'd heard, I pretended I didn't know. "They want your old man? What the hell for? What did he do?"

Quin shrugged. "It's about Agnes May. They say he had something to do with it."

"How'd you get away from Baggie?"

"Kicked him. Tried for his nuts, but he flinched, but I got him in the side of the knee." Quin touched his cheek and winced. "He pawed at my face as he went down."

"So now they're after you? Are you sure? Not your old man?"

"My old man mostly. But then I gave that kick to Baggie. When he buckled, I ran for the brush behind the trailer. The other one told Baggie, 'Let him be. He won't get far. We'll collar him by nightfall.' They saw which direction I headed in. You think they'll search your place?"

Sheriff Braddawl's words were still in my ear: the Republicans would be trying to connect my father with suspicion about Quin's old man…through me!

I said, "You're right. They'll be sure to search here," knowing my father would never have allowed it. "You can't stay here, Quin." My ears burned with lying.

His eyes flattened. "But, your old man…he's got to help me, Eugene."

"You kicked a deputy, Quin." I'd overheard enough legal talk to make it sound like I knew what I was talking about. "Now that you did that, my father would have to turn you in."

"But, your old man's a lawyer."

I shrugged. I couldn't let him near my father; not with the election coming up; not with what I'd heard through the register. I hoped he didn't see how red my ears were.

Quin's shoulders drooped. He stared at the floor. "You're good at figuring things, Genie. What can I do?"

After dark, along the side road down by Quarrel Creek, I gave the secret knock at Old Lady Hough's garage door: two hard, two soft.

Quin let me in.

One half of the place was taken up with the old lady's '49 Ford station wagon, the car we Dumble Doers had borrowed one night last June. The other half, behind a partition wall, was a room she had once used for a business of taking in washing. The last time I'd seen it, it had been layered in dust and dirt and droppings. In the circle of a flashlight beam, the place appeared to have been cleaned up. Sink, with a pitcher pump mounted on it, old Maytag wringer-washer, knee-high wood stove for heating water and irons—all had been recently relieved of years of cobwebs and grime, and the floor had been swept.

"You cleaned the place?"

Quin only stared. Grabbing the bag I'd brought with me, he pawed among the blankets and foodstuffs, and grabbed a jar of peas I'd stolen from Grandma's cellar. To his twist of the lid it hissed and popped. Tilting it to his mouth, he drained all the water, Adam's apple bobbing to rapid swallows.

"I never thought I'd like these much," he mumbled through a mouthful of green.

"You can keep this." I gave him the flashlight. "Be careful not to shine it around in here. It might draw attention to any-body passing by. Only shine it down on the floor."

"I'd better not use that stove, either. Somebody might see the smoke from the flue."

"Just have a small fire at night, after dark. That's when it's gonna get cold in here."

He swept the light-circle across the floor. "A trap door."

I pulled the ring, and it opened easily to a waft of musty air. A chill went down my spine—something moved away just as the light found the cellar's dirt floor: rats?

"Must be where the cistern is," I said, and shut it back up.

Quin suddenly said, "What if Old Lady Hough's daughter comes back? She must be the one who cleaned everything."

"Not likely, Quin. The old lady's daughter lives clear over in Susquehanna County."

"But her mother's been ill. The daughter is bound to look in on her."

"So, keep your eyes open. If you see anybody coming, drop down into the cellar."

He grew quiet. Then he said, "I don't know. Down there...I'd kinda feel like I was trapped in a hole."

"I should go. My parents will notice me gone, and they'll wonder what happened to me."

His hand touched my shoulder. "Genie, you going to ask your old man? Ask if he can help me somehow?"

"Sure. I'll ask him—see what he can do for you."

In the dim light his eyes widened. He took his hand away. "But, you *can't* ask him, can you." His voice lowered. "Like you said, he would have to turn me in, then."

I shrugged.

Quin said, "With him running for judge, he can't be connected with the likes of me right now, can he."

"I gotta go, Quin."

Quin stood between me and the door, quiet. The way his eyes looked into me, I was grateful for the darkness. He put his hand on my shoulder. He said, "I don't know how I'd ever make it without you as my friend."

As I trekked back home, climbing the hill under a dim quarter-moon, I avoided its pale light. I didn't need it to find my way home. I followed the shadow cast by the hedgerow that lined the road.

## Chapter 48, Think It Over Real Hard

Deputy Hollander held his hand to the back of my neck. Not a tight grip: beefy thumb under my ear on one side and sausage fingers on the other reminded me that I was under his control. No doubt he was used to escorting people through the drab-green hallway of the ancient limestone County Jail. Calluses and lumpy knuckles guided me to a room where a woman sat in a steel chair, rustling papers from a yellow folder in her lap. She didn't look up. The deputy closed the door with a clank. A lone bulb glared from a caged fixture in the ceiling.

I sat in the chair opposite her. Both chairs, the only furniture in the tiny room on either side of a sand bucket holding stubbed cigarettes, were bolted to the concrete floor, which looked like it had once been painted the same drab-green. Except for the corners and directly under the chairs, it had been worn away to gray cement. The old stone walls were speckled and splotched with stains, a coffee-color splash looking recent, as if a cup had been tossed across the room, leaving drip marks, some of them running all the way to the floor where they had puddled and dried. High up, a window no bigger than a paperback book was opened inward, allowing a glimpse of daylight through bugged-up screen. No air seemed to move through it, though, to disturb the room's atmosphere of ash tray and old sweat. The woman didn't seem to belong here, not in a pale-blue dress-suit, rimless glasses, red lipstick and long-flowing black hair that cascaded around her shoulders.

Squaring the papers by tapping them on top of the folder, she looked up. "Let's introduce ourselves, shall we?" Her glasses enlarged dark irises to the size of black olives. She spoke with a British accent, words forged deep in her throat rolling forth in baubles of sound.

"Eugene," I nodded.

"Dolores Kettering." She smiled and reached a plump hand into the space between our chairs. "Just Eugene?"

"Eugene Ahern." I took her hand. It was warm and doughy. "How do you do, Missus Kettering."

She laughed. "Oh, no. It's Miss Kettering. And let's not be so formal, shall we? I'll be Dolores, and why don't you be—" she consulted her papers. "I understand they call you 'Genie.'"

"One friend calls me that, but nobody else."

She smiled. Her eyes wandered away, but the smile stayed in place, all those teeth gleaming white except one with a crack in it, a line of accumulated brown discoloration. She looked past me to the wall, then far past the wall to some other place, eyes darting back and forth. "The spirit world has few formalities," she said softly. Her eyes came back from wherever they had gone. "Boundaries are very fluid."

People thought she had some kind of special powers, my father had said. She had a sharpness to her expression that had me supposing maybe she really did. The way she peered into me: what if she could read my mind? Did she know, right at this moment, that with all her smiling she reminded me of a collie? My ears were growing hot from her stare. Would she suspect, even before we started talking, that I might be a liar? And she was working for the cops. Suppose she did have weird mental ability, could suck from my brain everything I'd ever done. What about all those times I'd stolen cigarettes from Widmere's? And the night we'd taken Old Lady Hough's car for a ride and vandalized the Reverend's road grader? This could end up being a whole lot more serious than a simple interview by a clairvoyant.

"May I be excused to go to the bathroom?"

The collie grin vanished. "Young man, you certainly may not."

She suddenly sounded like a teacher. She was now on ground that I was familiar with. Her eyes dropped to the papers in her lap, and she started fingering their corners. My fear of her vacuum-cleaner brain began to wither away: this wasn't some horror movie; she might have been an oddball, but she was no alien who had drifted in on a comet. I hastily reminded myself that she was a clairvoyant who traveled the fair circuit, taking people's quarters. My own brain started to feel a bit safer in the presence of hers.

Placing the papers on her lap, Dolores gazed into me and asked questions, wanting to know about school, my friends, my parents and even Grandma, what I did when I was alone and whether or not I remembered my dreams. I answered as I would any grownup, telling as little as possible but tossing a few made-up morsels to liven it up and make it sound like I was really trying. One of the morsels—that I always slept with the window shade down to avoid accidentally waking up and seeing the Milky Way—seemed to interest her, had her picking up the papers to scratch a note; had me secretly thanking Miss Hendershott's interest in astronomy for inspiring a story that no kid would have been likely to fabricate while under tough questioning.

Her eyes came back up, went past me, and through the wall behind me. They started bouncing back and forth like before, but now I wondered if she was doing that on purpose. She spoke in a whispery voice: "Once a session begins, you see, we mustn't disturb the energy field if at all possible. When you asked me to use the bathroom, I was already in the midst of detecting a sense...a sixth sense, some call it, though that's not really what it is. It was imperative that we commence with questions."

"It's okay. I can hold it," I lied. I didn't have to go anyway.

More questions warbled at me from a pink hole made of moving teeth and lips under that steady-eye glare of hers: Was Agnes May my friend? Yes, I knew her from school. Did I know her in any other way besides as a school chum? I wasn't exactly sure, since the only chum I was aware of was Chet Morton in the Hardy Boys books. A special friend, then? Adam was my friend, and I knew she was very special to him, her loving brother. That one seemed to curl the clairvoyant's lip, making me suspect that she really could tell when I was lying.

"You see, I possess much more than an extra sense. It's a gift — as much a curse as a blessing — a gift bestowed on me from the origins of time itself."

I nodded.

"I immediately picked up on bundled energy. Young man, an aura surrounds you: vestiges of an experience, so strong it almost forms into an image, yet we've barely begun to know each other." Her eyes widened, bored right into me. "You must have very strong feelings for her, Eugene," she whispered.

"For who?"

She jerked her mouth into a not-funny smile that says a grownup already knows the game a kid is trying to play, and is way ahead. "Why, for Agnes May, of course." Her eyes narrowed. "Oh, you mustn't hide it. I know it's embarrassing, but you can trust me; no need to pretend. The image is already strong...very strong."

"Image?" I saw Agnes May's eyes, brown and flecked with bits of other colors, like shiny creek pebbles. I was suddenly missing her. "What does the image look like?" My voice wavered without my intending it.

She closed her eyes. "I've not used the correct word. Forgive me. It's so much more than just an image. A spiritual essence that surrounds her fully engulfs the mere visual aspect." She had a sudden intake of breath. "A pulsation," she said. "No, a pulsation double in strength...the beating of two hearts...the rapid beating of two hearts. Ah! It's a strong force, this intertwining of two spirits, two young heartbeats." Her eyes opened, she blinked at me, then lowered her head, stared at the dirty floor between us.

Static and muffled syllables coming through the door from radio calls at the dispatcher's desk down the hall had me looking that way. In the crack of light at the bottom of the door, two shadows betrayed the feet of someone standing there, listening.

The woman said nothing. Not a sound. Her head went lower still. Was she all right?

I said, "Dolores." Nothing. "Miss Kettering!" in a louder voice.

She jerked up, eyes wide open. "Am I—? Oh!" Recognition came to her face. "Eugene." Bringing her hands up, she pressed her index fingers on either side of the bridge of her nose, pushing at the corners of her eyes. "Oh, Eugene, the essence is so clear for just an instant: two auras...two auras melded into one. In a field of grass...a boy, a girl."

How could she have known about it...that we had been in a field, down in the pasture together through much of the summer? "Do you see the trench I dug?"

Eyes wide, boring into me, she said, "A depression...a long depression in the grassy field. Beside it, two auras twined together there. And now they separate, yet each aura drags with it a bit of the other, leaving a long, stretched-out elasticity of light between them. And now..." She lowered her head again, and placed palm over forehead. "A deep, dark place, and oh, it's cold and wet...cold and wet. The young girl calls out, 'I'm here!' She is cold and wet and shivering, trembling from the cold, and also from fear. She holds onto...she has managed to grasp it with her hands."

"What is she holding onto?"

"She's holding on, and it keeps her from sinking down any further. She holds onto it with her hands, clings to it...and she...her very soul reaches out, and clings to the residue of light from the aura. 'I'm here,' she says. 'Genie, I'm here!'"

Dolores leaned forward, placed her face in her hands. A moan came out of her, like one of the wails I would sometimes hear in the middle of the night from wildlife down in the woods.

From the back seat of the patrol car I studied the lines on Sheriff Braddawl's neck in the waning light, as he swung the big Plymouth into our driveway. He turned the car around in our yard so that it was pointing back toward the road and parked by the porch. As he squeezed himself out from behind the steering wheel, he said to the deputy sitting beside me, "You wait outside, DeVerl. I'm going inside to talk a spell with our future judge." Then, he went up onto our porch. Lowdown barked from inside.

Deputy Hollander unlocked the rear door on my side and let me out. Leaning his lanky frame on a fender, he rolled a cigarette. I went to the garage and found the back-up flash-light hanging by its cord-handle on a nail. As I crossed the yard, the end of deputy's cigarette glowed under his wide-brimmed hat in the growing dusk, and the smell of tobacco came across the yard.

Rounding the barn, ducking under the electric fence, I headed down through the pasture, which was in the hill's shadow cast by the meager twilight still clinging to the sky behind me. The latch on the pump house door clicked as I lifted it, hinges squeaking. Stepping into a cube of blackness, I raised the flashlight.

How could Miss Kettering have known about this place?

The light beam came on, and showed the well cover firmly in place. On my knees, I put the light down to lift each half of the cover. The well released earthy dampness. I pointed the light down inside. A single galvanized pipe, shining bright, centered the tube of darkness down to where it disappeared in the water surrounded by gray stonework. I leaned further over the opening.

My breath stopped: a face! I backed away. I closed my eyes.

Had I really seen it? A face? A face, eyes staring, at the surface of the water about ten feet down. My ears roared with my own heartbeat. I leaned over again, and forced myself to look. A face, eyes open, looked back up at me. I lowered my head further into the well. The face went into shadow. I moved to one side...it moved with me.

My breath came back. After replacing the well cover I sat for a while on the floor of the pump house.

I stood up and went out, latching the door. More tobacco smoke, and a tall shadow in a wide-brimmed hat was down here with me in the pasture. DeVerl took a drag on his ciga-rette and said in a low, gentle voice, "You got something to tell me, son?"

"This is one of my chores: check on air pocket in the tank," I said and turned away.

Staying a few steps behind me, the deputy huffed with ef-fort of climbing the hill. Half-way up, I suddenly stopped. He stopped. I turned to face him. He stood still, a long, dark shadow a few paces downhill from me. The end of the cigarette glowed, partially lighting up his narrow face.

"Agnes May has never called me 'Genie.'"

He threw the roll-your-own into the grass, where it made a shower of sparks. "Huh."

Back up in our driveway, the Stippils' Power Wagon was now parked behind the sheriff's car. The Reverend had just come out of the house. He stood on the porch peering into the darkness at the sound of us coming around the barn.

As I approached the porch, Reverend Stippil said, "Young Ahern," and stepped down onto the gravel. "You're the one I want to see."

I stopped short of him by a few feet. Deputy Hollander went to the patrol car and leaned against it, rolling himself a new cigarette. The Reverend pulled a rag from his back pocket. Raising his cap by the bill, he wiped his forehead.

"Saw the sheriff passing my house," he said in a slow nasal twang, "so I came on over here to see what he's learned about my Agnes May." He wiped his hand over his mouth and chin, making a scratchy sound from rubbing a few days of whisker growth. "So far it ain't much." His voice dropped to a rasp. "Not much at all."

He said quietly, "Eugene...is that your name?"

"Yes. Eugene."

"Well, Eugene, the sheriff just told me the state police are taking over. They will be calling you boys in, first thing tomorrow. So I'm asking..." His voice choked up. "I'm here asking, Eugene." He wiped his forehead again, and his voice rose up in pitch and sounded shaky. "My little angel has disappeared. My heart is surely in pain."

I looked away while the Reverend sobbed a moment. He blew his nose in the rag from his back pocket.

"I'm here asking," he said more clearly, "that tomorrow, you tell it all. Whatever you know, you tell it, no matter what it is. The sheriff thinks you might know more than you've said, that you might know where that Sloot kid is hiding out. He is the son of the Mexican that's likely took her. If we find the kid it might just lead us to Agnes May. Think on it tonight, Eugene. Think and pray over it real hard."

He stepped toward me—then settled back on his heels again. "That's all I'm asking." With shoulders slumped he lowered his voice. "I'm asking for my angel back."

## Chapter 49, The Door Clanked Shut

The person behind the window cage, according to the name tag attached to small hooks under the window ledge, was Officer Lloyd Drithers. He sat in a cubicle, looking through folders and jotting down notes, occasionally responding to crackling radio calls by pressing a button and speaking into a chrome microphone that stood on his desk. And once in a while, he would look up and peer through the cage fabric to eyeball Hangy and me in the waiting room.

"Special Investigator Bolerjack has not yet arrived from Harrisburg," he'd informed us when we first came in, and had us sit in two of the wooden chairs that formed a semi-circle just inside the front door. He spoke with a forceful accent from down-state, where people tended to more spit their words out instead of just saying them.

The Wyotanda State Police Post was nothing like the Wilmot County Jail. A single-story brick building alongside Route 6 a little west of town, it looked more like a large ranch-style house than a police station. There was even a small patch of lawn, split by a sidewalk that ran from the parking lot up past a wooden sign with a yellow keystone painted on it. The area where we sat looked like a doctor's waiting room.

"Hope this doesn't take long," Hangy said, eyebrows drawn down. "I've got corn to get in from that low section that's finally dried off. You know the place I mean?"

I nodded: two low-lying acres, which would always bog up if we got much rain. He'd had to leave it standing two weeks ago when he'd run the chopper through the rest of the field. Hangy, whenever I did get a chance to see him these days, would talk a lot about farm problems. He hadn't even known that the Yankees lost the World Series to Pittsburgh. Ever since Old Man Hobbes' death, he was no longer the same kid at all.

"How's Lucinda?" I asked.

He shrugged and looked away. Nobody had seen her since she came back from North Carolina. So far, she'd stayed out of school, stayed home, and kept to herself.

Then, he looked at me and said, "You know, she actually helped with the milking yesterday morning, and then again today. Maybe she's coming out of it. She's even been nicer to our step-mom...not a *lot* nicer."

When Drithers got involved in a long radio call, I changed the subject, speaking in a whisper. "Don't tell the cops anything more than what you know about Agnes May disappearing. Anything else you say could make trouble. That's what my old man told me to tell you."

"But I don't need a lawyer," he whispered back. "I don't know anything about her disappearing."

"It oughta be easy for you, then. We just don't want them knowing some of the other things we've done."

Hangy nodded.

My father had given me that advice—as if I was one of his clients—as he had dropped me off at the police post. "They will try to make you think they already know everything you've ever done," he had said. "The idea is to get you blabbing yourself into a corner that might incriminate you. It doesn't matter what it is, or even if it's related to the case they're working on. Often they think their job is to just put somebody in jail. Easier you—sitting right there in front of them—than going out and finding somebody else to do it to."

"Dad, can't you be with me?" I'd said.

"You're not a suspect." Then he'd thought for a moment. "It would be better if you didn't have to have me there. If at any time you think you need me, you tell them, and then clam up tight. But, I trust Lieutenant Grimm on this."

When Drithers was done with the radio, we saw him eyeballing us. Hangy was not the one I was worried about. It was Adam. What if all that evangelizing and giving testimony at church had gotten him into a confessing mood? Would he open up about all the things we Dumble Doers had done? If he did, my guess was that the cops would let Adam off, first for telling, and then because they'd feel sorry about his sister's disappearance, and also because his old man was the Reverend. As for the rest of us: I could see the cops rubbing their hands together, see them licking their chops.

We heard a vehicle door close in the parking lot. Soon after, Adam came in, his father behind him. The Reverend caught my eye, and stared at me. I nodded hello.

"All present and accounted for, I see," Drithers said as he came out of the cubicle. "Sorry, Reverend, I have to take the boys back now. Best if you wait in your vehicle."

Looking like he wanted to spit, Reverend Stippil turned and left. He tried to catch my eye again as he went out the door, but I wouldn't let him. I was supposed to rat out Quin's hiding place. What if Quin's old man really *had* kidnapped Agnes May, took her down to Texas to sell her to sweaty oil workers?

My insides quivered.

Drithers took us back to a room that had six wooden chairs around a rectangular steel table, and told us to sit down. He returned to his cubicle, from where he still kept an eye on us. The walls of the room were painted the same green as the County Jail's walls, but here everything was spotless, the room smelling like floor wax.

Adam put his head down, face on his forearms. Hangy and I looked at each other.

"Don't know what it's like to lose a sister," Hangy said. "Must be tough on you. I've lost my old man. I know what tough is, all right."

Adam looked up at him briefly, face drooping, and then put his head down again.

Hangy looked at me and shrugged.

We heard someone enter the waiting room, and saw Drithers in his cubicle peer through the cage fabric.

I recognized the voice: Sheffield Hoy. "That fatality on the bridge Friday night," he said to Drithers. "A copy of my report."

Drithers said, "You the fire chief on this one, or the coroner?"

"Coroner," Sheffield said. "You're kinda new here, aren't you, Lloyd. You'll get used to seeing me. I have to give your lieutenant a copy of my report as coroner every time somebody in the county dies on the highway."

We could see Drithers reading through the folder. "So, the truck driver died of a heart attack?"

"That's what it all adds up to: dead at the wheel before the crash."

Drithers wagged his head. "Can't believe they let a township fire chief be the county coroner too. You have any medical training at all, Shef?"

"Sure. Army medic," Sheffield said, and chuckled. "Gave lots of physicals."

Drithers laughed. "A lotta fingers up guys' asses." He wagged his head again.

Shef said, "And that's not counting six weeks undertaker school. Nothing can beat the Army for training, you know."

"Yeh, that qualifies you, all right."

"Well, this here ain't Philadelphia, Lloyd. Welcome to the countryside." Then Sheffield said more seriously, "But I don't always get the last word, you know. Doc Willingham still has to sign off on what I do. If he doesn't like what he reads in my report, he won't scribble his name on the last line. Not until he's done some serious cadaver cutting and sawing on his own."

"Well, he did sign it," Drithers said. "So I'll add it to the file and give it to my lieutenant."

Sheffield, having seen Drithers turn to check on us, said, "Got somebody interesting back there?"

"The kids on that missing girl case. They're sending Special Investigator Bolerjack up from the burg. He's late. You don't suppose he mighta gotten lost on all these winding roads that seem to go forever around here?"

"Could be, Lloyd. He's not a local."

"Well, Shef, I've been assigned to this post a month already, and whenever I take out a cruiser I'm still lost plenty more than I'm found."

Sheffield chuckled. "Like I said, this ain't the city up here, kid. You'll get used to it. You mind if I take a look?"

"Be my guest."

Sheffield came across the hall and looked in on us. He said nothing at first. He just stared, gray eyes blank. Adam, sensing his presence, looked up.

"I hear a special investigator is on his way from Harrisburg," Sheffield said. "You know, they don't send him into a case like this until they're ready to wrap things up, ready to put somebody's sorry ass in jail." He leaned against the door jam. "Just a word of advice to you boys: no doubt he's already pretty well figured out what's happened to Agnes May; and who's responsible. You can bet on it. It would be a damned good idea to not hold back anything; a damned good idea for all your own sakes to fess up what you know."

He eyed each one of us until we couldn't look back at him anymore. "You know what you've done. And so does he. You can bet on it."

He stepped out of the room and went back across to the waiting room. Adam put his hands under his legs and rocked back and forth, glaring down at the table top.

"What's all the radio chatter?" Sheffield said.

Drithers answered, "That's from the County's frequency. I keep one ear tuned to it while I'm monitoring our own calls."

"Sounds like something's breaking."

Drithers turned a knob, raising the volume. "Don't know for sure, but I think that's your brother on there, Shef. He's jabbering about picking up some Sloot kid."

"The Gutierrez boy?"

"Dunno...wasn't paying attention to the details."

"Gotta be. He's been obsessed about him. You'd better tell your lieutenant. He'll be wanting you to squawk in on the County's calls to get him over here. That kid is with the bunch you've already got back in the room there."

Drithers scraped his chair on the floor and went out of sight. Following a conversation muffled by the walls of the place, he soon returned to the tiny cubicle, post commander Lieutenant Grimm on his heel. He got on the radio, raising Baggie Hoy on the County's frequency. "Bring him in to the post here," he said.

I recognized Grimm: one of the referees at Melody Falls High School basketball games.

"Aw, shucks," Baggie's voice crackled back. "Was hoping for a little fun at the jail first."

From somewhere out in the county, Sheriff Braddawl's heavy voice broke in. "Listen to me, you bag of puke, get him to the State Police Post, pronto!"

"Heading that way, Sheriff."

Lieutenant Grimm wagged his head. When he turned and saw us listening, he came and closed the door. My stomach sank. So, they had Quin now. A reunion of the Dumble Doers of Greater Melody Falls: they would now have us all rounded up at the Wyotanda State Police Post. Maybe it was a good time to say I needed my father.

Adam's rocking grew faster — then suddenly stopped. He looked down at the floor, closed his eyes and stayed frozen in that position for a long moment. Tears ran down his cheeks. He lowered his head and sobbed. I'd never seen him show those kinds of feelings for his sister before. Now that she was missing, new feelings seemed to be coming out. He sobbed louder, snot stringing from his nose to his lap.

"You okay?" I said.

He jumped up. Head back, he suddenly screamed like a woman, lips shaking. Bubbles broke through the snot. Lieutenant Grimm burst into the room, Drithers right behind him. They took positions on either side of him. Grimm placed a hand on his shoulder.

"What is it, son?" he asked in a quiet, even tone.

Drithers looked on, eyes like shiny half-dollars. Sheffield stood in the doorway, watching.

Adam suddenly sat down on the floor. He drew his knees up, folded his arms over them and put his head down. "She's in the truck," he cried into his knees.

The lieutenant kept the same steady tone. "In the truck? Who's in the truck, son?"

Adam raised his face, eyes red and puffy. "My sister. She's in the truck."

"She's in the back of your father's power wagon?" he said gently.

No answer, only sobbing.

"Adam," Grimm said more firmly, "where is the truck that your sister is in?"

Adam suddenly looked at me, as if I knew something. Grimm and Drithers and Sheffield all glanced my way, then back to Adam. Adam said, "The truck in Eugene's field. The truck that's broke down near Hobbes Woods."

"Jesus," Sheffield muttered. "Baggie's dog-catcher truck. It's got a compartment in the back where he locks up the strays. It's been—how many—eight days?"

"Get him onto a cell," the lieutenant barked.

Drithers lifted Adam by his arms and took him out of the room and down the hall, where a door clanked shut.

## CHAPTER 50, JUST RATS

I wiped my chin, and realized that I was swallowing over and over, trying to keep my stomach from rising to my throat. What did he mean, in the truck...for *eight days?*

Muffled voices came through the walls from the cell where they had taken him. Conversation, words back and forth, and occasionally a shout from one of the men would allow me to hear a word or two. And then came a very distinct shout from the Lieutenant Grimm: "WHAT KIND OF SHAPE WAS SHE IN?"

Quieter tones followed.

Across the hall, a man who had come into the waiting room put his brief case down on the floor. He stood with arms crossed, brown, bug-eyes searching through dark-rimmed glasses, sweeping the room. His gaze came briefly to where Hangy and I sat, and settled on us for a moment before returning to a dance that seemed to be in tune to the muffled noises from the cell.

We heard the door open and close again with a clank. In the moment that it was open, I could hear Adam's voice, reciting something, as if he was reading a poem.

"He's shut down on us," Grimm said as the three came back up the hall.

"Suddenly got religion," Drithers wagged his head.

The lieutenant, noticing the man in the waiting room, told Drithers to take care of him. Then he and Sheffield came in and stood over us, eyes angry.

"So, where's this truck he's talking about?" The lieutenant placed hands on hips.

"Down at the south edge of our farm," I said. "Baggie was driving around down there when his engine —"

"How did you fellows leave that girl? Was she still alive?"

Hangy and I looked at each other.

"Your buddy is not going to answer for you!" he spit at us. "I'm asking each of you separately. What kind of shape was she in when you boys were finished with her? It won't go so hard on whoever answers first."

"Lieutenant," Drithers called from the waiting room.

"It'll have to wait," he said over his shoulder, then to us, "How 'bout it?" his face red.

Hangy and I looked at each other again.

"LOOK AT ME!" he shouted. "Are we going to find her alive?"

Neither of us spoke for a moment. Then Hangy, eyes wide, suddenly cried and said, "I've gotta get the rest of my corn in."

"Lieutenant," Drithers said again.

"One goddamned thing at a time," the lieutenant spit out. Then to Sheffield, "You know what they're talking about... where that truck is?"

Sheffield nodded that he did.

A different voice, a low baritone, came from the waiting room: "Lieutenant."

Grimm spun around, neck and ears crimson.

The baritone, the man in the suit, said, "Does this involve the case I came up here from Harrisburg for?"

The lieutenant exhaled a long breath. "Sorry. Didn't real- ize who you were." He stepped across the hall and extended his hand. "Lieutenant Grimm, post commander."

"Special Investigator Bolerjack."

"I've certainly heard of you," Grimm said respectfully. "Glad you're here."

"By the looks of things, something big just broke."

"In just the last few minutes," the post commander con- firmed.

Drithers pointed at Sheffield. "Thanks to this man right here," he said with a wide grin.

Bolerjack stared at Sheffield, "And you are?"

"Sheffield Hoy. Just stepped in on Coroner business, and—"

"Don't know how he did it," Drithers cut in. "Whatever he said to them popped that kid's lid like a shook-up soda, and he couldn't spill himself fast eno—"

Drithers, the three men glaring at him, went quiet.

Bolerjack said, "What is your involvement, exactly, Mister Hoy?"

"I was just in here on other business." Sheffield said. "I'm the Wilmot County Coroner."

"You don't say. Well, Mister Coroner, did it occur to you that you were interfering in an official state investigation?"

Sheffield squared himself to the other man. "You don't say. And does it occur to you, Mister Special Investigator, that stand- ing here seeing who can piss the farthest brings us no closer to getting back the missing girl?"

Before they left, Grimm had instructed Drithers to keep Hangy and me in the room. After a while, Drithers gave each of us wa- ter in a Dixie cup, and then took some down the hall to Adam.

The radio erupted in chatter. Calls went back and forth between Lieutenant Grimm and Drithers and, once they'd gotten the Sheriff's Department vehicles to tune to the state police frequency, between Braddawl and Grimm and Braddawl and Drithers.

Agnes May wasn't in the truck.

"Looks like she mighta been locked in the back, all right," Grimm's radio voice said. "Somebody sure as hell kicked the latch apart from the inside."

The Sheriff talked about bringing the hounds back from Potter County.

Baggie Hoy broke in. "I've got the Sloot kid here…I'm just pulling up to the state post. Give me half a chance and I'll get some answers outta him."

"Put him in the room with the others, Lloyd," Grimm barked over the radio to Drithers.

"Baggie, once you've delivered the kid, you stay there," Sheriff Braddawl crackled.

When the front door opened a minute later, Baggie came in. He laughed to Drithers, "From the sound of his voice, looks like maybe I'll be getting yelled at. Well, that's what it takes, I guess, to do good police work. No matter how effective you are, the boss is likely to get a sore ass about it 'cause he's not getting the credit."

"So, where's your prisoner?"

"Got him hog-tied in the back seat. Where do you want him? "

"Hog-tied? A kid?"

"It's my own personal vehicle. Can't have him thrashing around."

"You heard the lieutenant: in the room with the others."

Baggie left and came back with a person who looked like he was dressed in rags, shirt pulled open, tee shirt ripped, dungarees filthy and torn. His hands were behind his back, and the rope around his waist had a lead that Baggie used to jerk him along in whatever baby steps bound ankles might allow. His mouth was taped. Quin's dark eyes glared through hair fallen forward into his face.

"Jesus, Deputy," Drithers said as he carefully removed the tape.

Quin took a gulp of air through his mouth, shoulders rising and falling. Drithers untied him, brought him into the room with us and had him sit in a chair.

He turned to Baggie, hands on hips. "You go sit in the waiting room until the Sheriff comes to get you," he said matter-of-factly.

Baggie gave me the swirl-eye, winked, then turned and, with a laugh, did as he was told.

Drithers brought water for Quin, who gulped it down. "Want some more?"

"No," Quin gasped, chest heaving, still trying to catch his breath. "He fired on her."

"Who fired? Who fired on who?"

Quin pointed across the hall. "Asshole," he gasped.

Baggie stood up and started toward us from across the hall. "Sit down!" Drithers said to him, and Baggie stepped back.

"The deputy fired on somebody?"

Baggie bellowed, "That lying sack of Sloot shit—just rats. Caught the kid hiding in Hough's laundry. Opened the trap door to the cistern, and heard the rats skittering down below."

"HE MUSTA KILLED HER!" Quin shouted, tears rolling down his cheeks. "He fired that over-under into the cellar—both barrels!"

# CHAPTER 51, SAGGING WITH TIME

"Delirious," I heard Sheffield Hoy say to my father through the register. "Delirious when we first found her, but Doc Willingham says she's come out of that part of it, at least on the surface. Time will have to tell, Owen. Who knows what it may do to her in the long run."

My father lit his pipe.

"On the face of it," Sheffield said, "she's lucky. A wound from shotgun pellets, a piece out of the upper fold of her right ear...almost looks like an animal took a bite out of it."

"Jesus," my father muttered.

"Lieutenant Grimm was the first one to get to her, down in the cellar under Old Lady Hough's garage. She was cowering in the corner, blood from the wound running down the side of her neck, soaking into the top of her dress. She was clinging to a pipe that led from the cistern up to the laundry sink. He had to pry her hands free."

"I hate to ask it, Shef."

"I know what you want to ask. Well, we can only guess what actually happened. Nobody is telling: not the girl, not her brother. The Reverend won't give consent to the doc for a real examination."

"Her brother could be put away, at least a few-months stint at Barry Town," my father pronounced.

"Not to be," Sheffield said. "He's the Reverend's son, and especially not with everybody keeping mum about what he actually did to her."

They were quiet, my father rasping the pipe.

Sheffield said, "And as far as the Gutierrez boy goes, she won't say anything about that, either."

"Well, I doubt anything would have happened there. I know Quin pretty well."

"All I'm saying is that nobody is talking. Quin and the girl were together in that garage for two days and nights. I'm not saying anything did happen. She just won't open up about it. And he won't either."

"But, Shef, how did the two of them end up hiding in the same place? You think they planned it?"

"Doesn't look like it," Shef said. "Too many different things were happening to them. Looks to me like it was just a coincidence they ended up both hiding in the old laundry. She hid out there first, and then Quin came along a few days later."

"They told you that much?"

"Not her, just Quin. She's not saying much. Quin either, but he did tell me that he went there to hide out, and then he discovered the girl hiding in the cellar. Apparently, she had gone down there when she heard him approaching the building."

A long quiet settled in with the aroma of Prince Albert wafting from the wall register.

I was unaware of my neck growing weak, head falling forward on my shoulders, until my brow plopped against the register.

"What was that?"

"Old air conduit in the wall," my father said. "Sagging with time, I suppose."

"Yeh, I know the feeling. I feel like I'm sagging with time too, Owen."

My father breathed a short laugh. "Suppose you were to actually win the election. You sure you would want to be the new Sheriff?"

Sheffield didn't say.

I raised my head from the register. Suddenly I had to see her. Suddenly, somehow, I had to see Agnes May.

## Chapter 52, Love Not the World

That next week at the Wednesday evening service, the dirt lane leading to the Melody Falls Watchful Christian Fellowship Church would normally have had, at most, two dozen cars parked along the driveway. But by six-thirty, the drive was already jammed with vehicles parked three abreast, overflowing out onto both sides of the road.

Many of them were people I'd never seen before. I had no trouble going unrecognized as I entered the vestibule, where I sneaked up a rickety wooden staircase inside the dark steeple. Climbing up into the shadows, I crouched into the familiar hiding place from where Quin and I had once spied on a Protestant service. It was a housing that held a massive fan designed to exhaust muggy heat from the church in the summer.

Folks filled the pews below. It wasn't long before standees lined the side aisles, and then began to clog the main aisle in the center. Joe Reed, one of the members of the church, who was also a Melody Falls Fire Department volunteer, called a halt to allowing any more inside. Though it was a cold, rainy night, he opened all the windows so those he turned away could still hear what was going on from under their umbrellas, standing outside along either side of the building.

The vent housing's shutters, which were supposed to open only when the fan was on, had long been stuck open by the goo from thousands of insects battered by three-foot steel blades. It would no longer close completely when the fan was off. Through vertical openings, I could easily observe from my hiding place the goings-on down below without fear of detection by the worshipers. I felt safe. Safe from discovery, and also safe from the mortal sin that my own religion imposed on attending a Protestant service. I wasn't really in the church itself, after all, so my hiding in the fan housing couldn't possibly be counted as participating...could it?

We'd been told in catechism that most Protestant services included lots of hymns. Not here. The Christian Fellowship was against hymns, or music of any kind, which they saw as a way for your mindfulness to drift away from a duty to focus on salvation that started with testimony, which proved how unworthy you were to be saved in the first place; at least, that's what Adam had tried to explain to me once. Noise rising from below told me that these people were not against talking in church, though, while waiting for things to get started. They didn't believe God was present, Adam had said. For the Christian Fellowship, God would only be among them if the assembly did a good enough job of praying and scripture reading and giving testimony. So, right up to the start of the service, the folks were visiting back and forth, all talking at once.

The Reverend stood up. Things quieted. He stepped forward to the lectern and turned around to face the people, his only vestment a white surplice over his everyday blue work clothes. The church had no altar, just the lectern centered in the sanctuary, along with two empty chairs, one on each side of it, facing the congregation.

Near the space in the front pew where he had stood up from, I recognized the back of Adam's head, Missus Stippil next to him. And Agnes May was next to her mother, in a flower-print dress, the new one that she had worn at the fair. In her braid, a bit of red hair was visible even from this far away. She was not wearing her bonnet.

I'd heard Sheffield tell my father that, after two days on a special hospital floor in Williamsport, Adam would be sent home in the custody of his parents. And here he was: usual clothes, blue shirt and dungarees, same as his father, a smaller version of the Reverend. Here he was, just like he would have been if none of this had ever happened. And here was Missus Stippil, the same as she always appeared, identical dress to her daughter's, identical braid, wearing the gray bonnet she always wore as the preacher's wife, head bowed before her husband.

My eyes kept returning to Agnes May, even if it was just to see her from the back. I had to look at her. She appeared so small from up here. So, she had been with Quin for two days and two nights in Old Lady Hough's garage. I just had to look at her. Agnes May, identical dress and braid as her mother, but no bonnet because the top of her right ear bloomed a large white bandage.

The Reverend cast his gaze over the flock. Humanity's noises tapered down to a cleared throat, a scrape of shoe on pineboard floor, a cough…then, silence.

The Reverend spoke in a forceful voice, almost at a yell, though at first his voice sounded small in such a large crowd, "It is no coincidence that the Lord in his mercy has gathered so many of us together on an evening when our humble assembly overflows out into the yard, just a few days after the conclusion of recent events."

People shifted, heads looking around at the packed assembly. Faces peered in through the windows.

"No coincidence at all," he said, voice growing. "We are here to worship, yes. And we are here to be saved, yes. And our redemption tonight shall begin with dispelling of untruth, uprooting and casting it out of our midst."

Lifting a worn Bible open to a section that he did not have to put his eyes on, he proclaimed: "Love not the world, neither the things that are in the world. If any man loves the world, the love of the Father is not in him. For all that is in the world, the lust of the flesh, and the lust of the eyes, and the pride of life, is not of the Father, but of the world. John, Two Fifteen."

Nods of approval.

"...not of the Father, but of the world," he repeated.

The nodding spread out in a wave among the folks, some of them turning to each other in agreement.

The Reverend started in a small voice again, "Listen when I tell you here tonight," that quickly rose in pitch and ended in a shout: "the Word of God is MEANINGLESS!"

The congregation gasped in unison.

His eyes seemed ready to burst forth with fire.

"MEANINGLESS!" he shouted again, "if not put to the test by experience of the world, the world that is not of the Father; if not put to the test by touch, by sight, by smell, by taste, and by hearing."

A collective sigh turned into more vigorous nods of approval and low mutterings, "Yea, brother..."

"We share our five senses with the beasts of the field. For them, they are the tools of survival. But I put to you here tonight: for us, the fallen creatures of God's creation, what are those five senses the tools of?"

He looked around the church. No one spoke.

"For us, for fallen mankind," he said, "the five senses are the tools of SATAN! Yes, SATAN, the sworn enemy of our heavenly Father, SATAN, who uses them to separate us from the Word."

A tiny muscle behind my ear jerked every time he yelled, SATAN.

"I say unto you, our senses are tools of SATAN, the evil one, who seeks to render the Word of God MEANINGLESS!"

Somebody stood and shouted, "THE WORD OF GOD, SAVE US!" and soon another, and then a chorus of people all shouting it out.

When the noise settled, the Reverend put his head back, closed his eyes and waited for quiet. "Our Heavenly Father," he groaned. "You see before you a people in distress. Your people, two of whose children, having suffered in the flowering of their youth the onslaught of Satan's wiles, who now must endure the vicious rumors that abound and travel among us, wagging tongue to wagging tongue." He put his forearm over his eyes and shouted, "REDEEM US, DEAR LORD, AND SAVE US FROM SATAN'S WILES!"

A roar from the assembly echoed the words.

He brought his head forward, opened his eyes and extended both arms toward the front pew, palms up. "Come forth, children. Come forth and suffer unto Him. Come forth and give testimony that you may acknowledge sin, yes...but that you may put an end to rumor. Come forth and be saved, REDEEMED IN THE NAME OF JESUS CHRIST!"

Adam and Agnes May stood and went up to the lectern. Adam, at his father's right, faced the congregation, head bowed. Agnes May stood to his left, facing her father, her face flushed, until he motioned her to sit down in her chair.

At last I could see her eyes. As she looked out at the crowd, she looked above their heads. Could she...was it even possible that she could see my eyes too, way up here; see me in my hiding place beyond the partially stuck-open exhaust fan shutters?

Adam, one hand stiffly crossed over the other at his belt buckle, raised his eyes to the gathering. "I have sinned!" he complained. "I have sinned before the Lord. I stand here before you to share my shame, to ask you to pray for my forgiveness before the Lord."

Tears came to his eyes, and he winced, like somebody was pinching him. The Reverend called out to the folks to say the Lord's Prayer. The congregation burst with recitation in one voice that hurried the words out of their mouths.

"Watch and pray," the Reverend intoned at the prayer's conclusion, "so that you will not fall into temptation."

"Amen!" the congregation said as one.

"For the Spirit is willing, but the flesh is weak; Mathew, Twenty-six, Forty-one."

"Amen!"

Adam, shoulders rounded, bowed his head and tears flowed from him.

"Even this young man," the Reverend said, "whom you yourselves have often seen helping me deliver the Word of God right here in this church, can fall victim to the evil posed by Satan. Does it not bear witness to how perilous are the evil one's temptations?" His voice lowered, and people leaned forward to hear him. "Are we powerless before Satan's wiles?"

"NO!" a man in brown coveralls shouted. "LET US REPENT. THE WORD OF GOD, SAVE US!" Others joined in, repeating the call.

"No indeed!" The Reverend said. "The serpent may, in a single moment, surround any one of us, wrap a man in suffocating coils, confuse him, and make him think he has been cut off from God."

The man in coveralls stood up. "THE WORD OF GOD SHALL SAVE HIM!"

Folks shouted approval.

"Though the evil one may have turned a youth's own senses against him, caused him to see his sister as a temptress to be dealt with; though the evil one may have turned affection, the pure, simple affection of a brother for his sister, into anger, do you think God has abandoned one of His own?"

"NO!" someone shouted, and the crowd broke into further shouts that slowly tapered away.

"Though the evil one may have turned a young girl's own senses against her, caused her to be blind to the failings of her female nature; tricked her into presenting herself before her brother as an alluring object of this world; though she may have allowed that angelic form to project onto the male eye even a small glimmer of the lewdness that has beset every woman since the fall of Eve, do you think God has abandoned her?"

"NO!" The man in coveralls shouted. "THE WORD OF GOD SHALL SAVE HER!"

Agnes May's face flushed, streaming with tears. She bowed her head and put her hands over her eyes.

Praises to the Lord and biblical phrases stirred a plume of noise that lifted up from the assembly. After it slowly settled back down, the Reverend motioned for his son to sit in his chair. He turned to her. Face in her hands, she was hunched forward and shook with sobs.

The Reverend, into a crisp silence, called out, "Daughter of Eve," and extended a hand toward her. She did not budge. "My angel," he said more softly, "the assembly awaits your testimony."

Removing her hands from her face, she looked up through reddened eyes. She looked up, past the people, over their heads. Her lips curled, then her mouth opened, formed a sound…a high-pitched wail: "MOMMY?"

Missus Stippil, suddenly at her side, put an arm around her daughter's shoulders. She helped her stand up. The two of them slowly made their way across the front of the sanctuary, and out the side door.

Silence that had frozen the moment now broke apart and fell into shards of chatter.

The Reverend pointed directly up at where I was hiding. "Can't you see?" he hollered. "My daughter has been overcome by the stuffy air. Too many people are crowded in here. Please! Somebody turn on the fan!"

I heard a click...and quickly stepped backward onto the steeple floor, as bug-smeared steel blades went into motion.

## CHAPTER 53, FRIEND FOR A DAY

"Get in."

Baggie was parked in front of the school on the wrong side of the street. I eyed him through the half open driver's window. When I'd told my parents I could easily hitch a ride home, I hadn't expected him to be one of the rides.

"Don't want to be seen with me all of a sudden?"

I said nothing. Baggie had read my thoughts.

"Get in," he said exactly as before. He looked away, finally, and peered through the windshield into the distance. "Yeh, I figured as much. Ole Baggie is down, tripped up by the assholes that run things around here, just for trying to do his job, and now you're gonna give him a kick too."

"I'm not going to give anybody a kick."

"No different than your old man. For a while there, I thought you mighta been different. Now here you are, scared off by what people might think if you let ole Baggie give you a ride home."

"I'm not scared."

"Scared. Just another coward, just like the old man."

"He's not a coward," I said, a hot bubble crowding into my voice.

"Get in," he said for a third time. "This ain't over, not by a long shot. It's not over until the election is over." He gave me the swirl eye.

What would he do to ruin the election? He kept saying he had something on my father.

"So, young Ahern, we still friends or not?"

What a liar I was. Whenever he'd approached me, I'd always let him think I didn't mind, as if I didn't think he was an asshole. I had let him give me rides home, let him show me his peep hole at the fairgrounds, let him call Quin a Sloot, even let him talk the way he did about Agnes May and me...all without saying a word.

So much for me being a friend to anybody else. I deserved what had happened with Quin and Agnes May. Once Quin had found her hiding there in the old laundry, had they clung to each other? I had already proven how easily I could abandon a friend.

What difference did it make if Baggie thought I was his friend? I might as well be. Were we so different, he and I?

I walked around the front of the car, engine huffing through the grill with uneven idle between chirps of a worn fan belt. The passenger door complained with a high-pitched squeak as I opened it. I stood in the street beside the car and looked at Baggie, edge of the car door pulsating in my hand, the old Dodge Coronet's engine throbbing. I wanted to slam it shut...slam it and say, "To hell with you, Baggie Hoy," and that would be the end of it.

He had said, with what he knew about my father, he would ruin the election. Whatever it was he knew, if he thought I was his friend, maybe he would tell me, and then I could warn my father.

I got in. Baggie put the car in gear and we headed away from the school, two friends riding together through busy Wyotanda Friday afternoon traffic.

I turned to him. "Stop saying that about my father."

He said nothing, staying quiet as he drove, roughly slamming the transmission through the gears. He peered through the windshield as if I wasn't there, and slowly nodded to himself. We went out of Wyotanda and up the highway, climbing the east slope of the mountain without a word. Near the top of last grade, Baggie downshifted and made the turn-off at the rock-cut. As we moved north on the winding road along Belknap Ridge, he kept it in second gear, as if to be careful on the loose gravel left from recent passes by Reverend Stippil at the controls of the Galion grader. Being careful was not like Baggie. He usually drove the dirt roads, loose or packed, like a maniac.

"Everything can be traded," he said in a voice deeper than normal, and finally looked at me with round, expectant eyes.

I avoided looking at him.

"It's time my little Ahern pal learned that. Like your old man, you pretend to be honorable. Well, honor can be traded too, like anything else. So can truth. Hell, you're old man is in the truth-trading profession, now ain't he."

He looked at me. I did not look at him, and didn't answer.

"So, what have you got to trade, son of honorable Owen Ahern, Attorney at Law?"

"Trade for what?"

A laugh jumped out of him, like it had squeezed his lungs by surprise. "Hell, how bad do you want it, little Ahern; to turn your old man's honor into His Honor? You want it so bad you can taste it, I know."

"I want him to win, that's all. If he loses, I don't want him to be stopped by a pack of lies."

"Lies!" Baggie laughed hard. "I'm sure you don't want to think your old man's a coward, but that really don't matter to me. What matters is what you've got to trade. You willing to pay the price, little Ahern? Pay me to keep my mouth shut?"

"What do you mean?"

He waited a while before he said, "Tell you what," in a voice that was suddenly gentle, almost like he wanted to be nice about it. "Maybe there's something you can do for me. You do for me, and I will do for you."

He reached and brushed my cheek with the back of his hand. I jerked, and faced away, which made him laugh. Hand back on the wheel, he fell quiet, deep in thought, and the car seemed to slow a little.

We passed the Christian Fellowship Church, its muddy driveway still puddled with angry ruts from the gathering two nights ago. The ancient Dodge Power Wagon was parked alongside the Stippil house.

What were they saying to each other inside that house with drawn curtains and panes of glass that threw back the daylight? Maybe the Reverend was shouting Bible verses at his family. Or was Missus Stippil, arms around her husband and children, speaking in soft whispers? A vision came to me, then, of the four of them sitting in the far corners of the house away from each other. And Agnes May was looking at me the way she had looked from the far end of the church through the exhaust fan shutters.

"Here's what you can do for me, young Ahern."

Baggie glared as he took the car out of gear and let it roll to a stop by Hobbes Woods. He said nothing more, until I looked at him.

"Here's what I want," he said. Eyes narrowed and peered into me, his mouth cracked into a grin. "Everybody's down on ole Baggie right now, down on him for just doing his job. But you can be his friend. Can you do it, young Ahern? Be his friend for a day? "

I shrugged.

"Well, these are your choices. Once you get outta this car, I can drive on home. Or I can stop by Missus Tull's place. If I stop by Tull's, well, I figure by nightfall about half of Melody Falls Township, and by tomorrow night, half of Wilmot County, will know all about your old man. They will know what he really did during the war. Everybody will know. Everybody."

I looked away.

"Which is it, young Ahern? Should I stop by Tull's?" His breath fell on me as he leaned closer "Or just go on home?" he said softly.

I moved against the door. If only I knew what my father had done during the war, knew what the hell Baggie was talking about. But my father would never talk about it. Baggie stayed put, a few inches from me, until I looked at him again.

"Go on home," I heard myself say. "Please don't tell Missus Tull."

The grin grew wider. He finally sat back in the seat. "Tomorrow, noon."

He looked at me again, and I looked at him.

"Tomorrow, noon?"

"The fairgrounds," he said. "Not our secret viewing area" he said, as if we shared his peeping activity, as if I was a peeper too. "No, you come right in the shower facility front door, into the little foyer. Won't be anybody else around. It'll just be you and me. We'll make a day of it."

"What are we going to do?"

He chuckled. "Now, don't you have me spoiling it for you by telling ahead. An adventure. You just be good and ready to be ole Baggie's pal for the day, that's all I'm saying. Be my friend when everybody else is kicking ole Baggie. Best if you get out of the car right here, don't you think? Wouldn't want your old man to see you with me."

"I'll be there, but only if you tell me, once and for all, what my father did, and you never tell anybody else."

"Sure." He grinned. "You show up by noon, and ole Baggie will tell you the whole story."

The door squeaked. Loose gravel from Reverend Stippil's grading job met the soles of my feet.

"How old are you?" Baggie said.

"Twelve," I said and stood to my full height. "Twelve and a half...or three-quarters, actually. Almost thirteen."

"Twelve and three-quarters," he said and laughed. "What a perfect age for an adventure," he said, and drove off.

It didn't seem like a perfect age to me. I wished I was older. I wished I was wiser to what grownups were talking about when they went into their code language: "Perfect age for an adventure." What did *that* mean?

A chill came from above. Pine boughs, swirled by the wind, sounded angry. Descending into the creek-wash, I gripped the tree-root hand-holds tightly. At the bottom, I crossed the stream and climbed the other side. Gnarled wood felt slimy, hard to hold onto. I struggled to reach the top of the embankment, and when I finally did, I lay face-down a moment and breathed in the smell of forest floor. I easily could have fallen just now, slipped off the root-holds, split my head open on the rocks in the creek bed. How many times had I made the same climb without ever thinking about that? Trees above let out a roar as the wind ripped away more leaves. Cold rain started to fall, pelting Hobbes Woods…pelting me.

## CHAPTER 54, SWEET CREEK

In the morning, I went out to the porch and sat on the Adirondack chair. Not in it, but on the curved end of it, elbows on knees. My hands seemed so tired, wanting to droop toward the floor. I soon took off my jacket. Last week, I had helped my father replace all the screens with storm windows from the attic—all twenty six of them—and now bright morning sun in October slant warmed the porch like an oven.

But Grandma, in her wicker rocker, had a woolen blanket over her knees and wrapped around her feet as she rattled the *Clarion*.

"I figured you'd be sleeping in," she said. "Oatmeal is on the stove."

"I'm not hungry."

She glanced around the paper. "In a hurry to go somewhere... without any breakfast?"

"I'm just not hungry, Marja."

"Just like your father and your uncle when they started to grow up. They would forget everything else to go see their friends."

I wasn't about to tell her that I was going to see Baggie Hoy. She had never liked him, not even when he and my father had been kids playing together a long time ago.

She put the paper down and stared at me. I felt my face flush from her look, and I turned away.

"Something's troubling you."

I shrugged.

"That girl?" she said softly.

"What girl?"

Her smile drew me to look at her. I couldn't deny her quiet demand that I look her in the eye. Somehow—through a secret grandma power—she knew about Agnes May. Better to have her asking me about Agnes May than suspecting that I was about to meet up with Baggie today.

"Did you think nobody knew about her?" she said.

I shrugged.

The smile fading, her blue eyes deepened, drawing me in.

"Would you listen to an old lady's advice?"

"Sure, Grandma."

"Go to her."

My face flushed, and I looked away. "But, Marja..."

"No buts about it. Go to her. Is she your friend or isn't she?"

I didn't know the answer.

"I know what you're thinking," she said. "You're thinking about all that's happened to her, and that maybe you should stay away, that she is damaged."

I nodded. I was thinking about all that had happened, all right.

"None of us may ever know the particulars," she said. "But the particulars aren't needed, not for a friend. What matters is that the girl has been harmed. Don't go thinking something is wrong with her, or that it is all her fault."

I had to look away, my face hot.

"But that's not what a friend does." Grandma was trying to make it into something so simple.

She picked up the *Clarion* and started to read aloud. The lead article on the front page—continued on page six—was about the Sweet Creek Project, which involved rerouting the highway where it came out of Wyotanda and began its long climb up the mountain, heading westward.

In that moment I decided to tell her. Marja was my best friend. I would tell her about Baggie, about our conversation yesterday, what he had been saying about my father, and my plan to meet Baggie today. I sat back in the chair and waited as she pronounced each word, wanting to tell her everything, feeling my body relax as I gave in to the need to talk with my Grandma—really talk with her for the first time in a long time.

The article had her full attention. It was a continuing saga that the whole county had been talking about. In recent days, my father had been talking about it over supper. Mechanical shovels had unearthed what appeared to be human remains, which stopped the Sweet Creek Project cold. Sheffield Hoy, wearing his County Coroner's hat, had climbed down into the hole, and soon decided to call for an expert: an archeologist from Penn State. The engineer and the foreman, having sent the crew home, stood around their construction trailer scratching their heads over the delay. By week's end, the expert announced that the site contained some human bones, all right, and a treasure trove of artifacts from a native settlement hundreds of years old.

Mister Johns suddenly had found himself chosen by a scattering of other locals with Susquehannock heritage as their spokesman. Descendants of a people that had been mostly scattered, a few of whom had stayed put by marrying white settlers, now claimed to be closely related to the original inhabitants of the village.

"The professor from down state says he will lend his full authority to our concern," Mister Johns had exclaimed from the window of the Bookmobile, eyes bright, last Saturday as Marja talked with him in our yard.

The following Monday, the engineer had conferred with the West Wyotanda Township Supervisors. The Supervisors conferred with Wilmot County Commissioners. The Commissioners conferred with the inspection official that the State of Pennsylvania, appointed as Harrisburg's eyes and ears on the project. All that conferring concluded with a business luncheon at the Wyotanda Motel, in the Knotty Pine Room. Just as dessert was brought out—canned pears topped with dollops of cottage cheese in hexagonal glass bowls—the attendees came to a consensus: the road project could not be stopped or delayed over a few old bones and shards of crockery.

So now, according to today's article about it in the *Clarion*, the project would soon be back on schedule. The new section of highway would open in a year, with the two-mile piece of old road being turned over to Wyotanda Township and designated Lost Village Trail.

Refolding the paper back to the front page, she held it up for me to see the center photo: men in suits, my father's opponent, County Commissioner Bill MacKenzie, among them.

Grandma's crooked index finger pointed him out. "A bit smug, don't you think?"

The group smiled broadly, having gathered at the site for a photo straight from the conclusion of their Knotty Pine Room meeting.

"If they can do that to Mister Johns' people, nothing can stop them from doing whatever they want to anybody," Marja complained.

In response to my silence, her face pinked up. "You should be thinking of these things, Owen."

"Eugene," I corrected. Lately, she'd been calling me by my father's name.

"Well, you're soon to be a man. You must begin thinking like one," she scolded.

The controversy was something from the far past, an ancient settlement that was important only in the memories of folks like Mister Johns. They were upset about something buried so long they had even forgotten the location of it until a contractor accidentally dug it up. I had my *own* thoughts to think. Real ones, from right here and now. I wanted to tell Grandma about Baggie Hoy, about his threat to hurt my father, her son. But she insisted on reading her paper, and there seemed to be no good opening where I could put forth my concern carefully. She started reading aloud again, a new story, about space scientists having shot off a test rocket from Hampton, Virginia two nights ago, causing many citizens along the East Coast to phone the police and report a glow in the sky.

And I wanted to tell her about Agnes May, some of the particulars, about how her fluttering around my life like a butterfly had opened up such emptiness. Maybe the telling could have helped to soothe the sharpness of it. But, as I sat and listened to her read, her voice was not soft today. It had a scratchy shrillness to it, like the harsh rasp grain makes when it goes down a chute.

Through the glass, in the distance, Hobbes Woods had lost most of its leaves to yesterday afternoon's storm. Just a day ago, the woods had been fluffed out with reds and yellows and purples. Suddenly, not much was left of a sky full of celebrating itself: gray limbs and branches, now like bony arms and hands that reached up, a few pieces of flesh barely clinging.

Grandma had stopped reading, and stared at me. Her glasses had fallen askew, a little away from one eye. The paper plopped into a crooked pile on the floor.

"Are you all right, Marja?" I got up and stood by her.

She looked up at me and blinked, one eye enlarged through optics, the other not aligned with its lens. "What did you say, Owen?"

"Eugene."

She looked at me with surprise, eyebrows arched. Then she laughed, forgetful of her missing tooth. But the laughter quickly drained from her face.

"Marja?"

"Promise me, Eugene." Her voice shook.

"Promise you?"

"Promise me."

"Promise you what?"

She held her breath for a moment. "Don't let them take me away."

"What? Take you away?"

Her voice grew angry. "I don't ever want to leave my farm!" Glasses falling into her lap, she looked at me with one eye afire, the other seeming to have gone cold.

"But, Marja, why would anybody want to take you away?"

She turned and looked through the window out at the yard. "That's what they do nowadays."

"But, what if you get sick, or something? The hospital."

"No!"

"But, the hospital. I mean, if you get sick, you might need to go to the hospital, and then come home after you get better."

She was quiet, eyes welling with tears. Then she said, "If I get sick, I'll get better right here. They have nuns at the hospital. They might find out, you know."

I put my hand over hers, over her fist as it drew a piece of the woolen blanket into a ball. Slowly, she relaxed her grip on the fabric and put her hand in mine. Wet, bloodshot eyes looked up at me.

"Grandma. Who is going to find out? And *what* are they going to find out?"

She blinked rapidly over and over. Tears burst forth, ran down her cheeks, found and followed her wrinkles the way a rivulet finds its way among leaves and twigs to the cracks in the dirt when rain starts. She grasped my hand with both of hers, fingers icy.

"The promise I broke, Owen. When I was young."

I didn't remind her that I was Eugene.

"The promise?"

"What if I'm discovered? Suppose they realize who I really am: will I be punished?"

"Punished! Nobody would punish *you*, Marja. Punished for what?"

"Breaking the promise," she scolded, as if I hadn't been listening. "The promise I made to Father Duda after Mass that day in the barn. He arranged my passage to America."

Her hands, like claws, dug into mine. I stood there, wanting to climb out of my own jumpiness.

Grownups had so many secrets. They seemed to be layered in them. Why had I supposed she was any different? Something had surely disturbed one of the layers deep within her.

She quieted down, wiped her tears on my sleeve. Pulling a bunched-up piece of toilet paper from her apron pocket, she sniffled into it.

"I promise," I said. "I won't let anybody take you away from here."

She gripped me tighter for a moment, then relaxed and let my arm go.

Gathering up the *Clarion*, I handed it back to her. "Would you still like to read your paper?"

She did nothing at first. After a long time passed, she rattled the pages, found her glasses and started to look for where she had left off. "Could you take the blanket away, Eugene?"

I folded it, laid it on the Adirondack. In a softer voice, she started reading aloud again, another story: this one about Sheriff

Braddawl reopening an investigation into the fire that had burned down the Wyotanda Grain Elevator back in 1954. An old man at the County Home, thought to be senile, had suddenly come forth, mumbling details that only the authorities had known about.

It was getting late. I left the porch by the storm door, and put on my jacket. I wouldn't be able to talk things over with Grandma. I had to meet up with Baggie Hoy. No getting out of it. If I didn't, he was going to spill the beans about my father to the whole county; *what* beans, maybe I could find out.

"Shouldn't you wear your down coat?" she called to me, tone muffled from beyond the window glass. "The paper says it will turn colder."

I waved goodbye over my shoulder. How would I ever be able to keep my promise to her to not let anybody take her to the hospital? I was just a kid. Maybe about as well as the professor from Penn State had kept his promise to the local descendants of the Susquehannock.

As I walked around the house to the garage, gravel crunching underfoot, the image of my grandma sitting there reading the paper on the porch was soon crowded out by Baggie Hoy, the way he would roll his head on bowling-ball shoulders, and look into me with round eyes and a crooked grin.

I stopped by the garage. In my father's tool box, under the leather-wrapped box wrench set, I found a screw driver just the right length to be concealed in my jacket pocket.

"Go for his eyes..."

Just one eye would do, if you shoved the blade in well past the socket.

# PART FOUR:

# WHEN LAST WE WERE TOGETHER

## CHAPTER 55, ANCIENT ROOT

I turned at the sound of a vehicle. A shiny green Willys pickup rounded the curve, black license plate from Texas on the front bumper. It slowed and stopped. I studied the driver through side-door glass. Quin's old man.

"You're back." I climbed in.

The cab of the truck had a new-vehicle smell mixed in with sandwiches and coffee and motor oil and sweat. Bert grinned at me, showing a gap between his two front teeth that I'd forgotten. It had been so long since I'd seen him smile. His face was sun-darkened.

"Got in this morning. You seen Quin? He ain't at the trailer." Putting the truck in gear, he headed us down the road.

"Did you ask Mister Rollheis? Quin's been doing chores for him."

Bert's eyebrows drew together below the bill of his red hat. "Been handymanning for Rollheis? I expected Vern to look in on him while I was away. Didn't expect him to put Quin to work."

"He's been paying Quin to help with the milking. I don't know what else." I avoided letting on that Quin and I hadn't been talking much lately.

"I sure hope the boy's not neglecting his schooling," he said. Then his eyes lit up. "How d'you like my new truck? Four-wheel-drive. Traded in the old Studebaker. This is just what I need for the job."

"When did you start, Bert?"

"Two weeks ago. Pipe welder on a cross-country line, seven days a week, big overtime check. I'm based outta Big Spring. That's in Texas."

So, that's where he'd gone.

"How long are you back for?"

"Got a few days off to get things squared away. Took two to get home and it'll take two to get back. That means I have to get everything done today. Now, don't you be tellin' Quin 'bout my job if you should see him before I do. I want to be the one to tell him."

"I'll keep mum."

The bottom of my stomach dropped. So Quin would be moving to Texas. Today?

"Where you headed?" He talked like we were old friends. I'd only ever been on the outer edges of conversation between him and my father, and had seldom spoken directly with him myself. He had always been so quiet.

"Fairgrounds," I said.

Coming to a stop sign at Route 6, he downshifted and braked. "Fairgrounds? This time of year that should be pretty well closed up."

"Gonna meet somebody there."

"Well, now that you mention the fairgrounds, I been figurin' to do one last check there myself on that septic system. Just take a look down inside, make sure everything's okay before I leave here. I owe that much to your dad. He has always been nothing but good to me. Your whole family's been good to me, both me and Quin."

Where Belknap Road joined the highway at the rock cut, we headed down toward Wyotanda. Bert put his shiny green truck through smooth gas pedal and clutch and gear-shift motions, bringing it up to speed. The vehicle gave off the sound and smells of newly machined and freshly painted metal, and soon the scallop-tread tires were singing.

"Bert, are you moving for good, then? You and Quin?"

He was quiet except for soft lip-smacking noises of a man thinking things over. "Not quite sure yet about Quin," he finally said. "I'm out on the pipeline night and day. We sleep in shifts in a construction trailer. Got me an apartment, all right, back in Big Spring, but sure hate to drag Quin all the way down there and then leave him for weeks at a time all by himself."

I felt like I was supposed to offer to have Quin stay with me. But that would never work, he going to Stephen Foster and I to Saint Agatha, and the two of us not getting along lately. I wondered if Bert was aware of what had been going on around here. Did he know about Agnes May's disappearance, and that, at one point, the deputies had wanted to question him?

"Your uncle," Bert said, "Father Dan. He gave me good advice in the past. You know, he also sent me a letter when they found my Missus. Most folks just stay away from a tragedy like that. Not your uncle. He wrote me a letter all the way from Indiana. Gave me his phone number and said to call him for any reason at all. I've got a hankerin' to do just that, maybe ring him up out there in Indiana. Have him weigh in on what he might think is best for Quin."

He stopped the truck in front of the fairgrounds main gate. "Who you meetin' with, Eugene? The place looks pretty well closed up to me."

"Baggie Hoy, over at the showers building."

Bert's eyes narrowed. "Baggie? What the hell doin's you got with the likes of him?"

I opened the door and stepped out. "Just for…well, he's going to give me some information, that's all. Aren't you going to check the septic tank?"

Bert looked off in the distance. "Got nothin' with me I can use to open the access." He rubbed his chin. "I'll swing by the hardware store first."

I was about to shut the door when he said, "Eugene." His eyes bored into me. "You be careful 'round him, you hear? Baggie ain't nobody to fool with."

"Sure." I shut the door.

As I approached the building, my stomach quivered. Baggie's blue Dodge Coronet was parked around the side, so he was here. I felt for the screwdriver in my jacket pocket. I went up the stone path, opened the building's front door and went inside. He had set up the foyer like a living space: cot against one wall, card table and a folding chair, electric space heater, food packages scattered about, two Old Crow bottles, one empty and one almost.

"Didn't think you'd show up," he rasped. "Thought you'd be a coward, like somebody else we both know."

"Stop saying that."

He laughed from deep in his throat as he leaned back in the folding chair, face puffy and flushed. "Not a coward? Ha! So, what did he tell you about the war when you asked him. You did ask him, like I told you to."

"No."

"There you go. I dared you to ask, and you didn't follow through."

"I'll ask my grandma."

More raspy laughter, and then he took a swig from the bottle. "Now, that ain't quite the same, is it."

It was hot in there with the heater puffing. I took off my jacket and laid it on the table.

"Just for laughs, ask your old man, not his ma."

He took another swig, belched and laughed at the same time. "But then don't hold your breath waiting for him to talk. He started to tell his old pal Baggie once, and then realized he'd better shut the hell up. That happened the day we saw each other after we both came home from the war in Europe. That was back before he fancied himself up, became oh so respectable. It happened when the two of us were lying in the hay mow, drinking straight bourbon, in your grandpa's barn."

"My father doesn't get drunk."

"No, not any more. Not after that day he opened up to his old pal Baggie about what he did in France. He'll never make that mistake again, never get drunk and spill what a coward he was."

"No. You've got it wrong." Tears welled up in my eyes.

"Aw. You gonna cry now?"

"He wasn't a coward," I said, my throat wanting to close. "It's not possible."

"Then you tell me why, in France he dressed up, pretending to be a priest. I'd call that being a coward, wouldn't you?"

"A priest?"

"A priest. A Catholic goddamn priest, while everybody else was stepping on mines, getting shelled, strafed and shot at by Germans."

"But you weren't even there. You told me once you were in Italy."

"Italy? France? What's the difference?"

"But you told me you were stuck in supply; that you never got to see any action."

His face pinked up, eyes bulged. "I did my job. Not any fault of mine I didn't see action. If I had, I sure as hell would have done my job there too. Not like Owen Ahern, who took just one shot at a Kraut and then couldn't squeeze another round off."

"You don't know that," I managed to say, my throat wanting to close up. "He never tells anybody about the war."

"Those Krauts had to be stopped, just like you'd have to stop a crazed wild animal. I'm tellin' ya, put the Baxter Hoys into action. Send the Owen Aherns back to supply. Ole Baggie won't be wringing his hands over it—no sir—not when there's even one rabid dog left to be killed."

He stopped, chest heaving, as if he'd almost worn himself down, eyes still bulging.

"My father would never run away."

"While the rest of us did our jobs, your old man had the garb of a priest, even a black prayer book he carried around. Quite a gig, I'd say. You know, plenty of them Krauts were Catholic, so it was pretty smart of him."

"No!" My scream sounded like a woman. I put my hands over my ears. I shut my eyes. I shut my eyes and saw, on one of my snooping forays through his office, a cassock, crucifix, prayer book, all under a cloth cover on a shelf in the closet. At the time, I'd told myself it was my uncle's things. But why would Dan have left that stuff at home, where he always wore normal clothes? And the cassock looked too small for Dan anyway.

I heard only my own breathing and roughness of my heart pumping away. I opened my eyes. Baggie stared evenly at me. Then a grin stretched his fleshy face.

He changed his tone to soft and gentle. "Now, don't get your jock strap, size small, in a bind. Just because I know all about it doesn't mean I have to tell anybody. Like I was saying yesterday, little-boy Ahern, I'm willing to trade…that is, if you are."

"Trade what?"

"You think you're man enough? Think you've really got what it takes?"

"Got what WHAT takes?"

More laughter. He raised his voice again. "At age twelve-and-three quarters, I'm thinking you haven't quite got the balls for it."

"For what?"

He stared at me, then spoke gently again. "No, you ain't got the balls. For a trade. For being grown up enough to know the cost. What it would cost for my silence, so your old man won't be ruined one week before election day."

"I will trade for you to keep mum. I will trade whatever it is you want for that."

Laughter. "Whatever? You sure you know what whatever is?"

"Whatever!"

"So, let me see. I'll keep quiet about what I know. For whatever. Maybe ole Baggie had you figured all wrong. Maybe we'll find out if you've got some balls after all."

"Whatever," I said again, not recognizing my own voice.

His eyes rounded out and looked straight into me. "You."

Was the whiskey affecting him? "Me? What's that mean?"

"You." His face turned blank, leaving just the glare of his eyes. "For a good ole friend's GUAR-AN-TEE of keepin' the secret."

I turned away, unable to look at him. He was drunker than I thought, making no sense. "I don't understand," I said.

"Tell you what. You just gotta give me a little something. A token. Let me have just a sign that you're ready to be ole Baggie's friend. You know, a guy gives the shirt off his back for a friend."

I looked at him.

"Just a symbol," he said evenly. "Your shirt."

He wanted my shirt? For his silence, I unbuttoned it, felt it fall from my shoulders, slip from my arms. I handed it to him.

He neatly folded it and placed it on the table. "Now the tee shirt."

"You just said my shirt." In his drunken state he was making no sense at all. "You're not getting my tee shirt. You said you'd guarantee silence in exchange for my shirt. Just a sign, you said."

I never should have taken the jacket off. I should have kept the screwdriver close at hand.

"Shirt off your back. I distinctly remember saying that." He turned aside as if talking to someone else, "Now, didn't I say that? Shirt off his back?" Turning back to me, "Yeh, I did say that for sure. Shirt off your back." He pointed index finger at the floor, stirred the air with it. Eyes narrowed. "Now the tee shirt."

So it was a game. All right, I would play. For now. I pulled it over my head, but held onto it. "Your silence then? Your silence for my tee shirt, and that's it. You'd better not be too drunk to remember."

He gave a short, one-syllable laugh. "Sure. Why not." He grinned at me, eyes rounding out, and full of fun.

I handed it to him. In the same motion, I picked up my jacket and felt for the screw driver.

He folded the tee shirt and put it on top of the other shirt. "You ain't fooling ole Baggy," his voice suddenly turned serious. "You don't come all the way down here on a Saturday and pretend you don't know what's what, pretendin' you aren't eager, at age twelve-and-three-quarters, for your first big-boy adventure." His eyes narrowed and swept over me.

Pin pricks rose in a wave on the back of my neck. I felt for the opening to the pocket, and found the handle of the screw driver.

The door slammed open. Bert Gutierrez banged into the room. He looked me up and down, eyes afire.

Baggie laughed, his whole body shaking with it, like a fat Santa Clause. He got on his feet with an "Uh," raised a fist and stumbled toward Bert. Bert put his arm up, palm flat on Baggie's chest. As Baggie rushed at him, Bert stepped back and let his elbow bend, absorbing the force of the heavier man. Baggie's drunken try at a punch found only air. Bert set his feet, and stiffened his body. With a grunt, he shoved. Baggie, windmilling his arms, slammed into the wall, head snapping back atop his beefy shoulders, thud on ceramic wall tile.

Bert picked up my clothes, handed them to me. "Get the hell out," he said, spitting the words, "and don't come back. Go get in the truck and lock the doors."

Baggie, easing down the wall to a sitting position, suddenly heaved, throwing up onto his round belly. As I hurried away, I heard him slur thick words at Bert, "Sloot-humping son of a bitch."

In the cab of the truck I shivered. I put my shirts on, then my jacket. I craved warmth, but Bert had told me not to go back in there. More than just the chill of the air had me trembling. Raw realization ground at me from the inside. Goose flesh ran over my skin. It was like the time I had slipped and almost fallen from a rung near the top of the silo as a little kid. How close I'd come to sliding off the world as I knew it into — whatever — chasm yawning, eager to devour, a place that I would never be able to come back from.

I wanted to go back, but Bert had told me to wait here. Rubbing my arms through the jacket did no good. To get my mind off the shakes I picked up some papers from the middle of the seat:

"American Petroleum Institute," the top page said, and under that, an official-looking document. "Roberto Gutierrez is hereby certified for the Shielded Metal Arc Welding process to butt-join pipe of all thicknesses from 2 to 60 inches diameter in any position..."

It meant nothing to me. It did nothing to stop my trembling. I had to go back, had to have some heat. And I had to know what was happening, regardless of what Bert said. I left the truck and went to the building. Nobody there...what had happened to them? Suppose Baggie had managed to get the jump. Slipping hand into pocket, I gripped the screwdriver. Around the side of the building, beyond the old Dodge, one of them was crouching. I couldn't see which one. I sneaked along the side of the car. I saw Bert in his red hat. The septic lid was open, a big box wrench and shiny, black new crowbar, on the ground. I moved closer. Bert held Baggie's Old Crow bottle upside down, dribbling the last of it into the septic tank access hole. He dropped in the empty, and jerked his head toward me.

"Wait in the truck!"

"I had to—"

"In the truck!" He pointed for me to leave, eyes like shards of glass.

I turned away and did what he said. A few minutes later he came along and clanged the tools into the back, then climbed into the driver's seat and started the engine. He smelled sweaty, even in the cold.

We rode in silence back up the mountain. We turned off at Belknap Road. With Bert's smooth operation of the gas and clutch and gear shifter, the quivering in my stomach slowly eased up along the way.

When we stopped in front of my house, he looked at me. "Just so you know," he said quietly. "I seen what he was up to with you. So he decided to leave town. He's gone from these parts for good. The varmint won't be coming back. Ever." He continued to look at me without blinking.

I said, "Back by the septic tank, I saw his car was still there."

Bert's eyes dropped away and then came back to me. "Sure. Too drunk to drive. Best to not wait around, not wait to sober up. Wise of him, I'd say. He went looking for another mode of transportation outta here."

He turned and looked out his side window. The quiet of a long moment filled up with tremor of the truck's engine at idle.

He turned back to me. Eyes softening, he said, "You and I gotta have a deal, Eugene. What happened back there is not what you'd want folks talkin' about. So, I give my word I won't ever tell. And I figure you won't ever tell either."

He looked away, letting me think about it. At last, I felt my breath coming back to normal.

He looked at me again without blinking. "We got a deal?"

"Deal," I said.

He reached, grinned at me with everything but his eyes. I shook his hand. It was crooked and lumpy and callused, like a piece of ancient root turned up by a plow, yet warm and welcome.

## Chapter 56, For a Lousy Smoke

"Something's not right with Eugene."

No kidding, I tried to say, but filaments of sleep had me tongue-tied. I struggled to break through groggy webbing as I lay on my bed atop the covers, in my clothes, in the dark, my left arm numbed by weight of a book that had closed on it.

"What do you mean?" my father echoed through the register.

"Haven't you noticed?" my mother said.

I had fallen asleep under window twilight while reading an assigned chapter in the seventh grade science textbook. I'd been dreaming:

Astronomers discovered another planet, one that we hadn't known existed on the opposite side of the sun from us. They'd noticed oddities in the pull between Earth and the Sun. The only possible conclusion: a twin planet that nobody had ever seen through a telescope because the sun had always blocked it. So, the Army had attached a spacecraft on top of bundled Redstone rockets and sent a crew of two explorers to see what was there. And then, in the middle of the journey, the rockets misfired.

Halfway through the dream, I realized that it was me out there. I was one of the explorers. We had spun far off the planned trajectory. Adrift, stripped of its purpose, our spacecraft had become just one more grain of space dust. We did not expect to be alive much longer.

As I emerged from the dream, the other explorer, my sole companion, just a few inches from my face, puffing sour breath: Baggie Hoy. I woke struggling to get away, yearning to be with Grandma Marja and Quin and Agnes May and Uncle Dan and my mother and father and—

"I suppose I have noticed," my father's voice came up the cold air return.

"I don't know how to describe it," my mother said. "Something's just wrong."

"I've been too occupied. I admit it. Now that you bring it up, his demeanor's been nagging me too. I should have paid closer attention."

I turned over and slid along the covers to be nearer the register.

"Just think about it. The Hobbes boy's father dies. Quin's mother's body is found. His little friend, Agnes May, vanishes, and then Quin comes under suspicion for that. So much has been going on in his life, Owen. My goodness, the police question Eugene, and even allow that clairvoyant lady from Leaning Stone to ply her hocus-pocus on him—you never should have allowed that."

A click of my father's lighter.

"And then," my mother said, "it comes out the Stippil boy did something to his sister. Well, what must it seem like to Eugene? The sky has fallen down around his ears."

"I think something's going on between him and Quin, too," he said, "if I read the signals correctly."

"And who knows what else could be happening in our son's young life." She sighed. "I haven't told you about his notebook."

I shifted closer to the register. My mother had been in my notebook?

"His notebooks are kind of private, don't you think?"

"I'm his mother."

"But, his notebooks—"

"I'm his mother."

He drew on the pipe.

"A penis," she said. I'd never heard her say that word before. It didn't seem that the sound of it should be coming from my mother's lips. "Right there alongside all those strange calculations he was doing all through the summer."

"They're not strange. Just batting averages. During the season, he likes to keep up on batting averages from the box scores in the paper. Don't worry about it, Veronica. I did the same thing when I was a kid. Questionable drawings, too."

"I'd say a bit beyond questionable. Don't worry? A massive, erect *penis,* veins and all."

I winced to myself.

My father coughed.

"And a tiny man, to whom the thing appears to belong, holding on with both hands like it's a runaway horse."

My ears burned as I listened. I remembered drawing that picture one day in the summer, a mindless doodle, my ear to the radio as Mel Allen called a game from Yankee Stadium against the Orioles.

"Well, I wouldn't worry, Veronica. You're a girl. It's not all that unusual."

"Owen, it's a sign that our son needs a vacation," she decided. "He needs a break from all that's been building up in his life. And it would do him good to get away from this election business of yours. So much tension in the air."

"Can't just take him out of school."

"For a day or two? Make a long weekend for him. Send him out to visit Dan. You know how they adore each other. And maybe...just maybe there's something there in our son's future, like we've talked about."

After a long silence, my father said, "I know we've talked about it. Dan's a busy man, but maybe you're right. I'll call him and see if this is a good time to send Eugene out there for...well, a retreat."

So, they had been thinking of sending me to visit Uncle Dan. When were they going to tell me about it?

The train arrived in Buffalo at the end of the Lehigh Valley line in the dark of morning. My parents had put me on the train at Wyotanda last evening and I had ridden through the night, occasionally nodding off but then jerking awake again, my mind still being pestered by Baggie Hoy and his swirl-eye.

Through the station and out to the street, I found a bus marked CENTRAL DEPOT, just as my father said I would. After a bumpy ride on dark streets, I was just one among the flood of sleepy passengers the bus disgorged to a massive building, one corner of it a tower of office windows that reached into the sky. We entered into a broad terminal where the size of the place allowed the push of people to relax and spread out, footsteps and voices bouncing off enameled surfaces.

The clock on the pedestal was right where my father had said it would be, all of its four faces showing 5:19. "Used to be an information counter around it," he had said. "That was gone last time when I went through there, so you might have to watch the board on your own."

But a man in a red tie and green vest with a gold name tag stood near the clock. He looked at me, and figured right away that I probably didn't know what I was doing. Asking to see my ticket, he pointed across the terminal at a gold statue of a bison about to charge.

"Departs at 7:27. Start listening for the announcements before that. You'll go past the buffalo, turn right and down the concourse to Track 4."

So far so good. Other instructions from my father: "Keep your wallet and ticket in your front pants pockets, hang on to the gym bag, don't let strangers talk you into going anywhere with them."

The wallet and ticket presented no problem. But at the urinal in the men's room, holding onto the gym bag proved too awkward, so I placed it tightly between my feet. When I was finished, I realized that, right beside me, a man in a brown suit and fedora had been watching.

As I turned to leave, he mumbled, "Earn a quick bill?"

"No, thank you," I said. The hair on my neck stood up, like it had the last time I was with Baggie.

I found the waiting room and a bench to sit on and wait.

At 7:15, I stood and joined the swell of people heading toward the golden buffalo. On Track 4, I mounted a step into the car and found my seat on the right side. As we left the station, gray daylight began to fill the windows. While the train moved along the western shore of New York under a cover of clouds, Lake Erie went in and out of view. We crossed the Pennsylvania chimney and moved into Ohio. Except for Cleveland, the stops along the way lasted no more than a few minutes. In between, my eyes wanted to close, but thoughts kept racing to open them again.

Would Baggie just go away as Bert Gutierrez believed he would?

I suddenly awoke from a short nod-off to the loud voice of the conductor coming through the car, announcing that we were in Indiana as he called out upcoming stops: Elkhart, South Bend, Gary. His voice was cut off when he exited the other end of the car.

My hand, as if not connected to my brain at all, checked my pocket to feel for cigarettes that I'd forgotten to bring. I got up and went to the lavatory in a small lounge fitted with green sofas at the end of the car. After I came out of the toilet, I found a space beside a man who was loudly describing to the others that power steering was hottest new feature of his product line. His briefcase proclaimed in burnished lettering, OLIVER FARM EQUIPMENT COMPANY. When he finished his cigarette, he quieted just long enough to use the butt to light another from a pack of Camels.

"Whitey Ford smokes those," I said, and smiled.

The man looked at me. "Sorry to hear it. Maybe I should switch to another brand."

The others laughed at that, and new conversation arose around the recent World Series. The men in the group soon clamored to take turns jousting and jawing with each other.

"Where you from, kid?" the man asked.

"Pennsylvania."

Their eyes lit. Somebody said, "Hey kid, how 'bout that Mazeroski!"

The tractor salesman jerked his Camel pack, coaxed a few cigarettes to slide out part-way and offer themselves up. Each of them took one. The man raised his eyebrows when I took one too. Here I was, pretending I wasn't a Yankee fan, just for a lousy smoke.

## CHAPTER 57, ACHE IN MY KNEES

The train arrived in South Bend in late afternoon that had a hard time deciding between bright and dreary, sun going in and out of the clouds. A man waved to me from the platform: Uncle Dan, long black coat not quite covering the skirt of his cassock. For an instant, he didn't appear to be the same man at all who would come home to the farm, don dungarees and work shirt to help me feed the Percherons and shovel manure.

We rode together on a rattling city bus out to the university.

"Your father must be on pins and needles," he said, "with election day so close."

"He's pretty quiet."

Dan smiled. "That's Owen. Not a man who reveals himself."

Before arriving at a circular drive that marked the entry to campus, the bus took us past the red-brick stadium standing far in the distance in a vast, empty parking lot.

"You'll be seeing the stadium tomorrow," he said as we got off the bus.

Did that mean he would be taking me to a game?

"Meanwhile, we'd better get moving if we want to make it in time for supper," he said. "You'll be spending the night at the little sem."

"The little sem?"

"That's what we call the one for high-school-age seminarians."

We went briskly across campus to a cinder path beside Lake Saint Mary, a distant walk that had me shifting gym bag hand to hand along the way. The path led up a small incline past an athletic field with a chain-link backstop. The little sem appeared as a hodgepodge of old buildings stuck together from different centuries. Inside an aluminum and glass facade, a sign greeted us: SPES UNICA—ACROSS THE WORLD WITH HOLY CROSS. We met Father LaSalle, a short, broad man with black-framed glasses and a five-o'clock shadow, who appeared to have been waiting for us. Dan introduced him as the seminary superior.

A seminarian took my bag. At the sounding of a loud bell, students erupted out of side-halls, doorways and dark staircases that funneled them from mismatched levels into a main corridor. Nobody said a word to disturb a whispery flush of shoe-sole on highly waxed floor. We followed along and entered a dining area, the refectory, I later learned. Father LaSalle ushered me to one of the tables and muttered instructions to a blond-haired seminarian, who motioned for me to stand by my chair.

We all faced a crucifix at one side of the room, near to where a number of priests stood at their own table. My uncle, who normally took his meals at a campus dining hall, stood among them. When the mass arrival of people abruptly ended, total silence overtook the assembly standing at attention, most of them a head or more above me. The superior intoned a Latin phrase, and eager voices responded as one, also in Latin. When it was over, we sat down, but remained silent for a student at a lectern to read a religious passage. Suddenly, at a clang from the priests' table, the room burst into conversation.

"Mike McCreary." The seminarian beside me put his hand out, a broad smile on his face. "I'm a freshman here. Father LaSalle chose me to be your shadow."

"Eugene Ahern."

Shadow? But I would be visiting with my uncle. What was a shadow? Why would I need one?

Eight of us sat at the table on creaky wooden chairs with circular seats and bentwood backs. About two dozen similar tables were arranged in rows throughout the room. Students were neatly dressed in ties and jackets. The fancier priests' table was off by itself.

"Eugene Ahern," said the mature voice of a senior, who announced himself as the table head. "So, you're a relative of Father Dan?"

"He's my uncle."

All eyes turned to me, seemed to say I was okay, as if to offer immediate forgiveness from feeling awkward about my young age, smaller stature and lack of spiffy clothes. It was obvious that, around here, Father Daniel Ahern was somebody, all right.

After supper, blond-haired McCreary — ever at my side — kept me from running afoul of a myriad of customs and rituals of the place. I learned as many as I could, all the while wondering when I would join Uncle Dan again. McCreary showed me what parts of the facility were off limits to seminarians, where and when to maintain silence, how to stand straight and motionless and, at prayer times, to forget about putting hands together in favor of a Holy Cross custom of simply folding your arms. I even learned to skip a space at the urinals so no two people ever stood side by side.

Just before a night-prayer assembly in the chapel at 9:30, McReary explained that the whole place would soon be under Grand Silence, which meant that nobody would be allowed to talk for any reason. When the prayer was over, he signaled me to follow him to the basement, where seminarians crowded in front of lockers to get ready for bed. In the gym bag I found the pajamas that my mother had packed, tags still on them. I stripped. McReary suddenly put a robe over me and hastily rasped, "We don't do that here!" Realizing that he had broken Grand Silence, he looked around to see if he'd been caught at it, but was only met with a few chuckles. Then, with hand signals, he demonstrated an awkward procedure of putting the bottoms on while wearing the robe. With a bit of fumbling, I was able to master it.

We slept in a dormitory on the top floor, a large room with thirty beds in parallel rows. Exhausted, I gave up wondering when I would see my uncle again or why they had sent me here. I just hoped to quickly fall asleep. I must have dozed off for a few minutes, and was reawakened by brightness slowly filling the room from lights that shone through the east windows, followed by the distant drone of a plane. I came fully awake again as the light grew brighter, the drone louder. In a moment, the room lit up, panes began to rattle, throb of multiple propellers beating the air. The glaring white light broke into window-cast rectangles that swept across the floor in the opposite direction of an aircraft passing close overhead. A sudden drop in pitch sent the plane away, heading west.

"Mike," I whispered. "What was that?"

"Northwest Orient," McCreary whispered back. "And right on schedule. We're under the approach path for South Bend."

From a bed in the corner of the room, deep voice of the senior who had been assigned to keep order in the freshman dorm, "*Magnum Silentium!*" Chuckles from among the rows of beds, and then the place filled with deathly quiet.

I started to doze again. But Baggie Hoy, his round face, glare, raspy laugh, would not let me fall all the way to sleep. For hours I was alone with him in the dark. And then I was taken away in a dream:

Agnes May and I sat together at the back of the pump house, the art book from the library open across our bent knees. On one page was the photo of the marble statue of a woman with no arms, and on the opposite page the urn whose fine lines had always reminded me of Marja and Uncle Dan. Agnes May studied the urn intently, tracing its shape with the tip of her finger.

"It is perfect," she said, turning to me, her breath touching my cheek.

A shadow came over us. Baggie stood in his dirty boots and deputy uniform, wide leather belt sagging from the weight of a holstered pistol, staring down at us from under the brim of his hat, lips grinning over yellow teeth above the fat chin.

She saw him and grabbed my shoulder. "Ah!" She said in a high pitch.

She was naked. She crossed her hands over herself to cover up, thin arms decorated with a fine white down. I grabbed to pull my shirt off and cover her. But I was naked too.

Baggie laughed, rolling his head on his big shoulders. I knelt up, facing her, and pulled her to me, wrapping her with my arms to cover her from his gaze. She started to cry. I grabbed her more tightly and pulled her against me, her flesh giving off heat.

Baggie laughed. "Now, there you go, young Ahern—there you go!" The toe of his dirty boot was between my legs, nudging me from behind.

I sat up. Darkness was filled with breathing seminarians. After awhile, I lay back down. The night, ever so slowly, overtook me.

The next day, after a sleepy Mass, and then a more wakeful breakfast, I helped McCreary with his assigned chore. His daily responsibility was for one of the seminary's many odd staircases. Saturday—and no school—meant the job was more than simple herding of dust bunnies into a pan. On our knees, we scrubbed and waxed by hand every square inch of every step and landing from third floor to basement. When we were finished, my knees complained: What had happened to Uncle Dan? What was I doing at the little sem?

When it was finally time for lunch, my uncle was not at the priests' table. Instead of saying grace, the seminarians and priests stood through recitation of the Angelus Prayer in Latin, one of the seniors clanging a bell. After the meal started, Dan appeared in the doorway, then came through the refectory and stopped by our table.

"A little late," he grinned. "My Saturday class ran over." He looked at me with a big smile, "So, what do you think so far?"

I didn't have an answer. What had I thought about WHAT so far? Wasn't I, his favorite nephew, here to visit with my favorite uncle? Other than time spent together on a lurching city bus, that hadn't happened at all.

He waved for us to be seated.

"Oh, he's really enjoying it here," McCreary said. "Especially scrubbing and waxing the stairs."

Everyone at the table laughed. Dan winked at me, and went away to sit with his fellow priests.

Just what was I doing here at the little sem?

The Table Head looked at me with a serious face. "What do you think so far, Eugene?"

I didn't have an answer. I smiled and said, "Nice place, all right."

McCreary's face melted into a grin, and the others at the table were all looking at me. "It's not all praying and washing steps around here, you know." He pulled something from his pocket: tickets to the game, arty blue-ink print of Notre Dame Stadium on them. "Just one of the benefits of being a Holy Cross Seminarian."

All eyes were on me, savoring my surprise.

Sure, I smiled, but I did not want to be one of them. I was here to visit Uncle Dan. Wasn't I? And after visiting him, I wanted to go home. Home, where I would go see Agnes May as soon as I could. I had to be with her. I would go to her, to the sound of her voice, and the feel of her hand in mine. I would go to her, just like Grandma Marja had said. She had been harmed, and I had not gone to her.

The high school seminarians, their seventh grade guest from Melody Falls, Pennsylvania in tow, found their seats, which were scattered around the stadium at the top row, up against the wall where a cold blustery wind blew in from the North.

"It will never fill up," McCreary assured me as we watched the band leave the field. "Too cold today, and the Irish haven't been winning."

He was right. The two south-corner sections had almost nobody in them, and after kickoff we easily found seats down there closer to the field, although the wind was now blowing into our faces. A man with a round, ruddy face, wearing a heavy overcoat, sat nearby. At first glance he looked like Baggie. Baggie was turning up everywhere: at the urinal in the Buffalo Central Terminal, in my dream, and now here at the football game. This one had ear muffs, a plaid tam o'shanter, and a binoculars case.

On their first two plays of the game, Notre Dame lost yardage, thanks to Pittsburgh's Number 89, who tackled the ball carrier twice behind the line. Through the wind and the noise of the crowd, the announcer's pronunciation of the player's name sounded like "Itka." On the third play, the same Panther player, Mister Itka, tall, big-shouldered and agile, forced the Irish quarterback to hurry his throw, which fell incomplete.

"Looks like I'm gonna need this," the man said. Flipping open the lid to his case, he unscrewed a silver cap from the binoculars, put it to his lips and took a long pull, wiping his mouth with the back of his hand…like Baggie would have done.

I'd never been to a big football game before, not even high school; Melody Falls was too small to have a team. I was surprised that from down by the field in the stands, you could hear the whacking and thudding of hits, see the spray of saliva. Into my mind's eye spilled the memory of Baggie falling against the wall in the foyer.

After a Notre Dame punt, the Pitt Panther quarterback lofted a long, high pass across and down the field. The entire stadium stood up as one to watch the play unfold. Number 89 — that guy again, now on offense — caught it on his fingertips, pulled it in, and continued down the sideline with a green-shirted Irish defender riding his back until they finally stumbled out of bounds together, just short of the goal line.

"Jesus!" the man yelled at the 60-yard play, and took another pull on his fake binoculars.

A minute later, Pitt led 7-0. By half-time, they led 20-0. And by the start of the third quarter, the score had found many of the cold, wind-blown fans without a reason to stay. We looked for new seats above mid-field, and binoculars man, having adopted us as buddies, came along.

A new strategy that put two players against Number 89 changed the game. On defense, the Irish stopped Pitt, and the offense was finally able to move the ball. In the fourth quarter, Notre Dame, on a come-back, brought the score to 20-13. With just over a minute left, they stopped Pittsburgh's last attempt on offense, which loosed a roar from the student section.

As the final Irish drive got under way, the crowd was on its feet. Enlivened fans, standing and shouting in unison, sent quivers into the structure's concrete and bricks. Three quick plays were short sideline passes. The noise grew deafening, "HEAR COME THE IRISH!" I was pulled into the sound, into the feel of it. It swallowed me whole into the belly of a magnificent, pounding roar so much bigger than me. I was on my feet, rhythmic excitement skipping through every nerve. Clock ticking down, the excitement rose to a scream as a green-shirted Irish receiver streaked to the end zone. The quarterback planted his feet and — Number 89 plowed into him. The ball fluttered to the ground. The clock fell to zero, Pitt now the winner. Crowd roar echoed around Notre Dame Stadium like a dog trying to decide where to lie down, then fell silent.

McCreary and I, in a state of numbness, turned for the exit. We finally managed to leave our companion, who sat down, alone. Having earlier drained his binoculars, he could do little else but mutter to himself, elbows on knees, head in his hands, tam-o'shanter wagging.

Working our way through the crowd, we crossed the campus to the cinder path along the lake, where we joined others strolling back to the little sem in small groups. Gray wind moaned through dark, bare tree limbs, its bitter chill mocking the ache in my knees from all that scrubbing of stairs. Up ahead I spotted my uncle's blond hair, seminarians gathered round him, all of them talking about the game.

## Chapter 58, What Anybody Thinks

We left the little sem after early Mass on Sunday morning. Dan was taking a few days leave to be with our family on election day, so he was allowed use of the Studebaker Lark again to make the drive home.

We made good time through Indiana and along the lake in Ohio. On Route 20, in Ashtabula, we stopped for fuel at a Sohio station. Once gassed up, we parked next-door, at the Vinifera Diner. Passing through the murmur of a handful of table-customers, we took seats at the counter.

A round woman named Sandra in a stained white uniform used little squares of waxed paper to retrieve the doughnuts we asked for from inside a glass case.

"You sure you don't want some coffee?" Dan said as he swallowed from a heavy mug.

I sipped orange juice. "Don't really like coffee."

"You've been quiet the whole trip, so far," he said.

Sandra served them on small plates, two each, waxed paper between them. Dan's were jelly-filled, one grape and one apple. Mine were both regular doughnuts covered in chocolate icing, Grandma Marja's favorite. I had inherited her love for chocolate.

The words popped out of me: "Why in the hell did you put me in that seminary?"

I'd never said hell to a priest before, and certainly not to my uncle. As soon as I said it, I couldn't look at him. I stared at the doughnuts on my plate. The more I looked at them, the less they looked like Grandma's.

He breathed hard through his nose as he took a bite, swallowed and gulped some coffee. I knew he was looking at me, but I couldn't look up from my plate. He didn't take another bite, but remained perfectly still. I was supposed to look at him now, but couldn't.

"Eugene," he said, and put his hand firmly on my shoulder. "What's going on?"

I hadn't ever cried in front of him, not counting the time he hit a grounder to me that took a bad hop, smacking me in the mouth. But as I turned to look at him now, a tear materialized and ran down the side of my face. "I thought it would be just us."

~ 347 ~

The grip on my shoulder softened. "It's a case of ruined expectations. Learning how to deal with it is one of life's important lessons, Eugene."

I wiped my eyes with my sleeve. "I don't care about important lessons. I thought we were going to be together, you and me."

Sandra stared at us. Dan pulled a dollar from his pocket. "Could you get me a copy of the—what do you have—the *Cleveland Plain Dealer*? Keep the change."

We ate and drank in silence. These doughnuts didn't taste anything like Grandma's. The murmur of the diner, which had quieted, picked back up again. Sandra plopped a thick Sunday paper, wrapped on colorful comics, on the counter. Dan flipped to an inside section, and glanced at the headlines.

"Looks like it would take all day to read that paper," I said.

"It lasts all week," he chuckled. "One of my few pleasures in life: Sunday papers."

"Dan, I don't think I want to be a priest."

He put the paper down. He looked at me. And so did Sandra. His arm went around my shoulder, then a heavy squeeze pulled me to him for a moment. He let me go, but held me with soft eyes. "Your parents and I just thought it would be okay to let you see what the little sem is like."

I shrugged.

He looked into me and said, "We should have asked you first. That was disrespectful of us. I'm sorry, Eugene."

Sandra looked from Dan to me to Dan.

No priest had ever said he was sorry to me. He hugged me again, and we suddenly laughed at each other. The waitress tore a page from her pad and placed it on the counter. "A dollar sixty-seven," she huffed, and went away to attend to one of the tables.

Back on the road, the land began to rise and dip as we approached Pennsylvania. Just across the state line, we turned off Route 20 to a northern extension of Route 6, which took us inland, away from Lake Erie and on to the main route.

In the road quiet, I suddenly asked, "Were Dad and Baggie Hoy friends when they were kids?"

"They were inseparable as kids. I was your dad's pesky little brother, and Shef Hoy was Baggie's pesky little brother. We tried to follow them around. They got to be pretty good at losing us," he laughed. But something made him uncomfortable. He took his eyes off the road for a brief look at me.

"Baggie said the voters just wouldn't stand for a guy like Dad becoming judge, once they knew the truth about him. A coward would never be able to send a killer to the electric chair."

Dan's face went cold, eyes frozen to the road ahead. "Why would you be listening to the likes of Baggie Hoy?"

"Did you know Dad has a cassock in his office closet?" My voice quivered as I spoke. "It has a cape with it, just like yours, a Holy Cross Fathers' cape. I know it's not yours. The cassock is too short for you, but it would fit him just right. And a breviary. A dog-eared and worn breviary."

Dan stared through the windshield. After a while he said, "And what do you make of that?"

"Why would he have that stuff? Why would my father have a set of priest clothes and a breviary?" The whine in my voice was a mixture of complaint and accusation.

After a long silence, he said, "Have you asked him about it?"

"No."

"Why don't you ask him, then. I believe he'll tell you why he has those things."

"I can't ask him, Uncle Dan." Blood rushed to my ears. "I only know about the breviary and cassock and cape because of my snooping around in there."

"He doesn't always keep it locked?"

"I know where the key is."

Dan laughed; a laugh that said he recognized my predicament, and I felt better. He had never seemed to mind if I saw him as just another human being like me. He said, "That does complicate things, all right."

"You see me as your good little nephew. But I'm a bit dishonest, sneaking around in his office. A real liar, you might say."

"You're not alone, Eugene. And think about it: it can't be a very big percentage of the time that you're a liar, now can it. Everybody realizes at one time or another that he's not been genuine."

We drove through a long period of quiet into the mountains of western Pennsylvania. We left Route 6 for Route 59, a shortcut through the Allegheny Forest.

"Once they finish the dam, won't be long before this will all be under water," Dan said as we passed through Kinzua. "The whole town has to be moved. The Seneca people — Quin's mother's relatives — are very upset about it."

Thirty miles later, on the eastern downhill slope of a mountain, I felt the car slowing. We came to a stop on a short bridge that was only about two car lengths. A crooked, rusty sign poked up from a freshly painted railing: BLACKSMITH RUN.

"That's where they found Frances Gutierrez," Dan said. For a few minutes we looked over the railing into the streambed.

A recent gouge in the thick undergrowth showed where they had pulled her car out of its seven-year hiding place.

"Uncle Dan, how did you know — all the way from Indiana — that this was the place?"

He said nothing for a while. Then he turned and said, "Well, I do keep up on the news from home."

After rejoining Route 6 at Smethport, we went on through Coudersport. The Studebaker climbed a windy hill eastward until we stopped at Potato City. It was an agricultural institute that Dan was familiar with from his biology studies. It also had a restaurant. Blue and white Nixon-Lodge posters were taped to either side of the front door.

"Tell you what," Dan said as he stirred his coffee. "I'll help you off the hook with yourself on this one. But in return, you promise to keep a secret. And afterward, it'll be up to you to go straight with your father."

"People are always telling me secrets."

"That means they feel they can trust you, Eugene."

"That's what Grandma Marja says."

"If that's what they think, and if you have lived up to it, you have no call to be hard on yourself. You can't be such a terrible liar if you can be trusted."

I thought about it. "What's one more secret, then?"

We looked at each other, the two members of a club that included only Dan and Eugene Ahern.

He sipped his coffee, then put the cup down and, elbows on the table, looked aside in thought. He said, "The secret I'm about to tell you is your father's secret. He has never asked me to not tell it, but I never have because I'm his brother. I will tell you because you are his son. It's up to you whether or not you let on to him that I've told you. Or, maybe he will tell you himself someday. Meanwhile, keep it to yourself."

I nodded. As the waitress refilled his coffee cup, he looked at me with Grandma Marja's eyes.

"Okay," I said. "I promise."

Dan looked out the window for a time, then back at me. "Your father and Baggie were friends when they were kids, all right. His younger brother Sheffield Hoy and I were friends too. Matter of fact, Shef and I, though we have gone in much different directions, remain close friends to this day. As for your father and Baggie, they also went different ways, as kids always do, and as I'm sure you will do with your friends, or maybe you already have had that experience. My big brother Owen was always driven: excelled in sports, in his classes, wanting to ever prove himself, and improve himself. Baggie, if he was driven at all, it was to avoid doing much of anything except be entertained by life. He grew cynical, made fun of your father's increasing accomplishments. They remained friends in spite of it—a childhood friendship can run deep—until they were both back from the war. They went out drinking one night. I don't know what happened, but they were suddenly no longer friends."

It didn't seem like much of a secret. "Baggie says Dad ran away from action in France. He told me he could ruin Dad's election chances by spreading the truth about him."

Dan's face reddened. "Your father never ran away! Is that what Baggie told you? Why were you even listening to him?"

"Something about Dad not being able to pull the trigger."

Again, Dan's face reddened. He swiped an open hand over his hair, front to back.

"Is that true, Uncle Dan? My father was a soldier. I mean, how could a soldier not pull the trigger? Weren't they fighting the Nazis? Isn't it like facing a rabid dog that's trying to get into your house? I mean, aren't you supposed to kill it, no matter what?"

He glared at me. Then he laughed, not a laugh about anything funny; a short laugh, quick escape of air for two or three syllables. He looked away from me, looked out the window as he rubbed his hands together.

I was not willing to let him leave it there. "Uncle Dan!"

I hadn't meant to speak in such a harsh voice. The level of dining room hubbub suddenly lowered. It drew a nearby couple to turn our way, a man in a black suit with white hair, a black hat resting on the table. He looked like Hopalong Cassidy. A freckled female red-head, much younger, sat across from him. They both glared at me.

Neither of us said anything for a while. When conversational noise came back up, and when Hoppy and his mate resumed eating, Dan finally looked at me again.

"Uncle Dan," I said quietly. "There has to be something to what Baggie told me. What did my dad do?"

He sipped his coffee, placed the cup carefully in the saucer. "The cassock? The breviary? Some of the other things he might still have: all part of, well...call it his cover."

"Cover," I repeated, but hearing it in my own voice did little to help me understand.

"Did you know the religious order I belong to, the Holy Cross Fathers, is from France?"

"You are part of a French order of priests? Why not an American one?"

"Most religious orders are based in Europe, Eugene. Anyway, that's where the university got its name—Notre Dame du Lac—founded by French missionaries."

Our conversation paused as the waitress took our orders.

"In 1940, a Holy Cross priest from Lemans, Father L'Hereux, was over here in America as a visiting Professor of Languages. Owen, your dad, was one of his students. He had him for three semesters. Then Owen enlisted in the army in the middle of his sophomore year, as you may know."

"I didn't know. He doesn't talk about it; doesn't talk about the war at all."

Dan looked into his coffee, gave it another stirring. "No, I suppose he doesn't." He looked up at me. "Just after Pearl Harbor, many young men enlisted, abandoning whatever they were doing or planning to do. Owen said good-bye to the spring semester. In fact, so many students enlisted at the same time that the university came close to going belly up. And, Father L'Hereux went back home. Then, in the summer of '44, your father was moving across France with the invasion force. That's when he contacted Father L'Hereux for help."

"What kind of help?"

"Authenticity. He was determined to look the part. Eugene, that book you saw in his closet was a real breviary, or certainly would have appeared that way. And it was unlikely that any Vichy policeman or German soldier would have been fluent enough in Latin to examine it closely. The pages were loose, like most books that suffered from a bad job of binding during the war. Removable pages, Eugene. A perfect means of carrying papers—instructions, plans—among prayers of the Divine Office, everything in Latin."

"My dad? Some kind of—"

I felt Hoppy and Red looking our way again. When I turned toward them, Red smiled at me with green eyes. I waited for them to go back to their dinners.

"Why would Baggie say he had run away? And run away from what?"

"Baggie is…well, Baggie is Baggie." His face said there was more to it, but that he wasn't about to tell me.

So here I was, having believed Baggie, that my father hid some terrible shame. Here I was, confused by lies that surrounded me, a kid snooping in his father's things. It was the liar's labyrinth that Father Kearns had warned about. Only it was a whole lot more complicated than he had described. He could not have possibly described it in detail. He had warned me about it, and it had been up to me to avoid it. I had not, and so now here I was, caught up in it, all right. Here I was in the middle of a maze of my own making.

"Uncle Dan, I just wish Dad would talk about it. I wouldn't have to wonder."

Dan shrugged. "Maybe someday he will. Up to now, he's just not ready to."

"But, if he could talk about it—not just to me, but to everybody—then nothing Baggie would say could hurt him. Everyone would know the truth."

"Eugene, the election is only two days away. It seems to me that Baggie, if he was really capable of doing damage, would have taken his best shot by now."

I hadn't heard anything from Baggie in a week, as if he had fallen into a hole. Not since Bert had saved me from whatever Baggie had wanted to do to me. Bert must have been right: Baggie had seen fit to just leave for good. I felt my insides relaxing.

"Besides," Dan said, "truth does not depend on what anybody thinks. It's bigger than that."

## CHAPTER 59, SUBJUNCTIVE MOOD

It was dark when we turned off Route 6, headlights sweeping the country blackness. The Studebaker whined at dips and rises and grumbled at graveled turns of Belknap Road. My parents and Grandma Marja noisily welcomed us with Sunday dinner that they had held until we arrived.

At the table, my father and uncle talked in excited tones about the election two days away. My mother and Grandma glistened with approval at all the reasons Uncle Dan came up with for why his brother would surely whip MacKenzie at the polls. My father's estimations of how badly he would do caused wrinkled faces that turned away from him. When talk turned to the national election, Grandma spoke firmly that Eleanor Roosevelt would have made a much better candidate for President than a rich kid from Boston who seemed to be a bit of a smarty. Her comment left in its wake a few moments of quiet, giving everybody a chance to dig into the lamb chops, boiled red potatoes, and early June peas direct from her canning shelves in the cellar.

My mother turned to me. "Sister Aloysius called. Tomorrow, you will have to stay after to make up the math exam you missed on Friday." Her tone was scolding, as if it had been my idea to miss a day of school to go on a 1200-mile trip all the way out to Indiana and back.

After dinner I went upstairs to bed. I'd been gone for only three days. It seemed so much longer. I was home, back among grownup voices buzzing against the ceiling below, smells of my family, familiar feel of my room, and the warmth and little pinging noises of the hot water radiator whose whispers of heat softly nudged the window curtain. But nothing was quite the same. I settled under the covers, all that had happened tugging at me. Emptiness gnawed: loss of Quin, loss of Agnes May, loss of the kid I had always been. At best, I was a distorted version of myself. My father had once told me, in one of his stretched-out explanatory moods, that fire does not send smoke up the chimney, but a natural draft from outside draws air against the embers to make them flare up. I drifted toward sleep on those words, flames licking at a hollow space within. The sky — all of the limitless sky — wanted to draw me up the flue.

Monday after school was the math test, and by the time I met up with my father at his law office, the sky was already lavender. We drove home in the dark. As we passed the Stippil house, a curtain glowed from an interior light in a downstairs window. Seeing me gaze out the passenger window of the Buick, my father told me he'd heard that Agnes May was still not back in school, that Missus Stippil was keeping her home, would not let her out of her sight.

Passing Agnes May's house, not having seen her except from a hiding place in the church, and then in a trembling dream at the little sem, put an ache in my chest. The ache rose up inside me, and asked why I could not go to her, to hold her hand and walk with her in the pasture and smell her hair and look into her brown eyes and listen to her breathing and the way she spoke so precisely. After a long pause, my lungs, on fire, forced me to breathe again.

As we rounded the bend by Hobbes Woods, I wanted to ask my father about Baggie Hoy. Had he been around in the few days prior to the election? But, of course, I didn't. If Baggie had carried out his threat to expose my father, I surely would have heard people chattering about it. To ask about him now would be like poking a stick into a rat hole. Had Bert Gutierrez really scared him off? A chill ran down the back of my neck. Baggie's eyes appeared before me in the blackness of the windshield, eyes rounded and bulged out at me as I took my shirt off in the shower facility foyer. "Won't be anybody else around," he said. "We'll make a day of it."

Tuesday, Uncle Dan picked me up from Saint Agatha at 3:30, and took me straight home to be with the family on election night. We had a quick dinner — my father nibbling salad and pushing the rest away — and afterwards gathered in front of the television.

While I'd been away, my parents had brought a bed down from the attic and put it in the living room so Grandma would no longer have to climb the stairs. It was the sick bed Grandpa Carroll had spent his final days in long ago. Marja, getting herself ready in the spare bathroom behind the kitchen, came to the living room and climbed into bed. She directed me to turn one of the cranks protruding from the heavy steel frame, which raised her head up so she could watch election returns with us.

Through the evening, politicians dropped by in dribbles to wish my father well. As it grew late, the stream of visitors dried up. At 11 o'clock, Douglas Edwards yielded coverage from CBS in New York to fifteen minutes of local news. From Channel 12 in Binghamton, station newscaster Ed Kane droned about all the other area-wide results before he finally mentioned us. Like the presidential race, the struggle for Wilmot County Judge "down there in Pennsylvania" was still undecided, still too close to call. Grandma Marja was snoring. The other three grownups were quiet. My parents sent me to bed, and I soon fell asleep.

In the morning, the news had not changed. In the afternoon, as I was sitting in class, Sister Miriam said, "For example, you should always seek to be a virtuous person. Now, that is much different from saying you are, or you were, or you have been a virtuous person."

Her movements in front of the classroom were like that of an actress, voice breathy and determined. "Do you see the difference?" Her eyes swept over us and settled on Tommy Tanager.

Tommy seemed to suddenly come awake, and nodded.

"The subjunctive mood, Mister Tanager, unlike the indicative, is for expressing what may not be quite real." Her eyes left Tommy in search of someone else to home in on. "The subjunctive lives only in a world of possibility, of expectation, of what would or could or should be, not what is or was or will be."

The principal, Sister Aloysius, burst into the classroom, her gray eyes larger than usual.

"We have a president," she said in wavering voice. "Mister Kennedy has won."

A hush of sighs and shoe shuffling went around the room.

She raised an open palm to us, and the hush died down. Her lips cracked into a smile. She looked at me, her voice now sharp and clear: "And His Honor, Owen Ahern, is our new judge!"

All eyes turned to me. Beginning with Sister Miriam, applause erupted. Tears ran more quickly than I could wipe them away.

Sister Miriam led us in an Our Father and a Hail Mary in thanks for America's new President, and then again for the new Wilmot County Judge. "From among our own," she sighed. "At last."

## Chapter 60, Casey Stengel

"Thirty-four!" My mother screamed. "Thirty-four votes!"

Uncle Dan said, "Only thirty-four? Will MacKenzie demand a recount?"

"I assume he will. It's never over till the Board of Elections says it is." My father studied the legal pad where he'd scribbled down the numbers. "Yesterday, a good day for the Irish, all right. The new President may have lost Wilmot County by a hundred thirty-one, but won the national election. Nixon finally conceded this morning." Leaning back in his chair, he seemed to relax a bit. "It looks like I'm more popular with my friends and neighbors than Mister Kennedy himself."

Everybody laughed. He stiffened again, humor evaporating. "With a recount," he said, gaze unfocused, "MacKenzie would have a hard time overcoming thirty-four votes. But still, you never know. Besides, let's say I do win..."

"What do you mean!" my mother stood up, chair sliding back. "What's this 'let's say' nonsense? Owen, you won!"

Grandma laughed at that, and forgot to cover her missing tooth. She looked around the room, a gleam in her eye, but only the right. Her left eye, too tired to be a part of it, didn't want to come along.

My father allowed himself a smile. "Okay, I won."

"You're damn tootin!" my mother said, and raised her arm like the Statue of Liberty.

"Okay. But all things are temporary, you know."

Uncle Dan chuckled and pointed into the air like an orator. "*Sic transit gloria mundi.*"

"Stop it, both of you." My mother looked back and forth between Dan and my father. She threw up her hands. "Oh, you...you Irish!" Standing behind my father's chair, she placed her hands on his shoulders forcefully. "This moment will never be temporary. This moment will be forever. This moment belongs to one Owen Ahern." She kissed the top of his head. "And to his wife, and to his son, and to..."

Marja said, "I wonder what Bridget Kelly thinks of us now."

Nobody reminded Grandma that her mother-in-law, Great-Grandma Bridget Kelly Ahern, had been dead for thirty years.

My father's eyes regained their focus. "I mean, look at Casey Stengel: ten pennants in twelve years; seven World Series victories. Last month, Mazeroski homers in the ninth inning of the seventh game, and you know what? Ole Case is no longer fit to manage! I tell you, everything is temporary."

My mother rolled her eyes. "This is not the World Series. This is right now. Whatever happens in the future cannot change that!" She kissed his head again.

Dan said, "Owen, you mean that article?" He reached for the *Plain Dealer* that he'd bought in Ashtabula on Sunday. It had settled into an awkward pile on a side table. Rattling the sports section, he opened it and scanned down through the newsprint. "Here it is."

"When asked for a comment, Casey confessed to turning seventy in mid-season. He admitted that in doing so he had run afoul of the Yankees' new emphasis on youth. Stengel promised that he would never make that mistake again."

The adults laughed, except Marja, who did not understand baseball.

Dan picked up a salt shaker and pointed it at Grandma. "This reporter is now in the Ahern home, and I have here the victor's mother, Marja Ahern. Tell us, Missus Ahern, what you think of your son being elected County Judge?"

Conversation paused. Distance in her eye shortened up, came into focus around the table, her face forming not quite a smile. "Carroll would be so pleased," she said softly.

"And that's the news from the Ahern household," Dan said, putting the salt shaker down, and we all laughed.

"Would he?" My father sat back. "How would we be able to tell for sure?"

"Oh yes," Marja said. "He would not tell us with his words—that stubborn Irishman—but he would surely be proud." Her eye glistened.

"*Kulta*," my mother said. "Even to this day you are still so much in love with him."

Grandma looked at my mother, her face flushed.

My mother moved behind Marja, then, bent down and embraced her neck, arms around her, cheek of younger woman touching older woman's cheek, blonde hair briefly twining with white braid. Momentary quiet allowed only the sound of breathing.

After a while, my mother went back to her own chair. Marja looked around the table at us. Her left eye seemed to have awakened from its stupor and came into focus. She spoke in that tone of hers that said nobody had been listening to her—not really listening—over the years: "Why do you think my Carroll escaped from that awful Hazleton coal mine?"

When nobody responded, I spoke up. "To become a book-keeper."

Her eyes turned to me, twinkle acknowledging that I had listened as well as anyone. "When I met that crude Irishman on the train in his ill-fitting suit, sitting across the aisle, and he said he was on his way to the Sheshequin Institute, well, don't you see, I knew right away."

"You knew what right away?" my father said.

"That he would never become a bookkeeper, of course; he kept returning to the newspaper that someone had left on a seat, to a full-page land-sale advertisement. And him with a pocket stuffed in cash saved up for his schooling. Some twenty years before, lumber people from down-state had stripped all the trees off these mountains around here, don't you see, and because the regrowth wasn't fast enough for them, owners were now eager to sell off the land to would-be farmers."

I had a hard time imagining the mountains around Cloven Hill Farm without their woods.

Dan curled his lip. "You're saying he *wanted* to be a farmer? Never seemed that way to us, did it Owen?"

My father said, "You could have fooled me. I'd always figured he was pretty unhappy farming."

She clucked her tongue and wrinkled her brow. "He never wanted to be a bookkeeper. That was his mother's idea. And he never really wanted to be a farmer. That was my idea. He wanted... well, he wanted respectability, something his people never had."

"Respectability?" Dan said quietly.

"Respectability. And the grouchiness that you two boys criticize him for...well, what would you expect of him, scratching around in these rocks and dirt his whole life? He was a man, you know; a man who yearned to see something of life beyond his own calluses and dirty fingernails."

My father and uncle both stared into the tablecloth.

"And he has found it," she said softly. "Through this old woman's eyes, my brooding Irishman can see clearly at last. Tonight, he sees you. Tonight, he is so proud of both his sons."

The brothers looked up from the tablecloth and found their mother's eyes.

My mother said to Grandma, "You've never told us what you were doing when you met him on the train that day. Where had you come from? Where were you going?"

"Time for my bed," she said, struggling to slide her chair back.

Dan stood and helped her up. On his arm, she made her way to the bathroom behind the kitchen.

My mother shrugged away the unanswered question.

Lying by the door, Lowdown sighed, raised her head, perked up an ear. A minute later, lights swept past the windows as tires crunched driveway gravel. The dog's tail plopped twice against the floor. My father got up and went to the door, had it open by the time the visitor was out of the vehicle and up onto the porch.

His voice boomed, "So how'd you do?"

Sheffield Hoy came in. "Even better than you, Your Honor." A grin broke through his tired face.

The two men grabbed each other's arms and laughed.

Dan went to his brother's side. "Thirty-four votes! How close was yours, Shef?"

"Sixty-six."

The three men shook hands and then hugged each other. Sheffield stepped further into the dining room with them. As they talked, my mother opened a bottle of wine and poured it into glasses.

"None for me, thanks," Sheffield said.

"Just a celebration sip?"

He smiled with his lips, but his face was not part of it. "No, really, Veronica. I can't tonight."

Dan's brow furrowed. "What's going on?"

Sheffield exhaled, looked around at my mother and me, then at my father. "Gotta talk to you."

My mother held out a glass of wine. "Not even sworn in, and already all business."

Sheffield didn't take the glass. He smiled again, with just his lips. Then, he turned as Grandma came out of the bathroom in her nightgown. "Evenin,' Missus Ahern."

"Evenin' to you, young Sheffield. Or should I address you as Sheriff Hoy?"

He smiled, all of his face opening for Marja. "Not till the first of the year, Missus Ahern."

Grandma's face brightened. "Your parents would be very proud, young Sheffield."

"Thank you, Missus."

Conversation waited as Dan helped Grandma make her way through all the people crowded into the dining room. She waved away the offer of a glass of wine and went into the living room, closing the double doors.

My father motioned Sheffield in the direction of his office.

"Sounds like important business. I'll stay out," Dan said.

"It's business, in a way," Sheffield said. "But I'd like you there too."

Then, the living room double doors opened back up. Grandma announced, "No, I've never told anyone what I was doing on that train."

The grownups all stopped and glanced at each other.

My father said, "It always seemed like you never wanted to say." He stepped toward her. "What is it, *Kulta*? Are you feeling all right? You look a little flushed."

"We were on the Lehigh Valley," she said in a strong voice. "Sister Irene and I boarded in Scranton and would be changing trains in Buffalo, over to the Nickel-Plate, they called it, into Ohio." She looked into the distance. "Oh, my goodness: I hope I didn't get Sister Irene into a lot of trouble."

"Sister Irene?" Dan said.

"Sister Irene was escorting me out to Fremont, Ohio, to the mother house there."

Dan and my father looked at each other. Dan said, "*Kulta*, why were you going from Scranton to Fremont, Ohio? Who is Sister Irene? And what's this about a mother house?"

"Because I knew some German. Haven't you been listening, Daniel? I could speak German just a bit. And lots of German immigrants went to western Ohio, you know, filling up the Catholic schools with children who knew little English."

She grew quiet, peering at each of us one by one. She turned to go back through the double doors, but stopped again and came back. "Sheriff Hoy, you would know if anybody came looking for me."

Sheffield turned to Dan, to my father, then stepped toward Grandma. "Missus Ahern. I haven't officially taken office. Who would be looking for you, Missus?"

"Why, Sister Irene, of course! How frantic she must be. I mean, to have a young postulant she was responsible for disappear from that train with a coal miner."

Sheffield rubbed his chin, peered from under lowered eyebrows. "Well, now Missus Ahern, I won't be Sheriff until—"

My father motioned with his hand. "That's okay, Shef. A small technicality."

"But you were only twelve when you came to America," my mother complained. "Was this Sister Irene supposed to be taking care of you?"

"The Sisters of Mercy," Grandma said. "Oh, they took very good care of me for the three years I was with them. They didn't send me on the train for Ohio until I was pretty good at English. But I never even made it out of Pennsylvania, not with that lumpy Irishman in a suit across the aisle talking to

Sister Irene, looking past her all the while and glancing at me."
She suddenly laughed and covered her missing tooth.

We were silent.

The soon-to-be new sheriff wrinkled his brow at my father, my uncle, then at my grandma. "There's the statute of limitations," he said, adopting an officious tone. "Isn't that right, Judge?"

Grandma said, "Does it apply if you lie about your age at the marriage license window?"

"Without a doubt," my father nodded.

Grandma sighed through pursed lips. "Well, that's good to know." She turned and went back into the living room, shutting the doors.

We were quiet, listening to Grandma shuffle around in her new bedroom.

My mother said in a hoarse whisper, "She just blurts things out lately. Hard to tell if it's real or not, what she just told us."

"It's real."

All eyes were on me now. After a long time they stopped looking at me. And nobody said any different. When Marja was settled, she called out for someone to put out the light. My father nodded to me. I went into the room and found the corner lamp too far away for her to reach. I turned it off.

"Young lad," she whispered.

I went closer. "What is it, Marja?"

"About the girl…I've forgotten her name."

"You mean, Agnes May?"

"Agnes May," she said, savoring the sound of it. "How are you and Agnes May, lad?"

"I don't know what to say, Grandma."

She reached out, found my hand and wrapped it in icy fingers. She allowed me to just sit with her, not trying to make me talk. I put my other hand over her fingers and felt them slowly grow warm between us.

Without meaning to, into the darkness I suddenly said her name aloud: "Agnes May."

"Agnes May," Marja repeated. "And tell me, lad. Is she as pretty as her name?"

"She is, Marja." My voice was shaky.

"You are so young," she said. "Nature is not convenient. She seldom waits for just the right moment, often making a move when you least expect it."

Before long, her breathing grew drawn out and deep. I stood to leave. Undoing our hands, I placed hers under the covers.

"Eugene," she whispered. "Are you going to kiss me goodnight?"

"Of course, Marja. I thought you were asleep already."

"Well, almost." She reached out for me.

"Goodnight, Marja," I said, leaning down to her.

"You see? I'll not complain at being wakened by a young lad's kiss." She breathed a tiny laugh to herself.

As I neared the door, she said, "You haven't let them talk you into that seminary, have you?"

"No. It would be another two years before I could go there anyway."

"But that gives them plenty of time to try to talk you into it," she warned.

I closed the living room doors and went up to my room.

The only sound coming up through the cold air return was the click of my father's lighter. The men were quiet. Had I missed something?

He drew on the pipe, the way he did when he was in thought. "His car was parked there, you say?"

"Beside the showers facility," Sheffield said. "A deputy, Joe Holland—you know him? —on a routine patrol, noticed the gate hanging open. It should have been padlocked. He went in to check around and found the old Dodge back there, sideways against the building."

"What else did Deputy Holland do? Didn't disturb the scene, I hope."

"He called Dolan Braddawl immediately. Doley called me. Election be damned: we both had an unexplained death on our hands, and went through it together. Inside the facility, a cot, some of his clothes scattered around, a package of stale cinnamon rolls; a number of them, actually, two or three crumpled ones on the floor; some cans of tuna fish; bottle of Old Crow, empty, of course...one of the two bottles we would find on the scene."

Dan cleared his throat. "Shef, I'm sorry for your loss."

"Thank you, Dan. Baxter and I weren't close, you might say, but still..."

"Baggie was your brother," Dan said.

Sheffield's voice wavered. "He was my brother. Very kind of you, Danny. Yes, he was my brother, and now he's, well...death is so final."

They were quiet for a while, my father rasping on his pipe. "It doesn't make sense, Shef. I checked the grounds myself after the fair was over last summer. Bert Gutierrez had bolted that lid down secure."

"Yeh, I know that, Owen. Doley figures it coulda been kids. They coulda gotten in there and got it open. We were all kids once. Did any of us ever need a reason to do dumb things?"

"So Doley figures the lid was open, and your brother just fell in. You accept that?"

Sheffield was quiet for a long moment. "No. No, I don't. Neither does Doley. A passer-by did see a green truck parked there on Saturday—not Pennsylvania plates—but didn't see what state it was from. And, somebody said they mighta seen Bert Gutierrez driving a green truck."

"Not likely," my father said. "Bert hasn't been around for some time, now. Besides, he would be in that old Studebaker he fixed up."

"We don't know if that's anything or not. We're sure going to look into it. Anyway, Baxter was on a serious drunk. He could have stumbled around, maybe not even knowing where he was. Doley and I both figure, if somebody did push him, or if he mighta just fallen in, well, either way, once he was in, it wouldn't have taken long in those fumes...you know, like dying in your sleep."

"Jesus Christ," my father said. "Sorry for the language, Dan."

"Understandable, Owen."

"Found him in the sludge, face up." Sheffield's voice was shaky. "That second bottle of Jim Crow I mentioned...it was on his chest, empty, of course."

## CHAPTER 61, OVER-UNDER

In the morning, the sky was just beginning to lighten when I heard through the register my father's movements downstairs. I got up and went down to his office, and closed the door.

"Make it quick," he said. "Meetings all morning."

I sat down in the leather chair across from him. I'd been in here with my father at times when he had closed the door, and I would know I was in for it. This time, I was the one who closed the door. His face was one I hadn't seen before: uncertain. I'd never known him to be uncertain about anything.

It didn't last long, though, soon transforming into a more familiar expression, one I'd seen many times, jaw set, eyes piercing, the face I'd seen when I'd watched him in court. I was afraid, so I looked away

"You have something to tell me?"

He didn't ask if I had something to say, but if I had something to tell him. And why not? He'd spent much of his legal career defending every kind of human being. When I finally looked up at him, the face had softened. I suddenly wanted to fall into that softness, the way, when I was a kid, if I got hurt, I would fall into Marja's softness and feel it surround me. She would hold me in an embrace of softness: warm, ruddy cheeks...her breasts and arms...

"I'm a liar."

His expression did not change. "Oh?"

I looked down at my lap. I didn't see my hands now. My vision conjured up Baggie's eyes, lifeless eyes reflecting back the light of the day; and Oriane-Florisse's huge eye from that day in the forest when she had died because of us Dumble-Doers doing something dumb.

"I have to tell you, that's all."

"And why is that?"

Baggie and Oriane-Florisse: those eyes stared, unmoving, unmoved.

"I can't help it," I said, and realized that tears fell down my face.

I was aware of shadow in front of the window, and of him standing, coming around the desk. A folded handkerchief appeared. He went back to his chair as I wiped my face and balled the handkerchief in my hand.

"Whenever you're ready," he said after a while. He seemed to have lost his hurry to leave for important meetings.

"I don't know what to tell you," I said. "There's too many things."

He laughed. "So, you're in lies up to your ass."

I laughed. I'd never before laughed and cried at the same time.

"Look at me."

I looked up from the balled handkerchief.

"You're allowed to find yourself lost now and then, Eugene. You just aren't allowed to let yourself *stay* lost."

We looked away from each other and quiet took over the office.

"I'm just tired of it," I finally said. "I'm tired of lying."

"Well, that's a beginning. The important thing is: what's next?"

I shrugged.

He leaned back a little, thinking. "When you're outnumbered, take on the biggest one. You'll find the others will start to shrivel and shy away. Lies are all cowards."

I said, "Cold air return."

I looked up. His brow was drawn in puzzlement. And then, I told him about how I'd been listening through the cold air return all this time. And I told him about all the snooping I had done, about the priest garb I'd seen in his closet, and the photos of a woman in the folder.

He didn't look at me. He looked off somewhere else, looked at the wall, then seemed to see right through the plaster at a far-away object.

I didn't tell him any more than that. The cold air return and my snooping in his office made up my biggest lie, and maybe that would do it. I didn't tell him about Baggie. By telling him all about the cold air return, maybe my secret about Baggie would shrivel away on its own. Not right now...but someday? When I was as old as Grandma, maybe then I could finally tell someone what had happened with Baggie, the way Marja had finally told about running away from Sister Irene when she was a girl in training to become a nun.

He stared blankly, in thought of how to form the words for what he would say next. He was suddenly different: jaw less firmly set, eyes more distant. A stranger took up his physical being, one who looked like him but was not my father at all.

His eyes tightened, settled on me. "By the time I was your age, I was pretty good with the over-under. My old man gave it to me for my birthday. I practiced and practiced. Pieces of wood, corn cobs, tin cans, bottles...nothing was safe."

He laughed. He was my father again, and I laughed. It felt good.

Eyes drifting away for a moment, he studied something afloat in his vision just over my shoulder, then back to me. "I got so I could hit a crow from 20 yards with the twenty-two. You get one, and the rest of them try to take off. That's when you open up with the four-ten."

He was my father again, but I'd seldom heard him talk this way, like you'd hear from one of the neighbors, or even us kids, not in lawyer tongue at all, so distant from his usual style fashioned around logic and rubrics of fine elocution. He'd called Grandpa Carroll his old man. He was my father, alright, but that stranger I'd seen a moment ago was mixed up in him too.

"The four-ten, its shot would scatter out and take down more of 'em. I only had to do it a few times before the crows learned to stay outta the two fields where I'd shot their relatives. It soon got to be, if they spied me anywhere around, they'd be just as happy to steal seed outta the Tull's or Hobbes' fields. Crows aren't called smart for no reason, you know."

He laughed again, focused on me, eyes glistening. "They remember things. I can't figure how they do it, Eugene, but crow memory seems to pass down. Even years later, I could walk out to the fields, and the crows would take flight before I got within a hundred yards, but they couldn't have been the same ones that survived my over-under, 'cause too much time had passed. Makes you wonder if maybe something in the mother's memory gets fed right into the chick while it's forming. I asked Dan about it, once. Figured with his biology studies he might know. But he doubted there's much scientific proof of what I was saying." He looked away. "He promised to noodle around in the ornithology journals, but he never did get back to me." He suddenly took up a legal pad, flipped the page and scribbled a note, reminding himself to ask his brother again to look into that.

"What happens now, Dad? If you walk out to the fields, do they still take flight before you get within range? Do they still realize it's you?"

He thought about it and said, "You know, son, I just haven't tried it in a long time," and his eyes hazed a bit. Swiveling his leather chair around, he adjusted the blinds and looked beyond the yard out to the fields. The only sound was our breathing for a while. Then he spoke into the window glass. "Baggie and me, we wanted to see what would happen, so we grabbed a few muskmelons out of *Kulta's* garden; beautiful gold-green melons, soft and juicy and sweet, you know, like she grows every year. Almost ripe. Just needed a day or two more. No doubt, she'd been eyeballing them for picking. Woulda been the first ones of the season. We took them around back, down to the manure pit."

His voice quivered. "The twenty two cracked, and went thud. But the four-ten, it whomped. Mist sprayed out, floated up, hung in the air for a second or two, and pieces flew, bits of yellow flesh and juices. The life that had lived in those melons got sprayed out in onto a stinking pile of manure."

From behind, I saw him wipe his sleeve over his face, like a kid would do. I looked down at my hands. Those eyes were there, empty eyes, Baggie's eyes and Oriane-Florisse's. And here my father was sad about shooting Marja's first melons of the season...must have been thirty years ago. In thirty years, what kinds of things would I have done that would still come back to haunt me?

When I looked up, he'd closed the blinds. He turned to face me again. His arms hung low, like you might do when you're tired, like the weight of his arms pulled on his shoulders. "I was trained as a sniper," he said quietly. "Do you know what that is, Eugene?"

"Shoots people."

"Yep." He seemed to hold his breath a moment. "Shoots people from concealment. Battle is not like a movie. People seldom even know they're being hit."

He changed. Right before my eyes, he changed into that stranger. He was still my father, alright, but with a different face. It was like looking at the Hobbes twins: they were exactly like each other, but when you looked at one and then the other, and went back and forth, you knew you saw two different people, two pairs of cheeks, smooth and colorful and soft, like ripening peaches, but couldn't say exactly how they differed. My father's face, rough and lined as he sat before me, changed into the face of another man, just as rough and lined as his, but a stranger, as if he had a twin.

The twin said in my father's voice, "In some ways, similar to a bombardier. Choose the target. Look through the scope. Calculate. Release. 'Cept, through the scope on my Springfield, you see the stubble on a man's face. You see a guy with dirt on his ear where he musta brushed it with a soiled hand, maybe where he tried to scratch an itch just a few minutes earlier."

He swallowed, and looked at me. "You know, a little thing like that makes you wish you could somehow tell him. He probably doesn't know. He would likely do the same for me if he could, if he saw me like that. It would be downright embarrassing to let a fellow not know he's left a big smudge on his ear. Since he doesn't know about the smudge, he's not embarrassed, so you feel embarrassed instead."

He swallowed. Two faces, my father's and the face of that other man, the twin, changed places, came back and forth, and couldn't seem to settle on one or the other.

"After I got down outta the steeple, well, I'm still seeing him clear as when I first studied him through the scope...seeing the smudge on his ear."

"What steeple?" I asked.

He turned away from me, rubbed his hands over each other, and blew into them like they were cold. He looked back at me.

"I put down the Springfield." He looked away again.

A large quiet filled the room. I spoke into it, "What's a Springfield?" So much quiet seemed to swallow my voice.

He had heard me. He stared at me. "Sniper piece. Highly accurate. Springfield sniper rifle that was issued to me."

I should have known that, should have figured it out, shouldn't have asked, shouldn't have interrupted.

He spoke in a steady, even voice: "I told the lieutenant he'd better call back, get a new man assigned. I could have been in for bad times by doing that if anybody else had been in charge, but Kowalski, from Ohio — he'd been a foreman at Hupmobile — he'd been around, knew people, knew tough situations. I could see it in his eyes right after I said it. He knew I was for real."

"Smudge on his ear." He looked away, then back at me. "Those glasses — I still see them — that Kraut's eyes through his glasses. Round lenses. The way he looks out at everything, eyes moving, eyes in tune to his thoughts, movement made out of things that he's accumulated in his life up to this moment, this very instant, you know. And him not even knowing he's got a big smudge on his ear."

He stared at me. Anger came into his voice, not loud anger, but soft. A firm complaint, as if something had gone wrong: "They shoulda changed somehow."

I could do nothing as he spoke. He gazed right through me.

"I mean his eyes, behind those glasses of his, you know? The man at least coulda...you'd think there'd be the smallest bit of recognition from him. I never even thought, just never thought that it woulda happened that way."

He looked straight at me. "That dumb Jerry kid never even heard the shot."

He raised his arm and turned his face against his inner elbow, not quickly enough to stop tears that ran down his cheeks, fell off his jaw, and made wet lines down his shirt. He tried to finger something out of his pocket.

But I was still holding the handkerchief, balled up in my hand from before.

## Chapter 62, "Don't," She Said.

On Friday afternoon, at the end of the school week, once again, Dan picked me up in front of Saint Agatha.

"Your father's tied up in meetings," he explained. "Now that the election has been decided, everybody needs to talk with him."

I got into the front seat and pulled the passenger door shut.

On the journey out of town, up the mountain and along Belknap Road, Dan's voice leapt quickly from topic to topic.

"Your folks will now have a steady income," he said, "instead of living off the hard earnings of a small-town lawyer."

He reminded me that, as the son of the County Judge, I would have to be especially careful about how my actions might reflect on my father's upgraded importance. I would have to be aware of how others would be eying every member of the Ahern family.

And then he went quiet, and we gradually slowed down to about three-quarter speed on the gravel road, as if the car were listening, intent on reading my uncle's thoughts. He said, "Oh," when the speedometer caught his attention, and sped up again.

"I'll be leaving tomorrow," he said quietly, "heading back to Notre Dame."

"Tomorrow? I didn't think you'd have to be back till Monday."

"That's true," he said. "But I need to make a detour first, down to Scranton. Then, from there I'll head back to Indiana."

He didn't say any more about it, and I didn't pester him like I would have in the past. Things had changed between Dan and me. I was still his favorite, alright, and he mine, but a quiet had emerged between us.

In front of the Stippil house we stopped for the school bus approaching from the opposite direction, red lights flashing. Adam jumped down from the side door and, looking away from us, walked up the rutted driveway.

No Agnes May. She was not back in school, still being kept home by her mother. Seeing Adam was an unexpected event, one that rubbed into my face how much I missed his sister. It pulled at me. Grandma had said that nature is not convenient, and seldom waits for just the right moment, but often makes a move when you least expect it.

I pushed open the car door and stepped out.

Dan looked at me with steady eyes. "Something you have to do?"

I nodded. "I'll be home by supper time."

He nodded back. I shut the door. When the bus moved on, he drove away, frothy exhaust scampering along behind the Studebaker.

I made my way up the driveway behind Adam, stepping on the high spots in the scrabble of ruts left from last week's rain-soaked Wednesday service, now hardened in place by the cold. He passed through the front doorway's rectangle of yellow light that disappeared when the door closed. In evening shadow beside the house, the Reverend's Power Wagon eyed me as I approached, crooked headlights, first one, then the other, following each step. My knock roused stirring from inside. The door opened. The Reverend's gray eyes looked me up and down.

"We're not open to having company just now," he said in a low layer of gravel voice. The door closed.

From inside, I heard Hughla Stippil ask who it was, followed by a low-mumbled reply. The door opened again. "Just a moment," Hughla's lips spoke into the cold, and then she disappeared from the narrow opening.

The man's voice rose up, "We don't cut all that firewood so we can heat the whole township!" And the door slammed shut.

I waited. It opened just a crack, then more. Wrapped in an army-surplus wool blanket, Agnes May held the gap in front, close around her face. Like a small nun, she stepped out to the porch and pulled the door closed, eyes downturned.

"My mother said I should see you," she said quietly, lips and teeth precise in speech. "It wouldn't be polite to let you stand out here alone."

Then she did look up, just briefly. In an instant, the last time we had seen each other rushed back into existence, that moment down by Hobbes Creek, as if all that time suddenly vanished.

"Agnes May," my voice was shaky.

She didn't look up.

"That day I took your hand," I said, "and you didn't want me to, and then you did let me, and we walked together..."

She turned away from me, a quick breath into the cold. A laugh?

My ears burned with awkward feeling: I should have gone home with Dan.

"I had to see you." My throat tightened. "See you up close."

"You can't, Eugene," she complained. "You just can't."

"Yes, I can. I can and I do."

"Things have happened. You just don't know."

She bent her neck forward and sighed, slumping her shoulders. I moved closer and touched her, my fingers forming to girl-softness that rounded the rough blanket.

"I do know," I said.

She turned around, eyes sharp and wet. "You do *not* know," she rasped. "Only my mother, and even she—I couldn't stand to see her face so twisted, and I couldn't tell her all of it."

"I *do* know, Agnes May. You cried out in the church, and you looked up at me. From all the way up in the bell tower, I heard you, I saw you, and I *do* know."

Her eyes softened, and I looked into them.

"And I still see you and hear you."

"You were there, Eugene?"

Her eyes filled with tears. The blanket opened, loosening around her face. She felt both of my cheeks with her fingers. Our breaths mixing together in the cold, she quickly kissed my lips.

"When I'm falling to sleep, Agnes May, I still feel your hand with mine. I still smell your hair."

"Don't," she said, placing fingers over my mouth. Tears ran down her cheeks. She suddenly turned away, went back into the house, and softly closed the door.

## CHAPTER 63, FOLDED CLOTHES

Saturday morning, I struggled to finish breakfast.

I went back up to my room and tried to read a history assignment. It was about the Battle of Lake Erie in 1813, the kind of subject I would have normally found myself deeply absorbed in. Not today...

I lay on my bed, thinking: I had to settle this. I'd been plain lucky, that day on the slope, to get a good grip on Quin's legs and topple him. He would never let that happen again. This time, if he got the best of me, I might have to take a beating. My stomach fluttered. I was not going to give in, no matter what happened. Nature had made its move, like Grandma said. Agnes May and I would be together. How it was going to happen, I didn't know. But, that was the one thing in my life I was sure of.

Quin answered my knock on his trailer door and let me in. A faded green duffel bag was propped on his bed.

When he saw me looking at the faded black stencil, ROBERTO GUTTIEREZ, he said, "My dad's. Everybody calls him Bert, but he's actually Roberto, same as me."

"Roberto," I said. "But your name is Joaquin."

"That's my middle name. My parents went by it so I'd have a different name than him. They shortened it to Quin—remember?—so people won't know I'm a Mexican."

"I forgot you were Mexican."

He laughed, "Half Mexican...Guatemalan, actually, and other half Sloot, or, did you forget that too?"

"Sorry, I forgot that too."

I'd never said sorry to Quin for anything before. After we'd been so pissed off at each other lately, it felt good to say it. But that didn't change things. Agnes May and I would be together, no matter what. Today, I was going to settle it: put an end to whatever was between her and Quin.

He mussed my hair. "Don't be sorry. Any more than I'd be sorry for not thinking of you as Irish."

I said, "Mostly Irish, and Finnish, from my Grandma. I don't think about you and me that way. I don't really know where Guatemala is, or Finland."

"I don't either." His eyebrows bunched up. "But things are different now, Genie. The way grownups look at us, they expect one set of things from you, and a whole different set of things from me. Don't you see that?"

He placed folded tee shirts into the half-filled duffel bag, and said, "You take care of Agnes May."

What did *that* mean? He said that like he was leaving, and she was a pet that he was giving away.

"I didn't tell her," he said. "You can tell her for me. She doesn't know. Nobody does, except, well…one person, who's helping me get away, but it has to be a secret. And, of course, I had to tell you, Genie."

"You're leaving?"

He nodded and looked away.

"But Quin, maybe you even saved Agnes May's life. How can you just go away and not tell her you're leaving, and expect somebody else to tell her?"

"So, I helped her out. I didn't let on to Daggie that she was down in the cellar. Isn't that what you'd do? You know you'd do it too, if someone needed you to."

Two small stacks from his bed, folded socks and underpants, went into the bag. I'd never known Quin to fold his clothes before.

He laughed. "She's a tough girl, your Agnes May. That's why that crazy brother of hers couldn't kill her by locking her in that truck. It's not like she was afraid of breaking a fingernail when she smashed her way out."

The way he talked about her burned in the middle of my chest. I tried to keep it out of my voice. "You think Adam really tried to kill her?"

Quin shrugged. "Who knows? Adam went a little crazy." He wagged his head. "All that preaching, and then what he did to his own sister."

Heat choked my windpipe, wrenching my voice. "So, Agnes May doesn't mean anything to you. You don't feel anything for her, like an old tee shirt you won't wear anymore."

His jaw tightened. He stopped packing, rested his forearms on top of the bag, and put his head down a little, breathing low against himself. "It isn't like that, Eugene. Maybe I have an eye for her, sure. You can't help noticing somebody who's pretty. I can't help noticing her sometimes, but not the way you notice her. It's more than that for you. And you sure are more than that for her."

So, she had talked with him about me? I felt my chest settle.

"Quin, why did we fight?"

He shrugged and looked away.

"All this time," I said. "I was thinking about you and her together."

He laughed. "Now, how could I know that you were doing a fool thing like that, Genie? Me and Agnes May? And you're supposed to be smart."

"You mean we fought just out of pure craziness?"

"Well, not like Adam crazy. It was just us. A you-and-me world. You and me, Genie, we have our own world that doesn't fit well into the real one...not anymore."

I'd never known Quin to lie to me.

"Not because you wanted to be with Agnes May?" My voice sounded like it came from someone else, squeezed with complaint.

"Cripe'n-itey, Genie: me and the kid-brat?"

How could it look like one thing one moment and then something else the next? So, he didn't want to be with Agnes May. But, he sure hadn't wanted me to be with Agnes May, either.

He neatly folded a white dress shirt. What had happened to the hand-roll method of folding as long as no grownup was around to catch you?

He said, "Remember? I told you about it down in the woods at the retreat: that animal inside of me. No telling where it came from, but it has hollowed out a place inside of me and it makes me crazy, makes me want...makes me want what I just can't have."

"What can't you have?"

He laughed from his mouth, but his eyes hesitated. He finished folding the shirt and placed it with care on top of the other items.

He looked at me. "You, Genie."

"Me? What are you talking about, me?"

"I can't be you."

"Well, I can't be you either, Quin."

He turned and mussed my hair. "You don't get it, do you?"

"Don't get what?" My voice cracked.

"Don't you feel it? It's reaching down and grabbing at us. The world, the one the grownups live in, is making us be a part of it. Agnes May turned from a kid-brat into somebody who has an eye for you, and you for her. And the animal inside makes me crazy for what I can never have."

"She has an eye for me?"

"Dipshit," he laughed. "Don't tell me you don't know that."

"Sometimes I do. And sometimes..."

He wagged his head at me. "That's the grownup world, for you. You can't ever be sure, and like I said, it's reaching down and grabbing us up into it."

Quin was way out front of me this time, not because of how well he hit a baseball, or swished a basket. This time, he had out-figured me. I'd always been the one who did the serious figuring between us.

He turned and looked straight into me. "You have feelings for Agnes May, Genie. It's up to you to make them real. You never know when the world might just do a flip, and whoosh! — it's all gone."

I suddenly saw before me Agnes May's eyes, and she wanting me to look into them, even as she said, "Don't."

"When will you be back?"

He peered at me under his eyebrows. "I won't be back, Genie."

"Not ever?" My words came out as a squawk.

"Ever is a long time. I know what I have to do, that's all."

A hollow opened up inside of me. "What do you have to do?"

"Make it real. I'm not the son of a judge and an artist. I don't even have parents. My only parent is gone."

"But he's gone to a new job, Quin. Once he saves up some money, you can be a family, you and your old man, you and Bert."

He eyed me. "Are you so sure, Genie? He was back for a day, and then disappeared. Did you know the sheriff is looking for him again? Not the just the old sheriff. The new one, too. Shef Hoy has been around, asking if he's been back, and wanting to know where he went."

"He didn't go back to his new job in Texas?"

Quin looked at me with surprise. "Nobody's supposed to know about that, Genie! I thought I was the only one who knew."

"I saw him, Quin, that day he was back. He told me about the welding job."

Quin's eyes widened. "Something happened that day, Genie. He wouldn't tell me what. He just said he had to get away fast, and that I was not to tell anybody he'd been home, or where he'd gone."

His face turned scarlet, eyes darting side to side. "Genie," he said, breathless. "Did you tell anyone you saw him that day?"

"No," I said. I had tried to forget all about that day. "So much was going on…the election, and everything. I'm sure I never mentioned it."

His face calmed a bit, but his voice wavered, "You can't ever say that you saw him, Genie. A clerk at Van Shoor Hardware says he thought he saw him, and that he was driving a green truck, but didn't remember for sure. So, that leaves only

you and me. Genie, promise me, you'll never tell anybody —
and I mean, never!"

"I promise, Quin. Never!"

"Somebody's going to help me find a way out of this. I
can't tell you who, because he told me not to tell."

He continued packing, not saying anything, his face dark.

When he finished, he looked at me. "I'm not respectable,
Genie. Don't you see? That's the worst thing you can be in the
grownup world, not respectable. The grownup world has come
down to get us. So, I have to go. You know? Gotta go and
make my life real for myself. Somebody is giving me that chance,
and I'm going to take it."

I couldn't look at him. I lifted the chain from around my
neck, and the medal he had coined for me at the fair. The copper oval was warm from having lain against my chest, where
it left a green mark that I had to scrub off every few days.

I handed it to him. "You have to give this back to me some
day, you know."

I watched him take it, chain curling up in his palm.

## CHAPTER 64, CUP OF COFFEE

Crossing the Hobbes farm, I didn't have time for whatever Lucinda wanted, up there waving at me from the top of the hill. I had to get to Agnes May: her eyes were out in front of me, asking me to look into them, pulling me through the brown autumn grass. I just had to get to where she was.

Lucinda, still waving, hadn't asked, "What are you lookin' at, squirt?" in quite a while; not since before running off to North Carolina. In fact, she hadn't said much of anything to anybody since she'd returned, all of Melody Falls Township snickering. Whatever she wanted now, up there on the hill behind the Hobbes barn, didn't matter.

"Euge-e-ne!" Her voice came to me over the distance. I finally looked up. She had her hands cupped around her mouth. "Euge-e-ne!" again, but I kept walking, grass whipping my pant-legs, dry cockle burrs hitching a ride.

She waved to me with something in her hand. I kept going, shook my head, "No!"

She recupped her hands and yelled something else, too many syllables for me to understand. But in the mix, over the distance, came the words, "Agnes May."

I stopped. She waved again, waved something yellow at me. When she saw me stop, she burst into a hurry toward me, ran down through uneven pasture, jumped over stones, depressions and tufts of grass, ignoring the zigzag cow trail, just came straight at me.

I stood still...perfectly still. And the rest of the world stood perfectly still too, except for Lucinda running at me.

She got close, and slowed. Her face red and puffy with exertion, she looked with darkened blue eyes, eyes that said they did not want to look at me at all, that looked away and then briefly back again. Her final steps were hesitant. She reached out without getting too close, reached out with fully extended arm, handing it to me, looking quickly again with those reluctant eyes, just eyes, the rest of her face wanting no part of it. I had to reach, stretching to take the yellow paper from her. She turned and went some distance away, bent and picked at a milkweed, suddenly took interest in it, stripping leaves from stem, playing her fingers in gooey white pith that oozed out of the wounds.

It was a yellow, lined paper, folded. Inside was familiar cursive in blue ballpoint ink...

When I finished reading it, Lucinda was beside me. We climbed the hill together, no words between us. Real sight and sound wanted to disconnect from me, as if we were just two characters in a movie...

In the Hobbes kitchen, she stood by the stove, eyes having lightened up, looking at me. Her step-mother, Crystal, and brother, Hangy, were down in the barn. It was evening milking time, after all, and with Old Man Hobbes gone, everything was up to them these days: no matter what's happened, you can't just not milk the cows twice a day.

My own voice surprised me, sounding so normal. "They don't need you down in the milking parlor?"

So, I wasn't in a movie. I was at the Hobbes kitchen table, a rectangle of yellow lined paper resting on the blue oilcloth in front of me. On the stove, the coffee pot's glass knob suddenly "blooped.".

"They'll be all right for a while, milking without me. That whole time I was away, well, they did fine, just the two of them. You know, Eugene? When I was away, down in North Carolina."

I did know. The whole township knew. She had been hiding ever since, from all the looks and the laughter. And now Lucinda talked about it freely here in the kitchen, not embarrassed to remind me.

The coffee pot grew impatient, gurgled hurriedly, steam puffing out of its spout. She waited a little longer before turning the burner off, then poured two mugs and brought them to the table.

"I don't drink coffee," I said.

She turned away and took something out of the refrigerator.

The outside door opened. The twins, Elsie and Elise, came in, big eyes staring at me.

Lucinda sat down across from me and placed a small tin measuring cup beside one of the coffee mugs. "Your first time," she said. "You might need this."

I poured some in and watched the liquid wrestle with itself, changing color, inviting me to at least taste it.

"You sure they don't need you down in the milking parlor?"

"Oh, I suppose so," she said. "Crystal will send my brother to come looking for me before long. But right now, Eugene, I think you need...we both could use a good cup of coffee."

The twins removed their coats and climbed onto her lap, one on each thigh. "You don't have to read the *Clarion* to us, anymore," Elsie said to me. Elise nodded, "Our big sister reads it to us now."

Elise sucked her thumb. Lucinda wrapped them in her arms and kissed each of them on top of the head. She looked at me, blue eyes glistening, no longer reluctant. She quietly looked with her whole face, a gentle face, with eyebrows and lips and round-ness of cheeks. That dimple on her left one was part of it too.

I slid the tin of cream toward her.

"No, thank you. I recently learned to drink mine straight," she said.

She eyed me through the curling vapors as she reached around the girls and raised her mug. Holding it sideways, she wrapped her fingers around it and let them poke through the loop, leaving the handle to stick out as she sipped.

I felt their eyes on me as I looked at the swirl of liquid in my mug.

Lucinda said, "Okay, little sisters. You can help me throw hay down."

"Or the cows will go hungry," Elise announced, taking her thumb out of her mouth for just long enough to say it.

Lucinda quickly sipped once more from her mug, and then the three of them got up and left for the barn, spring-loaded outer back door whapping shut.

I sat in quiet. The note in yellow lay before me. It was creased across its middle, two halves bowed a little from having been folded before I'd opened it down in the pasture.

I tasted — carefully — the warm mix of coffee and cream, bitter and sweet.

Flattening the paper, I read it again, a note in blue ballpoint cursive:

Dearest Eugene,

I couldn't tell you on the porch. We are moving to Arkansas. That's where we are from, and still have family there, in Bald Knob. Mama called on the public phone out back of the Esso Station and talked with somebody down there about us staying with them. We will take the Power Wagon to the Lehigh Valley station early Saturday morning. She figures the Reverend will be occupied in the church prac-ticing the Sunday service with Adam, and they won't notice us leaving until it's too late so we can get away.

Love, Agnes May

PS. Remember the book I told you about? It's the story of a woman they named a theorem after. I promise I'll send it back to Mr. Johns as soon as I'm finished reading it. Please don't tell him that I took it all the way to Arkansas. I just hope nobody asks for it at the Bookmobile. I have to tell you something: I decided I'm going to be a mathematician instead of an architect.

There are so many other things I wish I could tell you.
I love you,
Agnes May

## 2016 – Melody Falls, Pennsylvania

Inside the FedEx envelope was another envelope, faded manila, with a hand-written note taped to the front:

Eugene,
Thank you for talking with me this morning. I called the number you gave me and spoke with your uncle's caregiver. We decided it would be best to send it to you. If I can be of any assistance, please feel free to call on me.
Best Regards,
Rev. Timothy Turley, C.S.C.

On the front of the manila envelope, there it was: "Give this to Daniel Ahern, if I don't make it back." My turning it over caused something to slide around inside, and when I pulled up the flap, the item fell out, tap-tap onto the table surface. It was a folded piece of paper the size of a matchbook with something inside of it, taped shut. I then slid out a two-page letter fastened with a rusty paper clip.

Robert J. Walters, C.S.C.
Casa de Santa Cruz
Santa Maria Nebal
Guatemala
June 16, 1982
Dear Dan,
To say I'm frightened is an understatement. Disappearance squads have begun to target clerics, even sisters. What could nuns have done to offend anybody? Do I hear correctly that such brutality is an extension of our own President's policies?
It is late here, the hour when I should be turning in after another exhaustive day among my urchins. Though cot calls to me from the corner, fear intervenes, overwhelms fatigue, and condenses my brain down to primitive alertness. And, my soul, too, is alert.

You know how I've complained in the past that my true spiritual nature seems forever to elude me? Could I have finally found it, as you promised? You said it would only come to me if my struggle was pure. I wish I felt pure now, Dan, but I'm just plain scared, trembling at approaching thunder. Yet, I must be thankful to those who force this moment upon me, a moment that overwhelms my thoughts, allows the soul to emerge so keenly aware.

Today I played soccer in a muddy patch at the dump, a sanctum so far not violated by men with guns. Yes, with all that goes on around us, I played soccer. Don't ask me to explain the workings of it, but it seems the simple act of trying to keep up with ragged children in the sucking mud brought forth an epiphany. The eagerness on their faces short-circuited time and resurrected the youth within me.

When I was twelve, I was a child at play too, and in the midst of play, my youth was suddenly interrupted. I thought I'd been singled out. I felt dismissed from my own childhood. I'll never be able to thank you enough, Dan, for responding to my dad's call for help back then, for taking it upon yourself to ensure my well-being and safety with the sisters at the orphanage. But this afternoon, I discovered that I am still the child I was. I've been slumbering, dormant, having hidden myself down so deep, wrapped in layers of pretending. We grownups are so clever at pretending, you know, so crafty compared to children, who easily accept its border with reality.

You see, today, I fell in the mud. I looked up, and all those clear, unpretending eyes stared down at me. In that moment, their eyes became my eyes. These orphans (and all of us are orphans to some degree) who insist on playing soccer at such a time as this, refuse to be defined by what is likely to be done to them at any moment. Isn't that what the Teacher tried to teach us? "...as we forgive those who trespass..." We are what we do, and especially what we do to others, not what others do to us. It suddenly seems...well, so simple.

Brother Lawrence and I both received our orders in this week's mail: get out! It seems our Superior wants us safe, "back home in Indiana." But imagine the spectacle it would present to clear, unpretending eyes: their fallen priest just gets up from the mud and runs away.

I've asked Brother Lawrence, who is leaving in the morning, to act as courier and see to it this letter is saved for you among my stored personal effects — just in case. May it never find you. I'm sure many opportunities await us to be together again in person.

My wind-up Westclox loudly ticks away the waning night. If you do hold this letter in your hand, it means I am done trembling. Father, do not pray for me. It means I am at peace.

And, Peace be with you also.

Walt

PS: Enclosed is a medal I've saved in my pocket all this time. Genie gave it to me when last we were together. Please return it to him. He is the one who always loved me, the one who will always know my name.

The tape gave way. Crinkled paper opened. The copper piece was worn, lettering almost gone: *In Hoc Signo Vinces.*

ABOUT THE AUTHOR:

Patrick Lawrence O'Keeffe was born in Towanda, Pennsylvania, where he attended Saint Agnes School through the eighth grade. Raised on a dairy farm three miles west of Ulster, he was one of nine children in a family that also included three orphaned cousins. When he was a teenager, his parents sold their farm and relocated to the San Francisco Bay Area. O'Keeffe studied for the priesthood under the Holy Cross Fathers at the University of Notre Dame, where he received frequent encouragement from his teachers to become a writer.

Later embarking on a career in industrial fabrication, he lived in Indiana and Michigan, and finally settled near Akron, Ohio, where he and his wife, Karen, raised five children. They now reside close to Lake Erie, in Port Clinton. O'Keeffe participates in activities of the Firelands Writing Center, and reads his work at the Center's monthly gatherings at Mr. Smith's Coffee House in Sandusky, Ohio. Along with poetry that has appeared in various journals, he has also contributed humorous essays to the *South Bend Tribune*, as well as book reviews for the *Morrow County Sentinel*.

In 2016, he authored and co-edited *History of Ottawa County, The 1ˢᵗ 175 Years*, a comprehensive work that tells the story, in photos and narrative, about the settling of one of the final frontiers in Ohio, which largely arose from the Great Black Swamp and the Lake Erie Islands. He is also the editor and publisher of the *Scribbler*, a monthly historical and literary paper for Ottawa County readers. *Cold Air Return* is O'Keeffe's first novel. He is currently at work on a second.

# BOOKS BY BOTTOM DOG PRESS

# Books By Bottom Dog Press

### Appalachian Writing Series

*Brown Bottle: A Novel* by Sheldon Lee Compton, 162 pgs. $18
*A Small Room with Trouble on My Mind*
by Michael Henson, 164 pgs. $18
*Drone String: Poems* by Sherry Cook Stanforth, 92 pgs. $16
*Voices from the Appalachian Coalfields* by Mike Yarrow and Ruth Yarrow,
Photos by Douglas Yarrow, 152 pgs. $17
*Wanted: Good Family* by Joseph G. Anthony, 212 pgs. $18
*Sky Under the Roof: Poems* by Hilda Downer, 126 pgs. $16
*Green-Silver and Silent: Poems* by Marc Harshman, 90 pgs. $16
*The Homegoing: A Novel* by Michael Olin-Hitt, 180 pgs. $18
*She Who Is Like a Mare: Poems of Mary Breckinridge and
the Frontier Nursing Service* by Karen Kotrba, 96 pgs. $16
*Smoke: Poems* by Jeanne Bryner, 96 pgs. $16
*Broken Collar: A Novel* by Ron Mitchell, 234 pgs. $18
*The Pattern Maker's Daughter: Poems*
by Sandee Gertz Umbach, 90 pages $16
*The Free Farm: A Novel* by Larry Smith, 306 pgs. $18
*Sinners of Sanction County: Stories* by Charles Dodd White, 160 pgs. $17
*Learning How: Stories, Yarns & Tales* by Richard Hague, 216 pgs. $18
*The Long River Home: A Novel*
by Larry Smith, 230 pgs. cloth $22; paper $16
*Eclipse: Stories* by Jeanne Bryner, 150 pgs. $16

### Appalachian Anthologies

*Unbroken Circle: Stories of Cultural Diversity in the South*
Eds. Julia Watts & Larry Smith, 200 pgs. $18
*Appalachia Now: Short Stories of Contemporary Appalachia*
Eds. Charles Dodd White and Larry Smith, 160 pgs. $18
*Degrees of Elevation: Short Stories of Contemporary Appalachia*
Eds. Charles Dodd White and Page Seay, 186 pgs. $18

Bottom Dog Press, Inc.
P.O. Box 425 / Huron, Ohio 44839
http://smithdocs.net

CPSIA information can be obtained
at www.ICGtesting.com
Printed in the USA
BVOW03s1059110617
486604BV00001B/54/P